UNDERTOW

Other novels by Lesley Grant-Adamson

PATTERNS IN THE DUST

THE FACE OF DEATH

GUILTY KNOWLEDGE

WILD JUSTICE

THREATENING EYE

CURSE THE DARKNESS

FLYNN

A LIFE OF ADVENTURE

THE DANGEROUS EDGE

DANGEROUS GAMES

WISH YOU WERE HERE

EVIL ACTS

THE GIRL IN THE CASE

LIPSTICK AND LIES

Non-fiction

TEACH YOURSELF WRITING CRIME AND SUSPENSE FICTION

A SEASON IN SPAIN
with Andrew Grant-Adamson

UNDERTOW

Lesley Grant-Adamson

Hodder & Stoughton

First published in Great Britain in 1999
by Hodder and Stoughton
A division of Hodder Headline PLC

10 9 8 7 6 5 4 3 2 1

British Library Cataloguing in Publication Data
A CIP catalogue record for this book
is available from the British Library

ISBN 0 340 74807 9

Typeset by Hewer Text Ltd, Edinburgh
Printed and bound in Great Britain by
Caledonian International Book Manufacturing Ltd.

Hodder and Stoughton
A division of Hodder Headline PLC
338 Euston Road
London NW1 3BH

To my mother

They believed the worst and they had to blame someone so they picked on him.

As proof was more elusive than prejudice, they made do with rumour. Over the years rumour hardened into the legend that he had got away with murder.

The unresolved fate of the victims, and the memory of a murder trial without a body, clouded the villagers' lives. Then, last summer, he decided to break his silence.

Chapter One

This time the lightning showed a boat in the churning bay. Perhaps not a big boat, perhaps not a boat at all. A glimpse was as much as the night allowed.

It kept Alice at her bedroom window, hand cupped to face, a robust and level-headed young woman watching frantic white waves careering ashore, and waiting to be scared. She had done this as a child, nearing thirty she was equally enthralled. Charles, though, curled up on his half of the bed, had stirred when the tumult began but descended into sleep. She was a light sleeper and he was not, one of many contrasts discovered during their months of living together.

Storms thrilled her and the history of this coast was told in storms. They had redefined the bay, shaped villages and people's lives. One great storm had plucked a hamlet from its rock and pulverised a harbour. Another had cast up a pebble ridge and abandoned a seaside village inland. Lifeboats and freighters had been lost to these furies.

The tales she had heard were rich although language was insufficient for the telling. People recounted merely the physical damage – roofs being carried away, dead animals fetching up further along the coast, and the road that was their lifeline to the world being captured by the sea. They lacked vocabulary for the things that mattered more – the daunting sense of their own inadequacy, their smallness in the natural scale, and the chilling moment when excitement turned to dread that they would not live to survey the wreckage in the morning.

Storms were their history but were also resonant in everyday life. They were the reason for a pond where swans swanked and a lane made a detour, for moorings high and dry in the saltings and a farmhouse lonely beside its drowned fields. They accounted for widows and poverty, as well as for a network of deep rhines chopping the land into rectangles. The local word for these big drains, pronounced reens, had quickly slipped into her vocabulary.

Alice had marvelled at the contrast in the landscapes the first time she travelled to the peninsula. Within two miles of a conventional village, in feminine, leafy orchards, she had entered a world governed by water. Stark Point was a straggle of farmhouses and cottages on a spit of flat land between the sea and a river mouth and beneath an enormous sky. It looked vulnerable, even on a calm day when the water was a placid grey mass without a lick of white to enliven it.

Used to living in a city in a cuddle of hills, she felt uncomfortably exposed. Wherever she turned there was nothing, and there was no consolation in such emptiness. At the end of the causeway a silo sprouted from a dark clump of evergreens but the other buildings of Stark Point were hazy in a feathering of windbreak trees. The bay, on her left, was a sweep of yellow sand curving round to the buckled strata of a low cliff and a grey rock that resembled a crouching cat. A dark horizontal, like a mark in soft pencil, drew the line between surf and sand. And somewhere indeterminate beyond that the waters of the bay and the channel commingled. Far out in the channel rose the limestone humps of indistinct islands.

While distant headlands gave the coastline some shape, everything was remote and vague. Looking back the way she had come, she was surprised to be deprived of landmarks. Stone churches and their villages had blended into the backdrop, giving her the impression of gazing over unpeopled country, all five miles of it, to the hills. With a tingle of apprehension she had understood the bitter isolation of Stark Point.

Given a simple choice, she would never have gone to live there.

Lightning. She saw a savage sky, waves dying in fields, and a boat, yes, surely a small boat flung high and . . .

Darkness.

A rasp of thunder. Alice rested her forehead on the cold pane.

She waited, alone with the sounds, thinking: The boat *was nearer. The wind's driving it ashore, people might die.* She flushed with guilt at enjoying the spectacle.

Just then the cacophony changed. An alarming new note, a thin high screaming, broke in.

She flinched. 'A child?'

But she immediately rejected the idea, took a few paces to the landing window, pressed her palm over a cracked pane and smothered the cry.

Outside was a dense mass of sheltering evergreen, blocking her view. She let the wind come wailing through again and retreated to her bedroom window. The pitiful sound set her teeth on edge. She invented ways of patching over the crack but could not tear herself away from watching the storm to try any of them.

Lightning. She gasped. A boat was hurtling through the air, propelled towards her in a white maelstrom.

Then nothing but sound, intensifying to a frightening clamour. She could no longer distinguish the slam of water against the walls of the village from the desperation of lurching trees or the raging of the wind. One sound alone was clear and that was the one inside her house, the heart-rending misery of a child.

She dared not leave the window, the storm compelled her. She puzzled why this should be when other people hid beneath bedclothes and muttered mantras to help them endure a horrible experience. But she always felt a heightened existence, which was inexplicable as part of the excitement was facing her own mortality or, at the very least, inconsequentiality.

This storm had come without warning, preceded by a breezy bright day and the sort of calm evening when a brassy haze glows behind blue hills. There had been no anticipation, no sense of the heavens pressing down while people grew fractious and muttered; 'We need a good storm to clear the air.'

The flare. Waves creaming across the road. No boat. Just water and flailing branches. Thunder.

The landing window screeched. Alice jammed a folded magazine against the pane. Tentatively, it held.

Lightning. There was a longer delay before thunder rolled and when it came it was weaker. The storm had moved inland. Cold, Alice climbed into bed and fell asleep.

The storm spent itself in the hills to the south east, petering out an hour or so later in staccato showers which disturbed the sleep of farmers on the high land, filled field drains and flooded lanes. Down on the coast, the white waves continued to batter the shore until, gradually, their energy failed and towards dawn, after the tide turned and the wind veered, a quiet day was born.

The only sound was water and it was water running away. It dripped from leaves and faulty guttering, scurried along ditches, teemed across the road and made all haste to reach the bay. Now and then the sea flung it back, but each breaker that arced onto the land was less effective than its predecessor. By the time light streaked the bay, the flashing menace was no more dangerous than memory.

Departing waves fussed around a black shape. Sometimes it travelled a few feet with them, sometimes they failed to shift it. In the end, they had to go and it was left there alone, a cold finger of sunlight pointing it out to anyone who was up early and curious.

As the sun lifted into the sky, waders picked their delicate way across freshly washed sand. When they paused, they used the upturned hull as a vantage point to survey the wet expanse of their hunting ground. Their piercing calls seemed squeals of amazement as the sun revealed an average day after such a night.

A dog fox went to earth in scrub where sand gave way to soil. Miles away, headlights raked the sky as a vehicle climbed an incline. For a while the sea was paler than the land because there was nothing to cast shadows on it and the water exaggerated the light. The phase passed, sun lanced the grey light, and shades warmed and intensified until the sky and the sea were touched with gold and the land with shining green.

Alice opened her bedroom window. The air was rich with the earth's fragrance. A teasing breeze from the west played with strands of her fair hair but barely stirred the plants in her garden. Petals had gone, though; her first sight of damage was a denuded clematis. She scanned the beach for the alarming thing remembered the instant she woke, but failed to see a boat and wondered all over again whether it had been real or imagined.

Village and coast appeared dishevelled, as though the familiar scene had been jiggled until bits and pieces rattled loose. Shreds of plastic and paper were hooked onto walls. A beer can bounced along a gushing ditch. Sky was reflected in a pond where, surely, there ought to be a road.

She dressed quickly, eager to run out and explore but the stairs were creaky and once she was down she heard movement overheard. Charles soon followed her, wearing the woolly dressing gown that transformed him from a slim and sleek thirty-year-old into a podgy bundle with middle-aged solidity. His face was screwed up in annoyance, as it invariably was when he discovered he had to face another day. Crumpled and wan, he put her in mind of a discarded toy: Toby, a knitted thing she had loved until her mother put him through the washing machine too many times, and his vibrant colours leached out and his woolly clothes and body unravelled.

'Sorry,' Alice said, 'I didn't mean to disturb you.'

She had a habit of apologising to Charles first thing in the morning, her only way of handling his mood. The rest of the time he appreciated her cheerfulness, although he did not quite share her optimistic and ironic view of Stark Point, but early mornings were tricky.

There were two Charleses and for almost a year she had lived with them both. The one she got to know first was a relaxed, confident fellow with a quick mind, a well-rewarded salesman who loved parties, jazz and country pubs, and was jovially satirical about his own achievements and much of life besides. It was his joke that his life was marqued out, meaning the more business he won for his employers, the pricier the car they allotted him. He was witty about his clients and colleagues and, when he told stories, he would take off all their voices brilliantly. His humour matched Alice's, and they enjoyed a lot of laughter.

Unfortunately, the second Charles was self-centred, tetchy, and could not raise a smile if you paid him. Each day Charles the second held sway for an hour or so until he was deposed by Charles the first. Alice teased him about his duality but only when he was Charles the first.

He sat at the kitchen table. 'Are you making tea?'

'Yes,' she said, postponing her outing.

Over her shoulder, while she did the business with the Morning Time herbal teabags and the pot, she asked whether he realised there had been a storm.

He said: 'It kept me awake half the night. How could anybody have slept through that racket?'

Oh, he was sounding *very* Charles the second. She smiled broadly, although when she spoke there was no inflection to give away her aumusement.

'You didn't get up, though.'

'What for? To see a lot of rain?'

'Well, I watched it.'

'In the dark?' He yawned.

'No, there was lightning. It was fantastic, Charles. I couldn't bear *not* to watch.'

But he was uninfected by her enthusiasm. He yawned more loudly and put the conversation into limbo.

Once tea was on the table, and she was studying the sopping garden through the window, she tried to revive it.

'I always said Stark Point was at the mercy of the elements.'

He snorted. 'They weren't showing much mercy last night.'

With a laugh she agreed. 'That's true, it's what made it so thrilling.'

She waited. He didn't reply.

She drank her tea, thinking: '*How strange that he's taken such a fierce dislike to this place.*'

By 'place' she meant both cottage and village. They might have appealed to him, as they offered tranquillity and space, qualities he grumbled were virtually impossible to find in the city. The cottage was pretty, too: whitewashed walls and red tiled roof, standing in an old style garden where flowers jostled for attention. Yet Charles loathed staying in the countryside, whatever he claimed to the contrary, and she was reluctantly accepting it.

Whether he had accepted it himself she wasn't certain. She hadn't devised a way of asking without sounding challenging, and to misjudge the tone might lead to an argument. Good-natured and peaceable, she skirted squabbles whenever possible.

He said, when she had quite given up expecting a response: 'I suppose the Starkers will talk of nothing else for days now.'

She ignored his disparaging tone, saying lightly: 'I'm keen to know where it rates on their index.'

'Oh, Alice, they're never going to admit last night's was as bad as it gets. They'd ruin their best stories if they did that.' He yawned again, demonstrating boredom plus tiredness. In a good mood, he would have done his impressions of the Starkers discussing it in their rough West Country burr.

She was not willing to concede he was right, that history was routinely tailored to suit the teller and, when the process was complete, the result was legend.

Instead she said: 'I wonder whether I was the only one who found it exhilarating. They might have grown blasé because they've lived through so many.'

'Which is about all the living most of them do.'

She let the gibe pass. 'Being exposed to the elements gives me a new perspective, something city dwellers miss out on.'

With another yawn he pushed his empty mug away and scraped back the chair. 'I expect Starkers get a buzz from the turmoil of the city.'

She doubted it but did not object and listened to him walk away. A loose stair tread creaked. Bathroom pipes glugged. Alice pulled on boots, lifted her macintosh from the hook on the kitchen door, tied back her hair with a ribbon from the pocket and went out.

She lingered in the garden, mentally recording the scene. The wind had appliquéed fragments of leaves to the wooden door. Her roof appeared intact although a piece of broken ridge tile on the path raised suspicion. The lawn squelched as it took her weight. Herbs were indeterminate soggy blobs. Near the de-flowered clematis was a mess of saturated earth and pottery, previously a dwarf rose in a terracotta tub. Of the plant itself there was no sign.

'*Will I meet it in the lane?*' she wondered. '*Or has the wind presented it to one of my neighbours who'll plant it in recompense for whichever of his own shrubs took flight?*'

Laughing, she entered the lane. An uprooted sapling and branches ripped from other trees were sprawled in the road, holding up a queue of cans and plastic pots, plus a few brilliantly coloured children's toys. Alice clambered across the debris and headed down the lane, keeping close to the rushing ditch because much of the roadway was flooded.

She wanted to be absorbing details of the scene, the tentative writer in her finding phrases to express it, but she was forced to concentrate on the physical act of walking. Once, looking up, she saw a face at a cottage window. Friendly by instinct, she raised a waving arm but there was no answering movement. There never had been, not on any of the occasions she had greeted the woman.

Alice felt sure it was a woman, although all she ever saw was a pale face. She kept meaning to ask about her but it was difficult to know who best to approach. Minor embarrassments during her early days at the cottage had made her wary of seeming nosy or critical. Incomers at Stark Point were discouraged from asking questions.

Shortly before water engulfed the lane she turned right by a field of buttercups where finches fluttered. A worn wooden bridge took her over a rhine, one of the big drainage ditches, and onto a slippery path through tall grass. Two men were ahead of her, their top halves gliding over the grass. Abruptly they turned, scolding an invisible dog.

'Hello.' She waved as she called.

There was a hesitation before they responded, a slight one. She chuckled, thinking: '*A couple of months ago they'd have pretended not to notice me.*'

How long, she wondered, before the Starkers, as Charles had dubbed them, greeted her first?

A brown and white collie came thrashing through the grass, intent on inspecting her, sniffing, shoving its muzzle against her legs to hurry her, treating her like a laggard in his flock. She stooped to pat him but her outstretched hand was misread as a threat. The animal jinked away, barking, and raced after its owner.

Alice didn't see him again until she emerged from the high grass onto the stubby vegetation covering the saltings, and he was a streak of energy on its way to join figures brooding over a wrecked boat. By the time she moved from saltings to sand, the men had drawn into a tight knot, their windblown voices as devoid of meaning as the cries of oystercatchers. They were short, down-at-heel people, thin but with heavy features, and so it was their lack of animation that was the most striking feature.

'*Elsewhere people would skitter around showing their excitement but here there's only heavy pondering.*'

Dickens, she thought, would have lampooned them mercilessly.

The men stood in her way but she saw enough to deduce that the wreck was twenty feet of pleasure craft rather than a boat that did business in coastal waters. Drawing close, sand merging into mud and the mud sucking at her boots, she noted how the overturned hull, balanced at an angle on its cabin, was bedding down. A messy thing, it was daubed with tar, smeared with green slime and liberally encrusted. Even Alice, no sailor, knew its keel was long overdue for scraping.

'*This is local legend in the making,*' she thought. '*An event becomes local history, telling it refashions it as legend.*'

She joined the men, saying a cheerful general hello. Subdued replies, in most cases bleak nods, admonished her for being far too jolly in the circumstances. There was silence for a moment, except for the swish of the sea.

The dog owner, a stubble-chinned, bullet-headed man of forty, broke it, voicing almost everyone's prediction. 'The next tide will take her.'

'Jacko will be here soon enough.' A thin man muffled in a fat anorak answered him.

On cue Jacko, the fisherman, appeared on a tractor. He left it high up the beach and jogged towards the boat, ropes and tackle dangling from one hand, a cigarette in the other. The wiry, monkey-faced Jacko became the lead player in the drama, the hero who knew how to secure the boat, raise her and drag her to a point from which the sea would be unable to snatch her back. He ruled out the dog owner's suggestion of turning her over to allow her to slide more smoothly.

The others deferred to him, as Alice had assumed they would. She was fascinated by the way the village accorded everyone his own special role and certain unchallengeable knowledge to accompany it. Jacko was their expert on storm and tide.

She fancied there was a timelessness about him because each generation had produced a fisherman who was guardian of the same information. At a glance, Jacko's appearance was unchanged, too: trousers stuffed into long boots, coarse woollen jersey and waterproof jacket. His pockets were weighed down, she supposed with traditionally useful odds and ends, including items not in dictionaries because his terms were purely local, peculiar to a few miles of coast or possibly Stark Point alone.

Alice kept a little apart, noticing how water oozed into the groove gouged by the wreck as it was tugged free. Gulls spiralled down, seeking morsels in the disturbed sand. Men buzzed around the boat, easing her, steadying, putting an unnecessary hand to her to assure themselves they were important in the day's adventure. They got muddy, they got scratched. Through all their warnings and plentiful advice to each other, the tractor droned. Jacko was inching the vehicle inland, sitting twisted on his seat to study the antics in the bay.

The boat snagged. The tractor halted too. Bending figures investigated, conferred. Jacko walked down with a spade, a man went to meet him, the spade changed hands. Soon the boat was lifted clear of the obstruction. The tractor crawled up the beach again.

When Jacko was satisfied, he cut the engine for the final time and strolled down to gather in his rope. He lit another cigarette, cupping the flame in his hand, listening to the prattling of the others speculating where the craft had come from. Its name and registration had been obliterated. Eventually, he gave them his version, speaking in his usual leisurely drawl that suggested a wisdom he might not actually have possessed.

'She's from up the channel, sure to be. The way that wind blew last night, anything up that way didn't have a prayer.'

Men concurred with nods and grunts. As Jacko's words didn't amount to anything, Alice expected some of the men to put questions. They didn't. They stared hard at the hull and waited for him to offer up more.

He drew on the cigarette, then: 'Could have been torn from her moorings, see.'

Murmured agreement again but he spoke over it, saying: 'Or she could have been making for harbour and run into a squall. There's no saying how long the sea was tossing her around before it dumped her here for us to take a look.'

The cigarette rose to his lips. He exhaled luxuriously before adding: 'I rang the police when I saw her at first light. Could be a body or two on board, I told them.'

People shifted from one leg to the other, making perceptible movement away from the wreck. Jacko was planted firmly. 'Either the crew tipped overboard and they'll be coming in on the next tide, or they're trapped in here.'

He slapped his hand on the hull, then scanned the sea with the attention of a man who makes his livelihood from it.

Everyone else looked with dismay at the wreck they were now convinced was a coffin. The collie confirmed the theory by scrabbling around it, barking, refusing to come away even though his owner remembered an urgent reason to be at home and sidled off.

Jacko, reacting to the threat of losing his audience, threw away his cigarette and mustered another opinion. 'It's like the great storm in sixty-one. Now what you've got to remember about the tidal flow in these parts . . .'

A telephone beeped. With a simian scowl, Jacko delved into a pocket Alice had assumed full of fisher-folk clutter. Then his wife's voice was squeaking across the bay. His expression tightened, he barked a terse 'All right' and hung up. As he stooped to pick up his rope, he told them what they knew, that he had to leave. Before they could ask anything, he was gone.

With his departure, a new leader took centre stage. An unemployed youth, Sam, who hung around the village described his first sight of the boat.

'She was like a toy chucked around. And those waves . . . they were thundering ashore, smashing like water cannon. Pulverised our back fence, they did. Half of it's swilling along the rhine and God knows where the other half's got to. And that wind . . . it came at us every way.'

Alice was interested because his story tallied with hers, but apparently he had told it already and no one else was willing to hear from him. He kept on, though, so they started up rival conversations, trying to contain in words the unimaginable ferocity of the night and where it figured on the local scale.

'It was worse than eighty-three when the barn roof went.' This from a beer-bellied chicken farmer who narrowed his eyes as though remembering back as far as *eighteen* eighty-three.

'Ah, but eighty-three took two days to blow herself out, Doug.' Cavil from the lean and hungry salesman for an animal feed company.

'Hm, Pete's right, this one was quick. Sounded like we had the artillery out here, the noise of it exploding against the cliff. And, if you ask me, the flooding's due to the drains. Folk don't care for them like they ought.' The retired farm labourer did not need to mention names, they understood which folk were being blamed.

Backs were turned on the youth, leaving him only Alice and a deaf elderly man with wonky teeth. Alice used the dog as an excuse to escape, following him around the wreck in a useless attempt to distract him from it. When she was on the far side she saw movement at the foot of the cliff. The beachcomber.

That's what she called him, the beachcomber. Often she saw him from her bedroom window as she rose in the morning. Occasionally, she spotted him later in the day but always distant and by the sea.

He invariably wore a brown knitted hat, which might once have been topped by a bobble, and a green waterproof jacket, but it was his gait that made identification certain. He pottered slowly along, hands clasped behind him, body tilted forward as his eyes raked the beach. She had never seen him with a companion, and on the occasions anyone else arrived on the beach he had shied away, taking cover by the cliffs or in the scrub.

'That's what he's doing now, because we're here,' she thought. *'Tucking himself out of sight.'*

She guessed he had been first to approach the wreck. Jacko could have telephoned the police without leaving home because his house enjoyed an unobstructed view over the bay. But the beachcomber had probably found it, and surely it was the most remarkable sight since he had taken to prowling the water's edge.

Alice did not know his name although she had asked two people, separately, shortly after she had moved into the cottage and become aware of him. His isolation and singlemindedness intrigued her, therefore she asked. One man claimed not to know who she meant, which was incredible, and the other avoided answering.

'It's as though I don't exist,' she had thought, *'or as though the beachcomber doesn't. Maybe neither of us does.'*

The dog came pestering, rounding her up. Amused by the creature switching allegiance to her, she ran with him up the beach. Her goodbyes went unanswered. Too cheery again?

'I'm getting used to it,' she told the collie. 'Beaming at implacable faces, addressing taciturn curmudgeons.'

But she wasn't and the indifference startled her whenever she met it. Telling her friends, she made the characters buffoons and life at Stark Point comical, and she kept to herself the unpleasant undertow.

For a young woman who could not help striding through life with a smile on her face, it was unsettling. She had caught the smiley habit from her mother. 'You're so alike,' friends and family told them, which was wrong.

Her mother was lean and dark, Alice was tawny and rounded. It was the happy cast of their features, and a way of crinkling the eyes in amusement, that performed the trick. Mother and daughter appeared to smile, even when their minds were far away; and the world smiled back at them. Although not at Stark Point.

The dog owner had lingered by the saltings, expecting the animal to peel away from Alice. Instead, it stayed with her, chivvying with an occasional nudge of its nose. The man shouted but it ignored him and he had to wait until Alice caught up. She arrived with a comic apology for stealing his pet, and took advantage of the situation to begin a conversation. Rapidly, before they reached the single file path through the tall grass, she slipped in her question.

'That man who was sitting under the cliff, the beachcomber, can you tell me his name?'

'Beachcomber?' He turned to call the dog who was threatening to stray.

'Yes. He's often here, wearing a brown hat and wandering around the bay.'

Silence. She filled it with an urgent 'Oh, you must know who I mean.'

'Old fellow?'

'Yes.' She was afraid she sounded impatient but they were nearing the narrow path and once on it there would be no prospect of conversation.

'Beachcomber, you say?'

'I believe he lives in the village. I mean, if he doesn't he must walk a long way every time he goes on the beach.'

It annoyed her to be rattling on rather than getting him to talk. He scratched his stubbly chin in a contemplative way, as if working out the man's identity or, more probably, deciding how much to share with an inquisitive outsider.

When he spoke he was dismissive. 'Can't say I know of a beachcomber.'

'Oh, but surely . . .' She cut herself off as she realised there was more to come.

'The brown hat, though. That puts me in mind of Joe Keenthorne.'

She echoed the name.

'That's it,' he said. 'Can't think of anyone else it might be.'

They reached the path and she let him go ahead, for the sake of the dog who was already whisking through the grass. He strode off, leaving her and her unsatisfied questions in his wake.

She recited the name, to make it stick in the memory. 'Joe Keenthorne. Joe Keenthorne.' It set up a marching rhythm as she tramped home.

When she had come to Stark Point, owing to a twist of fate that resulted in her inheriting Spray Cottage, Alice had anticipated being lured into fact-finding conversations with her neighbours. After all, it was human nature to focus on a newcomer and drain them of personal information. She had prepared herself, deciding it would be necessary to admit to writing poetry because they would see her mooching around with a notebook.

Family history, though, she meant to skim over with a simple statement that she was Bella's niece. There was no need to explain she had not been acquainted with this aunt or that the intended beneficiaries had been killed off before Bella succumbed to a heart attack.

Her planning was wasted because the villagers showed no more curiosity about her than they wanted her to show about them. Precious theories about human nature collapsed. She was mystified.

Alice bent to adjust a sock which had slipped down inside her boot and formed a lump under her arch. The socks were Charles's and too big for her. He did not know she had borrowed them and he had made a fuss the previous time. She plotted to creep indoors and remove them before he found out. It would be no good if he saw her come in and offered to give a hand pulling the wellingtons off, as he frequently did.

She walked on, cautiously because it was boggy. It was bothering her that she had been too reticent about asking after the beachcomber. The logical approach would have been a general enquiry, when she spotted him, to let one or more of the group supply an answer. By instinct, she had known that was useless.

She was entertained by the idea that each one would have pretended to be blind to what she saw, and thus freed himself from the obligation of answering.

'*But it isn't funny, their reluctance is sinister,*' she thought.

Worse, their attitude was influencing her. Because of it she had avoided speaking at the opportune moment and questioned the dog owner at an awkward one. But was the problem that the Starkers declined to speak to her or that they were determined not to discuss the beachcomber?

'*That's three times I've been rebuffed when I've asked about him.*'

Yet, for all she knew, there were a hundred other topics that would make them clam up, study the hazy islands in the channel and wish for all the world she would go away and take her nosiness with her.

She had never encountered anything like it before. But then, as she reminded herself with a shrug, she had always lived in the city, hugger-mugger with people who realised that outgoing friendliness was not a sign she took undue interest in them.

'*Perhaps,*' she thought, as she stepped around a steaming reminder of the dog, '*the rules are different in the countryside and two hellos in a week is regarded as harassment. Maybe somebody will tack a notice on the board by the chapel demanding my sort of behaviour is put a stop to before it spoils life at Stark Point for everyone.*'

The petty things people complained about, anonymously, on that noticeboard amazed her. A radio played too loud in a bedroom was a nuisance – although you had to be on the footpath crossing the rear garden of the house to hear it. Spare vegetables and flowers, offered free to passersby, were deemed a hazard because their box might topple off the garden wall. Property owners were urged to fix chains across their entrances to prevent cars which had strayed into the village turning round and heading back where they preferred to be.

The Stark Point vigilante, as Charles called him, had a fresh winge every week. Oh yes, it made perfect sense for an edict to be handed down demanding an end to the nuisance of grinning and being pleasant to people.

Alice began to giggle, on the verge of hysteria, not caring if she was heard. The dog owner marched on, his upper body bobbing above the high grass. Three figures advanced on him, strung out at intervals. Everyone was looking down, except for the occasional glance, but no eyes drifted her way save those of the dog who responded to her hilarity. With barks and leaps he merrily accompanied her the rest of the way to the lane.

Recovered, she managed to send him away to his owner. Her wave of farewell was answered by the man with a movement that barely raised his arm above his waist.

'*I'm doing something wrong,*' she thought, plodding along the road, wellingtons squelching sludge. She revised that, refusing to take full responsibility.

'*No, I mean I'm failing to grasp something about this community. I'm misunderstanding.*'

That was usually at the heart of a problem, not mean-spiritedness or a fundamental difference in nature but sheer misunderstanding. She frowned, worried how many more gaffes she was destined to make until anybody enlightened her.

Such guessing games were new to her. In her work in the city, a job for a local radio station that might have been fascinating but wasn't, people talked constantly, told each other what was right and what was wrong and what might happen and what was never likely to. Abruptly, coming to Stark Point for a few months instead of renewing her contract, the chatter had been cut off.

She was discovering loneliness. No longer living in gossiping clamour, she was enveloped by a silence relieved only by the rhythm of the surf. It might be interrupted by the odd snatch of conversation, the purr of a vehicle, a dog's bark or the moan of cattle. But unless she spoke, switched on her radio, played music or telephoned one of her friends her life now was very quiet.

Oh, that was weekdays. For weekends there was Charles.

Yes, there was Charles who ought to have carved out an office space in the cottage and installed himself for weeks on end. He could, as he had agreed, do his work as a sales rep for an engineering company just as easily in the country as the city. More easily, given his yearning for peace and adequate room to spread his papers. And yet he hadn't and he wouldn't.

'He needs to keep his working environment separate from his home,' she decided. *'Many people do.'*

A black thought, like a cloud on sunlit water. *'No, it isn't that. He can't bear being at Stark Point.'*

One day, while he was taking one of his rare walks around the bay, she had cleared out a room for him, dragged in a table to be used as a desk and made all the fiddly rearrangements he had talked about but put off. Then she had hung up his slick business suit and his painstakingly chosen ties – sombre enough to look serious, flamboyant enough to be memorable. Alice thought it amusing that he put so much effort into this impossible balancing act, without ever standing out from the crowd or looking anything but a salesman.

Coming back, he had poked his head into the room and said: 'Thanks. Yes, that's fine.'

Then he had produced reasons not to move in there right away. He had to make a trip next morning, one he had not mentioned before. He needed to fetch a desk lamp from his flat and . . . Oh, they were thin to the point of transparency.

Alice had cajoled him for the truth. 'If you're leaving me, I'd rather you said so.'

'Good lord, no. It's just . . . Well, like I said . . . The meeting. And the lamp. And . . .' He had taken her in his arms. 'Alice. Darling. *Of course* I'm not leaving you.'

He made it sound the absurdest idea and they ended in hilarity.

But Alice thought, soberly: *'That's how he'll do it, though, it's his way. He inches away from relationships, I've always known that about him.'* The question was how much quiet disentanglement went on before Charles himself realised what he was doing.

Alice splashed up the flooded lane. Vapour was rising from wet fields as sun warmed the earth. Hesitating, where the sapling blocked the road, she sensed she was being watched. She offered the face at the window a bright smile and then clambered across the obstacle, concerned to reach her own gate without providing extra entertainment, such as falling down, ripping her clothes, tripping into the ditch or any of the comic disasters that routinely befall human beings who feel a critical eye upon them.

The scowl on the face at the window deepened. She pressed knuckles against her mouth to stifle her misery, but in her head the words ran on anyway.

'It isn't fair, Alice living in Bella's cottage. She shouldn't be there, it isn't right.'

A lot of things seemed not to be right and they confused and embittered her.

The confidence of young women amazed her. They were so open about their lovers, they did anything they wanted, they had it all. She had not manged to have it all herself. She got the baby but not the husband. People drank too much on carnival nights, that was how it happened. Of course, she did not admit to that. She had invented a farmer who loved her but would not make the necessary sacrifices to marry her. The story earned her a modicum of sympathy and, before long, she too had believed in him.

'But these young women, no one cares who they go with or how they live, they don't have to hide anything. It isn't fair.'

She stayed there a while thinking over and over that nothing was fair, and fostering a secret hatred of Alice.

Chapter Two

Alice blurted out her news while he helped her off with her wellingtons.

'You'll never guess, Charles. There's a wrecked boat in the bay. Jacko and his tractor pulled it up the beach.'

'Who's Jacko?' It was remarkable how much grumpiness he squeezed into the two words. Apparently, Charles the second still reigned.

'You know, the fisherman.'

'Oh, yes, the one that looks like a monkey. Presumably that's why they call him Jacko.'

He tweaked the right boot off.

She said, 'He believes the bodies of the crew are trapped inside.'

Charles was sceptical. 'Why anyone should have taken a boat out in that weather is beyond me.'

'Jacko said they could have been caught in a squall before the big storm blew up.'

'Anything's possible.'

The left boot came free. He looked at the socks, his socks, but did not comment.

Alice, to distract him, had switched to describing storm damage in the village. She was mentioning the tiles missing from the chapel roof, when he butted in.

'Did you say the road's flooded right across?'

'Yes, completely. There's a lake stretching from the beach to the far side of the big field. I saw three mallard on it.'

He frowned. 'But it can't be any depth or you wouldn't have walked through it, even in these boots.'

Alice mocked his solemnity. 'I didn't say I went that way. No, I took the path down to the saltings. The roadway's hopeless.'

'Oh.'

She picked up where she had left off, with the damage to the chapel, but he interrupted again.

'Are vehicles getting through now? I mean, the water's probably gone down a lot since you went out.'

'I don't know. I didn't notice any vehicles, except for Jacko's tractor.'

'It wouldn't affect him. His house is the other side of the flood.'

She began saying the state of the road didn't matter to them either because they were not planning to go anywhere, but she broke off.

Preoccupied, Charles missed her change of tack. When she talked instead about the mess the storm had made of her garden, he joined in, joking about the possible whereabouts of her flyaway rose bush. He was keen to help tidy up.

'Get yourself some breakfast,' he suggested, 'while I make a start on it.'

'Have you eaten?'

'Hours ago. You were away for ages.'

If he had not mentioned food, she would have skipped it. She was always trying to lose weight. While she ate her cereal and made a pot of coffee, she glimpsed him flitting back and forth outside the kitchen window, busy and efficient. When he came in, it was to fetch a hammer and nails to secure a loose stave on the gate.

'You don't want it collapsing and letting cows wander up your path.'

He bustled out. Alice heard hammering.

In a while she joined him and discovered he had transformed chaos into order. Paving and paths were swept and rubbish was tied up in plastic bags. New nails shone on the weathered wooden gate. Fresh twine held climbers up against trellises where they ought to be. Shards of broken pottery were in a bucket in the shed, ready to be used when plants were potted up in future.

'Now there's only the roof, which obviously I can't do,' he said. 'Looks like your chance to meet the local builder.'

They talked about ridge tiles and insurance claims, then fell silent.

Alice said quietly, 'I went upstairs, Charles.'

'Ah.'

'You've packed.'

He draped an arm around her. 'I really do need to work tomorrow.'

'And you can't do it here?'

'Afraid not. But I'll be back before next weekend, you know I will.' He gave her a nervous glance, having said this before and let her down.

She was laughing, though. 'What makes you think you can leave? Stark Point is now Stark Island, remember?'

'But the water's sure to go down soon, isn't it?'

'I honestly don't know.'

'Let's trot down to your lake and see if we can pick up some clues.'

They tramped down the lane. Since her last outing someone had dragged the sapling to one side of the road and kicked debris into a heap beside it. A plastic doll had toppled into the ditch and lodged against a stone.

Whimsical, he asked: 'Ought we to dive in and rescue her?'

'No,' said Alice, poking with a stick and disappointed the doll was stuck fast, face blurred by the rushing water. She gave up, saying: 'Let's hope the little girl who owns her doesn't see her like this. It could lead to a lifetime of nightmares.'

Charles said that's how he felt about being stuck on Stark Island.

Alice objected. 'You aren't stuck. Maybe your car is but you're free to go.' Mischievously, she pointed to a path beside a cottage wall. 'Follow that over the fields and you'll hit a tarmac road within two miles. I guarantee it.'

He was not fond of walking, his idea of exercise being squash with a colleague. He snorted. 'If I can't drive along it, it isn't a proper way out.'

They came to a sky coloured sheet of water. The number of ducks had risen to four.

'Oh dear,' said Alice, without being dismal. 'No mucky tidemark, no reduction in water level.'

'Wade through it and show me how deep it gets.'

She looked alarmed, as if he had asked her to walk through fire.

He said: 'Well, *I* can't because I haven't got rubber boots on.'

For answer, she took a few steps. It was disconcerting to be walking without having any notion what unseen hazards she might be stepping on or into.

'*Perhaps the tarmac's caved in,*' she thought, '*or the crew of the wreck were cast ashore here.*'

She turned back.

Charles was impatient. 'You didn't go very far.'

With a flash of inspiration she pointed out what she had not consciously noticed until this minute. 'It's too deep. Look at that wall, it's half sunk. Normally it's all visible.'

Charles said 'Oh, yes,' and agreed they should retreat.

He began muttering it was absurd there was only one road.

'Charles, it's a peninsula. One road's all it requires.'

'Untrue. It needs back-up during the great storms they're so fond of boasting about.'

'Hush, someone might hear you.'

'Who? There's no one around, there never is.'

'Over there. Look.'

'Oh, right. That guy patting his cow. I wonder whether he knows how long that lake's going to stay there.'

But by the time they drew near enough to ask, there was only a cow.

Charles revived his argument in favour of an alternative route in and out of Stark Point.

Alice argued it would flood as badly as the existing road. 'Don't forget, the one we have is raised on a causeway.'

They looked round at the overnight lake. A third of the way along it, the bank had been breached. Low tide, now, and yet the swell was still noisily energetic.

'Oh God,' Charles groaned. 'All this bloody water and more on the way.'

The rest of their journey was passed in silence, regularly interrupted by the waves.

Being cut off, as he considered it, chafed at Charles. He made several telephone calls in which Alice heard him exaggerating their plight. He sought out neighbours who were no smarter at reading the future than he was. He stumped about the garden tidying what had already been tidied, trying to find useful occupation until he was released from his prison.

Alice sat and read poetry, curled up in a chair by the window where the light was best. Outside, Charles ran out of things to do and paced. Suddenly he dashed in the direction of the gate. Investigating, she found him quizzing an anoraked farmer who had brought his tractor to tow away the sapling. The project was abandoned while they discussed the depth and duration of the lake.

'There's another way out, mind,' the man said.

He echoed Alice's assurances about a track through the fields, and Charles did a reprise of his earlier disdain.

'No use,' he said. 'I *must* drive my car out. I've got heaps of stuff to take.'

'I wouldn't even risk it in my tractor. The bank's breached near a ditch, and the last time it went the road fell in.' His eyes narrowed. 'But if you're determined to get away from here, luggage and all, there *is* a way of doing it.'

Charles appeared ready to shake the information out of him.

The man said: 'Jacko will ferry you over the water in his dinghy. He took two out this morning. They had a friend with a car waiting on the other side.'

Conflicting emotions whisked over Charles's face. Revelation. Anticipation. Frustration. He said drily: 'Unfortunately, I haven't a friend on the far side.'

'No, but you can telephone for a taxi, same as anyone else.'

Charles settled on anticipation. 'Brilliant! I'll take a taxi to the railway station.'

'Well, if that's what you decide, you need to phone Jacko and arrange about the boat first.'

An hour later Charles escaped from Stark Point, rowed over the flood by the monkey-like fisherman. A third of the way across, a telephone chirruped and Jacko thrust the oars at Charles and reached into a pocket. His wife's voice carried over the water to the small audience of this mini-drama: on one side of the lake Alice, a cow and a couple of damp children, and on the other side a cigar-puffing taxi driver.

Charles fumbled, the boat pirouetted and a drake skittered out of the way fanning water. Jacko said a harsh 'All right' and hung up, simultaneously plucking an oar from Charles and fending the boat off a rock.

Before entering the taxi, Charles flung up an arm and Alice waved back. Then he was gone. She returned home feeling pleasantly alone and enjoying the soft murmurs of the afternoon tide easing in.

Charles had lavishly vowed to telephone every day and return before the end of the week. Plainly, he felt horribly guilty about abandoning her and, before he stepped aboard Jacko's boat, hugged and kissed her like a sailor heading for a war zone.

Soon she would miss him but not before relishing the special pleasures of being alone in her own home. To shift from talking about writing to achieving it, she must concentrate, and company meant distraction, even the company of someone with faith in her untried talent. Charles was not that man. She had foolishly imagined he was because he had not discouraged her reading or enthusing about poetry. His attitude, though, had altered to mild derision once he realised she was intent on turning herself into a writer.

He had thought it charming that poetry books tilted beside her bed; and that the last thing she did at night, after they had made love, was read herself to sleep; and the first thing she did in the morning was step over the pile.

Yet to his mind there was a gulf between reading and writing. 'Poetry? Whatever for?'

Defending herself, unprepared, she had asked a question back. 'Whyever not? You know I like reading it.'

'Reading's different. Anybody can read.'

She narrowly avoided snapping that most people don't. Charles was no reader.

He said, 'What makes you think you can write?'

He had caught her, the way that question always catches people who have yet to prove the matter either way. Squirming, and disgusted with herself for doing so, she mumbled: 'I don't know, it's a feeling I have. Anyhow, I'm going to try. That's all I mean, Charles: I want to try.'

'But why now? Writers make up stories and rhymes and things all their lives, but you haven't. How can you suddenly decide you're going to be a writer?'

Of course, he was wrong about the suddenly and about the stories in her head, but she would never enlighten him. Instead, she answered the easiest of his questions.

'I haven't really had the chance until now.'

The accurate answer was that she had not felt ready, but she realised the pointlessness of saying that. With a writer or a painter, say, she might have referred to the welling-up of creative energy which produced first poems, novels or pictures. Fond as she was of him, Charles lacked the experience and vocabulary for that conversation. And she, not yet a novice, could not hope to explain.

She let him assume she meant the practical changes in her life. Moving into his flat, no longer squandering time driving across the city to the radio station, and forsaking some time-consuming duties for a charity had reshaped her days. Charles was content to believe those things had made the difference.

The day he first saw her with a notebook, he could not curb the temptation to tease, which made her forget the phrase she was about to write down. By the time she remembered it the shine had worn off. She set it down, swiftly and faintly, then turned the page and jotted fresher thoughts unsullied by his interference and her self-consciousness. She had wondered then whether self-consciousness was a phase writers passed through or whether it crippled them all their writing lives.

What had truly made the difference to Alice and her dreams was the gift of Spray Cottage. The timing was excellent too. Her short contract at the radio station was coming up for renewal, so she arranged to work on another programme starting in the autumn and move into her cottage for the summer.

Once on her own territory rather than his, Charles's attitude was less wounding. She grew tougher and cheerfully told him to shut up when she needed to make a note. The days of sneaking out of the room to do it clandestinely were over. In fact, it became acceptable for her to say, sorry, she did not fancy driving to a pub that evening, she planned to work on a poem.

He did not beg to see the poems, sensitive enough to understand she could not tolerate sharing them until they were finished. About once a week he asked whether she had completed one.

She invariably said: 'No, there's nothing ready to show.'

And he replied: 'Never mind, perhaps next week.'

Her writing was pushing them apart, not drawing them closer as it might have done if Charles had shared her delight in wordplay and observation. The morning after the storm, for example, while she was sealing the window pane, she had mentioned the noise of the wind through the crack. 'Pitiful, like a little child screaming.'

Ruffling her hair affectionately, he mocked her tender heart, then added: 'Sounds more like a cat caught in a mangle.'

His levity prevented her confessing she felt haunted by the boat flung about during the storm. But, after Jacko had helped him on the first leg of his complicated journey home, she dreamed up phrases to encapsulate the scene and the feelings aroused in her. The actual boat, wrecked on the sand, was less powerful in her imagination than the mystical one glimpsed during the storm, in spite of the horror of bodies trapped within the hull.

'The wreck's a tragedy,' she reasoned. 'But the night boat was a thrill and a mystery.'

Playing with the image that afternoon she identified it as a metaphor for her own life in which she had frequently felt tossed this way and that, incapable of controlling events. Although never afraid to take decisions or make choices, she found it very disconcerting to be proved wrong about ideas or people.

Friends claimed she bounced back with admirable speed from the occasional blows, and that her sunny personality was of inestimable help. Alice, inevitably, felt differently. True, she faced the world with her mother's confident smile but there were days when it was deliberately misleading, a mere ruse for surviving the low points.

The lowest of the lows was the collapse of her marriage to Rod. For five years she had centered her life around his needs, always more pressing than hers, and he had been heavily dependent on her. During their time together he set up his own business designing computer programs, a far more demanding venture than either anticipated. Alice let her own career mark time, realising that, if she were to put herself under equal pressure to succeed professionally, home life would become intolerable.

She became their social secretary and kept up with friends, so they did not lose them through neglect, and she also took on responsibility for Bonny and Camilla. Bonny was an exquisite Burman cat, a whisp of thistledown that Rod acquired from his mother who developed late onset asthma and had to forgo pets. Camilla was Rod's daughter from his first marriage.

She was five when Alice became her stepmother. A taciturn, staring child with a slack mouth, she came for only one weekend a month but her sulky aura hung around the house. As did random toys and the odd sock. Alice coped by pretending to find her sweet and by being careful not to get pregnant herself. She found Bonny easier.

In time, Bonny's moulting and finicky ways became tiresome and Camilla grew more interesting. Alice gave Camilla treats and took her on outings. She taught her to swim and to ice skate. Rod, hard at work, missed it all.

'We're having a party next time she comes,' Alice warned him over a nightcap one Sunday evening. She had just returned from driving Camilla home.

He looked as though he had misheard. 'A party?'

'It's her birthday.'

'Well, of course I know that.'

She doubted it. Possibly he realised the child was coming up to ten but he was blank about dates.

He said: 'But does she know anybody here to invite to a party?'

'Camilla knows lots of children. From swimming, from skating, the neighbours' children . . . Lots.'

His face showed he could not conceive how this had come about.

Alice said: 'We've picked eight, that allows for a couple of sick-wicks on the day. We're doing the food ourselves.'

'You don't have to, you can buy whatever you need.'

'Yes, but she wants to do it. Especially a chocolate cake she's learned to make. That's my present to her, the party.'

There was a tightening of his mouth. She wished she had phrased it differently, including him instead of taking over both treat and daughter in one possessive remark. But it was too late to undo so she said nothing.

The party was a triumph. None of the guests cried off and, because it was winter and they were cooped indoors, the number was perfect. Camilla made her chocolate cake and that was perfect too so Alice did not need the emergency substitute hidden in her bedroom. Rod stayed home throughout the day to be with Camilla and was nonplussed to be considered surplus to requirements until she sent him on errands: buying flowers, ferrying the friend who had the most awkward journey, so on.

'Alice, that was fabulous,' Camilla said when the debris was stashed in the dishwasher and she was surrounded by presents and sleepy but resisting bedtime because she could not bear the day to be done.

'Yeah,' said Alice, scrunching a wrapping paper lurking under the sofa. 'And that's only your tenth. They get better as you grow older.'

Whenever she reminisced about Camilla's birthday party, Alice's heart ached. It was the first and last they shared. She did not know whether Camilla's others were better or not, she did not know Camilla any longer. The day after the party Rod told her he was leaving.

He left her for his secretary, the only flash of originality being that Ruth was twelve years older than him and eighteen years older than Alice. He offered peculiar reasons for splitting up, apparently failing to understand his own motives. A couple of his reasons stuck in her memory. One was that she took no interest in his work. The other was that she was too involved with his daughter.

Alice's friends said she coped marvellously.

During her abruptly enforced solitude she revived an interest in poetry and, soon after, a long-buried conviction that she was, at heart, a writer. She remembered herself at school, in a class of bright girls destined for good degrees and the professions, but not one among them in whom she could have confided her wish to be a writer.

Had she been blessed with one of those intuitively guiding teachers into whose hands successful men and women tend to fall, her life would have played differently. Unfortunately, no one remotely like that worked at her comprehensive and her ambition fluttered briefly and died. Cast adrift by Rod, she found the impetus to try.

However much Charles questioned and wondered, she could not tell him that story. For one thing, it sounded self-pitying and she was nothing of the sort. For another, he failed to appreciate that being a writer was a state of being and not a matter of training. She did not grudge him his jokes about her falling into 'poetic moods', but it was a shame her passion for language was incomprehensible to him. Was being blinkered to it a state of being too?

No matter, there was good to be gained from their conflict. She ran no risk of being a self-indulgent writer because her poems would fall under the most critical eye.

Curiosity drew her down to the bay for a second time the day after the storm. Was the lake draining away and what had become of the boat?

The lake looked the same except that the ducks had left. The wreck was tipped onto its side, safe from the waves that were already slamming into the Cat Rock. The only person on the beach was Mrs Aley, a rugged widow who lived at the far end of the village and was never seen without gumboots, red headscarf and a couple of lurchers. By local standards she was chatty so Alice was always pleased to spot her. For once, they were walking in the same direction and she waited for Alice.

'A fresh day after a nasty night, Alice. Not as bad as the storm of eighty-three but more than enough for this time of year.'

Mrs Aley carried straight on with a remark about the boat, gesturing at it with her walking stick. 'Jacko reckoned the crew were lying dead inside it and the police sergeant from Downhill had to climb in and look.'

'And were they?'

'Course not. Washed overboard, I reckon.'

She swung her stick at the tumbling surf, and Alice saw in profile the big West Country nose on one side balanced by the sharp point of the scarf on the other.

Mrs Aley said: 'Can't see anything coming in on the tide but we'll know for sure when it goes out again. Extraordinary what the sea throws up here. We've had a couple of bodies from sea burials, you know.'

'Ugh.' Alice's wince pleased Mrs Aley.

'Oh yes, buried at sea but not far enough out for the current to leave them alone. Jacko found them.'

An objection signalled in Alice's mind. *'Jacko again, not the beachcomber, although I see him most mornings, most evenings, scouring the beach for the pickings.'*

Aloud she said 'I was wondering . . .'

But the lurchers set up a commotion and Mrs Aley's interest centered on them.

'I hope my boys don't find the crew for me. That's one thing I can do without. Animals don't think of that, though, do they?' When she laughed it was like listening to one of her dogs.

She yelled at them. 'Bingo! Lotto!'

They ignored her as dogs will. Splashing through the surf they worried a hunk of driftwood until the water retreated, leaving it dead and drying at their feet. Triumphant, they abandoned it in favour of chasing gulls which was as good a reason as any for more barking.

By then Mrs Aley was describing other tragedies. 'Folk try

and walk across the bay when the tide's out. Holidaymakers, usually. Looks easy, see, but the water comes in that fast they can't run ahead of it. And the mud's sucking at them . . . And there's nasty currents.'

'Oh, that's horrible.'

'The mud slows them down and then the water's over their heads in no time. We've had a few die like that. The sea washes them up and dumps them on the beach.'

Alice repeated her horror.

'There was a nasty one, backalong. Washed up over to Cat Rock and the eels got to it. There isn't much left of a face when an eel decides it's hungry. Takes the eyes, the lot. Took a time to find out who it was, because who can identify what the eels leave?'

Alice stammered out a question. 'Was he a holidaymaker?'

'No, he lived on a caravan site over that way. He'd picked up his rods and told his wife he was going fishing on the bay. Caught more than he reckoned on. Oh it's no use you looking like you're going to puke, Alice. The sea's a clean place and eels help with the cleaning. All dead flesh is good to them, never mind whose it is.'

Mrs Aley laughed but she was laughing at the antics of the dogs.

Walking dogs, as Alice had come to appreciate in her weeks at Stark Point, was an entertainment. Obviously, it was a bad idea if you wanted to study wildlife because they scared it off but otherwise there was much to be said for them. The fluffily posing Bonny had not offered anything to compare with this. Alice wondered, for the first time in her life, whether she might keep a dog.

She and Mrs Aley talked about the merits of lurchers, swapped notes about the storm, talked about the dogs, guessed at the duration of the lake and talked again about the dogs. The wind got up and the point of Mrs Aley's headscarf snapped like a pennant, a familiar noise she ignored although Alice had to raise her voice.

Eventually the animals went to rummage near the cliff. Alice snatched the opportunity to ask about her mystery neighbour, the face at the window. She did not mention the spying, merely asked who lived at Ham Cottage.

'Ah, you mean Iris Dottrell.' This was said with a sigh, a pitying shake of the head. 'Poor soul, you won't see her out. Had a bad turn backalong, she did.'

'Does she live alone?'

'Quite alone. A couple of folk in the village look after her – shopping and that – but that's as much as she allows.'

There was a finality about the remark that Alice sensed was a warning against getting involved.

From near the cliff came yelping. Mrs Aley strode forward, shouting, her scarf a flashing danger signal as she went. Alice was left to stroll where the foaming spray died on the sand.

The Cat Rock was inaccessible now and water swirled high up the bay. Light was fading towards evening. A sombre wash tinted the sky and flattened the colours inland. Alice struggled to put words to the sensation of life being colour, in nature, and colour being squeezed from the day.

In a corner of her mind Mrs Aley's lurchers continued to bark. All at once they came roaring into view and plunged into the sea, causing a tremendous rumpus and tearing Alice's thoughts away from anything requiring concentration.

'*What I'll do,*' she thought, on a quite different level, '*is take Iris Dottrell some flowers or fruit. Whatever I can find in the garden, if the storm's left me anything worth giving.*'

But she had the niggling suspicion that Mrs Aley had warned her off, and there was no chance to find out because Mrs Aley was disappearing into the scrub, her dogs gambolling after her. Alice, feeling she had been dismissed and left to make her own way in the world, sauntered along the beach in the opposite direction.

After a few minutes a cool breeze flattened her hair to her

head and she pulled up her collar, her pace quickening involuntarily. A picture of her cottage, with the curtains drawn and the stove lit, filled her mind. She ran up the beach.

Once in the village, protected from the breeze, her urgency dissipated and she went at a casual pace, pausing to peer at the doll jammed beneath the water. At that moment, she tingled with the sensation that someone was watching. Iris Dottrell. The spy had a name now.

Home, she cast around for a gift to deliver to Mrs Dottrell. Lilies were in flower but they were redolent of funerals and misery. Alice poked around until she had gathered a bunch of bright blooms, yellow, pink and blue, a pretty handful to brighten any heart. She took them to the spy's house.

But her ring on the bell was unanswered. Alice set the flowers down on the doorstep, then imagined them lying undiscovered by a woman who never went out. Instead, she left them on the kitchen window sill where they were certain to be spotted.

Eyes were on her as she walked away. The temptation to point to the flowers was almost overpowering but she stared straight ahead, and that was how she happened to see the beachcomber, on a path behind cottages in the centre of the village.

He was alone, as usual. She was struck by the thought that the people she saw at Stark Point generally were. It had taken the exceptional event of a boat being flung ashore to draw them into a chattering, questioning group.

The solitariness gnawed at her. She had known, from the day she first drove onto the peninsula, that it was a physically comfortless place but she had been unprepared for the way topography influenced the inhabitants. Not only was the village cut off but the dwellings were strung out; and not only were the buildings held apart but so were the people. One might have expected them to huddle together for the warmth of companionship but they preferred to be lonely individuals.

Alice puzzled whether this was their conscious choice or was forced upon them by their dangerous relationship to the elements. At Stark Point it was impossible to ignore a human being's insignificance in the natural world.

Other things perplexed her. How had her Aunt Bella managed? Did the Stark Point mentality account for Bella becoming estranged from most of the family? Did it explain why she overlooked closer relatives and bequeathed Spray Cottage to a nephew and niece she had scarcely met and who, as fate would have it, had predeceased her?

'If living here depends on loving isolation, I don't think I can do it,' Alice muttered. 'I can't help being sociable, I enjoy having neighbours. God, I'll go mad if life here really is as bleak as I imagine.'

The beachcomber was out of sight and no one else disturbed the emptiness of the landscape.

'*What on earth is it going to be like in winter?*'

Alice started to laugh but the sound was not a pleasant one. She realised she was shuddering.

Chapter Three

Next day Alice decided to speak to the beachcomber.

The Starkers' reluctance to acknowledge his existence had inflamed her curiosity, and when she saw him shambling close to where the surf broke on the early morning shore, she made up her mind.

'*It's as if he's part of the natural order,*' she was thinking. '*The filtering light, the swing of the tide, the high-pitched forays of the birds, and the beachcomber to check everything's doing what's expected of it.*'

And then the question. '*But why do I keep asking about him and guessing? It'll be the easiest thing in the world to meet him and find out for myself.*'

So she went, quickly, before he disappeared, as he was wont to, part-way round the bay, among the thorn bushes backcombed by the wind. She presumed there was a path there although she had been unable to discover it.

'*If so, it also explains my sighting of him behind the cottages. He doesn't walk through the village, he slinks past it.*'

Her quickest route was straight down the causeway but the lake was still there and she faced a poor choice. Go through the saltings or cut inland and hope to discover a path? Either way she risked missing him.

'*The saltings,*' she decided. '*This is supposed to be a chance meeting, and it won't be convincing unless it's on the beach.*'

She saw him as she came out of the high grass. He had his back to her and was going towards the rocks. At low tide there were rock pools, at high tide there was danger. She skipped along, willing him not to perform his vanishing trick.

He reached the rocks before he turned and saw her. Alice kept moving steadily over the sand, hoping he assumed she was going to the boat which lay between them. Scuffled sand around the wreck proved it had become one of the local sights. Word had spread, in the magical way it does, and people had driven down from the hills to marvel at the twin wonders of the wreck and the lake.

While she looked it over she kept him in the tail of her eye, aware he was studying her. Then she walked directly towards him. He shifted his weight, changed the direction of his body until he was poised to speed away inland. Alice called out.

'I've been looking at the boat.' Her words did not matter, the point was to hold his attention. She offered him her most generous smile.

He waited without moving. As she drew nearer she registered the tatty state of his green waterproof jacket, a rent down one sleeve fixed with safety pins; the white salt stains discolouring his boots; the way the brown knitted cap fitted so tightly over his scalp and ears that it might have been painted on; and the searching pale blue eyes. He stood with his hands clasped behind his back and let her come right up to him.

'Hello,' Alice said, still beaming.

She was surprised he was old, not the casual dawdler she had originally taken him for but a man in his sixties or seventies whose gait was slow and uneven because of age and physical neglect.

'Hello,' he said. 'You're that writer.'

The word gave her a pang. Nobody called her that. Oh, it was not true, of course she knew it was not, insofar as she was unpublished, but even so – *to be called a writer*. She checked herself, tried not to glow with the pleasure of the compliment.

'I'm Alice Wintle.'

He nodded, said nothing and she feared he would escape.

'The boat.' She snatched at a subject to stoke the conversation. 'Were you the first to find it?'

His eyes brightened. 'After the storm.' He gave a leftwards jerk with his head. 'She was right down there.'

'I know, I was here when the men towed it up the beach.' *'And so were you,'* she thought, *'sitting by the cliff, ignored.'*

He nodded. The wind got beneath his jacket and lifted it so he looked like a balloon being inflated. For the first time he released his clasped hands and beat at the jacket, flattening it. Alice noticed they were large hands in gloves whose thin leather was cracked and stiff. She felt a rush of sympathy for him.

'You're a writer,' he repeated. 'I've got a story to tell you.'

'Really?' Smiling, looking interested.

She had heard that writers were frequently offered stories. It was extraordinary, this man was treating her like a genuine writer. Her instinct was not to spoil it by explaining she was a poet, not a writer of tales. Besides, she was curious to hear the story.

But rather than spill it out, he waited for her to say more. Alice did not understand what. She caught at flying strands of her hair and anchored them behind an ear.

'Is your story a true one, about something that happened here?'

'Yes, it's about this place.' A pause. 'I've been here all my life.'

She gave an encouraging nod.

'They want me to go. They want me out of my house.'

'But surely . . .'

Just then his face grew wary. He shifted, ready to walk off. Down the beach something was troubling him. Alice twisted to see. Mrs Aley's lurchers were scampering through the saltings.

She heard him say goodbye. Useless to try and stop him, Alice could only note his route: up the beach, along the rim of the bay for a few yards and then into the scrub where foxes went to ground. Abruptly, he dropped from sight.

The lurchers came, barking, flinging themselves around, spraying damp sand, emptying the bay of wildlife. Rabbits fled in panicky jerks, birds wheeled away and a village cat scaled the crumbling cliff to sanctuary. Alice returned to the boat and soon met Mrs Aley.

'Talking to him, were you?' Mrs Aley surprised Alice by mentioning this before the weather, which was the usual preliminary to local conversation.

'I asked him about the boat.'

'Hm.' The woman used her stick to jab in the direction of it. 'He won't know anything. Jacko says the police are saying it came from right down the channel. Ripped from a harbour, it was. Anchored there but not good enough to withstand the storm.'

'Then nobody was on board, after all?'

'Course not. Jacko reckons only a fool would have set out in a boat that evening, what with the weather forecast the way it was.'

Alice spotted the discrepancy between Jacko's previous opinion and his hindsight, and Mrs Aley's too, but gave no hint. 'Well, thank heavens the crew weren't killed.'

Mrs Aley began yelling at the lurchers who were being taunted by the cat and not taking it quietly.

'Lotto! Bingo!'

After things calmed down, Alice said: 'I'm thinking of getting a dog myself.'

Mrs Aley strolled along the beach with her, talking about dogs. The tail of the red head scarf wagged in the wind.

'They're good company,' said Mrs Aley who seemed to do nothing but bawl at her pair from a distance. 'I got my two after my husband died. Not that I'm really alone, you know. I've got my brother and sister-in-law at the Point. John has the poultry farm by the chapel, you know the one.'

They walked on a bit further talking about chickens, neither of them mentioning the incongruity of birds trapped in a building in the midst of a landscape of air and water. Eventually, Alice asked where Mr Keenthorne lived.

'Over there.' Mrs Aley's stick swung in an arc that encompassed the entire village.

Alice refused to be fobbed off. 'Do you mean actually in the village?'

'There.' The stick shot up again.

'Does he also live alone?' Alice was remembering the pinned jacket, the cracked leather of the gloves. A man on his own might not trouble about such matters, although a woman probably would.

Mrs Aley was no more forthcoming than before. 'Yes, and he shouldn't be at his age.'

Stubbornly Alice pressed on. 'I heard people want him out of his house.' No need to mention she had heard it from Joe Keenthorne.

'They've talked to a social worker who comes out here, told her he can't look after himself. He ought to see sense and sell up, let folks who can manage the house have it.'

'Does he have family here?'

'Used to.'

Alice felt herself blundering without understanding why. 'He seems so solitary. Whenever I see him he's alone.'

Mrs Aley did not respond to that. It became important to shout at the lurchers who were digging a hole by the water's edge.

'*Cagey*,' thought Alice. '*She knows everything there is to know about him but she isn't going to tell me.*'

Since the lake had formed the only audible engines had been tractors but now she heard cars. Something was amiss, though, because they were shunting, not going anywhere. Mrs Aley caught up with her on the road.

'Vehicles are getting through,' Alice said, slightly sad that the phenomenal lake was seeping away.

'The men cleared a drain on Duller's land. By rights, it should have carried the water straight off but folk can't be bothered to look after them like they used to.'

As they turned the first of a series of bends in the lane, they found a delivery van confronting an estate car. The drivers had wound their windows down and were arguing.

Mrs Aley was oddly smug as she commented: 'Drivers who don't know the road always get jammed there.'

'It is a difficult bend.' Alice recalled Charles cursing on the day he sped round it and met a tractor.

'We used to have a worse one but that was straightened out years ago.' With her stick she showed Alice where it used to be.

The car driver was afraid of reversing into a rhine and the van driver was convinced he would brush a wall if he moved an inch. Alice expected Mrs Aley to intervene, using her expert local knowledge, but the woman preferred to gather her dogs to her and wait for the road to be cleared. It was Alice who persuaded the van driver to ease back and let the car through. The car was driven by a young woman who raced away without Alice having a clear view of her.

'Don't know who owns that car,' admitted Mrs Aley, 'and the van driver isn't one of the regulars either.' The fact that two strangers had come to an impasse in the tricky Stark Point lane gave her great satisfaction.

The car had pulled up at the side of the lane and, as Alice and Mrs Aley came round the next bend, a slender young woman jumped out and ran through a cottage gateway.

Mrs Aley gasped. 'My, that's her daughter come. Well, who'd have thought it?'

'Iris Dottrell's daughter?' Alice remembered the spying face and her own tentative gift.

'Yes. Mary Dottrell. Well, it's been a time since we've seen that young lady here, I can tell you.'

But Alice did not worry about the sarcastic edge to Mrs Aley's remark. She was feeling ridiculously pleased at the prospect of having a woman of her own age nearby.

* * *

She did not need to prompt a meeting with Mary Dottrell who called on her to say thank you for the flowers.

She appeared at Spray Cottage during the afternoon, a neatly dressed figure, her dark hair in a boyish crop. When she spoke she had a low and pleasant voice, with a restrained version of the local burr.

'Mary Dottrell reporting,' she said in a self-mocking manner, 'to thank you for the flowers and for getting that bone-headed van driver out of my way.'

Alice warmed to her. She invited her into the sunny sitting room, pushing her poetry notebook out of sight under a magazine while she offered tea. Mary said no thanks, having been drinking cups of instant coffee with her mother on and off since her arrival.

'My mother's grateful for the flowers,' she insisted. 'But she doesn't go out and she hardly answers the door. I suppose you knew that.'

A sympathetic nod.

'I tell her she's becoming a recluse but she doesn't care. If I could get her away from this place she'd be all right, I'm sure of it. Well, almost sure.'

Mary was assuming Alice knew far more than she did. Rather than let the misunderstanding build, Alice owned up.

'I've only been here a matter of weeks.'

And so they fell to talking about Alice inheriting the cottage and deciding to live there, about Charles who came and went, and about Stark Point and its peculiarities. They talked freely, like familiar friends.

Mary was the first person genuinely willing to discuss the village. In return, she sought Alice's impressions of it.

'I'm intrigued,' Alice said, launching into her fascination with the solitariness of the setting and the way this seemed to be reflected in the way people held themselves aloof. Once or twice Mary's brow puckered and she seemed poised to object, but she did not interrupt the flow and Alice was left to wonder afterwards whether she had imagined it and whether it had been significant.

One story that poured out at their first meeting was the wretched tale of Iris Dottrell.

'A few years ago Mum had a job in a pub, not behind the bar but in the kitchen,' Mary began. 'You'd think that would be safe, well away from any trouble and, believe me, they do get trouble in these country pubs on Saturday nights. Well, one evening they were short-handed so she asked her assistant to carry a meal into the lounge bar. And when the girl was crossing the public bar a man – all tattoos and earrings, that sort of customer – jumped up from a stool and snatched it out of her hands.'

'Drunk?'

'That was the excuse, if anything could excuse what happened. Mum heard the girl shriek and flew out of the kitchen. The man had the girl up against the bar and was threatening her. Mum told him to leave her alone. Then up jumped his two friends who began pushing Mum around. When she fell down, the three of them kicked her. On her back, in her side . . .'

Alice was aghast. 'But wasn't there anybody to stop them?'

'That's the worst of it, Alice. There were half a dozen other people in that bar, plus whoever was in the lounge bar. Not a soul intervened. And that's what did the real damage, you see, that nobody helped.'

'But the girl. Surely she tried?'

'Transfixed, like everybody else. They watched, that's all any of them did.'

'The barman?'

'Oh, he was on the phone to the police in a flash, but that didn't help Mum.'

Alice guessed from her face there was more.

Mary said: 'She recognised one of them. Not one of her attackers, I mean one of the men who wouldn't help her. He lives here, at Stark Point.'

'No wonder she shuts herself away.'

'Her world's shrinking, Alice. Immediately she came home from hospital, she said she couldn't face going into town, there'd be too many people there. I dragged her over there once but she kept fantasising she was seeing those youths. Then she had to be treated for depression. She's still prescribed sleeping pills. After a while she announced she couldn't bear walking around here either, because she's afraid of meeting the man who wouldn't protect her.'

'What does she do all day?'

'Radio, telly, does a crossword or plays around with an old computer of mine. That's about it. Her doctor told me it isn't unusual for the victim of a violent act to be destroyed psychologically, especially if they were left feeling worthless because nobody bothered to help them.' She sighed. 'I wish he hadn't told me. It's snuffed out whatever hope I had that this was a phase she'd pass through.'

The telephone trilled then, bringing both the sad tale and Mary's visit to an end. It was Charles enquiring whether Stark Island had been joined to the mainland yet and how soon he could be reunited with his car. When Alice said cars were driving through at last he said he would be down on the train that evening, if she would pick him up from the station. They fixed a time.

'How's your roof?'

'I telephoned a builder this morning. He promises to come in a day or two.'

Charles gave a disbelieving snort. 'Don't forget the form for an insurance claim.'

'I phoned for that this morning too.'

'Well. See you at the station at eight then.'

After she came off the line she thought about her conversation with Mary, and how touching it was that Mary was protective of her mother. Alice's own mother was the capable sort that other people turned to in troubled times.

'*Perhaps,*' she thought, '*it would be a kindness if I were to start calling on Mrs Dottrell. As she's letting her social contact dwindle away, a little gentle intrusion might be all to the good.'* She had another, less altruistic, reason. *'If she becomes familiar with me, she might drop the silly habit of spying.'*

Alice registered that Mary had said nothing favourable about Stark Point, her view seemingly coloured by her mother's experience. To know you live in a place where people lack the decency to stop a woman being beaten up by thugs was hard to bear. And yet Alice suspected Mary's attitude predated the attack. When Mary was leaving she had said, in her self-mocking way: 'Don't take any notice of me, I'm the one who got away.'

Had Charles not chosen that moment to telephone, their conversation would have ended with a plan to meet again instead of being chopped off awkwardly. Mary had been vague about how long she intended to stay with her mother but Alice hoped there would be time for them to explore the potential for true friendship. Initial attraction did not always mean a friendship gelled.

Alice read through her embryo poem about the boat in the storm. After a few reluctant minutes, during which her mind looped around her talk with Mary, she got to grips with it. Faults, which had earlier appeared nothing of the kind, glared up from the page. Her central idea was not thought through and, consequently, the poem was unfocused. Two phrases revealed themselves as trite and a third as absurdly elaborate.

For half an hour she grappled but it grew worse, not better. With a groan she tossed the notebook down and trailed through to the garden. Although the evergreen blocked her view of a barn, she heard cows lowing softly. Unseen birds filled the air with lazy song. Accompanying them, as ever, was the whisper of the sea.

An aeroplane glinted in fathomless blue. A dragon fly whirred into the garden, one of few places he would fail to find water. Alice was enticed to saunter through the bright afternoon.

For once, she walked the other way, towards the tip of the peninsula. The tarmac lane ended at a five-barred gate and continued as an unmade track through fields. Alice had only been as far as the gate once before, when she was driving and had to turn her car with difficulty. She opened the gate.

She lazed away the hours until evening sprawled on a rock, watching the sea nudging the shore, intermittently reading or looking across to a seaside town. From this distance, it was like any one of hundreds in Europe with its ice-cream-coloured buildings, the low long shapes of its terraces, where windows glowed gold in the sun. When the gold turned to fire she rose and began the journey home. She noticed then how hungry she was.

That was one of her discoveries about being alone. You were utterly free except for the regular call of your own hunger. When she had lived alone after her marriage broke up it was unlike this because she had gone out to work and been with companions all day. Only the occasional lonely Sunday had given her practice for doing nothing at Stark Point.

'But it's changing already. Whenever I get used to a situation it changes.'

She shuffled away from the thought because it brought to mind the botched poem. In that she had been struggling to use the storm-tossed vessel as a metaphor, and saying that sometimes she was content to be pushed around by events or other people's demands but other times she resisted and resented it.

The last few months had been a drifting time. The gift of Spray Cottage had encouraged her. She had been perfectly entitled to sell it yet she had let ownership of it re-order her existence.

'I imagine,' she murmured, as she closed the gate between the field track and the made-up lane, 'I'll grow bored with the house and sell it in a few years. However wonderful a thing is when it's new to you, it gradually palls.'

After a few yards she had the opposite idea. 'I might become rooted. If I really can write here, and especially if Stark Point is what inspires me, I'd be rash to leave.'

She ambled down the lane, fantasising about the villagers' reappraisal once her writing became a success.

None of this was shared with Charles when she collected him at the railway station. He rewarded her with a quick supper in a country pub, handed over post delivered to his flat, and spent no more time at Stark Point than it took to check his answering machine. Then he hopped into his car and swished away through the lake. The water was still shimmering and rippling when the car was a distant hum en route to the real world. Alice, torn between being offended and relieved, because she hardly wanted such an unwilling visitor, saw the funny side and gave way to laughter.

In the morning, the lash of rain against her bedroom window woke her. The light was weak, as though it were several hours nearer dawn. For a few minutes she lay there disgruntled. Her plans did not amount to much but she had made a few. With luck, another meeting with Joe Keenthorne in the early morning bay and a taste of the story he wanted to tell her. Mid-morning a visit to the Dottrells, to meet the mother and invite the daughter to tea. In between, a telephone call to Charles because she could not remember whether he had ordered the wood for her stove.

Rain altered everything. A light shower in the countryside was a delight but this was serious rain, slanting, slashing rain hurled by an onshore wind.

Alice pushed the curtains back. The scenery had dissolved. She wondered whether the downpour had raised the level of the lake or whether the cleared drain in Duller's field was emptying it at a faster rate than the sky was filling it. It was one of those school arithmetic questions, except they had featured baths and plugholes instead of lakes and drains.

By mid morning she gave up hope of the weather relenting and pulled on mac and rubber boots, armed herself with an umbrella, and ran through stinging flurries to Ham Cottage. To her surprise it was Mrs Dottrell who opened the door.

'Oh, you're drenched, my dear. Come in, come in. What a terrible day.'

Iris Dottrell's invitation was immediate, no hesitation for shy introductions or reassurance. She fussed around Alice, taking the dripping umbrella and helping her off with the mac.

'We'll put them here,' she said, lobbing the raincoat onto a hook that was too high for her to reach in comfort.

Alice smothered the hilarious thought that Mrs Dottrell had the action of a diminutive basketball player. Not only was she very short but the wrists scooting out of her sleeves were thin as twigs. The comic effect was enhanced by her lopsided skirt and the greying hair that was growing out a wire-wool home perm. Beside her Alice felt grossly oversized, a bouncy big creature of a different species.

She stood the umbrella in a pottery vase, apparently kept there for the purpose, and invited Alice to kick off her wet boots before going into the sitting room. Alice obediently dumped them beside a muddy pair of lace-ups. The stone flags felt cold through her socks.

The cottage smelled of cigarette smoke and yesterday's chips. Off the tiny hall was a chintzy sitting room the width of the house. Beyond it Alice glimpsed a kitchen where a radio was talking to itself. She saw no sign of Mary.

She sat on a sofa and Iris settled in an armchair with a tabloid newspaper on the floor beside it and an ashtray balanced on the arm. Alice read an upside-down headline about the dangers of nicotine.

Iris Dottrell stubbed out a half-inch of cigarette, saying, 'Mary's gone to the market to shop for me. I said to her, why don't you leave it this week, the weather's so bad? But she said no, her mind was made up and it was only a drop of rain, when all's said and done.'

She laughed and as she did so a strong look of the daughter came over her. 'She likes the sausages we get there, you see. Very fond of her food, my Mary is, not that she's any better at putting on fat than I am.'

Alice thought: '*They're like me and my mother, they have the same face.*'

Aloud she said: 'I'm sorry to miss her. We were interrupted yesterday and I'm sure we've lots more to talk about.'

'She enjoyed meeting you. You've made Bella's cottage very nice.' Smoke was coiling from the dying cigarette but she was oblivious to it, thinking how interesting it was to meet Alice at last having spent so much time watching her and resenting her.

Alice enjoyed the unwarranted compliment. All she had done to the cottage was splash a coat of white paint over dingy walls and ceilings. Well, she'd had no choice, there were light patches where pictures had been removed.

'You have a lovely sitting room,' Iris continued, 'with the sun streaming in and plants on the table by the window.'

Alice demurred although she was pleased Mary had delivered a good report. Presumably that was how Iris, who did not go out herself, knew. Alice said: 'Mary saw it at its best. It's dark in there today, I've had electric light on all morning.'

At last Iris was troubled by the smoke and ground the cigarette stub out thoroughly. Then she made mugs of instant coffee and apologised for the lack of biscuits which would not be available until Mary returned. Alice assured her she was perfectly happy not to be eating biscuits. In the kitchen the radio continued to chatter.

For a while they talked about the storm, its local rating which was not particularly high, and the unfortunate policeman who had climbed into the wreck checking for corpses. Soon they settled to talk about Spray Cottage and Bella.

The story of the bequest came up at the outset, as Iris intended. 'Goodness, you must have been amazed to get her house, if you never knew her.'

'Well, yes, I was rather. I mean, I still am. There are mornings when I wake up and think, "*Did that really happen?*"'

'Like a story in a book.' Iris seemed reflective for a moment, quelling her bitterness before she was able to add: 'She'd like that, you know, you hardly believing your good luck. She didn't want her property to go to just anybody. Lots of folk wouldn't have taken the house on, they'd sell up and spend the money elsewhere. Yes, you know, I'm sure Bella would have been thrilled at you moving in.'

Alice determined not to cast a shadow over this enthusiasm by mentioning she was to be a part-time resident. There was ample time to let those details slip into conversation before September and her return to the radio station.

Nothing was said, either, about Iris being repeatedly spotted at her bedroom window, even though Alice had waved to her cheerily enough. The flowers were mentioned, of course, Iris pointing them out in a lustre jug on top of the television set.

'Bella was fond of flowers,' she said. 'Well, you'll have guessed that from her garden.'

'Yes. It's one of the biggest clues to her personality. More than the inside of the cottage, I think, because people get stuck with furniture and houses they can't change. But a garden has to be made over and over again. It's obvious she chose to spend time on it.'

'You'll keep it up, won't you?' Spitefully, Iris doubted it.

'I will try.'

'It would be a pity if it were lost. There's scarcely a garden at Stark Point that hasn't got Bella's plants in it.'

Alice pictured her aunt counting small change after selling a few marigolds but Iris's next remark scotched the idea.

'Very open-handed, was Bella. She used to put a box of spare plants by the gate and let anyone take a few home. And if they admired anything in her garden, she was sure to remember and give them a cutting as soon as it was the right time to take one. In that way, her handiwork lives on although she's gone. Folk thought a lot of her, you see.'

Alice was hearing a new version of life at Stark Point. The

taciturn loners who had created her impression of village life were being replaced by generous and appreciative folk.

Iris spoke again. 'They gave her presents, or that's what she said they were but I think she accepted them because they didn't have any money for her. And anyway, she wasn't that interested in money, was she?'

Floundering, Alice muttered. 'I don't know.'

'Oh, don't you know she was a healer?'

'No, I know hardly anything about her.'

The admission comforted Iris in her secret loathing, because while Alice might have the cottage she had not had Bella.

'Well,' Iris said, 'when the doctor couldn't help, we used to go to Spray Cottage. It was meant to be a secret but everyone knew for miles around. Bella made you drink a confusion of herbs from her garden and you were cured.'

Alice begged for more, seizing on the chance to learn a piece of her family history. Sadly, her eagerness daunted Iris who became flustered and frowning.

'Oh dear, how can I tell you everything? I don't know where to begin?'

Cheated, Alice saw the story that had been dangled now being withheld. She cajoled.

Iris chipped in, too upset to talk any more now and afraid she was frightening Alice away. 'Come again and I'll have it all straight in my mind. Will that satisfy you?'

Alice said it would.

There was an echo of the beachcomber's words the previous day. '*I've got a story to tell you.*'

Chapter Four

'Every place has its stories,' said Mary Dottrell, facing Alice across the kitchen table at Spray Cottage. 'The thing is, how accurate are they? You know how people's minds work, one incident leads to half a dozen different versions.'

'*She's advising me,*' Alice thought, '*to be careful.*'

Aloud she said: 'True, but if I don't have the stories about Bella I won't have anything. She's dead. That's all that's left, the stories.'

'As long as you understand that. My mother adored her so you'll hear nice stories.'

'Was there a darker side to Bella?'

'I'm not saying that. But, knowing this place, if you asked certain other people you'd be told she was a witch.'

'Oh, come on, Mary, you don't mean that!'

'A healer, laying on hands and doling out herbs? Stark Point hasn't caught on to the New Age yet, Alice. Healers and herbs are strictly witchcraft around here.'

But she was pulling funny faces as she said it and making Alice laugh. If she'd been serious originally, she was no longer.

Mary had dropped in during the afternoon shortly after she came home from the market. The rain had slackened but settled into a steady drizzle. Alice had straightaway asked about the state of the road.

'All that's left is a huge puddle.'

'I might have to go out later on,' Alice said, explaining her concern about the depth of the water. She had not been able to reach Charles to ask about the firewood.

Mary felt in her pocket and put a flattish tin on the table. 'You don't mind this, do you?'

Alice rocked with laughter. 'Don't tell me there's a market stall selling cannabis.'

'Not exactly.'

'Your mother told me you go there for sausages!'

Mary, rolling a joint, said, 'Hm. I always have to remember to bring the sausages too.'

'But . . '

'Why don't I tell her? Her friend Bella having been a herbalist?'

'Exactly.'

A self-mocking smile. 'A girl has to have some secrets from her mother.'

'It isn't as though Iris isn't a bit of a smoker herself.'

'Life's full of ironies, eh?' She struck a match and offered the joint.

Alice shook her head. 'Not this time, thanks.'

Mary sucked on it, then said: 'This reminds me, among the local stories you'll no doubt hear from my mother is the one about three men and a boat, grounded off the Cat Rock with a cargo of cannabis. They say the policemen sent to guard it were out of their heads for a week.'

'Are the others as good as that?'

'Some. A great storm that blew the postman's sack up a tree is sure to feature, and probably a rigmarole about a cow in a ditch.'

'They sound comical,' said Alice, greatly heartened. 'If this is local history, I'm looking forward to it.'

'They *are* funny, if you look at them one way, but mostly what they demonstrate is a wilful lack of co-operation. For instance, the cow wouldn't have got near the ditch if the farmer who accepted responsibility for replacing the fence had provided a gate too.'

She inhaled again and checked whether Alice had changed her mind about having a puff.

'If you want a perfect example,' Mary said, 'take a look at the cottages on Parry's farm. You'll see their access is a shared drive. Mr Tims, who bought the one on the left, didn't own a vehicle and he objected to his neighbour parking a van up by the cottages, so he ran a strand of wire down the middle of the drive.'

'But it's narrow.'

'That's right. He prevented the neighbour using it. The wire was ripped down, and put up, and ripped down . . . They came to blows.'

'And in the end?'

'The wife of the van owner insisted on moving. By then there was a wooden fence installed. Before they left, her husband bought a heavy old truck specifically to smash down the fence and wreck his enemy's garden. He abandoned it so close to the door that Mr Tims could only come and go through a window until he'd had it towed away.'

Alice murmured that it was astonishing how far people would go. 'I wish you'd let me carry on thinking the stories were purely comical.'

Mary's face grew tense. She wished she could ensure Alice would take what she had to say seriously, not laugh it off. 'Actually, Alice, there's one that's absolutely terrible and I'm praying my mother won't feel she ought to tell you about it. It upsets her, you see.'

'I'll make sure she doesn't tell me. You'll have to give me a clue what it's about, though, because if I don't know I can't prevent her launching into it.'

Mary walked to the window and was silent for so long Alice suspected her attention had drifted. But Mary was working out how much to say, and wishing she need not say anything at all.

At last she gave a resigned kind of shrug and began to speak.

'A farmer and his wife disappeared years ago. The police believed they'd been murdered.'

'And had they?'

'Nobody knows what became of them. Some say they tried to cross the bay and were overtaken by the tide, but no bodies were found. My mother gets very perturbed whenever the subject comes up.'

'She knew the people involved,' Alice guessed.

'Stark Point's tiny. Everybody here knew them and they knew everybody.'

Her hard look deterred Alice from pursuing it.

'Mary might,' she thought, *'enlarge another time. If not, the village is full of people who know as much.'*

'Bloody weather,' Mary grumbled but in a good-natured way. 'You'd think it would let up for the holidays.' She reached for her raincoat. 'Sorry to rush off but Mum oughtn't to be left for too long, not while I'm here.'

Iris Dottrell had referred, with great pleasure, to her daughter moving back home but Mary's remark made it seem temporary.

Alice asked, 'Aren't you coming to live here?'

'No chance. I'm giving up my summer holiday to be with Mum but by September I'll be prowling the groves of academe again, or at any rate the corridors of one of London's minor universities.'

Reading Alice's face she added, 'Oh dear, you're going to tell me Mum's convinced herself her little girl's come home for good.'

'I'm afraid she has.'

'Damn. Well, I suppose if I'm honest I could see her running away with that idea and I couldn't bring myself to disillusion her.'

Alice suggested it was very difficult, when someone was delicate in the way Iris was, to dash their hopes.

'Terribly difficult, even when it's a ludicrously big thing she's hoping for. I mean, there's no logical reason for me to chuck up a decent job teaching social sciences, plus my social life, to burrow down at Stark Point with a woman who daren't leave her own house.'

Intuitively, Alice understood she was being fostered as the deputy daughter. She steeled herself to tell Mary: 'My own work takes me away in September, too.'

'But can't you commute? Bristol's not far.'

A shake of the head. 'I work awkward hours. No, I shall be ensconced in Charles's flat during the week and coming here for weekends, although even that depends on scheduling.'

Mary was dismayed. She did not care to hear the intricacies, it was enough to know her hope of companionship for her mother was a false one.

Alice admitted: 'Like you, I didn't spell it out to Iris. She made an assumption and I didn't correct her.'

She was thinking how easy it was to commit an unkind act while attempting the opposite.

'Don't worry, Alice, it isn't your problem. And it's weeks before either of us goes anywhere.'

Mary ran off into the rain, glum, quite unlike the chirpy young woman who had arrived at Spray Cottage an hour ago.

As soon as she had left, Alice tried Charles's number again. He sounded harassed so she kept to the point.

'Charles, have you ordered the wood?

'What wood?'

'My firewood. You were going to see Fred . . .'

'Oh, right. Firewood, yes.'

'That's great. I was afraid you'd forgotten to do it.'

'No, hold on. I mean I remember now. But I didn't order it.'

'Charles, you just said . . .'

'I didn't, honestly. I meant I . . . Look, Alice, your firewood is *not* ordered. Fred Phoenix was . . .'

'Partridge. He's Fred Partridge.'

'He can be Fred Budgerigar for all the difference it makes. I'm trying to tell you I went to the Falcon – why are these all bird names? – at the time he was supposed to be around and he wasn't. Therefore, no firewood ordered.'

'There's no need to address me as though I'm an imbecile.'

'All right, all right. I'm sorry. I apologise. But, Alice I'm drowning in faxes and I'm being bawled out by prima donnas and you're going on about firewood.'

She bit her lip before calmly saying she needn't hold him up any longer and goodbye.

'Prima donnas,' she muttered, venting her anger by punishing a cushion. 'Whenever he uses that word he means people are standing up to him. Which they ought to do and more often.'

She stepped back from the sofa and approved the plumped cushion. Hands on hips she told it: 'Well, now we know where we are, I can go and find Fred Partridge for myself.'

The Falcon did not open until seven. By the time her car nosed into what remained of the lake, a shower was veiling the hills and the evening had the special luminous quality reserved for the final hours of rainy days.

Alice let the car fly down the straight road, towards the hump-backed bridge where it turned an angle. Wet grass sparkled in the fields, green and gingery lichens brightened weathered stone. The rhines were silver bands tying the land into parcels. Slowing, near the bridge, she counted herons flying to the pond where swans floated. There was great beauty in this watery emptiness.

Her mind played with phrases to capture it. The mercurial aspect of it; the distinctive smell, a mix of sea scents and fresh water that moved so slowly it seeped rather than flowed; the airiness in which people led cramped lives; and the lure of the bluish hills to which all roads ran.

She came to a twisting section and a fork, the lane very narrow. Then her thoughts turned to the beachcomber. She pictured him sloping along the beach, close to the breaking surf, head down and hands clasped behind his back.

And then a little objection reared up, one she felt dense not to have registered before. For the rest of her drive, past villages, through the woods and into the car park of the Falcon Inn, it troubled her.

Switching off the ignition, she accepted the inevitable conclusion. *'He isn't a beachcomber. I've never seen him pick anything up and or carry anything. He paces the shore, that's all he does.'*

Depriving him of the purpose she had been convinced ruled his life was disquieting. *Now he's even more of an enigma.*

Alice entered the Falcon ready, after Charles's experience, for disappointment. Partridge was a man known to give a fair deal on well-matured firewood and, inconvenient as it was, it was said to be worth the bother of seeking him out. The Falcon was his base on two evenings a week.

Bored after half an hour, she finished her tonic water and went up to the bar for another. On her way back, she looked at quaint photographs hanging on the wall.

'I'll be reduced to reading the beer mats soon,' she was thinking. *'If only I'd brought a book.'*

But one of the photographs seized her attention. A man and woman were pictured with an old-fashioned car, in a traditional pose from the days when cars were prized possessions rather than necessary equipment. The man was standing beside it, square-faced, a solid citizen in every way, although the overcoat he was wearing probably exaggerated his girth. The woman was in the driving seat, sleek-haired and neat, a fur collar around her long neck and a bracelet spanning her wrist.

Undoubtedly, the car was the point of the snapshot. Even in an aged print, it gleamed with energetic polishing. Alice was not knowledgeable about cars and failed to identify the marque, but even she could tell it was an expensive car and would be more so now had it survived.

What tugged at her was the building in the background. Spray Cottage.

The picture was fixed to the wall. The landlady tried lifting it off, then fetched a torch in compensation. Alice scrutinised the scene.

At the bar a swarthy customer, arms ballooning from T-shirt sleeves, was downing a pint of cider in audible gulps.

'That car's a Talbot, pre-war model,' he announced. 'Had style, they did. Don't build them like that any more.'

Alice owned up. 'I'm looking at the house behind it. I think it's mine.'

The landlady said: 'You want to come in again when my Alf's here. He'll take it down for you, I'm sure.'

'Can't you get it off, Wanda?' Brawny arms reached for the frame.

Quickly Wanda discouraged him. 'I wouldn't like to try it without Alf's say-so.'

'Ah. Well, in that case, best not.' He gave Alice a wink and returned to the bar.

'Same again, Fred?' asked Wanda.

And that was how Alice discovered she had kept her rendezvous with Fred Partridge.

Business was soon concluded. Alice trusted she had put the right questions and paid a fair price, but this was the first occasion she had bought a year's supply of fuel for a stove and she was very much in his hands. Unfortunately, she would not find out the truth until she lit the first fires of Autumn.

Fred Partridge insisted on buying her a drink while they discussed the size of her firebox and the length to which he should cut the wood. She had already decided to ask him to cut it small enough. Her own experience with a saw-horse was nil and she fancied Charles's was no better. Besides, Charles detested Stark Point and threatening to turn him into her weekend woodcutter was a bad idea.

She wrote Partridge a cheque. Men, mainly older men, had been arriving in two and threes and greeting him. He had broken off to call back: 'All right, Jim?' or Jack, Paul or Dickie. No one came over, Fred and his customers being a familiar feature of the Falcon.

By now Wanda was fetching and bending and stretching as much as she might in a health club. When she was speeding up and down behind the bar, revolving this way and that, her roly poly figure reminded Alice of an animated Russian doll. She tried not to look, struggled not to laugh.

Fred wrote down her address with slow precision in a slim red notebook.

'About two weeks, then,' he said, closing it.

'I'll give you my telephone number, in case there's a change.'

'No, no, don't worry about telephones.'

His swift rejection convinced her they did not figure in his life. Well, it did not matter. He had access to the wood store in her garden whether she was at home or not.

She rose, bringing the conversation to an end and releasing him to talk to his friends. Jim and Dickie moved towards him immediately, and they were all talking and joking before Alice had taken two steps. The empty room where she had endured the long wait was transformed into a noisy clubby place.

In the centre, the man Fred had called Paul was spinning out an anecdote about last weekend's storm, loud enough to include in his audience an old man on a settle by the door. A red-haired youth was singing, a deliberately bad impersonation of a pop star. His giggly girlfriend was telling him to shut up. Someone was collecting money for a lottery syndicate, and two women were grumbling about the high cost of their water rates. Whirling Wanda was rushing at dizzying speed, almost keeping up with demand, but whenever she was winning the door swung open and another knot of customers entered.

Alice pushed through and went out into the cool evening. She wished she could stay, for the laughter and liveliness, but it would have been no good. The Falcon regulars were enjoying the fun of familiarity and she could be no part of it. Best to let them enjoy it.

It was twilight. The islands were suspended in a mist. A smudge suggested land on the far side of the channel. On the flat land between the hills and the sea, hamlets were pinpointed with lamplight. Later, the light from the villages would appear bold and ugly but for now there was a tender Japanese touch to the scene.

The lie of the land hid Stark Point from her. There was so little of it and even that seemed to have vanished. She could easily imagine it happening: a breach in a bank; a slight change of sea level swamping the saltings; the drainage system defeated and the peninsula sunk.

Alice drove down the hill. Orange lamps flared in village after village as the dove grey evening deepened towards night.

Iris Dottrell rested her bosom on her arms and hunched forward in her arm chair. Her head tipped to the right as she studied Alice and her question.

'Who lived at Spray Cottage before Bella?'

'Yes.'

'But Bella was there a good forty years. The Janners lived at the cottage before her. Rented it, they did, mind. Not many in the village owned their houses, if you start going back any distance. They didn't make the garden, though, only a few rows of cabbages and beans. Bella made the garden – herbs and flowers, those super bums . . .'

Alice smothered a smile at the unintentionally comical mispronunciation. She coaxed Iris to return to the question. 'The photograph I saw was taken in the 1940s, judging by the clothes.'

The corners of Iris's mouth turned down. 'Hmm. You've got me wondering whether it could be Bella herself you've been looking at.'

'No, it's not Bella.'

She felt silly for having rushed to Ham Cottage the next morning demanding identification, but until Iris screwed up her eyes and grappled with her memory it had seemed self-evident the couple were posing outside their own house. Now Alice wished Mary were there instead of buying mackerel from the fisherman. A third voice would have made the questioning easier, without poor Iris seeming to pass or fail depending on how much she recalled.

Iris was disappointed, too. 'Is there anything else you can tell me? All you've said is they were photographed outside the house in the 1940s.'

'Sorry, I assumed they lived there but they can't have.'

'They might have visited, mind. Folk would be photographed on visits, wouldn't they?'

'The car . . .'

'Car? You didn't mention a car.'

Feeling even more foolish, Alice explained. 'The car didn't seem to matter.'

'But they had a car with them?'

'A chunky old saloon, they were posing with it.'

Iris dropped her arms and let out a sigh that seemed too big for her skinny frame. Released, her bosom shuddered beneath her baggy jumper. 'Well, now, there was only one local family who owned a smart car backalong. What sort was it in the photograph?'

All at once Alice suspected Fred Partridge and his easy knowledge. She hedged. 'Possibly a Talbot.'

Expressions played across Iris's face like wind on water. After a minute, during which the only noise was the ticking of the kitchen clock, Alice pressed.

'Who were those people?'

Iris's voice was weak. She cleared her throat.

'Those were the Abletts, Alice.'

'I've never heard of them.' She paused to allow Iris to enlarge but eventually had to ask. 'Who were they?'

She saw Iris's shoulders rise, the way her daughter's did. It was not a shrug exactly, more an acceptance that something needed to be said, however reluctantly.

Iris cleared her throat again. 'They lived in a farmhouse down the village, on the other side of the lane.'

'Are they still here?' She was doing frantic mental arithmetic. In the photograph they looked in their thirties, but it was taken in the 40s, and the 40s were fifty years ago, therefore if they were still alive they would be in their eighties. Anyway, she might be wrong about their ages and the date of the photograph.

'No,' said Iris flatly. 'They went away a long time ago.'

Alice stifled a gasp. The change in Iris convinced her this was the story that was never to be mentioned. Less than twenty four hours since making her promise to Mary, she was begging Iris to dredge her memory for the farming couple who were missing, believed murdered.

Desperate to get away, she pretended to remember a telephone call she was expecting and fled.

Alone, Iris scrabbled to light a cigarette. She was breathing heavily, her fingers clumsy. Matches shot out of the box and sprayed over the table. Finally she got a flame to the tobacco and took shuddering gulps.

'Damn Alice, why's she got to go nosing after the Abletts! What's it to her what happened to them?'

She broke off muttering to suck at the cigarette again. Then, shaky, she sat down.

'She's trouble, that girl. Got Bella's cottage when she shouldn't have and now she thinks she can come to me with her questions about it. Always the same with incomers, the more you tell them the more they want to know.'

It hurt her to remember Bella, the friendship and the betrayal, but it hurt her more to think about the Abletts.

'They're long gone from here, that's all Alice needs to know. Someone ought to make sure she leaves them alone.'

Her lungs burned and for a couple of minutes she was racked with coughing but even that did not tear her mind away from

Alice and the need to stop her stirring up interest in the fate of the Abletts.

Alice banged in through her back door, angry at her blunder and imagining Mary and Iris breaking off with her, both distrusting her although for different reasons. For a while she hung around the cottage, drinking camomile tea and ordering herself to calm down.

As it happened, the telephone did ring. Her friend Julie, a chubby and untidy therapist, had time to kill between clients and craved a chat.

'How soon can you come?' Alice asked, as she always did.

'Oh, if only. I'd really love to, Alice, but . . .'

Julie had a string of reasons to delay seeing Spray Cottage. She was one of those people who affect always to be busy, overrun with commitments and work. Julie, though, spent longer on the telephone than anyone else Alice knew. A mutual friend had once wondered aloud why there wasn't therapy for telephone junkies.

This time they talked about Alice's discovery that her aunt had been a healer and herbalist. Julie was delighted, and Alice felt her own stock rising in her friend's estimation.

Then Julie confessed. 'A Mars bar on Friday, as a reward for doing my book-keeping.'

'Well, that doesn't count. Anyone who keep their books up to date deserves a reward.'

'And on Saturday a sticky toffee pudding after fish and chips.'

'Oh dear. No excuse for that one.'

'Your turn.'

'I've been saintly.'

Wailing. 'You always show me up. Why can't I have your will power?'

'It isn't that, Julie. I haven't got any shops, let alone a chippy.'

Two hours later, Mary came. Alice had spent the time since Julie's call engrossed with the boat poem. She was toying with a revised rhyming scheme, certain that unless she hit on a new treatment of the idea, the poem was lost. After two hours the table was littered with sheets of paper, each a brave but rejected attempt. A novice, she knew no short cuts and tested each idea by writing. And then Mary flashed past the window and rapped on the back door.

There was no time to tidy the papers. Alice pulled the sitting-room door shut and planned to keep her in the kitchen.

Mary's face stated as plainly as words that she was upset by the Ablett conversation. Alice immediately began apologising.

'I'm so sorry, Mary, it was an amazing gaffe.'

'It wasn't your fault. You couldn't possibly have known.'

Alice gestured her to a chair by the kitchen table but Mary, restless, ignored it.

'Mum's got herself worked up over it. She gets obsessed with things, you know, and I can't shift her. An idea lodges and it just goes round and round, and she can't break away. She . . .' She switched on her self-mocking smile. 'Oh, listen to me. If I go on about it any more you'll think I'm the one who's obsessed.'

Iris had told her about the finding of the photograph but Mary's interest sharpened when Alice said the landlady at the Falcon had suggested it could be taken down for her to see it properly.

'Borrow it and have a copy made.'

'I hadn't thought of that.' Alice was hesitant. 'It's a lovely period photograph but now I don't know whether I'm interested in it because of the house or the mysterious Abletts.'

'Hmm, the Abletts. I suppose you want to know more about them.'

Alice laughed before realising Mary was being serious, not teasing. 'I'll put the kettle on and you can tell me over a cup of tea. Rosehip? Blackberry? Or apple and ginger?'

'Rosehip, please.'

'I'm puzzled,' Alice said, filling the kettle, 'why the photograph should be in the Falcon.'

But there was no answer and when she turned she was facing an empty room. With a sinking heart, she trailed Mary to the sitting room.

'Poetry?' Mary was holding up a sheet of paper.

'Not yet.' Alice wished she could pluck it from her. Surely it ought to be understood that writing was private until finished?

'You said, though, didn't you, when we talked first? You said you were here to write.'

Mary put the page down and there was a difficult moment while she ran her eye over the others and Alice silently dared her to intrude any further.

'Come on,' Alice said firmly. 'We'll be more comfortable in the kitchen.' She moved away and heard Mary following. 'Back to the Abletts,' Alice said once they were seated.

There was a little lift of the shoulders before Mary embarked on her story. 'Very well. It goes back to the forties so, naturally, all I know is what my mother and older people in the village have told me.'

'Fair enough,' thought Alice, *'to caution me that pushing for extra details is useless. She can't have anything but hand-me-down rags of memory. And, anyway, we can only interpret history, not fully understand it.'*

Mary was relaxed now, fingers laced, leaning back in her chair. 'George Ablett owned Perrotts Farm. He inherited it from his father who had managed to buy it. What I'm saying is he was better off than the other farmers here because they were tenants of Sir Arthur Devrell's estate. Sorry, I'm rambling. You don't need to bother about the agricultural set up. The point is he was different from the rest, not a rich man but richer. Okay?'

'The smart car,' Alice said.

'Exactly. He had more money and he had a wife to help him spend it. They say she was the one keen on buying a car.'

Alice remembered the woman, the pose. 'In the photo she looks terribly proud of it.'

'That would fit, wouldn't it? Well, after a few years people were blaming her extravagance for running him into debt. And one night, in the spring of 1947, they got into the car and drove away, and that was the last that was seen of either of them.'

Alice was quiet, reflecting that the story fell short of what she had expected. She guessed Mary was calculating how much more was needed before she would be allowed to drop the subject.

'Murdered,' Alice prompted. 'You said last time it was believed they were murdered.'

'Yes, the police believed it. I suppose because there was no evidence of them being alive and hiding from creditors.'

'But what did the villagers believe?'

'Oh, some believed one thing and some another. My mother says . . .' She flushed, cross at this slip.

'What does Iris say?'

'That Stark Point has lived with the mystery for too long.' She was reading her wrist watch. 'Sorry, I told Mum I wouldn't be long and it's already been . . .'

'Yes, of course.' Alice lifted Mary's jacket off the hook on the back of the kitchen door.

She stood in the kitchen alone again, her forehead puckered. The story was a let-down and she did not entirely blame her own excited anticipation. By not rambling, as Mary had put it, she had not fleshed it out either. Indignant, Alice felt she was being fobbed off.

If she had been telling the story herself she would have wanted to spin it out, putting in the colourful details that made personalities shine. And she would certainly not have dismissed local rumour, as Mary had.

Was this, she asked herself, the difference between the writer she knew herself to be and an ordinary person, in Mary's case a teacher, telling a story? But no, that was patently untrue. Everyone who had ever been born enjoyed passing on a juicy story, and everyone loved a mystery.

It was inescapable that Mary did not want her to know about

the Abletts, and yet they had been photographed outside Spray Cottage. There *was* a connection, she was sure of it, whether Mary Dottrell realised it or not.

Alice went into her garden. Lovage grew tall by the wood shed, thyme sprawled over a low stone wall, furry looking borage flourished in a sunny spot, and evening primroses were yellow splashes beside the shed. Bella, of whom she knew next to nothing, had planted these herbs and used them to heal her neighbours, perhaps even the Abletts of whom she knew slightly more. It pleased her to realise she knew something Mary did not. She knew what the Abletts looked like.

'Is that why she suggested I copy the photograph? Because she wants to see them for herself?'

But her irritation with Mary was leading her into flights of fancy. All she could say for sure was that Mary had left her curiosity unsatisfied.

'And that's not a crime, is it?' she murmured.

She studied the garden carefully, happy to think of her shadowy aunt working there, caring for the herbs and using them to care for her neighbours.

'I will never,' Alice decided, 'destroy a plant or move one without finding out what she might have used it for. I'll buy a herbal, a decent one with clear illustrations.'

A phrase to depict the garden ran through her mind and she went indoors to write it down. Then an earlier, unconnected, thought revived. *'The Dottrells aren't the only ones who know about the mystery.'*

She peered out of her bedroom window and a broad smile spread over her face as she read a red signal. Without second thoughts, she set off.

The lurchers had frightened the gulls away from a drab object lying on the sand, and the gulls were retaliating by diving at them, screaming, claws dangerous. Some way off Mrs Aley was waggling her stick. Alice caught up with her easily although there was so much clamour her approach went unheard.

'What a glorious afternoon, Mrs Aley.'

'Oh, it's you, Alice. Yes, a calm day, I'm glad to say. Perhaps we can look forward to a proper summer now.'

Her crimson scarf was snapping like a pennant on a mast. Flickety-flick, flickety-flick.

After the preamble about the weather Mrs Aley stuffed her scarf into her collar and the wind sneaked it out again while Alice worked the conversation round to the mysterious Abletts.

'Oh, them.' Mrs Aley looked as though that was as much as needed to be said. She kept her eyes on the dogs.

Alice ignored her reticence. 'Were you here when they disappeared?'

'Here? Well, I've never been anywhere else. All my life at Stark Point. But I was only a girl, mind.'

Alice was thinking: '*You'd remember it, though. Anything remarkable sticks in the mind. It's the humdrum we forget.*'

Mrs Aley made several passes with her stick, and cried out: 'Bingo! Lotto!'

'It must have been very strange,' Alice suggested, hoping to wheedle a memory or two.

'Strange? You could say strange. Bingo, here boy!'

'What were they like?'

'Them? Oh, I don't know. He was a farmer. Big sort of fellow. Broad, I mean, not tall. There's not many tall folk in these parts.'

'No, I suppose not. And what did she look like?'

She felt idiotic asking the only questions she could answer for herself, until it occurred to her that the identification of the couple in the photograph was guesswork. There was a possibility the building was not Spray Cottage and the people outside it not Abletts.

Mrs Aley pulled a face, her big nose dipping down to meet her strong chin. 'Nice clothes, her hair just so. Would have looked very nice in a town. Too up-class for this place.'

'Not a typical farmer's wife?'

The scarf went flickety-flick. 'Not for round here. Put her on a big farm on good land, somewhere they make money, and maybe she'd have done, but here . . . If you want my opinion, that's what caused their trouble.'

'Mrs Ablett?'

'Wanting him to be what he wasn't. Raising them up. It doesn't do, that sort of thing. Folk don't like it.'

Alice was confused. 'I thought they were wealthier than most.'

'He bought the other farm, though, didn't he? Owned Perrotts Farm and then he bought the Little Farm. They say she couldn't grasp the money was tied up, good as gone. Still wanted to go on spending it.'

Lotto and Bingo had to be shrieked at before she could continue.

'Folk blamed her for everything, see. I'm not saying it was fair, I'm telling what happened. Delma got the blame. My husband, God rest him, used to say if George Ablett had stood up to her he'd have lived to a ripe old age, like the rest of us hope to.'

'But . . . I thought it was uncertain whether they're dead or not.'

Mrs Aley turned to her with a face that was very knowing. 'There were no bodies, so it wasn't proved. But there aren't many who aren't sure in their hearts those Abletts have been dead these good fifty years.'

Alice's next question died on her lips as an old man appeared. This was who she had come to see, Mrs Aley was a bonus.

Mrs Aley sniffed. 'Him again.'

'I was hoping to see him,' Alice said, anxious to catch him before he cut across to the scrub and sank from view.

'Don't bother asking him,' said Mrs Aley drily. 'He won't say anything, he never has.'

Alice, undeterred, was remembering Joe Keenthorne's eagerness to talk to her. He had offered her one story but today she needed to ask him about another.

She was out of earshot when Mrs Aley added softly. 'But if he does, I'd be interested to hear what he tells you. We all would.'

Then she advanced on the lurchers, her stick slicing the air.

Chapter Five

Rod was sitting on her doorstep waiting for her, hunched up like a pixie. She saw his car first, a red one she did not recognise. Then she was through the gate and there he was.

He looked up shyly. 'Hello, Alice.'

'Oh. It's you.' Nonplussed, she came to a full stop.

'I knew you hadn't gone far because your car's in the garage.'

'Oh.'

He got to his feet, laughing, a rangy figure taller than she remembered. She had become used to being on eye level with Charles, but Rod was a man she literally looked up to.

He said: 'You keep doing that.'

'What?'

'Saying "Oh", as though you don't believe I'm here.'

'I don't, Rod. I really don't.' She had still not moved a step nearer.

She studied the key in the palm of her hand. So this was the moment, this was the precise moment when she had to decide whether to let her estranged husband into her house and back into her life.

'Come on, Alice. Open up.'

Playing for time, she teased. 'Supposing I say no, you're not crossing my threshold. What then?'

For answer he reached out as if to take the key but her fingers curled around it. She slid past him.

'It isn't the key to the front door anyway.'

She heard him hurrying along behind her. Ridiculous thoughts were scampering through her mind. *'He'll hate the cottage, he's taller than Charles, the ceilings are low.'*

'This is,' he said, when they were standing in the kitchen and she was flinging her jacket on the hook behind the door, 'a quite amazing place.'

'The cottage? Yes, it is.'

'And the village. And the . . .' He spread his arms. 'The everything.'

'Tea?'

'Milk no sugar.'

'Rosehip. Apple and ginger. Or camomile.'

'Oh, *that* sort of tea.'

'That's all I have. Which, then?'

'You pick, I'm sure they're equally foul.'

She gave him apple and ginger.

'Explain,' she demanded.

But he disregarded her and wandered through the ground floor rooms. She winced as she remembered the sheets of paper scattered over the table by the sitting-room window.

In a minute or so Rod returned, still appraising.

'Well. An amazing place.'

'Yes, you keep saying so.'

'And your aunt – Betty, was it? – left you all this?'

'Bella. Who told you?'

Alice felt a nervous anticipation, understanding he had sought her out to discuss a divorce and was intent on discovering what she was worth since the inheritance. She had not seen him for several years, his choice rather than hers.

He refused to say who had told him and changed the subject. 'Camilla's thriving, quite the young lady now. But Bonny's dead.'

Alice's features flickered from pleasure at his daughter's progress to regret for the thistledown cat.

'And Ruth?' she asked, keen to get his mistress out of the way too.

'Ruth's fine.'

'Good.' She trusted that sounded sincere.

In truth, she had never liked the woman whom she had always suspected took too much upon herself for a secretary. Long before Alice learned they were lovers, she had resented Ruth's influence over him.

'All right,' said Rod, tipping most of his apple and ginger tisane down the sink. 'You want to know why I'm here and how I knew where to find you.'

Alice circled her hands around her mug, enjoyed the wafting scent of rosehip and waited for him to explain.

'*This is rather familiar,*' she was thinking, '*Rod doing things in his own time and his own way, which he judges to be better than anybody else's. With the exception of Ruth, though. For unfathomable reasons he sets great store by her opinions. There's no doubt who's the stronger character in that partnership.*'

He said, 'Charles told me.'

'Charles?'

'Yes, you know Charles. The Charles you live with in Bristol, the Charles who was here last weekend, *that* Charles.'

She wriggled with irritation. He was making fun of her surprise, yet surprise was the natural reaction.

'Rod, I didn't realise you knew Charles.'

'I don't. But I wangled your phone number out of a sweet girl at the radio station – Melissa, was it?'

'Melinda.'

'*Who ought to be fired,*' she thought, '*for handing out women's telephone numbers to plausible men.*'

She said: 'She isn't allowed to do that.'

'That's what she said, but I told her I was your husband and I had family news. I made it sound like very *bad* news.'

Alice groaned. Her suspicion that Rod's arrival was bad news in itself was hardening. She began rehearsing the response she would make when he mentioned divorce.

He was saying, 'When Charles told me about this place I thought I'd pop down and see it for myself.'

'And me, too, of course.'

'Yes. You're looking well, by the way, Pippin. Blooming.'

The pet name slipping out like that gave her a jolt, she had forgotten it ever existed. Pippin was a tease from their happy days, a joke about her apple-cheeked freshness.

It occurred to her that Rod, by contrast, was not looking well. His eyes were tired, fine lines that were new to her were scribbled across his face. She saw through his brightness, his nonsense. It was an act, a performance put on for her. '*Well,*' she thought, '*I did try to persuade him not to work so hard. I did argue there was more to life than making money.*'

Aloud she said: 'Life at Stark Point suits me. I have lots of fresh air and exercise.'

'And Charles? Does he spend much time here in the fresh air?'

Alice looked mysterious and declined to enlighten him about the state of her relationship with Charles.

That was near impossible, anyway, because she barely understood it herself. With the move to the cottage and the concentration on her writing, her life had shifted into a different gear. She felt dislocated from the world they shared in the city. That much she could have said, but not whether the alteration was permanent or whether Charles felt the same.

Unfortunately, Rod was being thick-skinned. He came at it twice more, obliquely, trying to wheedle information.

She thought: '*It's none of his business. Why won't he take the hint?*' And: '*You can't just pitch up in someone's life after years of silence and demand the secrets of their heart. How can he be so obtuse?*'

Eventually she saw that Rod's concern was not sheer nosiness, that it mattered to him that she was in a comforting relationship when he made the final, official break. She softened, no longer provoked by his persistence. She even made a shot at telling him about the gear shift and the dislocation.

'I don't know what's likely to happen to us,' she ended up. 'If I manage to make my life completely different, it may not be a life he wants a part of.'

'From what you've said, it's already completely different.'

'Yes, but this summer is only a temporary change. Like a long holiday from my real life, if you like.'

After that she practically heard him assessing the chances of Charles being around to provide support through her divorce. On the basis of one telephone call and what little she had revealed, he was working out what the other man might do.

Alice stifled a smile. As far as Charles was concerned, she meant to let events unfold, to let it be one of those times when she was content to drift. Obviously, that meant she did not care enough, but she did not care to care. Charles was a lover, a companion, but she did not regard him as the grand passion in her life, which is what she had allowed Rod to be. Because Rod had dumped her, she had not been able to grant Charles that chance.

At last Rod spoke. He said carefully: 'I've been thinking, Alice, it would be good to get back together.'

She was stupefied.

He said: 'Us, I mean. If you like.'

'I . . .' Incapable of thought, she ran out of words.

He tidied up her confusion. 'Alice, I want us to be together again. That's why I've come. To say, please can we live together.'

'I . . .'

She felt a gaping fool, who had misunderstood everything since his arrival and did not trust herself to comprehend now. But his words left no doubt or ambiguity.

With a nervous laugh he said: 'You don't have to say yes immediately or . . .'

'No.'

'Right, you don't have to say yes or no immediately . . .'

'No, Rod. I said no.'

Abashed, he said, 'At least think it over.'

'It's thought over. The answer's no.'

'But . . .'

'But what? But you don't accept my decision?'

'Alice, love, you haven't given yourself time to get used to the idea.'

Through her mind flashed some of the previous occasions he had spoken to her in this patronising tone, dismissing her views because they did not suit him.

Quietly she said: 'I've had lots of time to wonder whether I wished we could get back together, Rod. All the time I was going home to an empty house after you'd walked out on me . . . The answer was always no.'

'That was ages ago.'

'Yes, and what's changed for me is that I'm happier and I run my own life.'

His eyes were no longer meeting hers. He was looking vaguely around the room. She was acutely aware of its shabbiness. In her eyes, the hand-me-down furniture was pleasing for sentimental reasons, but to anyone else it was out of date but not good enough to be quaint. And to anyone with the sort of money Rod earned, she must appear to live in penury.

She defended her home. 'I'm perfectly happy sleeping in my aunt's bed and sitting on her chairs. I know nothing here is up to your standards, Rod, but it's what I've settled for. And, as I said, I'm happy here.'

Conscience pricked but she excused the exaggeration of her happiness. What did overstatement matter if it served to convince him she was unpersuadable?

Rod sighed, looked forlorn.

Alice feigned not to notice. In smaller matters her natural warmth would have rescued him, as she said the kind word or did the good deed. But he was proposing to tear her life apart, and she dared not risk him supposing his charm could be worked upon her. This time her instinct for self-protection was stronger than the habit of sympathy.

She succeeded. After only the slightest awkwardness they talked of other things. Rod requested a tour of the village.

As they passed Parry's farm, she repeated Mary Dottrell's story of neighbours feuding over the shared drive. Rod suggested villages were rife with such goings on, but Alice kept Mary's other stories to herself because she preferred him to continue liking Stark Point.

Bossy edicts on the noticeboard by the chapel spoke for themselves, though. The latest recommended everyone to gather up possessions scattered by the storm.

'Charles says they emanate from the Stark Point vigilante.'

'Do people obey them?'

'Hard to say. There are toys in the hedge and a doll in a ditch. Her drowned face stares up at you.'

Rod went to look at the chapel. 'No churchyard?'

'No. The locals, and bodies recovered from the sea, have traditionally been buried elsewhere, safe from flooding. It's weird. Usually, villagers continue to exist in a churchyard but here it's as though they've been carried away on the tide.'

They walked on, Rod remarking on the spaciousness. After Charles's sneering, Rod's pleasure in Stark Point warmed Alice's heart.

He said: 'To me, Stark Point feels like a place to be when you aren't being anywhere.'

'A gap between places?'

'Yes, that's it. A nothingness.'

He made a guess. 'Is it called Stark Point because it's bleak?'

'I wondered that. But when I looked it up in a dictionary of place names, it said it's a corruption of Start, from an Old English word, *steort,* meaning a tail or a promontory.'

'Topography, not atmosphere, then. A shame, in a way.'

They came to the gate across the road. Alice had privately

decided not to continue beyond this. She leaned her elbows on the gate, talking, telling him about the storm.

Taking the end of her story as a cue, he unlatched the gate and they started down the field track. Unlike Charles, he enjoyed a long walk. When they reached the other beach Alice named the seaside town across the water.

'I haven't been there but I suspect this is the most attractive way to see it.'

Then they were both remembering a detour to an Italian town, enticing from a distance but disappointingly choked with traffic. She had not intended to spark the memory but was not sorry.

'Did you ever go back?' he asked.

'No. Did you?'

'Passed by it last year. Still looks wonderful from afar.'

'With Ruth?' She felt it was time Ruth joined the conversation.

'Yes, we spent a holiday driving down the coast.'

Alice was glad they were side by side so he missed seeing her eyebrows rise. She had thought people did not take new lovers to the haunts enjoyed with their old ones.

He said: 'Ruth's been going there for ages. Her parents used to borrow a villa, and when her father became too unwell to drive she went with them as their chauffeur.'

Alice scowled. There had been an argument, she recalled, because they were supposed to visit Julie, then training in France, but Rod got a yen for Italy. Wretched Ruth, she realised now, had subverted him.

Well, she no longer cared whether he had been in thrall to Ruth, that was his problem; but it did make her cross that the bitch had picked her holiday for her. Alice kicked a stone out of her way, savagely. Were no memories to be safely invoked without Ruth's hand being revealed? She cast around for another stone.

Rod, a step ahead of her and oblivious to the stone-kicking, was watching the lacy waves. 'What colour do you call rippled light on water?'

The boat poem flooded her thoughts. Water colours were unnameable, hours searching for precise words had proved it. She did not own up to the poem, only to her failure to paint the scenery in words.

'I can't pinpoint what it sounds like either. Hissing, sighing, sucking . . . The sea doesn't resemble anything, it's the other way round.'

He said: 'You needn't be deterred by that. Modern writers don't go in for riffs of description. Doesn't seem to hold them back. Jokes, that's the thing. If you can wrap an idea in a joke, you're made.'

'Rod?'

'What?'

'Where on earth have you got all that from?'

'They don't end lines with prepositions, though, Pippin, I should warn you.'

They began to laugh, as they used to laugh, the years falling away.

'Come on,' she said, 'I want to know.'

She feared the answer was Ruth and she dreaded the coincidence of Ruth taking up writing too. But Rod tantalised and refused to say.

'If you won't tell me, I'm going home,' said Alice, who knew it was time to leave anyway. Shadows stretched behind them, the glitter from seaside windows was harsh.

They walked back, easy in each other's company. There was a great gulf in the conversation but she was unconcerned. He talked about years ago and about the things around them today, but he was not telling her what had prompted his extraordinary visit to ask her to revive their marriage.

In a while, she thought, she must demand an explanation. Curiosity would not allow it be otherwise. '*How can I let him drive off into the evening taking the answers with him?*'

They reached the cottage. While he groped for the latch on the gate, her eye fell on his car. This was a modest affair, what garage people call a runabout, and not new. Until this moment she had been so taken up with her astonishment at seeing him, she had not spared a thought for the car. But now it hit her that she had never known him drive an inexpensive one or a model more than a year old.

She blurted a question. 'What's happened to your taste in cars?' For a silly second she imagined Ruth declaring small old cars to be best, and Rod obediently swapping.

He said: 'I've borrowed it. Mine's been stolen.'

'Oh?'

'From a car park while I was in a meeting.' He shrugged. 'I'm lucky it hasn't happened before.'

Once indoors, Alice offered supper. He accepted. She asked where he was staying and he hedged. She was ready for that and offered her spare room. He accepted that too.

Titivating the spare room, she threw a protective glance at her computer on the table that doubled as her desk. '*Oh, don't be ridiculous,*' she scolded herself. '*He won't touch it.*'

While supper was cooking, they drank wine and she pushed him into explaining what had become of Ruth.

Rod looked tragic and said Alice must have realised it was over.

'Yes,' she said patiently, in an echo of the patronising manner he occasionally used to her, 'but a few details would set my imagination at rest.'

'What do you want to know?'

'Well, did you strangle her and bury her in the back garden? Or did she leave you for a younger man? Or have you had a blinding revelation that I am your true love? Or what?'

He wrestled with choices before replying. 'It just came to an end. What I mean is it was never right and it was bound to end.'

Alice looked interested and did not let him see she recognised these words, which he had spoken to her when he told her he was leaving. She wondered whether people who took their lover to the same holiday destinations were also prone to use identical phrasing to end relationships. Someone, she thought grimly, should investigate.

Later, she lay awake unable to concentrate on anything except Rod's presence in her second best room. There had been no question of him joining her. In fact, he had gone meekly in there and closed the door a while before she went to bed herself.

She sat up and plumped her pillows. For the first time since she found him on her doorstep, she was alone with time to think. He had ducked some of her questions, and several of the answers he had given were unsatisfactory, but she was not a detective entitled to winkle out the full truth. It was up to him how much he told her, and no doubt he avoided the parts that caused him pain or made him ridiculous.

What puzzled her more than the fate of Ruth was his attitude to Alice herself. He had asked her to live with him again yet there was a distinct absence of such words as love, and after she refused he recovered his bright good humour very rapidly. Alice could imagine a man in his position being embarrassed and slinking away whence he had come; or, if he stayed, being visibly miserable. Oddly, her rejection appeared to have no effect on Rod, as if he did not care deeply whether she said yes or no.

She listed questions to pose before he left in the morning. After that, she supposed, their contact would be the occasional telephone call, if he were so inclined.

Picturing his current life was difficult. She had to cancel her mental images of his offices because he had moved to premises in another city. 'We outgrew that space,' was how he had put it.

With the move, Ruth had abandoned any pretence of being his secretary and was appointed a director. Other people had been drawn in at a senior level too. The top flight clients he named had impressed Alice but not amazed her. Whatever else, he could not accuse her of having lacked faith in his ability.

She fantasised about the house he owned. 'In Wykeham,' he

had told her, naming a rich man's village outside an affluent country town. Apparently, the house had a paddock and stabling in addition to acres of garden. Ruth kept a couple of horses. Alice pictured a gabled house with a porch and ivy, and then tried to unravel what he had actually said from what her busy imagination conjured up.

Doing this, she at last fell asleep.

Waking up hours later, hearing footsteps on the stairs, thinking it was Charles and remembering it was Rod . . . This was a peculiar start to her morning. She stood at her bedroom window for a short time, idly watching the beachcomber and reluctant to emerge and face the day. There were arrangements to make, questions to ask, domestic duties to perform. She dodged them by skulking in her bedroom. Rod was not precisely unwanted but neither was she anxious to see him.

In the end he came to her, tapping on her door with a mug of Morning Time herb tea in his hand.

He said he had been up for hours although the footsteps on the stairs suggested this was a lie spoken to upstage her. She could not judge, she no longer knew him.

'I'll get breakfast,' she promised.

But when she came downstairs a very short time later he had eaten toast and said that was all he wanted. His behaviour was somewhere between first time guest and family, and she felt wrong-footed. She was glad he was to leave soon.

They both claimed to have slept well, and trotted through the morning pleasantries guests and hostesses usually exchange. Then she assumed he was up early because he was anxious to make an early start, but he said no, he was in no great hurry.

Alice plunged into a deception born of panic. The idea of being trapped in the cottage half the day, silently begging him to go, appalled her.

'Then I shan't be here to wave goodbye. I have to visit a friend.'

'What time are you going?'

'In half an hour,' she said, 'and I'll be away all morning, maybe longer.' This seemed best, to offer no hope of company or lunch. He would hardly want to hang around once she had gone.

Half an hour later she was putting her coat on and wishing he would show signs of packing.

'Don't fuss, Alice, I'll see myself out.'

'But the key . . .'

'I'll hide it outside. In the wood store?'

'No. No, I always keep it with me.'

He looked at the kitchen clock. 'You're making yourself late.'

She bridled but the lie had left her no scope for argument. Testily, she asked where he would put the key.

They went outside together and agreed on a ledge in the wood store. 'Right,' he said, 'off you go. And have a good time.'

'Er . . . thanks. And . . . um . . . thanks for coming. It was good to see you.'

Because he was standing close she planted a kiss on his cheek before she hurried away.

This was farcical. She had achieved the opposite of what she intended. Rod remained in the house and she was banished by mistake. There was nowhere she wanted to go, and she needed to be at home to see the builder if he came to fix the roof.

Alice sat in her car, but not for long in case he came to ask whether it would not start. She backed out, past his old runabout, and turned in the direction of the causeway. She decided to call on the Dottrells.

Mary's car was absent, though, and Iris chose not to open the door. She had to drive on, out of the village and through the diminishing lake. She pulled onto the car park by the beach.

The wind ripped at her clothes. Across the billowing bay she saw Joe Keenthorne, aimless now she was aware he was not a beachcomber. She thought of setting off in pursuit, to hear the story he had started to tell her the previous afternoon.

When she had left him she had raced home to write down what he had said. Instead there was Rod, seemingly washed up on her doorstep by the afternoon tide. Her notes had been forgotten, along with the Abletts and everything else.

She took a few experimental steps over the sand. The wind was swirling it, stinging her face. She would get covered in it, Joe Keenthorne might not wait for her, and she had no notebook although she had promised him one 'next time'.

Rueful, she returned to the car. If Rod was at an upstairs window he would see her. She could not linger here and watch for him driving away, she needed to go further afield.

Alice drove by the water where swans swanked, dawdled down the long straight road where she always saw herons, slowed for the bend by the hump-backed bridge, went with caution through the junction and headed up into sun-flecked hills. There was a layby with a view over the low lying land. She pulled in, jiggled the car round until she had a good view of the only road to Stark Point, and lay in wait for Rod.

After a few minutes she was bored, switched off the radio and thought over what Joe Keenthorne had told her. But she was afraid that if she became engrossed in his story she would miss Rod's departure. A better idea occurred. She trained her field glasses on Stark Point, hunted for Spray Cottage, and identified a reddish blob as Rod's car.

Angry, she could not decide what to do. Going home would mean more lies – My friend had to cancel. I got the wrong day. I forgot something I was supposed to be taking. Pushing him out might lead to a row and she hated rows. She was a woman who generally knew her own mind, so it bothered her that her tendency to avoid acting forcefully made her appear indecisive. '*I ought to learn how to deal with this contradiction*', she thought ruefully, and suspected she might not.

Rather than linger there any longer, waiting to see him drive away, she chose to continue over the hills and go shopping in the county town. Browsing, anyway. There was nothing she required and little she could afford. Rod and his rich lifestyle rankled. Two horses in a paddock. A big office at a good address. A successful business and the trappings to prove it. Huh!

As she drove, she pictured him hunched over her telephone, running up enormous bills which he would not realise were enormous because his life was on a different scale to hers.

Alice chided herself. '*That's stupid. There's no reason to accuse him of stealing telephone calls. This is Rod, the man I'm technically married to, not a sponging stranger.*'

Seeing the Falcon pub ahead took her mind off him. It was closed at this time of day but there was a van in the car park and Wanda, the landlady, was joking with the driver. Alice drew up beside them.

Ten minutes later she was waving goodbye to Wanda. On the passenger seat lay the photograph of Spray Cottage and the couple Alice believed to be the Abletts. Following instructions from Wanda's husband, Alf, she was on her way to a photographic studio for a copy to be made.

An hour after that she was buying a notebook in a stationer's and seeking directions to the pubic library. There she found a comfortable space and hammered out alternative lines for the boat poem, having spotted all at once a fundamental flaw in the way it was developing.

'*What I've written lacks vigour,*' she was thinking, '*and if I can't get the energy of the storm into this, then it's bound to fail.*'

A lively phrase came easily to mind, and she let the idea grow until she had three fresh lines. Then she fretted over the balance between the passivity of the boat and the fury of the sea.

'*It might be days before I have the answer. Do real poets have to wait and see?*'

She argued with herself about changing '*the angry brilliance*' of the sea glimpsed by lightning, perhaps swapping the adjective for a one-syllable word to improve the scansion. Before she could decide, memories of the smashed boat high on the beach intruded and with them came Joe Keenthorne. Alice tussled for a moment, then turned her notebook round, opened it at the back page and wrote a title on the top line

Joe's Story

Joe wants me to write this up as a story but I don't think it's going to be good enough, although, to be fair, it's too early to judge. We only talked for about fifteen minutes and then he said someone was coming. I don't know whether it was true. In fact, I don't believe it was because I didn't notice anybody and I stayed on the beach for a few minutes after he'd gone. Maybe he didn't fancy talking any more, just then I mean.

We're going to meet soon for me to hear the next part. I'm disappointed we didn't get far the first time. Fifteen minutes sounds a lot, you can say a great deal if you've a mind to. With Joe, I'm not convinced he does. He says *he does, repeatedly. And that's where the time went, with him saying: 'You're a writer, Alice. You can do the words. I've got the story to tell but I can't put it down. You could do that. You will, won't you?'*

And I had to keep reassuring him and encouraging him to press on with it. It was a juggling act: I didn't want to seem impatient and have him cry off, and yet neither did I want to be kept hanging around if he's simply a crazy old fool who has nothing to say or, on the other hand, a story he isn't actually going to tell. I still don't know which.

He was terribly dithering which could mean either. The only thing he was determined about was my ability to put the words down. Otherwise, well, it was hopeless. And it wasn't even obvious whether the story's about him or the village. I had to keep dragging information out of him, with him delaying and backtracking and then, finally, doing his disappearing act.

I tried pinning him down by asking: 'Is it your own story, Joe, something that happened to you?' I'd decided it was friendlier to use his first name, not that he'd told it me, not even when I asked him to call me Alice.

And he said: 'Yes.'

Then there was a terribly long gap and I had to coax him again, saying: 'I wondered whether it was about other people here.'

Another pause then: 'Yes.'

By this time I was I was sure it was useless but he said: 'They want me to get out of my house. They'll do it, see.'

He was agitated, his cracked leather gloves scuffling like mice as his clasped hands twisted. He was struggling to hold them steady. His eyes were narrow, very hot. I was rather afraid of him.

Gently, as though I was talking to a patient or a child, and for all I know he's both, I said: 'Who do you mean, Joe?'

But he wouldn't say. At least, not in words. His eyes flicked towards the village so I was in no doubt they were locals. And, of course, I was remembering Mrs Aley telling me he lived alone and ought not to. He does seem odd, and probably not fully capable of looking after himself, so maybe she's right.

That's guesswork, though, so I tried again, saying: 'Why do they want you to leave your house?'

The gloves did a lot more scuffling before I got a reply. 'They want the house, Alice. They've always been after it, see. Now they say I'm to go into a home and be looked after. But it's not me they're looking after, it's themselves. Like they did before, like they always do.'

Then he shrank into his shell again and I couldn't get details out of him. I tried a different tack, although I guessed it was a big risk. I said to him: 'Joe, are Mr & Mrs Ablett in your story?'

And he immediately said: 'Yes. They're in it, Alice. They're in my story. It's my story but it's about them.'

His manner changed at my next question, though. 'What do you think happened to them?'

He stuck his jaw out, glowered and started ranting. 'Nobody knows, never have done. What folk say is all wrong, always was, but they don't want to know any different. Most of them didn't know George Ablett, never spoke to Mrs Ablett. But I knew them, and I've never been forgiven for it, nor ever will be.'

I was nervous, having sparked this off, but then I thought I might as well pop in another question while he was fluent. I said: 'Are they dead?'

And he scoffed and stuck his arm out to sea and said: 'Low tide you can cross and pick up the road down the coast. Before cars, folk used it regular, now they forget. Nothing strange about going out over the bay.'

'But they owned a car, Joe.' My objection was out without thinking.

And just then Joe saw we were about to have company.

That's the sum of his story so far and it doesn't amount to more than a failing old man being afraid to accept help. Except for two things: he isn't truly old and he plans to tell me about the Abletts . . .

Odd though he is, I'll meet him again, chiefly for the sake of learning about the Abletts.

Chapter Six

Mary Dottrell carried the photograph to Alice's sitting-room window for better light.

'Yes,' she said. 'That's definitely this house they're outside. The shrubs have changed but you can tell from the roof and the windows.'

Alice answered her from the kitchen. 'The bit of porch behind the man's shoulder seems significant.'

'Oh, yes. There isn't any doubt, they're outside Spray Cottage.' She turned the print over, saying: 'Where did you get this copy made?'

'Dawsons, in town. I had to wait until late afternoon to collect it, but it was worth doing that rather than make another journey.'

'You can't have been home long then.'

The cork was drawn from a bottle of wine before Alice replied. 'Fifteen minutes.'

There was the sound of liquid pouring, then Alice took the glasses into the sitting room and set them on the table beside the photograph.

She said: 'I wish we could be equally certain these folk are the Abletts.'

'My mother ought to know but I'm nervous of asking her. She's been twitchy all day.'

'Is that why she didn't open the door to me this morning?'

'Yes, she's retreated into herself.'

'All because I let her stray into the Ablett story?'

'Crazy, isn't it?'

Alice said nothing. Half of her was guilty about upsetting Iris Dottrell's delicate equilibrium, while the other half was plotting to ask her to identify the couple.

Mary went off in a fresh direction. 'Your aunt treated Mrs Ablett. Mum remembers Mrs Ablett being in a great hurry to get away from a meeting one day because Bella was preparing a potion for her and she had to be there at the right time to drink it.'

'What was it for?'

'A rash, Mum thinks.'

'An allergy? Herbal treatments are effective for those.'

'Mum might be guessing. It was ages ago and the Abletts aren't people she likes to think about.'

Mary pushed the photograph away, a signal she preferred not to think about them any more either. She asked about Alice's visitor whose red car was parked outside.

'My husband. Just a social call.' Alice said smoothly. She had arrived home to find the car but not Rod.

'He'll be gone by the weekend, presumably.'

Alice queried with a look.

Mary said: 'Charles is due then, you told me. You're not going to have them here together, are you?'

A mock shudder. 'Perish the thought.'

'Rod's good looking,' Mary said. 'I wondered at first whether he was Charles but my mother said he was new to her.'

With misgivings, Alice pictured two faces spying from the Dottrells' window instead of one. She shoved the thought aside, unwilling to dwell on anything that might undermine their growing friendship. All one's friends did odd things, no one seemed perfect. If you waited for perfection, you had no friends.

But her views on this friendship were already altering. From being entirely open, Alice had grown slightly guarded. If she had been speaking to Julie, say, she would have shared her astonishment at Rod arriving out of the blue and her indignation at him lingering. The difference was, Julie had a context for the information, knew both actors in the drama. Mary, knowing Alice a little and Rod not at all, was incapable of reading the story accurately.

With that self-mocking tone that endeared her to Alice, Mary said: 'My ex was a nightmare. Trust me to pick one of those.'

'I didn't know you'd been married.'

'I wasn't, not exactly. The same as you're not exactly divorced.'

Alice acknowledged her half-lie with a smile. 'It's simpler to say I'm divorced than to enter into the ramifications of a relationship that's finished although not officially.'

Swishing wine around her glass, Mary softly challenged her. 'Inviting him to stay doesn't help finish it.'

'But I didn't . . .' She had been too quick, given it away.

'The uninvited guest?'

Colour rushed to Alice's cheeks. She did not want to say more but if Rod reappeared the situation could become terribly confused. An innocent remark from him might make her appear deceitful, and a few muttered words would not be sufficient to prime him.

Mary coaxed. 'Come on, Alice. I can see you're itching to tell me. Are you two getting together again?'

'No.' But she was blushing.

'You are. That's it, isn't it?'

'No, honestly.'

'What about Charles? Does he know yet?'

'No . . .'

'You have to be so careful about timing. I remember Simon went spare when he found out I was leaving him for Adrian. He couldn't see I'd been going to tell him when the time was right. He just couldn't see it.'

Mary looked pityingly on the stupidities of jilted men. Then she swung the glass up and poured the last mouthful of wine down her throat.

At that moment Alice heard footsteps on the path and Rod strode past the window. She flew into the kitchen to stop him bursting in on them.

'Rod . . .'

Seeing her consternation he rushed straight into apology.

'Sorry, Alice, love. I couldn't get away today. You won't mind another night, will you?'

'Er . . . What happened?'

Conscious of the listener in the sitting room, she was making a huge effort to be conversational instead of furious. Fury would keep for later.

He said: 'I was waiting for a phone call.'

'But you went out!'

'Only down to the beach for half an hour. By then it was too late.'

'For the phone call or for you to leave?'

'Both.'

'I see.' What she saw was that she was not being told the truth and there was no way of getting it.

'I'll take you out for a meal, Alice, to say thank you. Where's there a decent place round there, somewhere a bit special?'

Alice shrugged. 'I haven't looked.' Eating out with Charles was a matter of good pub food, not cringing waiters and heavy cutlery.

Remembering Mary, she realised the talk had gone on too long without introductions.

'Rod, I have a friend here. Come and meet Mary.'

Rod and Mary slid easily into conversation while Alice fetched another glass and the wine bottle.

'*They both have that facility,*' she was thinking, '*of establishing instant rapport with strangers. With Rod it's a professional skill, learned because in business personal contacts are important.*' '*In Mary's case,*' she thought, '*it was innate.*'

She sensed herself holding back, sitting on the sidelines to watch them exploring the new acquaintance. There was a pattern to Rod's behaviour. Everything he did and said seemed spontaneous, but in reality he was going around a course.

Mary she did not know about. Her only experience was her own initial meeting, but the plunging into topic after topic was the same and the amiability too.

'Alice, what do you think?' Rod asked, looping her into the conversation.

She offered an opinion without believing it was a useful contribution. Mary was bursting to jump in as soon as she had finished. Rod was also ready with a riposte although he let Mary go first.

When the wine bottle was empty, Rod lifted it up in mock despair and asked Alice whether there was another one.

Mary said: 'Please, no, not for me. I ought not to be here. My mother will . . .'

Knowing they understood, she did not bother to finish the sentence. Rod said he was sorry she had to leave. Mary winked at Alice as she left.

'So,' said Rod, stretching luxuriously, 'we can dine at the Foresters restaurant. That's the best one, from what she said.'

'She also said it's essential to book days ahead.'

'I'll ring them and check. People always say that but it's often untrue.'

He was moving towards the telephone so she had to get her protest in rapidly.

'Actually, Rod, I'd rather not go.'

'Oh, don't you feel well? You've been rather quiet.'

'I'm fine but I'm not in the mood for a smart restaurant. Why don't we eat at one of the pubs? I know several which do decent food and they're nearer than the Foresters. Besides, I've been into town once today already.'

Aware she was rattling on, assembling arguments when all that was required was a straight 'No, thanks', she brought herself to a halt.

Rod was sitting on the edge of the kitchen table, giving her a sheepish grin. 'You're cross with me, that's why you don't want to go anywhere special.'

She realised he was right but she denied it. 'It isn't that. If we go to the Foresters I'll have to dress up and eat a large meal, and I don't fancy either.'

'You'll enjoy it once we get there.'

'Don't cajole me.'

'You know you will.'

He picked up the telephone directory. For a few seconds Alice stood watching him tracking down the Foresters. Then, tight-lipped, she went through to the sitting room.

Every word reached her. The enquiry about a table. The pause for the answer. One side of a discussion about time. The query that confirmed the restaurant took credit cards. The clunk as he dropped the receiver onto the cradle.

Alice sighed, loathing being treated like a child whose preferences did not count. '*He used not to do this to me, why does he think it's okay now?*'

'It's all fixed,' he said cheerfully from the doorway. 'A table at eight.'

Her back to him, Alice clenched her hands. '*Nothing's fixed,*' she wanted to say, '*nothing's going to happen unless I go along with it.*'

Without waiting for her reply he went on. 'How long will it take us to drive there?'

'Half an hour. But Rod . . .' Her voice was unfortunately plaintive.

He laughed, came over and put his hands on her shoulders. 'Oh come on, Pippin, I'm taking you out for a treat, that's all.'

The situation was ludicrous and she felt she was making it worse by being provoked into bad humour. '*He's right, it's only supper and I ought to accept graciously. If I don't, he'll think up another treat so I may as well get it over.'*

She hesitated a moment longer before remembering her mother telling her as a child: 'It's always mean to prevent someone making a generous gesture.' All in all, it seemed better to let Rod have his way. Apart from which, there was the possibility she would actually enjoy it . . . Alice capitulated, laughing, saying okay, he'd won, and adding: 'But I haven't a thing to wear.'

'Not true,' he argued, 'there are heaps of wellies and macs.'

'And which will create the best impression, do you think?'

'Not the stuff with the salt stains.'

She feigned despair. 'In that case I'd better see what I can find upstairs.'

When she went to her room, she stood in front of the mirror, accusing herself of ingratitude, then exonerating herself because there was definitely something she did not understand. Ever since Rod had materialised on her doorstep the suspicion had kept coming and going.

With a shrug she opened the wardrobe and picked out a dress and jacket. In the pocket, untouched for months, were the earrings she usually wore with the outfit. It was while she was feeling for them that she heard the telephone ring.

Two rings, then it stopped. Alice cocked her head, wondering whether it was the call Rod was expecting.

She heard his voice briefly, then nothing. She brushed her thick tawny hair and twisted it up on her head, remembered that was the way he used to like her to wear it, pulled out the pins and tied it instead on the nape of her neck.

'*Good thing I realised in time,*' she was thinking. '*I can't afford to give any encouraging signals by mistake.*'

When she went downstairs the bill from the builder was lying on the kitchen table. 'He came this morning,' Rod called through from the sitting room.

'Did you pay him?'

'No, I said you'd put a cheque in the post.'

Alice, who had arranged to pay cash, hoped it would make no difference the next time she needed work done. She put the bill with her insurance claim form.

Rod was flopped on the sofa and holding the photograph. 'Was this your aunt?'

Alice explained.

He said: 'She looks like the actress in *Amber Light*. You know, that old film about an impostor claiming an inheritance. What was her name?'

Alice sought the resemblance. 'Yes, you're right. I hadn't noticed it before. What was she called?'

'Donna Lake,' he decided.

'No, Leake. That's who she was. Wouldn't it be fun if this turned out to be Donna Leake?'

'You don't mean that, Alice, you'd prefer it to be the mysterious Mrs Ablett.'

'There's nothing mysterious except the manner of her going. The Abletts were the most scrutinised couple at Stark Point.'

'And yet the Pointers saw nothing, heard nothing and said nothing. A bit odd, wasn't it?'

'There's more which I haven't told you.'

He adopted an expression of exaggerated interest, mouth open, eyes wide and head flung back in surprise. Laughing, Alice refused to say. They compromised. 'I'll tell you on the way to the Foresters.'

Shunting the subject aside, she added: 'By the way, I prefer Pointers. Charles calls them the Starkers.'

He groaned. 'Oh, *Charles*. He phoned while you were upstairs. I forgot.'

She choked back a complaint. 'What did he say?'

'I told him you were going out shortly and he said he'd speak to you tomorrow.'

She wanted to return the telephone call but hesitated. A table at eight. A half-hour journey if the lanes were clear which they were often not. Tractors. Cows. A variety of hazards threatened the driver in a hurry. Tomorrow, then. She would speak to Charles tomorrow.

Rod airily confirmed her thoughts. 'You can speak to him tomorrow.'

His attitude displeased her more than the overlooked message. Anyone could forget, but he had chosen not to call her to the telephone, and now this.

'Yes,' said Alice quite sharply, struggling not to lose her temper. 'But I prefer to do so now.'

She could not help making rueful comparisons. Charles would not have forgotten a message, if it had been the other way around. He might not have Rod's flair but he was meticulous, reliable and straightforward. With Rod she could never be sure.

Rod made a show of looking at his watch. Alice tapped out Charles's number but soon set the receiver down.

Rod said: 'He was going out, too.'

'The line's engaged,' she said, all her anger evident in the icy tone.

In a couple of minutes, she pressed the redial button. Once again she heard the engaged signal.

Rod did another performance with his watch. Alice ignored it.

Silently she was accusing him of cheek, high-handedness and interference. Twice more she pressed redial without success. When it was twenty-five to eight, she gave up and they set out for the Foresters, Alice still battling with her annoyance and Rod seemingly oblivious of the battle.

A few hundred yards sped away before she began, by describing Joe Keenthorne.

'You see, he regards me as a writer and he's rather anxious for me to hear his story.'

Rod said: 'Well, what's stopping you?'

A sidelong glance. 'You, Rod. I came home from my first session with him and found you.'

'Oh.'

She slowed at a tricky junction. Rod said: 'Go on.'

'I'm waiting for that contraption to pass.'

A tractor and loaded trailer trundled by.

Rod said: 'I meant go on with the story, not get us killed.'

Once she was over the crossroads and descending the far side of the hill, she said: 'Joe Keenthorne says he's going to tell me all about Stark Point and the curious things that have happened there.'

'Which you hope includes the Abletts.'

'It does.' She dropped into the local accent, mimicking him. ''Tis my story but it's about them.'

Alice slowed for a traffic hazard sign. Around the bend she joined a tailback of vehicles and pulled on the handbrake. Rod looked at his watch, surreptitiously this time.

He said: 'As Joe's an oddball, you can't be sure he'll tell the truth.'

'I've been worrying about that. Yesterday he claimed that what other people said was wrong because they hadn't known the Abletts. He may not deliberately mislead me but I'm sure he has a different version from the usual one.'

'Except,' Rod corrected, opening the car door, 'there isn't a usual one. Nobody's saying, not even your friend Mary. And you're even more of an outsider than poor old Joe.'

Alice watched him walk to the head of the queue where three drivers were standing by the red light and discussing the hold-up.

She felt small, isolated, abandoned. '*He's right,*' she was thinking. '*I'm more of an outsider than the man they shun.*'

Another idea disturbed her. By spending time with Joe Keenthorne she could ruin her chance of being accepted into the community. Very few bothered to speak to her and they might stop. Mrs Aley, in particular, had made her feelings towards him clear, if not her reasons.

Alice chewed her lower lip, wondering how much she risked by being seen with him and whether his story could possibly be worth it.

'There's a tree down,' Rod said, leaning on the roof of the car and talking down to her. 'Right across the road. Someone's gone to ask a farmer to drag it clear with his tractor. The consensus is there's no way round and we have to wait.'

She looked back. Half a dozen vehicles were lined up behind her. The lane was narrow with a stream on one side and a stone wall on the other. Alice said: 'I'll reverse past the tailback and turn.'

Rod guided her through a nine-point turn.

'Not exactly text book stuff,' she admitted as she drove away in the direction they had come, but she was pleased she had brought it off. In her rear mirror she noticed another car attempting the same escape, now that she had proved it was feasible.

'What's the time?' she asked, knowing he was reading his watch once more.

'Twenty past.'

'Either we phone the restaurant and say we're going to be embarrassingly late or we phone and say we can't get there. Which?'

Without hesitation he said: 'Late.'

Alice veered off into a network of even narrower lanes, dropped down to the coast road, joined a main road and approached the town from the opposite direction.

'*Why am I going to all this trouble,*' she asked herself, '*when it makes more sense to drop into one of the pubs we're passing?*' The answer was immediate. Rod was taking her for a treat and if she ducked out of it this evening he was certain to insist on another one.

'*I'm getting it over,*' she decided, '*so that there won't be any reason for him to stay tomorrow. He'll have repaid my hospitality and he'll go.*'

They returned to Spray Cottage in the early hours of the morning. Rod had proved good company and they had lingered over their meal, laughing and swapping stories just like old friends.

The Foresters was sufficiently expensive to have provided more imaginative alternatives for non-meat eaters, although she kept that criticism to herself. Rod, content with a large and bloody steak, did not notice.

Between her fish and the pudding, he recounted young Camilla's triumphal progress at school and the squashing of old Bonny beneath a lorry. Alice banned her mental pictures of Bonny and concentrated on Camilla but that too made her regretful.

'She's a stranger to me now. She's fifteen, I haven't seen her since she was ten.' And her mind tracked round a familiar course: shifting waters, perpetual change and so forth until she switched back to listening to Rod who was choosing between a chocolate pudding and a meringue. She put Camilla out of mind along with the dead cat and helped him to a decision.

Convinced the road home was clear, Alice took the short route only to find that besides a tree in the road there was now a tractor in the stream. The detour in the dark was boring as well as tedious. By the time they were splashing through what was left of the big puddle at Stark Point she was extremely tired.

They talked for an hour, though, after she let them into Spray Cottage. The jollity was over and matters which had been delicately left aside, for the sake of a happy evening out, now surfaced. Rod impressed on her that he was absolutely serious about wanting them to live together again. She was equally plain in her refusal.

He said earnestly: 'It doesn't matter about Charles'.

But Charles was not the impediment. She stifled a yawn and replied that, on the other hand, it *did* matter about Ruth.

'Ruth and I are finished,' he emphasised. 'That's over.'

'Yes, you said. But even if I wanted us to be together again, which I don't, Ruth would always be with us. And if not Ruth herself, then her equivalent. I can't trust you.'

He objected to her saying that, although it was patently true. She thought he was being absurdly optimistic to try to change her mind.

Tiredness overtook her and she had to apologise for breaking off and going up to bed. Yet she lay awake for another hour and more, re-running the discussion in her mind. They had stated their positions at the outset and neither of them had budged. Really, it was only a longer version of the conversation on the day he arrived. This time, though, he had talked about love.

Iris Dottrell had watched them come home, noted the lights switched on in separate bedrooms at Spray Cottage and had drawn unhappy conclusions.

She stayed at her window, smoking, wishing there were signs that Rod was likely to take Alice away.

'Maybe it's what she wants herself but men don't always do what's wanted. Even these young women, able to speak right out and tell a man what they want, they can't get them to say yes every time.'

With a bitter smile she remembered that the farmer who had fathered Mary had been like that, refusing to marry her and leaving her to the condemnation of her parents and the pity of her neighbours. She knew by heart his protestations of love and his awful, damning rejections.

He was so clear in her mind that it took a minute or two for her to remind herself it was all made up. The man had not existed, the words had not been spoken.

Iris opened the casement and tossed the cigarette end into the garden. The lamp was still on in Alice's bedroom.

'*Alice's* room. Huh! That's Bella's room, not hers. She's got no right there.'

Her fist clenched and she beat on the wall, muttering: 'No right, no right at all.'

But, then, people often got what they were not entitled to and they did not get what they wanted. 'That's the way it is. Always was.'

Then she forgot Alice and was recalling scenes from her early life, real ones this time. The heat of her adolescent passion was beyond recall, only the way her heart had broken on the scornful indifference of a young man in the village. Embarrassed, Joe Keenthorne had shown himself appalled and she had been unable to bear it. It was extraordinary how easily her love had turned to disgust, plus the occasional, still glimmering, urge to take her revenge on him.

Chapter Seven

The postman delivered four letters for Alice, all redirected by Charles. She telephoned him straight away, guessing what he would say.

'Sorry, Alice, I can't come down at the weekend, after all.' It was early, he was barely out of his grumpy Charles the second phase.

She pictured him at his orderly desk in a corner of the flat, and guessed which of his crisp shirts he was wearing and which of the many-splendoured ties. He was never a slouch.

She asked: 'What's happened?'

'A sales conference. I skipped the last two and now heavy hints are being dropped. I've got no choice, I have to be there.'

'Well, if you really must . . .' She did not disbelieve him, as she might if it were Rod with a similar excuse. Charles was not underhand.

'Sorry.'

'Won't you take time off later?'

'Not next week, if that's what you mean.'

She did. 'When will I see you?'

But he could not say and the call ended inconclusively without arrangements of any sort being made. She thought it fair to assume he was unhitching himself, consciously or otherwise; but also true to say she had not offered to go to him. Perhaps his busyness was creating the pause they both needed.

Alice opened the letters, threw two away as they were advertisements disguised as personal letters, and skimmed the third which was from her mother. Nobody was especially ill or especially unlucky or demanding anything. A nice, chatty letter to savour later on.

She went into the garden. Charles was not coming, Rod had gone and she was content to be alone. A lark was spiralling its song, an aeroplane scratched a white line and, as always, the sea pulsed. She . . .

'Hi, Alice!' Mary was peeping over the wall.

Together they walked to the headland, Mary talking about her mother's nerves and how awful it was to live in a village where you knew you were surrounded by folk who refused to help each other.

'It's killing her, and I don't wonder at it.'

Alice found the subject tedious. She was sympathetic to Iris Dottrell but Mary harped on it. Alice thought: '*It's always the same, she doesn't tell me nice things about the Pointers.*'

She diverted Mary. 'Where were you off to when you spotted me in my garden?'

'Oh, just wandering about. Mum's not at all bad today and I needed a breath of air. Such a pity for her to be inside on a day like this, isn't it?'

Wryly, remembering the Ham Cottage stench of tobacco smoke and chips, Alice agreed. 'But surely Iris can venture into her garden.'

'Yes, she can do that. Why don't you come and have coffee with us in the garden before you go home?'

'Thank you, I'd like that.'

While they strolled Mary recited tales of ill-natured Pointers, greedy ones and recalcitrant ones. Alice attempted to swing the conversation in other directions: the seaside town over the water, ownership of the wrecked boat, Mary's work at the London university, and her own struggles with her writing. No use. Mary was a repository of bad news and Alice felt doomed to hear it all.

'*It's like going for a walk with the Ancient Mariner!*' she thought.

She had already decided to say nothing about Joe Keenthorne and his scheme for her to write his story, being sure Mary would have some unfavourable gossip about him. Residual doubts about sharing the news were dispelled by Mary's lack of interest in Alice's writing. When Alice attempted to talk about her painful progress, she got a grunted reply before Mary launched into a tale about a woman who tied open a gate to allow her chickens to forage in her neighbour's vegetable patch.

Alice wondered whether Mary felt less enthusiastic about her now she knew she could not be groomed as a surrogate daughter to fill the gap when Mary returned home. Yet she suspected the truth was she had been over-eager to welcome Mary as a friend, and disappointment was almost bound to follow.

Her thoughts had meandered and she was startled to hear Mary saying: 'Oh, I meant to tell you earlier. Mum says it's definitely the Abletts in that photograph.'

'How . . . ?'

'Rod loaned it me. Didn't he tell you?'

'*Rod*? But when?'

'I called round to ask to borrow it this morning. Quite early but I know you're an early riser.'

Alice thought: '*The spy at the window. Yes, you would know that.*'

And Mary explained: 'You'd gone out but Rod gave it to me.'

Disgruntled but battling to hide it, Alice sounded lame. 'This is my first outing today.'

'Oh? You know, I'm sure that's what he said.'

Alice shrugged it off. Rod had been awkward that morning, hogging the bathroom and keeping her waiting. Presumably that was where she had been when Mary called. His cheek in handing over her property niggled, especially as he had done her out of the chance to show it to Iris Dottrell herself.

Hoping to sound casual, she asked: 'Where's the photograph now?'

'At Mum's. I left her poring over it.'

Alice checked herself, on the verge of pointing out that Iris was supposed to have been upset by the previous mention of the Abletts. Mary had apparently forgotten about that and perhaps it wasn't true.

'I'll collect it when I come for coffee,' Alice said instead.

They approached the gate where the field track met the lane. Mary folded her arms on it and settled to talk.

'Mum's been telling me more about them, the Abletts, I mean. Delma sounds rather splendid.'

This kindled Alice's interest, not least because here was Mary showing enthusiasm for a Pointer, albeit an historical one.

'Does she?'

'She had energy, intelligence, knew what she wanted and went out to get it. An independent spirit, unlike ordinary country-women of her day. He, of course, was another matter. George was born and bred here.'

Smothering a smile, Alice thought: '*So she's still jaundiced about Pointers. What saves Delma is that she was an incomer.*'

Mary lit one of her illicit cigarettes and gazed into the distance, oblivious to the ironic twinkle in Alice's eye. 'It was Delma who insisted on buying a car. She was the driver, not him. It gave her freedom. While Farmer George was plodding around the farm, Delma could be out and about.'

'Did Iris tell you all this?'

'Most of it. But when I saw her in that photo, I understood what people mean when they say she was a bit above him, had ideas, that sort of thing. She looks it, doesn't she? Proud to be at the wheel of that car. And he just stands there, a lump. Not a good match, were they?'

'Yet they made the match, it must have suited them.'

'Oh, that was money. Delma had some from her grandfather

and plenty more coming from her father. She was the only child, did I say that? Everything was to go to her.'

'Except,' Alice pointed out, 'nothing did. Missing, believed dead. They both were.'

Mary gave that special lift of the shoulders that showed she had made up her mind to deal with a problem. She inhaled deeply before saying: 'There's something I ought to tell you.'

'About the Abletts?'

'About Joe Keenthorne.'

She paused, forcing Alice to prompt. 'Well, what about him?'

'They say he killed them.'

'*What?*'

The exclamation made Mary jump. She gabbled a kind of apology. 'I know you've been talking to him, otherwise I wouldn't be bothering you with this.'

Upstairs windows. Long views. A patch of flat land where you hardly ever saw people and yet they saw everything. Alice felt chilled.

She failed to keep calm, her voice rising despite every effort. 'Why the hell didn't you say this before?'

'Because . . .'

'You've talked about the Abletts for days and you didn't mention it.'

'I know. I'm sorry. But it seemed best, that's all.'

Alice groaned, rested her head on her hand. 'No, *I'm* sorry, I shouldn't have snapped at you. But . . .'

She did not know the rest of the sentence. Was it '*but I feel cheated not to have been told everything at the outset*'? Or '*but I don't believe the story, in any case*'?

Meekly, she said: 'Please will you tell me the rest, Mary?'

'All right.'

But what Mary said was disappointingly succinct. 'The police suspected Joe Keenthorne. Obviously, people set them on his track. He was charged with murder, tried and acquitted.'

The cold was spreading through Alice. She heard herself echoing: 'Charged with murder?'

'And acquitted. People here put it differently. They say he got away with it. They say he should have hanged.'

Mary moved to open the gate but Alice stayed her hand. 'No, tell me the rest.'

And when Mary resisted: 'Please, I need to hear it.'

She was thinking: '*This might be my only chance to drag it out of her. I have to know, I'm supposed to be meeting him tomorrow.*'

'Very well.' Mary leaned on the gate again, puffed the cigarette. 'To begin with the Abletts seemed happy. George doted on Delma. As they say around here, there was nothing she couldn't have and not much she didn't want.'

'Like the car.'

'Yes. She used to drive over to see her family in the Vale. After a while people noticed she was staying away, for days or weeks. George said one of her family was ill and she was visiting. But then a rumour went round, saying Delma had a lover.'

'Did anyone see him?'

'Yes, she was seen in a hotel with a man and people were convinced it was him. I don't understand why she didn't go off with him, but she continued to live here and play her part in village affairs. She was terribly good like that, opening the fête when the lord of the manor couldn't be bothered, putting on events, organising outings for children, you name it.'

'And George?'

'Farming and feuding, I suppose. The two go together here, as you'll have noticed.'

But Alice shied away from further tales of malicious neighbours. With the photograph in mind she said: 'I can imagine Delma opening a fête or two, she had the presence for it.'

'Yes, that's it, she had presence and he was a simple farmer. Well, their trouble came because of the reckless way George was spending money to hold on to her. It's true he fell into debt, what's in doubt is what happened next. Mum says everybody believes they planned to run off and start anew where they weren't known, abroad probably. After that, though, opinion divides. Some say they carried it through together, others that Delma ran off with her man and George died going in pursuit, and the rest cling to the idea they didn't go anywhere because Joe Keenthorne killed them.'

A tractor was thrumming up the lane from the village. Alice listened to it for a moment before asking: 'Why would he want to do that?'

'The usual. Fractious personalities.'

'No,' Alice argued. 'If the neighbour you hate is planning to leave, you let him go. You don't kill him.'

Mary frowned. 'Unless Joe didn't know the Abletts were leaving.'

'*She's making this up,*' Alice decided. '*Part of it, anyway. The trouble is, I can't tell how much is invention.*'

The tractor came closer, a black and white dog perched on the guard above a wheel, and a pony-tailed young man at the controls. Alice stepped aside and Mary opened the gate to let the entourage through. The man lifted a hand in thanks and the dog barked unpleasantly. Mary closed the gate while Alice began to walk towards the village.

Disconcerted, Alice wished she could be alone to decide what to do about Joe Keenthorne. Maybe she ought to make an excuse not to go on with his story?

Mary jogged to catch up. 'I'm sure he's harmless.'

With a sidelong glance Alice asked whether that meant she believed him innocent.

The reply was swift. 'Oh, I didn't say that. My mother doesn't, though.'

'And you?'

'I think it's more likely he did it than not. They haven't turned up alive in all these years so I assume they're dead. And if they are, the finger's never been pointed at anyone except Joe Keenthorne.'

At that moment a lurcher burst through a hole in a hedge and Alice recognised Bingo. Then there was Lotto. Mrs Aley's voice was raised. 'Here, boys.'

Where a path met the lane, she was leaning on her stick, waiting for Mary and Alice. The dogs eddied around her.

Alice thought: *'Mrs Aley believes Joe did it, I'm sure she does. It explains her attitude to him. It explains everybody's.'*

But because Mrs Aley joined them on their way into the village, they talked of other things. The weather, naturally. Might the sunshine last until the weekend? Would a calm sea be better or worse for Jacko's fishing? Oh yes, there was always the weather, and why not in a place where it affected every aspect of their lives?

At Ham Cottage, Iris, veiled in smoke, the ashtray tilting dangerously on the arm of her chair, demonstrated she had yet to take heed of the tabloids' warnings. Playing safe, she had folded the paper open at the crossword. The photograph of the Abletts lay on a table. In the kitchen, the radio mumbled.

'Mum, I've told her,' Mary announced, once she and Alice had confirmed what a lovely day it was and how pretty the headland looked in sunshine.

Iris exhaled and peered at Alice through the fug. 'Not upset, are you?'

'Er . . . no. I was taken aback.'

'Well, you don't expect to hear things like that about folk you know.'

Alice came close to saying she did not really know Joe Keenthorne, but she resisted such pathetic dissembling. After all, she had been meaning to know him well, better than most of the Pointers.

Mary saved her, by chattering about making coffee and moving the garden table and chairs from shade to sunny spot. Alice picked up her photograph.

'It is my cottage, isn't it?'

'Oh yes, it's Spray Cottage. Definitely. And it's Delma and

George Ablett, no question. I remember that coat, you know. Hers, I mean. With the fur collar. To me, it looked very grand, I don't think I'd ever seen anybody with fur before. She used to wear it well into the spring, it wasn't just for winter.'

Alice said she was impressed by Iris's memory but Iris laughed it off.

'When Delma Ablett was about the place, everybody noticed. She wasn't one to come and go quietly.'

The folly of that remark brought her up sharp. 'Until the day in 1947 when she did exactly that, of course.'

'*Now,*' thought Alice, '*I can coax from her what she knows. A good day, Mary said, nerves not so jumpy.*'

'Iris, do you truly believe Joe Keenthorne had anything to do with the Abletts' disappearance?'

Iris stubbed out the cigarette. 'Yes, I don't see any room for doubt.'

Alice sagged, giving away that she had hoped to hear the opposite. A doubt would have done and, as he was acquitted, there must have been doubt.

But Iris was speaking again. 'He had something to do with it, Alice, I'm convinced of that. But I'm not saying he's a murderer.' She delayed, to let the distinction sink in. Then: 'Lots of folk believe to this day Joe killed George and Delma Ablett but they haven't proof. And what the police had wasn't good enough for a jury, now was it? So how could I possibly say he did it?'

'When you say he had something to do with it . . .'

'If I knew what it was, we wouldn't have mystery.'

'And Joe Keenthorne? What does he say about it?'

In the kitchen the radio programme changed to a noisier one introduced by a man with a badly modulated voice, and Iris rose from her chair. For a thin, weak-looking woman she was remarkably quick. Alice remembered their first meeting, when Iris had flipped a coat onto a hook with the grace of a basketball player.

As she ran, Iris was grumbling. 'You don't know where you

are with the radio since they changed everything around. And I can't stand him, always going on in a monodrone.'

Alice smiled at her facility for enhancing the language.

Coming back, Iris said: 'Joe hasn't ever offered a word of explanation. If you ask me, he's brought his troubles on himself. He leaves folk guessing and they don't like it.'

Alice was looking afresh at Delma in her fur collar. Bright eyes smiled in an attractive face and little hands rested lightly on the steering wheel. Beside the car, George was plonked like a shop window dummy displaying an unyielding overcoat.

Her impression was coloured by Mary's tale. The admired but wayward wife was showing off her favourite toy, while the unsuitable husband seemed to have strayed into the scene by accident. They were not, to use Mary's word, a good match. It was very easy indeed to picture Delma suddenly streaking away in the car and leaving dreary George alone in the lane.

Mary called them through to the garden.

Alice slid the photograph into her pocket, reluctant to part with it a second time. The three women sat around a battered wooden table, red paint flaking to reveal timber the colour of driftwood. In the background, the sea surged and sighed, surged and sighed.

Alice stormed into Spray Cottage and flung herself down on the sofa. Confused, undecided, she was increasingly nervous.

Over coffee the Dottrells had refused to say any more about the mystery of the Abletts and the role the outcast Keenthorne might have played. Having raised her curiosity to fever pitch, they had denied her and made her talk about mackerel and marigolds instead.

She could not say whether they had done it deliberately, because they were so new to her that she could barely guess how their minds worked. But she had a horrid suspicion they were toying with her, using her as entertainment.

After fuming for a while, Alice concluded the problem was that a number of things Mary had insisted upon had proved false. Iris *did not* suffer an attack of nerves when the Abletts were mentioned. Far from it, she had enjoyed sharing her memories of Delma and her fur collar. And then there was . . .

The telephone rang.

For a moment Alice resisted answering, fearing it was Mary with bad news of some sort. Then she lunged, knocking the receiver to the floor and grovelling to retrieve it.

'Alice?'

'Rod?' She was so relieved it was not Mary that she sounded absolutely delighted to hear him.

'I've lost a wallet, Pippin. You couldn't pop up and see whether it's in the spare room, could you?'

She scampered upstairs, whisked through the spare room, checking beneath the bed and on shelves. When she lifted up a book beside her computer, she found it.

Breathless, she reported: 'Yes, it's here.'

'Oh great. That saves a lot of bother.'

'Where are you, Rod?' His predicament was her excuse to escape from Stark Point. 'I'll drive to meet you.'

But no, he could not possibly allow her to go to such trouble. They wrangled. He won. Mildly disappointed, she set the receiver down.

Alice carried a mug of rosehip tea into the sitting room. He had said he was the other side of Bath, therefore she had ample time to do some writing before he reappeared. She focused her attention on the boat poem.

The storm was now vigorous, the boat was helpless in the wind and weather, and there was a pleasing tension, she felt, between the two. Perhaps the poem was working, despite her doubts.

By three o'clock, when Rod had not arrived and the poem had become struck because she could not settle whether to distil it in one tight verse or let it flow into a second stanza, Alice tossed her pen aside, groaned with the deepest frustration and went through to the garden.

'Quite possibly the best day of the summer and I'm forced to let it slip away.'

She repeated the groan, more softly. This was a land where people saw and heard and she did not wish anyone to know how she felt.

With a pang she foresaw she would learn to conceal her feelings, as the inhabitants of Stark Point concealed theirs. That, she decided, was how her aunt had survived.

'Bella camouflaged herself. She pretended to be as they are.'

Then she was thinking: *'Everything here is masked by suspicion or collusion. People don't say what they believe or show what they think. They are pretend people, not straightforward or sincere.'*

This was harsh. She flushed, conscious of tarring too many people with one brush because she was justified in questioning the motives of a few.

Annoyed with herself, she grabbed a notebook, a jacket, a pen, anchored a message beneath a stone on the front doorstep and marched down the lane. A light wind was blowing, unusually, from the north, and the smell exuded by the chicken farm soured the air. In the high grass, Alice sent up flights of scandalised finches.

Jacko and three men were by the wreck. She headed towards them, wondering whether it would ruin her poem if she knew the truth about the real boat. Her romantic nature, maybe her writer's nature, had evolved it into something other than a yacht snatched from bad moorings. In her head it had become mythical. How dare she risk learning that it belonged to a man at, say, Minehead?

Jacko was orchestrating his companions. They were talking about shifting it onto a trailer and towing it down the road to the harbour it had been plucked from in the gale.

'Knowing the currents, like I do,' Jacko was saying, 'it was obvious where she came from. Couldn't have come from anywhere else, not with that wind behind her.'

Apparently, its owner had been to the bay to claim it and had accepted Jacko's offer of help, Jacko being the local expert on all things maritime.

The slime on the keel was reduced to a grey stain, and the hull no longer had the look of a thing from the sea. Between the night of the storm and this hot sunny afternoon, its nature had changed.

Beep, beep.

Jacko broke off to answer his telephone.

Alice trailed along the rim of the bay, where sand merged with soil. Rabbits flashed scuts and fled. A cat loped ahead of her, unconcerned, as she walked where the land was tumbled and hummocky in the shadow of the low cliff. Behind the Cat Rock she entered a desolation of shattered stone and sea-eaten boulders. The tortured strata of the cliff had collapsed. Shards ran jaggedly out to sea and blocked the way along the shore. In this ruined scenery she met up with Joe Keenthorne.

'I knew you'd come,' he said, convincingly unsurprised.

'I guessed you'd be here.'

'Did you bring your notebook?'

Alice drew it out of her pocket. The sea sang, a long way out but on the turn. Things went away and they came back. Situations, people, tides. You had to deal with things, because they always came back.

'Joe,' she said, 'today someone told me part of your story.'

To her ears this sounded fair. No point in fiddling around with niceties, as he probably thought she had known it all along. It was best to make the situation plain.

He grunted and looked out to sea. She thought: '*People at Stark Point can always evade you by doing that.*'

She said: 'I didn't know earlier about the trial and I don't think I've taken it in properly yet. But if we're going to go on with your story, it's important you tell me about all that.'

Her insistence on her own discomfort rather than his embarrassed her. Her hope was that he did not remember what conversational conventions were.

She moved round, to stand between him and the sea.

He flung out an arm, not pointing at her as she initially dreaded, but beyond, out into the bay.

'They went over the bay. I told you that, Alice. They went that way to the coast road.'

She shook her head, recalling how their previous meeting had ended with her stressing the Abletts' ownership of a car. If they had wanted it to seem they had vanished, rather than walked over the bay, they might have left the car behind. Yet according to the story, the car vanished too.

'Look,' she said, 'my cottage has a grand view of the bay and so do others. If two people walked across the sand at low tide, they were certain to be seen. But the Abletts weren't.'

He studied her. His eyes were guarded, his mouth a mean line. He stood, hands behind his back in his habitual pose, trying to read his future in her face.

Alice reddened and was forced to turn away to break his gaze. As well as reckless, she felt feeble.

He said: 'I want you to write it down. How they want me out of my house. I've got a story for you.'

'Yes, yes, I know. But . . .'

Her impatience shamed her. She tried again. 'Joe, I will hear the story about your house but it would be easier for me if we begin at the beginning. Begin there and go right through to the end.'

For her, the story was a complex and terrifying one, and the surest way to absorb it correctly was to work through methodically.

Slowly he nodded. Then he gestured towards a flattish slab, created during a cliff fall. He sat on it and Alice perched nearby. She made a show of uncapping her pen, putting her notebook on her knee. If he was genuinely willing to tell her, he would not miss this opportunity.

Chapter Eight

'If I could do the writing, I'd set it down myself. But you're the writer, Alice. I'm a farmer, that's all I know.'

'I'll do my best, Joe.'

'You know about me being born at Stark Point and living here all my life, except the time I had my trouble?'

'Yes.'

She was already having qualms about the amount of detail he might offer. His childhood? Family and friends? Memories of storms and harvests?

'*That's a risk I'll have to take,*' she thought, '*because I advised him to begin at the beginning. Besides, if I steer him along, he might skip something vital.*'

He said: 'Most families at the Point have been here generations. Incomers don't stick, see. They don't prosper, like plants that look all right for a while but don't put down roots. You have to be born to it to be comfortable here. My father used to say that and it's true.'

'What was his name, Joe?' She decided to garner facts where she could.

'Clem. And my mother was Bessie, a Burge before she married.'

'Was she from the Point, too?'

'No, over to Lambwood. Never liked it here, did mother. Couldn't settle. She lived here thirty years and I swear, Alice, every day she looked at the tide coming in on her and she gave a shudder and said: "Damn this place, I don't know why the sea don't swallow it up and be done with it." But she didn't ever get away, not back to Lambwood, not anywhere. Took pneumonia and died.'

'Was this before the Ablett affair?' She felt pleased with 'affair', a nice neutral way of touching on what was appalling.

'Mother had been gone a year before that happened. If she'd been there still, things might have been different for me but once she'd gone I was in the house on my own. No one to say where I was or what I was doing, see. No witness.'

Alice nodded, assuming the significance would become plain later. Instead, she asked about his father and was told Clem had died of a heart attack two years before his mother.

He said: 'The estate was very good, they let his tenancy pass to me. Only a few acres, it was, enough to feed a few cows and grow a couple of crops but it was fair land, well-drained and not spoiled by the salt. Some land at the Point has the sea right over it every year but we were lucky. Well, you might say I'd have gone on being lucky if it hadn't been for George Ablett. Never thought I'd have that sort of trouble from a cousin.'

'*Cousin?*'

'Didn't they tell you? George Ablett was my father's sister's boy, an only lad. Knew him from a babby, I did. We used to play together, get up to all sorts. After his father, old Richie Ablett, died when his tractor overturned, George got the farm, years ahead of when he might have expected. His mother went away, over to Exeter.'

Alice remarked on the symmetry. 'Both you and George were left alone on your farms.'

'Yes, although the big difference was mine was a hand-to-mouth tenancy and George was outright owner. Richie had been offered the big chance and he'd grabbed it, bought the property off the estate one time when Sir Arthur Devrell – who was lord of the manor before this one – needed money in his pocket. It didn't happen often. There isn't much land at Stark Point that isn't owned by the estate to this day.'

Alice said she had heard this. She did not hurry him, though, being intrigued by the emerging pattern. Two cousins left alone on farms, one man a forever-poor tenant and the other granted the chance to build on family success. Rivalry, jealousy, resentment? Their juxtaposition provided scope for all those.

Joe was saying: 'Once George owned the farm, several girls looked him over but, suddenly, there was Delma and that was that. Met each other at a hunt ball, they did. She wasn't like the other women around here, was never going to fit.'

Alice chipped in. 'I've seen a photograph of her. Well, of them, I should say. And their car.'

He showed no interest, making her wish she had resisted interrupting.

He said: 'Well, if George started with a few ideas of his own, Delma knew how to encourage them. Folk used to say it was all Delma's doing, pushing him on, like, but that wasn't right. The minute that farm fell into his hands, George knew what he was going to do. Off to see the bank manager, he was, within the week. I won't say he went the day of the funeral, which some will argue, but he was never one to keep ambition waiting.'

He told her what George had done with the bank loan, and she appreciated how closely lucky George Ablett's spending had been studied by everyone who lived on the peninsula.

'First off,' Joe said, 'there was money poured all over Perrotts Farm: machinery, improvements to the drainage, walls rebuilt, brand new outbuildings. Then he looked around him and he saw Josh Piccott was lame, his land getting too much for him and his boy turning his back on it, settled in a nice job in an office in Williton. So George set his mind to getting the farm off Josh. We always called it the Little Farm because for weeks at a time the water lay on it and what was left wasn't much, as you might say. Folk have always said that one day the Little Farm will be washed right away.'

'Is it where the flood was this week?'

'Ah no, Little Farm is up along. When Josh Piccott's uncles bought it off the estate, folk said they were making a mistake. It was cheap because it was poor land in a bad situation, and the

Piccotts knew that better than anybody. The other thing everybody knew was that the estate didn't part with good land.'

Spotting a discrepancy, Alice pitched in. 'But I thought the farm George Ablett inherited was good one.'

'By George's time it was but when his father took it over the estate hadn't spent a penny on it for years. Richie had always said the drainage was wrong and if it was put right the soil on the three big fields would be in good heart. So that's what he did, dug a new ditch alongside. Proved himself right.'

'Couldn't the same thing be done to improve the Little Farm?'

'Ah no, it lies on the seaward side, Alice. That's salt water swilling over it when the tide's high. What Richie bought was land on the other side, where fresh water off the hills lies around, and decent drainage cures that.'

'Well, the Little Farm doesn't sound a good prospect. Why was George keen to buy it?'

His eyes creased in a knowing smile. 'The farmhouse has a good view of the islands and George wanted to buy Delma that view. She begged him to get hold of it and put up a new farmhouse, with big windows looking over the channel. The land wasn't worth a lot but the view was worth everything to Delma, so George went for it. Everyone said he was daft about her, that there was nothing she couldn't have and not much she didn't want. Well, in the end George bought the Little Farm but Delma didn't get her new house. He asked the council to let him build it and he wasn't allowed.'

'Really? I thought farmers were allowed to build more or less what they wanted.'

'They often were and George was relying on it. But some folk in the village objected, saying it wasn't necessary and Josh's old farmhouse ought to be preserved, anyway. A fine example of a local style, they said it was, which riled George because he claimed Josh Piccott had built half of it himself, which was true.'

Primed by Mary's stories of grudging neighbours, Alice guessed how George Ablett had been thwarted, taken down a peg by envious neighbours denied the opportunity to own property of their own.

Joe was saying: 'And that's when I came up against George.'

He paused to let her consider this although, to Alice it was obscure.

'Joe, I don't understand . . .'

A puzzled look. 'I thought folk had been talking to you.'

'Not about that.'

'Well, they made enough of it at the time.'

'What happened between you and George?'

'I used to graze the Little Farm, see. Josh wasn't making full use of it, what with being lame, so we reached an agreement. I would do jobs for him and in return I got the grazing. It let me rear a few more animals than I could have managed without it. But as soon as George got the farm, he put a stop to it. It wasn't a proper arrangement, he said, because I hadn't been paying over money.'

'Was he correct?'

He shrugged. 'I don't know. We had a row about it but he was determined I was to go, and he got his way by herding the heifers out into the lane and putting a padlock on the gate.'

Seeing Alice agape amused him. 'Oh, George had a reputation for being awkward, always had been since he were a babby. A lot of folk had reason to complain. But, like I said, I wasn't ready for that kind of trouble, him being a cousin.'

'The whole village must have known, with the cows in the lane.'

'Oh, yes, and when George went missing there were plenty of tongues wagging about that bad blood between us.'

'Wasn't he on bad terms with others too?'

'Yes, but . . .' He let the sea hold his attention. Then: 'You see, Alice, the one person who could have explained that things weren't as bad as they were making out was Delma. Delma knew we were rubbing along all right, despite that business over the Little Farm. She was one for smoothing things over, was Delma. "You and Joe are family," she said to him. "Family stick together." Well, he didn't say anything to that, not while I was there, but when he saw me in town on market day he spoke as though there was nothing wrong. And I thought, "That's Delma, that is." '

Alice risked deterring him with a challenge. 'I thought Delma was supposed to have made him look down on other farmers at the point.'

'That's true, Alice, she did. But she didn't like what she called unpleasantness between folk. If there'd been a row, she wouldn't put up with festering – that was her word for it. To her mind, you should carry on like it hadn't happened.'

'I see.'

'As for getting him to look down, oh yes, that was Delma too. Once he'd bought the Little Farm, he was farming more land than anyone at Stark Point and she wanted them to live as though they were the best. As well as a new farmhouse, she was after a car. Seems strange now but vans were good enough for anybody else out here who could drive, and several who couldn't went about with a horse and cart. Well, once Delma got going you didn't see George standing around talking to any of us, like he might have done before. Oh no, he was off making friends with the big farmers. You'd see him with them on market day, strutting about the town like he was somebody who counted.'

His eyes strayed to the sea again, looking far off at the hurt and the resentment caused by that successful duo, George and Delma.

Alice turned a page in her notebook. The breeze caught the edge and fluttered it. Joe's gaze swung to her.

'You see, Alice, it's what they did that caused my trouble. I often think: supposing she hadn't craved the view of the islands, my heifers would have stayed on the Little Farm. No row, and everything would have been all right for me.'

Alice spoke softly. 'Instead, nothing was.'

He became brisk, forcing the words out before he changed his mind about telling her.

'The police decided I was the last person to see them alive and I killed them because of that bad blood. "They've run away," I said. "They took on debts they can't pay and they've gone. Ask anybody." But the police wanted a double murder. And I was stupid, Alice, not realising my danger, just arguing there weren't any bodies. I thought you had to have a body to prove a death. Lots of folk believe that but it isn't true. I went on believing it up to the time they charged me.'

His face was contorted with painful memories. When his hands began twisting, Alice was afraid he was going to rush away.

She started to sympathise but, greatly agitated, he spoke over her. 'This book you're going to write for me, it's got to explain I'm innocent. I didn't kill anybody. You must make everybody believe that.'

'Joe, we need to talk about the case against you and the trial.'

The pitch of his voice rose. 'When you write my story you must put down everything about my life: coming back here after the trial, nobody speaking, the Chiltons trying to get the house from me. Everything.'

She made her own voice soothing. 'Yes, of course. You must tell me everything.'

'Folk have tried all sorts to get me off the farm and now they're saying I can't look after myself and I ought to be put away. But I know it's because the Chiltons want the house. They've always been after it, and since I had pneumonia last winter they see their chance of pushing me out. Told the doctor to see about me going into a home, they did. But you can put it right, Alice. You're a writer, you can put the words down for me. Publishers pay thousands, don't they, for books? When you've written it we can share the money, and then I won't be thrown out of my house. I'll be able to pay for the repairs they keep going on about, and fixing the heating and all sorts.'

She didn't disbelieve him. For one thing, Mrs Aley had mentioned an attempt to persuade the council's social services department he needed to be be taken into care.

With a sinking heart Alice at last understood her role in his scheme. '*Everything depends on me. I'm all that stands between him and disaster.*'

She confined herself to sympathetic murmurs. Joe's eyes were darting around the bay, to the roofs of Stark Point, the scrub where foxes hid and out to the islands. Checking over and over, she realised, to see from which direction calamity might, this time, strike.

Obsessively he let his words flow on, swamping Alice's mind with his fears and his protests. He was victimised, he was cheated, he was no killer. She was his only hope, without her book he was doomed.

With an inward sigh, Alice folded the notebook and stood up to put it in her pocket. Numb from the coldness of the stone, she rubbed life into her leg. Her shadow fell across him before he noticed she was on her feet.

She warmed him with a smile. 'It's getting late, Joe. We'll have to talk again soon.'

He drew a deep breath as he rose. 'Tomorrow.' A demand, not a question.

'In the morning?' She was calculating it would allow time for the rest of the tale. This session had been mainly preamble, they had yet to touch on the heart of it.

He suggested a time when the tide would be far enough out for them to walk round in safety. *'But he'll be in the bay hours before that,'* she thought, *'parading up and down the sand like a beachcomber.'*

Then she wondered whether he would volunteer why he did that or whether, in the end, she would be forced to ask him.

They teetered over friable stone, then dropped down onto sand. They had the bay to themselves, except for a cat sunning on a flat stone and waders patrolling the line of the surf.

Alice scanned the saltings for warning of dogs or people approaching but saw nobody. The shambling man beside her was calm.

Casually, although acutely aware how this detail had been withheld, Alice asked: 'Where do you live, Joe?'

He pointed, slightly right of the causeway. 'Perrotts Farm.'

The name struck hard. 'But you said that's where the Abletts lived.'

'The farm came to me.'

'Oh.'

'That's the law. After seven years they were officially declared dead and everything they owned came to me.'

Chapter Nine

Exhilarated, Alice trotted up the lane. Pictures spun in her head: Joe and George as friendly schoolboys; George introducing Delma and her fancy ways to Stark Point . . .

All at once she remembered Rod and his mislaid wallet. She put on a spurt for the final hundred yards.

Rod was not on the step this time, he was in his car listening to the radio. He opened the door as she panted up.

'Hi, where've you been?'

'Sorry . . . had to go out.'

He mocked her breathlessness. 'Who's chasing you? Hounds of heaven?'

Alice fumbled her key into the lock. She was mumbling about having forgotten he was coming, which did not sound kind and then she was trying to undo the damage by saying something had happened to take her mind off it. As she tore off her jacket, the notebook flew out of the pocket. Rod picked it up.

'Oh, I see. Inspired by a poem, were you, Pippin?'

She dived for it but he jinked out of reach. 'Rod, please.'

He flicked open the book. 'Prose, not poetry.'

Alice pulled out a chair from the kitchen table and sat down, resting her chin on her hand. 'I can write prose too. I forgot to explain that.'

'Ho, very ironic.'

He dropped the book in front of her. 'The great novel instead of the great poem, is it?'

'I'm working on poems,' she said patiently, 'but Joe Keenthorne's been telling me his story.'

'Tea?'

'Thanks. Apple and ginger.'

Rod grimaced as he poured boiling water on herbal sachets, and carried the mugs to the table. He was saying: 'And is his story about the mysterious Abletts, as you hoped?'

'Yes, very much about them. He was tried for their murder.'

Rosehip tisane sloshed over the side of Rod's mug and splashed on the wooden table. '*What?*'

Alice took considerable satisfaction in now being the one under control while he gawped. She fetched a cloth as she enlarged.

'Tried and acquitted. We did preliminaries today but tomorrow I'm going to hear about the trial and the case against him.'

'Good God. Did he do it, do you think?'

'Most people here believe he did, and Iris Dottrell suspects he knows more than he admits.'

'What if he confesses to you?'

Her scalp tightened. She had not considered this possibility.

'No,' she said, too quickly, 'he wants me to write a book that convinces people he's innocent.'

'I dare say, love, but suppose you realise he's guilty?'

She looked blank.

He said: 'What then? Will you carry on with *I'm Innocent, Says Joe* or will you shop him?'

Flustered, she sought escape. 'I'll have to decide when that happens. Which it won't do, I'm sure.'

Rod was being coolly analytical, seeing what she was not yet ready to see for herself. 'The odds are against his innocence, aren't they? The police and the lawyers must have had sufficient evidence to put him on trial, and the Pointers don't believe him. Did he say why they thought he did it?'

'No.'

He pounced. 'Alice, that's the way you pronounce no when you aren't sure.'

She gave a wry smile. 'I have to admit he told me what his motive might have been. He inherited everything the Abletts owned.'

In quick succession Rod looked agog, despairing and ultimately triumphant.

Alice wrung out the damp cloth, then poured more water in the kettle and asked whether he would like a fresh drink, while knowing full well he would refuse.

He answered from the sitting room. 'No thanks.'

'But you can't have much left.'

'It's all right. I had a proper cup of tea with Mary earlier on.'

'Oh?'

'You weren't here so I went over to Ham Cottage in search of you. Mary took pity on me. PG Tips and fruitcake, in the garden.'

This ought to have made her feel better about keeping him waiting, yet it did not. And there was another thing: Rod, who had ostensibly returned to fetch a forgotten wallet, was not the least cross about being held up. She recalled occasions when unnecessary delays in his plans had caused tremendous fuss. Now here he was, utterly unconcerned about being a hundred miles or so from where he ought to be and showing no sign of collecting his wallet and going. No, he was asking her again about Joe Keenthorne.

'Don't run any risks, will you?' he was saying. 'I know you're not generally careless about your safety, but this is an odd situation you've fallen into. You might find yourself wishing you hadn't.'

She had settled in the chair by the window, the pot of geraniums on the table beside her brilliant in sunlight. Rod was comfortable on the sofa across from her. Too comfortable.

She resisted being drawn into arguments about her wisdom in hearing Joe's story. 'Rod, why are you here?'

Her bluntness startled him. 'Because I left . . .'

Alice denied it with a curl of her lip. 'I've stopped believing in the lost wallet. You're here because you don't want to be somewhere else.'

He was no longer looking comfortable.

She went on: 'Stark Point is a place for people to be when they don't want to be anywhere else. We agreed that on the first day you were here. When we walked to the end of the peninsula, remember?'

He still did not speak.

Alice said: 'When I found you on my doorstep that day I was convinced you'd come to discuss a divorce. I soon discovered I was wrong about that but I realise I still don't know the truth. Why can't I be told the truth, Rod?'

He laughed derisively. 'You're too imaginative, Alice. I came to ask if you'd be willing for us to get back together. That would have been an incredible thing to ask if I wasn't genuine. I mean, supposing you'd said yes and I hadn't meant it?'

But she was conscious of gaps in her understanding, the subjects he had skirted, and she refused to be swayed.

'It's no use. You haven't told me everything and the longer you're around the more it matters.'

Julie picked that moment to telephone.

'Hi, Alice, how are you?'

'Julie. I'm fine.' She was going to offer to ring back but Julie was in full spate.

'Still being saintly?'

'Well . . .'

'Not me, Alice, I've just succumbed to a Mars bar. I'm telling myself it wasn't lack of will-power, it was provocation. I've had the most amazing woman here, problems with her back, neurotic, I'd say, but she's convinced herself I'm the only therapist in the country who can fix her up, so I've been twiddling her toes and . . .'

'Julie, I . . .'

'Oh, isn't it a good time?'

'Afraid not.'

'Sorry. You should have said, silly.'

'Well, I . . .'

'Ring me when you're free. Okay?'

Alice said okay.

Rod had left the room. She found him in the garden, fiddling with the clematis denuded by the storm.

'What variety is this?' He was not being serious.

'Storm-damaged.'

'Thrives around here, I should think.'

'Like nothing else.'

'Except murderers and mystery?'

'Talking of which, Rod . . .'

'Which, Pippin?'

'Mystery.'

'Ah, the Abletts.' He knew she was not referring to them.

'No, nothing so tragic. At least, I don't think so unless you tell me otherwise.'

He faded, gave up the struggle to be light. When he spoke next his tone was weary. 'There are other sorts of tragedy, apart from being killed off for an inheritance or whatever happened to them. Come to think of it, they were spared seeing someone else enjoying the fruits of their labours.'

She felt a wave of sympathy. 'How did she do it?'

'The usual way. Took up with one of the other directors, took over the company.'

Alice needed to spell it out, to make an end of muddle and dissembling. 'Ruth stole your business from you?'

'Perfectly legally. Ruth and a man she urged on me as a director now own it between them. I was edged out.'

'And the house at Wykeham?'

'It was rented. They live there together, they drive my car, and I have . . .'

He broke off and spread empty hands.

Alice's memory flew back to that first evening, the questioning about Charles and her new life, the appraisal of her possessions. At the time, she had silently accused him of totting up what she was worth, ready to claim a share when they divorced. Now she saw it differently. If he was reduced to owning nothing, she was comparatively rich.

She felt his eyes on her. Rather than reveal what she was thinking, she faked a question. 'Can't you get any of it back?'

'Everything's owned by the business. And I'm not married to Ruth.'

'But . . .'

A flash of anger. 'Do you think I haven't been into all that?'

She regretted her blunder. Obviously he would have battled to hold onto things. And she knew what a fighter he was, how he had made everything out of nothing but talent and energy.

'You're right,' she said, quietly. 'There are other kinds of tragedy.'

Their eyes met for a long moment.

A high wind gusted up the channel that night, a warm current that shook leaves loose from trees and made window frames creak. Alice got out of bed around three o'clock but there was little moonlight and nothing to see. An occasional thudding made her suspect a shed door was swinging free. She went downstairs, furtively so as not to disturb Rod. Once she hesitated, hearing a faint movement from the spare room but it did not come again.

There was a lamp outside the back door and she switched this on hoping the pool of light would flow as far as the shed. It did not so she went out.

The blowy, warm night cast her mind back to holidays when the hot breath of Africa had scorched the Mediterranean lands. Then the thud sounded again. She fetched a torch from a drawer in the kitchen and hurried to the shed. To her surprise it was secure.

Another bang.

This time she gauged the direction, and went down the side of the house, stepping over drifts of leaves and twigs. Rod's car was parked by the garage but hers was inside. As she drew near the wooden door swung out, clouted his car and bounced back.

'Oh, no!' Her words, escaping into the darkness, gave her a nervous start.

She darted forward, in time to brace herself against the door as the wind tugged it. But the power of the wind was too strong and she was forced off balance and flung across the car bonnet. Her grip slackened, the torch skidded over the metal surface, hit the ground and went out.

Cursing, she struggled free the instant the wind dropped, and slipped out of danger by running to the far side of the car. From there, she grabbed the flying door without being trapped. She ran her hand over it, feeling for the catch and missing it.

'Damn! The torch, I've got to get the torch.'

She padded around near Rod's car, making frantic guesses at the trajectory of the falling torch. By luck she stepped on it. She spun the beam at the garage.

There was a pale patch on the wood where the catch ought to have been. She whisked the beam over the ground but did not find it. Then she went into the garage, wondering whether the catch could possibly have ended up inside.

She stopped dead.

Her car was open. The oddments she kept in there were scattered around the interior. Front seats were tilted forward. The boot was raised and she could not say whether she had left it locked.

Feeling sick, she looked in the boot. There was a jumble but, strangely, everything appeared to be there. Whoever had ransacked the car had rejected her valuable field glasses along with her maps and waterproofs and the usual motorists' clutter. It was the same story inside the car: a mess had been made but nothing stolen.

The actual damage was limited to the garage itself, as far as she could see, because the catch had been wrenched off. The rest was sheer nuisance.

Her feelings garbled, she stood there worrying what sort of person would leave home on such a night to pester her and why?

An answer popped up straight away. '*It's because of Joe Keenthorne. I'm being warned not to have anything to do with him.*'

Then: '*But hardly anybody knows about that.*'

And then the correction: '*Everybody knows. They don't tell me things but I have no secrets from them.*'

Suddenly shaky, she fled. Around the car, up the side of the house, and into the kitchen where she shot bolts across the door, collapsed against it and listened to her anxious heart.

From above: 'Alice?'

Haste had made her noisy. Rod was on the stairs.

'Whatever's happened?'

Not wanting to appear frail, she tried to laugh it off. Her chattering teeth gave her away.

He held her. 'Tell me, love.'

Alice thrust him away, needing to feel free, not crushed. If he felt unkindly rejected she did not notice.

'The shed . . . No, it wasn't the shed, it turned out to be the garage . . .'

And so her story stumbled out.

Rod asked, at the end: 'What about my car?'

'I don't know.' She felt foolish not to have looked.

'I'll go and see. What have you done with the torch?'

'I don't know.'

They found it on the draining board, apparently dumped there as she burst into the cottage. His car keys were on the window sill. He picked those up, too, then asked her to lock up behind him and not let anyone in until she was certain it was him. Meekly, she agreed.

Once he had gone she felt disgusted with herself. '*What would I have done if he wasn't here? I'd have handled it myself, not let some man take over.*'

A question followed hard on that. Take over what? Someone untidying a car did not amount to danger, but someone loitering near the house at night and wishing her harm was very serious indeed. There was no knowing what she was up against.

Shortly, Rod called out and she let him in.

He told her: 'I've moved my car right up to the door to hold it shut.'

Not having thought of it herself, Alice decided that was quite clever.

'Is your car damaged?'

He shrugged. 'We can't be sure until daylight.'

He did not sound worried, for which she was grateful. Until a few hours ago she would have assumed a few dents and scratches on a runabout to be of no consequence to a high earner like Rod. Now she had to consider everything from a different perspective. It would not be easy getting used to that.

Rod made a performance of checking windows and doors, then making tea for her.

Studying the packets he sought expert advice. 'Which one's best for calming you down?'

'Camomile.'

'Camomile it is, then.'

This time when he handed the mug to her he resisted even the faintest grimace or quiver of the nostrils.

'You don't think,' Rod said tentatively while she sipped, 'that this trouble with your car could have anything to do with Joe Keenthorne and all that?'

'Good heavens no,' she lied. 'I expect it's just a lad in the village making a nuisance of himself.'

Rod nodded, looking unconvinced.

Alice yawned. Tiredness was catching up with her now the alarums were over. She fancied creeping into a warm bed and, as the wind had dropped, she stood a fair chance of sleeping.

'Why don't you change out of that?' Rod asked.

She looked down at her nightdress and was startled to see it was filthy. Fighting with the garage door and being thrown across the car bonnet had done that. She burst out laughing.

'I must look a fright.'

'You had a fright.'

She got up, draining her drink. 'I'm going to clean myself up and go to bed.'

He said he was too wide awake to sleep and would stay there for a while. She left him glancing through the previous day's newspaper but as soon as she'd gone he went into the sitting room and picked up the photograph of the missing Abletts.

For a while he stood holding it beneath a lamp, chewing a lip thoughtfully as he went over what Alice had relayed to him. He could not shift the idea that he was right and she was wrong, that the interference with her car was a way of telling her to steer clear of Keenthorne and the Abletts. It worried him that she was being over confident but he knew better than to tell her outright that she was reckless and ought to drop Keenthorne before she suffered anything worse.

Upstairs, Alice lay cheated of sleep. Light was tiptoeing around her curtain before she as much as dozed. Instead of fretting about the night's adventures or the extraordinary tales of the day, she reverted to an earlier interest: the romantic Mrs Ablett.

Whatever anybody else might believe, Alice liked the idea of Delma Ablett going off in her car to meet her secret lover and leaving stolid George to his heifers. It was, after all, mainly Delma's money which had made the Abletts the richest folk in the village. If Delma chose to squander some on a car and a fur collar, whose business was it but hers?

Alice shut her eyes and pictured Delma driving through the lanes to rendezvous in country hotels and secluded pubs, of which there was ample choice in the area. The characters in her head acted out the clash between George and Delma over debts – his, not hers – and his crack-brained scheme for them to escape the problem by fleeing.

They performed anguished discussions which resulted in angry resolutions. While George was to walk over the bay towards the coast road, Delma was to drive round to meet him and then they were to chase away into the night, driving south to catch an early boat to France and oblivion.

But the Delma character had had enough of this stupid husband and, although George took the footpath over the Little Farm to the shore, she had a better idea of her own. George's movements were controlled by the tide: he had to dash lest the waters of the channel came racing over the sand and the mud and caught him. Delma's were controlled by no one but Delma. As soon as George was out of sight, she drove out of the farmyard without her lights on, to avoid being noticed, but instead of looping round to the coast road, she struck inland to meet her lover. Although she just as surely headed for oblivion it was in a totally different direction and with another man.

This secret lover, whose face was obscured from Alice in her day-dreaming, was exactly the fellow for Delma. His own car was grander than hers, he was svelte and smooth, accomplished in business and the social graces. He was hers, had been for years. George was an aberration in her life, but this man was her true love.

He . . . Oh, how Alice wished she knew his name! Well, he awaited Delma at the entrance to a private drive through a wood. Her car turned in, she jumped out. They ran into each other's arms. Back in their separate cars, he led her into the heart of the wood, which was on his land, of course; and there, in a disused forester's hut, she parked her wonderful car. He locked the door. She hopped into his passenger seat and together they disappeared into the night. It was all intensely romantic.

Meanwhile, George Ablett waited on the coast road. Light was easing in from the east but his wife did not come. He feared a confusion, an accident. It was hours before he allowed himself to suspect treachery. Then, with a howl, he staggered away, avoiding roads, moving by darkness for days until . . .

Alice wriggled with dissatisfaction, thinking: '*This is all very entertaining but it can't be true. Not the George part, anyway. He's far more likely to have been caught by the tide and not have reached the coast road.*'

Less romantic, less appealing, it was, however, more probable. Alice pictured George, miscalculating the time it took to cross the bay. No doubt he had done it as a youngster and no doubt he was quicker in those days. Besides, the mud and the sand were not constant features, they changed position. A man tearing across in the evening, while he had light and before the tide came, would take the shortest route. What, though, if the shortest route had become mud and not sand? How many steps must he take before realising his fatal miscalculation? And how long would he flounder before the surf was swishing around his legs, his waist, his neck?

Horrified, Alice sat up in bed. The images were so sharp it was impossible to believe she had invented them and done this silly thing to herself. This hysterical nonsense was quite out of character. She prayed Rod had not heard her gasping distress.

'*It isn't real,*' she insisted. '*I made it up. I let my imagination run away with me and . . .*'

But, in a sense, it was true. That was the reason it was terrifying to dwell on it. People had died in precisely that way, a few hundred yards from where she was telling herself comforting lies.

She understood acutely that the fears you can brush off are the imagined horrors of the supernatural, say aliens from spaceships, anything unproven and speculative. The ones that strike deep are those that genuinely and repeatedly destroy human beings. And drowning, she believed, was the most horrible of deaths.

She went to the window, this time discovering the world revealed in filmy grey. High tide and water surged ashore but its sigh was faint as the wind was not coming from its normal direction. A little later, as day encroached further, a trick of the light made her catch her breath. But no, of course it wasn't a body being carried on the swell. Her imagination was primed for anything, she thought, however distasteful.

For George Ablett, though, there had been another option. *'Heaven knows why I didn't see it before. All that chatter about mud and tides and perilous paths, I suppose. But, obviously, what he did was take a boat.'*

She was very keen to walk over the Little Farm and check whether it was practical to launch one there. Not that she expected a jetty, but a rock or two in the right position might be enough.

Impatient for daytime and the chance to find out, she had abandoned all hope of sleep. From the window she watched early birds swooping down on the strip of shore, a fox ambling along and, finally, an old man in a woolly hat traipsing over the wet sand as though he, too, were an element of the dawn.

At that she curled up in bed again and soon, unexpectedly, fell asleep.

Rod let her sleep on. When she woke it was mid-morning and they argued about whose fault that was.

'You knew I was going to meet Joe Keenthorne at nine,' she shouted.

'I forgot.'

She did not believe him and said so. 'You think he's guilty of the murders and I should keep away from him.'

'Alice, yesterday you were telling me his motive for murder.'

'Inheritance isn't a motive unless you know you're going to inherit. He could have been utterly amazed.'

'Yes, all right, but either way he's an oddball.'

'You don't want me to go on with the book. That's what this is about.'

'No, honestly.'

But she was certain he was not being honest. 'You don't think I can write it.'

'I haven't said that.'

'You've been thinking it.'

He shrugged. 'How do I know whether you can or not? You might make a good job of it, for all I know.'

'So why interfere with my research?'

He shook his head, aware the doubts about her capabilities were hers rather more than his.

All the time they were bickering she was eating, drinking, gathering notebook and pen, draping her jacket over her shoulders and preparing to run off and catch Joe.

Alice raced out of the house, planning to drive to the car park by the beach but then rediscovering Rod's car blocking her garage entrance. With a growl of annoyance, she jogged down the lane. A couple of hundred yards on she felt eyes on her, and saw Iris Dottrell's pathetic face at her window. Managing a grudging wave, Alice raced by.

On the beach, Jacko and a trio of helpers were hiking the wreck onto a trailer. Alice detoured to avoid wasting time on conversation before it occurred to her that conversation was the last thing she could expect.

They did not have the bay to themselves as the weekend crowd had arrived. Three sand-streaked children chased in front of her. Dogs were seeking out other dogs to sniff at and squabble with. Two elderly couples had unfolded garden chairs and were unscrewing thermos flasks. A man and his girlfriend were paddling with rolled-up jeans.

Joe was not there. On several occasions Alice hunted for him without success, and it was days later when she clambered round the rocks one morning and found him staring out to sea.

She approached smiling, saying how sorry she was she had missed him.

He said: 'Did you bring your notebook?'

She plucked it from her pocket.

He pointed to a flat stone nearby and as she sat down he started speaking.

'After seven years they were legally presumed dead and everything they had came to me.'

Neat, she thought, Joe picking it up exactly where he had left off days before.

He said: 'You'll have been asking yourself why that should be.'

She pretended she had.

'That was George's idea. He reckoned if Delma didn't have children and he died young, like his father before him, what he owned ought to stay in the family.'

A screaming gull caught his attention as it dived on a fishy carcase discarded by the water.

Alice hated the anguished sound. She spoke to blot it out. 'Did he tell you that?'

'I saw him in town on market day. "Looking very smart, George," I said, which was what he liked to hear. And he said, "On your account, Joe. I'm on my way to see my solicitor about my will." And then he told me what was to be in it.'

The bird seared Alice's nerves again. She looked from the old man to the gull, then at her notebook but her pen did not move. Any hope that he lacked a motive for murder dissolved faster than foam on the sand.

Chapter Ten

Joe's Story

'You see, Alice, that's what George and Delma were like, couldn't help showing off what they'd got. George, especially. My mother called it flaunting, said he didn't have the sense to keep his business to himself. She used to laugh about it, saying, "Don't you tell George any of your secrets, Joe, because there's a man who can't hold onto his own."

Mind, she wasn't exactly right there. The thing was, George didn't see as they were secrets. Didn't occur to him not to come right out with what he was going to do at the solicitor's. I don't doubt he mentioned it to other folk too, but we were talking in the street, anyhow, folk all around us and anyone listening who wanted to.

See, Alice, once the police started asking questions it wasn't long before they were round to me, saying, "Oh, Mr Keenthorne, we understand you are the beneficiary of Mr Ablett's will."

"Who told you that?" I asked, because I knew I hadn't ever said a word.

"Never mind that," they said. "Is it true?"

"Might be," I said, thinking George was a wily sort and we'd had that trouble over the Little Farm and, well, what it came down to was what he told his solicitor to do one day he could tell him to undo another day.

Later, in court, it was: "Did Mr Ablett at any time tell you that you'd inherit property on his death?"

And I had to say "Yes." Of course, I tried to explain I didn't know for certain he meant it.

"Oh?" they said, being sarcastic. "Was Mr Ablett a man given to making jokes of that nature?"

"No," I said, "but I don't know that he didn't change his mind on it."

"Was there any reason why he might have wished to do so?"

So then they had me telling them about the trouble between us, although I did say it was all patched up which they didn't want to agree with.

"And another thing," I said, "George wasn't an old man. No matter if he were leaving his farm to me, I'd be a long time getting it."

That was a mistake, right enough, because they shot straight back at me on that one. "Not if you murdered him, Mr Keenthorne."

All I could say was "Maybe so, but I didn't."

What's that, Alice? Yes, it was mainly the will that put it into folk's heads I'd done away with George and Delma. It made it look bad, I can see that. I didn't know whether I really was named in the will or whether the police were going by talk in the village. Could have been either. I kept asking the police, "Am I in George's will?" They wouldn't give me a straight answer, although twice they said, "Don't you know you can't inherit from a person you're convicted of murdering?"

They kept going on about the day George and Delma went missing. "Where were you, Mr Keenthorne? Did anybody see you?" Questions like that, over and over.

It was stupid. "Look," I said, "how can I answer you? I don't know which day they went. Now if you'd like to tell me the exact day, maybe I can say where I was to and what I was doing."

George's men came to the farm and did their work each day, but the owner and his wife weren't to be seen. First off, folk were saying, as though it were gospel, Delma's father took sick and George had driven her to the hospital, but the old boy was that bad she was having to stay over and George, good as he was to her, was staying too.

But then there were decisions to be made and no one to make them. One of the men walked over to my place and said, "You're family, Joe, what do you know about Mr and Mrs Ablett being away?"

"Nothing," I said. I was with a lame cow at the time, one of my fine old milkers. I sent him away.

An hour later he was back. "Where's her family to, Joe?"

"Why do you want to know that?"

"Because George Ablett's got business to do and he isn't here."

Anyway, I didn't have an address, only an idea of the village Delma came from. Then a message was got through and after that folk were saying Delma's father wasn't sick and she and George hadn't been over that way for months.

Her family it was who called the police and reported them missing. We heard the family were disgusted nobody at Stark Point thought to do it, but to us they weren't missing, only gone off in their car.

Well, the big puzzle then was when exactly did they go? I hadn't seen Delma for weeks before the police were brought into it. Easy to say when I saw George because it was market day and he was leaving the bank as I walked by, and I thought: '*Now here's a chance, Joe. See if he's willing to lend that saw of his for an afternoon.*'

I asked him straight off, quickly before anyone could chip in and spoil my chance. He didn't look pleased to be asked, but with George that didn't always mean he'd refuse you.

"All right, Joe," he said. "You come round tomorrow about six."

Six was a good time. I'd have my day's work done and it

would still be light. But the weather turned the next day and we got a drenching, plus one of my milkers was lame, so I didn't leave the farm till gone eight. By then it was dark like night and the rain was coming sideways from off the sea.

You may ask why didn't I wait for a better day. The police asked me that. Well, they didn't know George. If I hadn't turned up he'd have been saying the saw couldn't matter much, and I'd have to be careful not to speak out against him because then it would be Little Farm over again, a disagreement going on for months.

Well, I ran into his yard and immediately I thought: '*Oh no, I've missed them. They've gone out for the evening.*' There were no lights on, you see. The rain was pelting down so I dashed into the barn and grabbed a sack to make a cape over my head and shoulders. Then I went round the outside of the house, hoping for a light at the back or upstairs but it was no good and I went home. Soaked through. A terrible evening. Nobody but a fool like me ventured out in that, I didn't see a soul the whole time.

Later, though, somebody was telling the police they saw me running away from the farmyard at night, hiding beneath a sack. They put it on the wrong day, though, said it was a Friday. It was the previous Wednesday I was there, which is obvious with market day being Tuesday. The Friday evening was another wet one but drizzling, not what you'd call terrible.

The police took it as gospel I was there on the Friday, although they didn't tell me why the Friday was important to them. I said I didn't know anything about George and Delma but it made no difference. They settled in their minds that George and Delma were dead and that I killed them.

"Tell us what you did with them, Joe," they kept saying.

Tiring me, they were. Same questions but not listening to the answers which were the same, too. They were coaxing me to say where the bodies were, saying I didn't even have to tell them how I did it, if I didn't want to, because they had experts who could work out those details, so all I need do was tell them what I'd done with the bodies. In the end they were claiming I was the last person to see George and Delma alive, and that when I was running from the farmhouse on the Friday I knew they were dead.

They spun it out for a few weeks and then, all of a sudden, just when I thought they'd been quiet so long they must have been busy chasing up somebody who really knew where George and Delma were, they charged me with George's murder.

That's right, Alice. Only George's. My solicitor said they didn't have enough evidence to mount a case against me for Delma's murder.

"I don't get it," I said. "It's the same difference. I didn't kill her and I didn't kill him, so there can't be any evidence of me killing either of them."

"Well," he said, "I see what you mean, Mr Keenthorne. Now it's up to us to convince a jury."

And, as you know, they did, eventually. I'd been in prison the best part of a year, on remand they call it, which means they've made up their minds you're guilty but they haven't got around to trying to prove it. That was a bad time for me. I didn't know how my farm was going on, who was looking after my animals or anything. Of course, I knew somebody would see about feeding the cattle, because folk will always look out for animals even if they can't be bothered with human beings.

No, I didn't get visitors, apart from my solicitor, although any folk who were willing could have come. But they'd decided along with the police, see. Me supposedly being the last person to see George and Delma alive had convinced them. So I sat there, near on a year, wondering what was going on. With George and Delma, I mean, and with the farm, too.

Whenever the solicitor came they took me into a room to talk to him, private like. And the only question I had for him was: "Have they found George and Delma yet?"

And every time he said: "No, Joe, they haven't."

After that we'd go over my story, what he called our evidence, and there was never a change because how could I tell him anything new when I didn't know anything in the first place? I began to feel sorry for him, always looking to hear summat he wasn't going to.

One man in there, a burglar he was, well he had a radio and I used to listen to the news. The local news, in particular, because I thought if they find our George and his missis, then it's sure to be on the local although I doubt the national will bother. I really thought one day I'd be lying on the bunk listening and the announcer would say: "The farmer and his wife missing from Stark Point have been discovered living in America."

I had it in my head it would be America, I don't know why unless it's because Delma once said she had a cousin living there and she'd like to visit. That was the time she opened the fête when Sir Arthur Devrell let them down. Put on a brown straw hat with a rose on the brim, she did, and drove up to Chapel Field in that car of hers, every inch the lady. Made a better speech, I remember, than those old Devrells ever did.

"Friends," she began, and folk liked that and listened up. "Ours is a very special village and one of the things we do especially well here is our annual fête. As you see all around you, we have a Wild West theme this year. Oh dear, I'm afraid I've worn the wrong hat! If I'd had more time to plan I'd have borrowed a suitable one from my cousin who lives in America."

That's how she went on and everyone was very pleased with her. After that, when they needed somebody to stand up and do summat, it was Delma Ablett they turned to first. I think they forgot she was only George's wife, not gentry and not much different from them.

What's that? Oh, yes. The trial. I ought to get ahead and tell you about the trial. But that's written down, you see. You can read about that, Alice. I think the book is going to need all I can tell you about George and Delma and what folk here thought of the case. It didn't finish for me, you know, when the jury said "Not guilty" and the judge said "You can go."

Best you read the papers about the trial. Newspaper write-ups, I mean. I've got them at home, in a big envelope. They'll tell you more than I can remember. I had two days of it in the dock, see, and although you think you'd notice every detail, you can't. Your mind's too full to take it in. Then afterwards, when you're thinking over it, you're asking yourself "What came next?" and you realise there are all these gaps.

I went to the newspaper office in Bristol and bought the copies for those two days. That way I could read over and try and make sense of it, you see. Mind, I needn't have troubled because when I went to live at Perrotts Farm someone shoved the write-ups through the farmhouse door for me, the ones I'd bought and others I hadn't seen, and also articles that had been in the papers while I was away.

No, I can't say who put them through the door. They did it quietly, see. At night. I'd get up in the morning and there'd be another one lying on the mat. That's how they did it, one at a time, once a week. For months.

Now, you read those papers, Alice, and take your notes from them. You must come to the house for that. No use if I bring them out here and they blow away down the beach and out to sea.'

Chapter Eleven

'You're not going,' Rod said flatly.

'But Rod . . .'

'Two people have already disappeared from that farm while he was there.'

'Oh, you sound like one of the Pointers! Ignore the facts, just rely on prejudice.'

'There's nothing wrong with a spot of healthy prejudice. If everybody in this village was against Joe Keenthorne there was probably a good reason.'

'Like he was a serial killer?'

'I wouldn't go that far, but listen . . .'

'No, you listen, Rod. The prejudice against him was tested for two days in court and it was rejected. He walked out a free man. Yet because of that prejudice his life's been a nightmare ever since. You've seen what a loner he is, how he's shunned. Now he's having to fight to hang onto his home.'

'So he says. You don't have proof that's true either.'

But she had heard Mrs Aley's version as they walked on the beach with the lurchers, and the essence of it was the same as Joe's. The man was not welcome at Stark Point and people were talking openly about the poor state of his house and his failure to look after himself.

Alice explained that to Rod. 'He blames a family called the

Chiltons who rent his land and want to buy that and the house.'

He sighed. 'All right, love, I accept what you say. If he's innocent, what you're doing is laudable, but I'm still worried about you going to his house alone.'

She bridled again. 'Don't even think of coming with me.'

'No, no, of course not. But . . .'

'But what?'

He ran a hand through his hair, exasperated. 'Oh, I don't know. I hate the whole thing. Can't you drop it? Make an excuse and not go on with it?'

Quieter, she said: 'I live here too, Rod. It would make me as bad as the rest. Worse, in a way, because I raised his hopes.'

'The book.'

'It isn't purely the book. It's what he believes a book would achieve – recognition of his innocence and also money to fix up the house.'

She realised she was touching on her own reasons for planning to go on with it. Her need for money and the opportunity to make her name as a writer outweighed moral issues or physical risks.

Rod was understanding. 'I think, Pippin, he's put you in an impossible position. He's dangled an interesting story, promised you a chance to prove yourself as a writer . . .'

'Hang on. He doesn't know that, he thinks I'm a writer already. No use making him sound calculating because he isn't like that. Naive, rather. It was astonishing listening to him recite his conversations with the police, for instance. He obviously didn't understand the impression he was making, and he still doesn't.'

'From what you've been telling me, he might actually be rather dim.'

'I imagine the peculiar life he's led since has had an adverse effect. Isolation does funny things to the mind, and in his case it wasn't voluntary.'

He indulged in a faint triumphant smirk. 'This is what I'm

getting at. Whatever he was like in the past, he's an oddball now. Heaven knows what you'd be risking if you shut yourself away at Perrotts Farm with him.'

'We're supposed to be reading newspaper cuttings.'

'He might freak out when he has to relive the case. After all, you say he keeps stalling, filling you up with chitchat about the Abletts. Why won't he get on? Most people with a good story come rushing out with it.'

She argued against that, thinking how some people were so bereft of story-telling skills they wearied their listeners by dragging anecdotes out with preamble and postscript, repeating themselves and not knowing where to start a story or end.

Even as she spoke, she realised he was correct. The hopeless rambling she had in mind was different from Joe Keenthorne's habit of paddling in the shallows instead of diving into deep waters.

'There's one way out for me,' she added. 'I don't fancy it but it might be better if I invite him to bring his papers here.'

Raised eyebrows. 'Would you do that?'

She had made a remark, when she agreed to Rod staying for a few more days, about the sanctity of her home and the pleasure it gave her to have sole right to say who crossed the threshold. It had been designed to dissuade him from thinking he could come and go as he pleased, which, as they were both aware, he was already doing.

She wrinkled her nose. At a pinch she could see herself and Joe Keenthorne sitting in her garden, but it was impossible to picture him in the kitchen or the sitting room. She burst out laughing.

'He's an outdoor person, I bet he'd hate it.'

'Then ask him to hand over the cuttings for you to bring them home to read.'

She winced. 'Why didn't I think of that?'

So that is how the decision was reached.

'This afternoon I'll buy a catch for the garage door,' he said. 'Where's the nearest hardware shop?'

She told him he would need to go into town. 'Some of the village stores stock a few items but I haven't noticed anything like that.'

'All right, I'll head for the town then.'

'And I'll do some writing.' She spoke quickly to prevent any discussion of her accompanying him. *'Better,'* she thought, *'not to treat his strange visit as a holiday.'*

On the day he had told her the truth about his break-up with Ruth he had asked, awkwardly, whether he might stay on. Her heart softened but she dared not be sentimental.

'Stay as a friend, yes,' she had replied. 'But we can't turn the clock back to being lovers, let alone a married couple.'

He had thanked her and kissed her cheek.

Alice went up to the spare bedroom and switched on her computer. Before she could start she had to move some of Rod's possessions off the table and his clothes off the chair. The room seemed full of him. She resented the way he was taking over, and then felt foolish to feel that because it was quite unreasonable. He was there at her invitation, even if he had wangled the invitation, and knowing the mess his life had turned into she could not possibly have turned him away.

She opened a file and named it Joe, then turned to the page of her notebook headed Joe's Story. An electronic page awaited her words and her hands were poised over the keyboard, but instead of capturing Joe Keenthorne's story Alice's mind was on Rod. She was wondering whether he was the culprit who had ransacked her car.

What made her suspicious was his fussing about her dealings with Joe. Who stood to gain if she became thoroughly scared? Why, Rod did. Julie was too busy to keep her company and her other friends were always less free in their movements. Charles was away at his conferences and travelling, and he avoided Stark Point anyway. Rod, by contrast, was desperate to stay. An Alice made anxious and unconfident was far more likely to let him.

She had more physical courage than Rod did – she had always

been the one to get up at night and investigate unfamiliar sounds – but it was one thing to be tough in a crisis and quite another to resist being undermined by someone playing on your fears.

And then there was the state of the car. Untidy, no damage and nothing stolen, unless you counted the catch from the garage door. A person who wished her harm would not be scrupulous about her possessions.

The matter of the mislaid wallet perturbed her too. Plainly, it had been a ruse to bring him back to Spray Cottage but how many other lies had it involved? He had claimed, during his plaintive telephone call, to be on the other side of Bath, well on his way to Wykeham. Yet later he had said he currently lived in a flat in Bath. She wondered where he had really been when he rang. Two or three miles away, keeping out of her sight until he could pretend to have driven across two counties?

She sighed, got up from the table and went to look out of the window. Sun, a summer sky, but for Alice the day was clouded with uncertainties as the days preceding it had been and those following would be. *'If I like, I can challenge Rod about the car but what good would that do when he would deny it and I won't know whether to believe him?'*

The root of it was that she did not trust him, had been unable to since the massive betrayal when he had deceived her for months and then ditched her for Ruth. Now, beyond the bald facts of his relationship with Ruth breaking down and him leaving the company, she questioned everything he told her.

He had built up a picture of the events that led to his downfall. In it he was depicted as working so hard for the business that he failed to see what was happening around him.

His anger, he claimed, had kept him going for a while. 'To begin with I was struggling to find a legal redress. In a way, the worst time was when I was forced to accept there wasn't one. Everything they did is legally acceptable.'

Naively she had asked: 'Why don't you start up again on your own?'

'All my work, my innovations that were the backbone of the business, I don't own them now. I don't have a right to use them. They've got everything, that's what I'm trying to explain.' He had sounded weary at repeatedly explaining this aspect which people couldn't believe.

Ruth was the villain of his tale, the one who had urged further expansion and introduced Cavendish, a man keen to invest. Rod had overruled his dislike of the man, taken his money and made him a director. Once Ruth switched allegiance, Rod was out.

Alice thought over her conversation with him. What stood out was Rod's emphasis on the money. Cavendish's plenty, Ruth's craving, latterly Rod's lack of it. '*He finds it easier to deal with the issue in business terms instead of personal ones,*' she thought. '*The only faintly personal touch was when he talked about not wanting to go home to his flat because of the bills piling up. Lawyers' bills, he said, and begging letters from Camilla's mother because he hasn't paid child maintenance for months.*'

Then an impish smile spread over her face. '*Whatever he hoped for, I didn't offer to pick up a bill or hand over a loan. If he's got problems, so have I.*'

The basic difference was that she was used to her financial position being precarious and was in that state largely because of Rod and his perfidy.

'*Oh no, I shan't be making any lavish gestures,*' she thought and went back to the word processor.

She tapped out a straightforward account of Joe Keenthorne's story as he had told it. When she slipped in her own observations and comments she enclosed them in brackets, because this would be helpful in future when she might be less clear about what he had said and what she had thought. All writers, she supposed, invented systems for organising their work.

Alice was painfully aware that for the book to succeed she needed to offer more than a rehash of an old story, and that Joe's griping about his life ever after was inadequate. Unless astonishing facts surfaced during their conversations, it would be up to her to contrive something. The idea was daunting, especially as she was already out of her depth.

Once or twice she broke off writing, overwhelmed by the scale of the task. A book seemed beyond her ability. Ought she to enlist a real writer, a practised craftsman who could grasp what needed to be done and the best way to achieve it?

'*There's a lot I can do before I face that question seriously,*' she thought, and worked on.

While she was writing Joe's description of Delma opening the village fête, Alice had a great desire to peer again into the little face encircled with the fur collar. She ran downstairs to the sitting room and took up the photograph.

'*I'm being silly,*' she was thinking. '*This whole scene is imprinted on my memory so why do I keep looking at it? It can't tell me anything new.*'

Yet the tantalising feeling persisted that it might.

Her eye was drawn irresistibly to the woman in the car rather than the man beside it. A smile not without warmth, a fur collar and a polished bracelet – how could anything extra be divined?

Tutting, she threw the photograph on the table ready to go back to her work, then permitted herself one last, long look. '*If only she wasn't sitting in the car. I can't even tell how tall she was.*'

A gasp. Alice snatched up the photograph. '*The car! Where is it? People say the Abletts ran off in it or that Delma alone did. So what became of it?*'

The number plate was legible and she had been told the make. That amount of information, she thought, ought to be enough to trace it.

Suddenly she was imagining herself walking up a drive to a house, finding the car in a garage, ringing a doorbell and coming face to face with Delma Ablett. It was less romantic than her previous notion, of it being secreted in a hut in a wood on her lover's estate, but more credible. A locked hut would have been opened in the intervening years and the vehicle discovered. But if it were under a tarpaulin in the garage of a private house, then it could have remained hidden.

Alice wondered how hard the police had sought the car, and whether the fact she had only now realised its potential usefulness in unravelling the mystery was because she was not a car-minded person or because it was irrelevant. She could not convince herself it was irrelevant.

She decided to start asking about it immediately. *'Before Rod comes back. He'll try to talk me out of it, given the chance.'*

Going down the lane, she was almost running. Waiting on Iris Dottrell's doorstep she was fidgeting with impatience.

Iris opened up. 'Alice. How nice to see you, my dear. Come in.'

Alice took a final breath of fresh air before plunging into the smoky swirl of Iris's home.

'Mary isn't here.' Iris stubbed out a cigarette as she spoke.

'It's you I'd like to speak to.'

'She's gone to do some shopping for me.'

Alice noted that Mary was a frequent shopper and wondered how Iris managed without her. The village women who normally helped her were unlikely to be dashing off to the shops every day.

'Iris, I've come about the Abletts, again.' She waited for resistance but saw none.

Iris spoke calmly, although Alice was unsure whether her words were rhetorical. 'What more can I tell you?'

'Actually, it's about their car. Do you know what became of it?'

'Well, they went away in it. They didn't leave it behind.'

'That's what I'm wondering, you see. They disappeared without trace but what about the car?'

As she said it she was thinking: *'No, I'm wrong. Human beings can't disappear without trace. There's always a trace, if you know where to look.'*

'I didn't hear anything about the car being found. Folk would have talked if there'd been news of it.

'What do you remember yourself, Iris, of the last day the Abletts were here?'

'I was young, Alice, only a girl. Mind, I heard the grown-ups talking. Ralphie Aley, who was father-in-law to Libby Aley who's got the lurchers, well he was saying he noticed a light in the farmhouse late afternoon one Friday, and that was the last sign anybody saw of them.'

'A Friday?'

'Yes, definitely a Friday. You see, he was driving bullocks up the lane and one broke away and ran into the Abletts' yard. Someone had left the gate open, a strange thing to do. Ralphie said he chased round after the beast and it was plain as anything there was a light in a room downstairs. Sure to be the kitchen, folk said. But Ralphie hadn't ever been to the house so he wouldn't put a name to it.'

'Weren't any of the farm workers there?'

'As the story went, it was a wet dark afternoon and the men went home early. Ralphie didn't see anybody, only a light.'

'The car, Iris. Where did the Abletts garage it?'

'They didn't have what you'd call a garage, just drove it in at one end of the barn across from the house. Ages after they'd gone you could see oil stains on the concrete where it had leaked.'

A long shot but Alice asked anyway. 'Did Ralphie Aley mention whether it was there while he was in the yard?'

Iris frowned. Her hand went for her cigarettes. She concentrated on the question while she lit up. Then: 'That I can't say. Not for sure. But the idea was the Abletts were indoors while he was in the yard and, if they were there, their car was in the barn.'

Alice pictured it. A stray bullock careering around the yard with a farmer in pursuit, a light in the house yet neither of the occupants coming out to see what was causing the commotion. She filed Iris's version of Ralphie Aley's story under implausible.

Then she switched back to the car but in a roundabout way. 'Were the Abletts the only ones at the Point who could drive?'

An astonished laugh. 'Lord, no. Any of the men who'd been in the services could drive and several of the women too. What made the Abletts different was they had a bigger car and it was bought for pleasure. Only Delma thought it right to have a car especially for going out and enjoying herself.'

Hardly had it sprung up than Alice's theory collapsed. One moment it had looked fairly easy to pinpoint who had driven the car away to hide it if the Abletts had not, the next it seemed half the population could have done it. She floundered.

Iris's next words jolted her. 'Writing a book for Joe Keenthorne, are you?'

'I . . . How do you know?'

Iris fanned smoke. 'Because you're a writer and he reckons a book will make folk believe him.'

Her voice faint, Alice forced a reply. 'And will it?'

'I doubt it. He had his chance to have his say and all he said was he didn't know. Now he thinks if it's written down it'll make a difference.'

Alice repeated herself. 'How do you know all this?'

A laugh, although the words were not said kindly. 'Oh, there aren't many secrets at Stark Point.'

Disturbed, Alice invented a reason to leave. Iris's taunts dismayed her. She had been assuming Joe Keenthorne was shunned but it could not be entirely true if people knew about his hopes for a book and someone had given him the inaccurate information that she was a writer.

Gnawing suspicion accompanied her as she clumped down the lane. Iris and Mary Dottrell were unreliable, Rod was untrustworthy and Joe Keenthorne was an enigma who might or might not have got away with murder. There was nobody in whom she dared put any faith.

'*I'll keep my plans to myself from now on,*' she thought grimly. '*If I don't tell anybody anything, they won't be able to spread it.*'

But it was not in her nature to be guarded and she hated the prospect. She consoled herself that in a day or two, once Rod had gone, she would not have to cope with concealing things from him or worry whether he was chattering about her to Mary. As she had not herself told Mary about the book, Rod was chief suspect. Had he not mentioned taking tea in the garden at Ham Cottage?

She strode on until she noticed the weakened lettering on a farm gate. Perrotts Farm.

A vicious gleam lit Iris Dottrell's eyes. Oh, how she detested Alice and her meddlesome ways.

Iris spied her heading for Perrotts Farm and wondered whether she would walk boldly in or keep watch, as Iris used to, from a secluded corner. Her mind drifted to the Abletts coming and going, and Delma spinning the car sharp left to aim it through the open barn door. Each time Iris had winced, expecting the crump of it smashing into the wall. But, no, Delma's aim had been sure.

'*She wasn't one to get things wrong,*' Iris thought, her admiration unfading. She wished she had thought of telling Alice about, Delma's confident car parking.

'*Alice will be at the farm by now, if that's where she was going.*'

She fretted at not being sure where Alice had got to. Then she pictured her at Perrotts Farm with Joe, and Joe telling her . . .

'That's her trouble,' Iris muttered. 'Nobody else listens to him, but she does.'

She thought, with an obsessive's conviction, about the despicable nature of Joe Keenthorne. Her skinny body shook with unspent fury. What she accused him of was confused and vague and, in a few moments, the thoughts had stopped forming and there was only the trembling and the fathomless, unreasonable anger.

This, then, was where the farmer had dashed after his runaway bullock. Alice lifted the latch and went into the yard. It looked like any other at the Point. They were dotted along the spine of the land that was, marginally, the high point of the peninsula. Fields were flung out over adjacent acres but houses and barns were necessarily here.

She was thoughtful. The good land of Perrotts Farm lay on the river side, not the seaward. Joe Keenthorne used a track alongside the village, instead of walking through it, so there must be an access behind the farm as well as this gate from the lane.

To her right stretched unexceptional outbuildings and beyond them a low farmhouse, perhaps three hundred years old. Whoever cared that the roofs of the other buildings were intact, gave no heed for the slipping red tiles on the house or its flaking paint.

Until now she had not appreciated how well the house was obscured from the lane by the buildings which had grown up around it. Near the centre of the village, it was private. Anything could have happened here.

The thought clutched at her heart. '*But whatever did happen took place decades ago, there's no harm in it now.*'

Except that it was home to Joe Keenthorne who had inherited from the cousin he was believed to have killed.

Alice scanned the buildings opposite the house. There stood the long barn. She walked slowly forward and as she did so she felt a dreamlike stillness in the day. It took a couple of seconds for her to grasp that she was out of earshot of the perpetual stirring of the sea.

She peered into the barn's shadowy interior. There were dusty beams, a scattering of implements rusting on the walls, and there on the flagstones was the tell-tale oil stain.

'Iris told me it was a concrete floor,' she recalled with a wry smile.

Well, it was only a detail. She would not hold it against her.

She looked over at the house. The romantic Mrs Ablett of her daydreams had lingered at those windows and looked across at the wonderful car, her passport to freedom.

These days it would be hard to see out. Mud splashes obscured the lower panes, and dingy curtains were drawn across the upper ones. Weeds suggested the front door had not been opened in a long time. A kinked drainpipe showed where a bracket had been lost to a wind. A gutter sagged and the wall below it was stained with damp. Joe Keenthorne had inherited everything from George Ablett and this is what he had made of it.

The discovery was dispiriting although not unexpected. Her inclination was to leave but the writer in her realised it was important to inspect where the Abletts had lived. She had no intention of coming again so she bullied herself to squint through a filthy window into a room blackened with dirt. It was one of the most alarming incidents in her life when she encountered Joe Keenthorne staring back.

All the warnings to keep away rushed into her head and sent her scurrying towards the gate, pulse leaping, breath stuttering. But when she was halfway there he called and she was forced to go back, a short way, not as far as the hideous house. She was anxious to stay out in the open, as near the lane and escape as possible.

They met in the centre of the yard. She looked into scornful eyes.

'You should knock, Alice, not go snooping.'

She flushed. 'I know, I'm sorry, I . . .'

Neither knew what to say next. She recovered first.

'I need to see where George and Delma Ablett lived. It isn't really snooping, it's research for the book.'

He pointed at the farmhouse. 'That's their house. Was. It's mine now.'

'Yes, yes, I see. It's very private here.'

'It would be if folk didn't come snooping.'

'I'm sorry.'

'Not you. You're a writer, you need to see for yourself. You're not here to argue about drainpipes.'

'No, indeed.'

'You were looking in the barn. Delma kept the car in there.'

'Yes, I know.' The stupid remark had escaped before she saw what it might lead him to infer.

'Who told you that?'

She blessed her quick wits. 'I guessed when I saw the oil stain on the ground.'

'Oil stain? That's done by a tractor. Delma's car was upalong.' His hand shot out again, indicating a closed door in the same wall.

'Oh, I see. And, er, is there a stain there?'

'I don't rightly know.'

Before she could prevent him he was leading the way over the yard and yanking open the door. More beams, more rusting odds and ends and another stain.

'*A concrete floor,*' she thought, but said nothing.

'You want to see those papers now?'

She dragged her attention back to newspaper cuttings. 'Yes, please, Joe. If you'll give me the envelope, I'll take them home to read.' She spoke encouragingly.

But he scowled. 'Ah, I don't know I'm willing to do that. They belong here, see.'

Her heart sank. The idea of stepping through the door of the old house, let alone spending an hour studying his papers, appalled her. She was afraid she would not be able to disguise her revulsion at the squalor.

She used all her tricks of persuasion. He was implacable.

'You come and see them,' he ordered, and set off to the house.

She was rooted. When he glanced round he caught her reading her watch.

'No time, eh? Nobody's ever got time for what I want.'

The reproach was a statement of pitiful fact. Alice took a deep breath, told herself to stop being self-centred and to show consideration.

'*A proper writer,*' she thought, '*wouldn't hesitate.*'

A visit to the Abletts' house, believed to be the scene of the crime, was not to be passed up because she was pernickety about cleanliness.

He held the door open. She entered.

Chapter Twelve

Neglect has a smell of its own.

She recognised it from years ago, visiting auctions at pathetic country houses with her mother whose job was to buy interesting relics for an antique dealer. The odour was a composite of several distinct smells: damp seeping through the old type of wall plaster; dirt accumulated behind undisturbed cupboards; the bitter taint of soot from dead fires; and matted carpets impregnated with the other smells in addition to their own unclean contribution.

Perhaps her mother found treasures – she did not recall – but what had impressed Alice was the antique grime. She had asked how many years you had to leave a house untouched to achieve that tacky, blackening accretion on every surface.

Tainted and barely breathable, the air trapped in the house at Perrotts Farm was similar. She left the door open behind her as she went in, worrying about a hasty retreat but immediately glad of the drought that pursued her. Joe, though, was quick to double back and shut it. Alice fought to conceal her distaste.

'A genuine writer would cope and, anyway, nobody ever died of a smell.'

While he fetched the cuttings, she concentrated instead on appearances. It was indeed like entering a grubby time warp. Later, she was to joke about her Havisham period and exaggerate the spiders' webs, while conceding that the stopping of the clock at two minutes past one signified only that it had run down.

She began an inventory. Deep ceramic sink by a window. Damp-stained wooden draining board angled over it. Green enamel electric cooker, badly chipped. Coarse-grained wooden table that surely was meant to be scrubbed. Ceiling light with metal shade. Dresser displaying layer of woolly dust on jugs and plates. Three unmatched wooden chairs, one with a smashed stave. Floor of grey stone slabs.

But she was not attending a sale of contents, this was where Joe Keenthorne lived, and where the Abletts used to.

Alice wanted to picture Delma Ablett in the kitchen but her imagination failed. She could not link the proud driver of the shiny car with this decrepit place. It took an act of faith to accept this as Delma's home.

No. It had actually been George's home and before that his parents'. Delma had acquired it on marriage, it was not of her choosing. Farmers' wives, like vicars, got the house that came with the job. Perhaps, though, Delma had bought the cooker. Oh, it was no use, Alice could not see her in there.

She looked around, noting the scuffed limewash on the walls and the brown-fringed stain between two of the ceiling beams. It was no surprise that water had come through the roof.

Joe slid a sheaf of yellowing paper from an envelope onto the table, gently, and beckoned her.

With a delicate touch Alice went through the cuttings, thinking: '*This is it, the heart of the Ablett legend.*'

There were Delma and George at their wedding, then again at a village fête. Delma's height surprised Alice. She was as tall as George. There was Joe, looking like a stupid, startled rabbit as a camera caught him unaware. Prosecuting counsel presented the Abletts to the jury as a fine, upstanding, hard-working farming couple. Joe he presented as the envious poor relation. Early on he put their minds at rest about trying a murder case without a body.

As she read she pictured the courtroom, the yearning faces of the twelve just men and women getting to grips with the intricacies of English law, and the sonorous tone of a man who spent his days in courtrooms addressing faces as determined and baffled as theirs.

'Every prosecution,' he said, 'requires a *corpus delicti,* literally the body of the crime, and what we mean by that is its elements and the circumstances in which it was committed. It follows, therefore, that the *corpus delicti* of murder is more than a mere corpse. In a murder case it must be shown that a death has occurred, the dead person is the one alleged to have been killed, and the death was caused by unlawful violence. Ladies and gentlemen of the jury, the prosecution intends to show that George Ablett is dead, killed by Joseph Keenthorne.'

The court reports were wordy and Alice skimmed, deciding it was best to make mental notes of which newspapers they had appeared in, because she might have to consult their files if Joe did not relent and let her take these away to study another time.

Headlines leaped out at her.

The Case of the Missing Body
Defendant Seen at Death Farm, Jury Told
'Bad Blood led to Farmer's Murder'
Cousin denies killing farmer
Keenthorne acquitted

Joe was talking to her, drawing her attention to important points but making it impossible for her to concentrate. She waited until he paused and then she asked again to be allowed to take the papers away to study carefully.

'No,' he said. 'They belong here.'

Alice read on for a few minutes. He had stopped talking but his breathing filled the room. She felt increasingly uncomfortable.

'*Death Farm,*' she was thinking. '*Here I am at what the newspapers called the death farm. The jury were told Joe killed them here, and here I am . . .*'

She scolded herself for inflaming nonsensical fears. She was not a jumpy sort of person, she was big and strong and she was not afraid of Joe.

'It's the atmosphere that's getting to me, but I shouldn't let it. I'm familiar with the smell of neglect, it isn't a mystery or a shock. It's essential for me to be here where the Abletts lived.'

She assembled the papers ready to put them back in their envelope, the clearest of signals that she was preparing to leave. Joe was loath to let her go, repeating points he had previously made. Saying anything to keep her there?

Alice got up from the chair and looked around, a way of changing the subject. She made a banal comment on the age and period features of the farmhouse.

She was thinking *'This room is a nugget of history, like a museum mock-up of an earlier period but genuine.'*

Her thoughts circled to those sales in dilapidated country houses when she had felt a pang of regret, witnessing family history broken up by the auctioneer's hammer. Lot this would no longer be part of the same household as Lot that. Accumulated possessions scattered. Thus it was that little people were deprived of their past.

Influential families, meanwhile, had ancestral portraits, papers, and centuries of family ownership of good houses to anchor their present to their past and their future. It meant that ordinary people, with remnants of hand-me-down memories, were freer to invent.

'They do because no one likes the black hole which is the history of most of us. So they elaborate and enhance, take fact and fashion legend.'

Joe said: 'You've to come again and take more time over it, Alice.'

She smiled faintly at being ticked off for skimping. 'Yes,' she said, plotting to avoid it. Just now, all she wanted was to step safely out of the time warp and into real life.

Chapter Thirteen

Being alone was an agony. Rod was out when she came home and she rattled around the cottage, bursting with things to say but no one to say them to. Then caution crept in as she remembered her vow to keep everything to herself because Rod had not been discreet, he had told the Dottrells about the book.

Calming her excitable mind, she wrestled with ways of tracing the car and hit on one that sounded infallible. '*There's bound to be a Talbot enthusiasts' club, all the old makes have them. If I feed them the registration number, they can probably tell me who owns the Abletts' car now.*'

There followed a bewildering moment when she realised how deprived she was at Spray Cottage: no Internet, no e-mail and no fax. Impose on Charles and ask him to do the searching for her? But she felt awkward about bothering him and accepted how steadily they had drifted apart. '*We're coming to an end,*' she thought. '*Not because Rod's reappeared but because of the ease with which we ignore each other. I've no more been on Charles's mind than he has on mine.*'

Julie, though, would enjoy searching for the car, providing she had time between clients.

'My two-thirty cancelled,' said Julie, insisting that helping Alice would be no inconvenience. 'But I can't believe you're into fancy old cars. What's this all about?'

Alice told her so succinctly, fearing Rod's return, that she stuck to the bald fact of the car vanishing and said nothing of murder. 'If you can do this for me, Julie, I'll so grateful I'll . . . I'll . . .'

'What?'

'I'll buy you a Mars bar.'

It gave Alice a frisson to read out the letters and numbers from the photograph, a sense of forging a link with the long-ago owners who had once posed with the vehicle outside her house. She left Julie to seek out the club and make a simple request: 'Please do you have a record of the ownership of this car?' They arranged to talk later, after Julie's last client had limped into her consulting room and gone away with a spring in his step.

Meanwhile, Alice went briskly down to the beach to fill her lungs with fresh air and sort through what she had already learned that day and what she ought to do. It was an hour or two short of high tide and there was nobody around. A few brown birds, jerking along the waterline, were edged inland by the surf. Gulls had given up and were white splashes on top of the rocks.

The route taken by the tractor and trailer, which had removed the boat, was carved in the sand. The only evidence of the wreck itself was the shallow trough shaped during the days it had settled into the soft surface. With a twinge of guilt Alice thought of her boat poem, squeezed out of her mind by Joe's story and reduced to a memory no more vivid than that of the smashed boat.

For her, there had always been two boats and now there were three. The real boat was the one cast up on the shore, upended and damaged; the mythical boat flew through the darkness in the rain and the lightning; and the third was the one she had tried but failed to write. It seemed impossible for her to go on with the poem. Surely the spell was broken? Its moment had passed, because events do not wait and the latest, crowding incidents demanded every ounce of her attention.

Alice stood near the furrowed sand, watching how the lightest breeze was sending a fine yellow scree down one of the ridges, beginning the long slow task of smoothing out the beach again. Then another movement caught her eye. A dog appeared near the Cat Rock. Alice swivelled and walked back towards the saltings. She could not face meeting Mrs Aley and being made to talk about Joe Keenthorne or keeping a dog. Even to discuss the weather would be too much. Alice sped away, veering from her usual path in obedience to an unexpected thought.

'Before the tide's in I can walk round to the Little Farm.'

She picked her way through stubby vegetation, over rocks that barely broke the surface of the sand, and crossed diminutive beaches of ochre sand. Shadows of gulls flew over blue water. The sea lapped a hundred yards to her left, and on her right the land raised itself enough to stay dry at high tide. Fields crumbled down to the sand.

But ahead, here and there, bolder outlines jutted towards the water. Rocks became real outcrops several feet high. In between them, colour-patched boulders thrust through the glinting sand.

'I've found the stuff of Stark Point,' she thought. *'This is the tough core that refuses to be worn away, that makes the difference between land and sea.'*

When she raised her eyes she saw the islands, vivid in mid-channel and when she turned her gaze inland she saw a tilted house. Alice clambered onto a boulder and looked up and down the shore. She had almost certainly found Little Farm but there was nowhere that seemed an ideal place to launch a boat.

Soon she came to a gulf of water several feet wide, one of the peninsula's rhines where water escaped in an urgent white flurry, flowed out over the sand, spreading and sinking until it was no more than a silvery pointer to the sea. Down there she could cross it very easily whenever she chose.

Secluded and peaceful, lulled by the sibilant waves, Alice sat down. Here was the Little Farm with the view Delma Ablett had coveted and George had bought. It was irresistible to believe he had sailed away from this shore in a boat, abandoning his debts and his disasters. Although willing to believe he survived, Alice tended to see him overtaken by a greater disaster.

'My book needs a theory,' she murmured. 'All good books of this sort promote a theory and I must have one.'

She already had the one about romantic Delma bolting with her lover and leaving George to a tragic fate, and she supposed that would do if she found nothing better. Presumably Joe would be content with it because he had not discouraged her when she touted it, although it was fair to say he had not put it forward himself. Also, it had the merit of being in line with local opinion.

'Fortunately, those stories about Delma didn't come out at the trial.'

She caught herself imagining what Charles would have said if she had asked him to search for the car.

'He would have demanded more answers than Julie did, I'm sure of that. So what would he have said about Joe Keenthorne?'

Unwelcome words popped into her head. 'Alice, I always said those Starkers were mad. You ought to get away while you've got a scrap of sanity left.'

She shrugged. *'That's what he'd say if he were being grumpy Charles the second. Though, obviously, if he said it as Charles the first, it would be a bleak warning.'*

Charles's voice again: 'You're always concerned about this Joe Keenthorne and what he wants, and you're ignoring the probability that he did kill George Ablett.'

She wriggled with impatience, thinking this was not what she wanted to hear and thus proving the point.

Coolly she put the question to herself. *'Do I have any special knowledge to convince me Joe didn't do away with George?'*

The answer was no.

'All right, supposing Joe killed him. Did Delma flee by coincidence that evening or did Joe kill him on the evening Delma had already fled?'

But there was no answer at all.

She sat there, planning the book in her head, the shape of the whole and a few individual chapters. She toyed with titles and wondered about contracts. She fretted again whether to haul in a genuine writer to help from the start. She worried at it. She indulged in day dreaming about it. She wasted a great deal of time.

When she was ready to leave, the tide was almost in, a racing grey swell that could trap the unwary. Here she was safe, though, because her route was inland. She mounted the few inches to the field behind her and walked alongside the rhine, wondering where it would join the lane and how much land it drained.

The sight of the sagging farmhouse overlooking the sea tugged her thoughts back to the book. It was not a marvellously antique house and more modest than Perrotts Farm had been before it fell into neglect. Alice was not disappointed when she noticed her path led her close to it.

She stood by the gate and ran her eye over the red-tiled house and its cluster of pleasing old stone buildings. A black and white dog dozing by an empty pig sty sensed she was there and lifted an ear. Alice turned for home.

Chapter Fourteen

The morning after her exploration of the Little Farm, Alice was crouching in the garden logging Bella's herbs, when the call from the car club came.

'It's for you, a man about a car.' Rod, in the kitchen doorway, was quizzical.

Alice scrambled to her feet. A chirpy elderly voice was on the line.

'John Hezzard, about the Talbot. Haven't caught you at a bad time, have I?'

'Not at all.' Involuntarily, Alice crossed her fingers. 'Any luck?'

'Not the answer you want, I'm afraid, Alice. The car's a 1935 Roesch Talbot 105 Airline. Nothing's been heard of it since 1945, when it was bought by a man called Clutton-Wray. He wouldn't have paid much. It had three owners before him.'

She echoed the name. 'This is odd. I know who owned it at that time and it was a man called George Ablett. He lived at Stark Point, where I am now.'

'No, that name isn't listed. Alfred Clutton-Wray bought it from a second-hand dealer in Taunton in April 1945. You couldn't have got the registration wrong, I suppose?'

'Hold on.' She fetched the photograph and read it out. It was identical to the number he had searched for.

She said: 'The photograph's absolutely clear.'

'Hmm. Well, in that case there are two possibilities. Either your car's carrying plates that don't belong to it or else you've been misinformed about the owner.'

Alice felt dispirited. He was stripping away one of the few facts she possessed about the Abletts. Most of what she had heard was opinion, rumour or long-distance recollection but Delma's car had seemed a certainty.

Hearing her sigh, John Hezzard said: 'There's no obvious reason why the plates should be false, is there? I mean, unless you're going to tell me your Mr Ablett was a bank robber.'

She giggled. 'Far from it.'

'Well, then. Take another look at the ownership angle. If he was driving around in a car he hadn't paid for, who might have bought it for him? A business partner?'

'No, that wouldn't be it. Oh, dear.'

'Raised more questions than you started with, has it?'

'I'm afraid so.'

'Sorry, I do that to people sometimes. Now then, there's one thing I can tell you which might be of interest even if it's not going to be of any practical help.'

A little flame of hope. 'What's that?'

'You're not the first person to chase after this one.'

A quickening of the pulse. 'Who else wanted to know?'

'A garage owner in Suffolk. It was back in the days when the only way to obtain a special number was to buy a vehicle with it on and switch it to your other car. He wanted to put it on a sports car he was giving his son because it was the boy's initials. Perfect, except we couldn't trace either the number or the old Talbot.'

Alice snatched comfort from defeat. 'At least you've saved me wasting any more time on it.'

He jumped in quickly. 'But if you should find it, you'll let me know, won't you? For the club records?'

She promised she would. They rang off.

Rod sauntered through from the sitting room. 'Good try, Pippin.'

'It's bizarre, though. According to his records the car wasn't owned by the Abletts.'

When she had told him the rest, conscious of breaking her vow of silence but unable to resist having someone to talk it over with, Rod said the obvious explanation was that the club records were inaccurate.

'You know how clumsy people used to be with computers – all those muddled names and addresses and computer errors that were actually operator errors? Well, I'd guess this is a mistake they haven't corrected yet.'

'But assuming his records are correct, I ought to be asking who Alfred Clutton-Wray was.'

'Who can you ask?'

She shook her head. No one.

Alice strolled out to the garden. At this time of day it was sharply divided, one part brilliantly sunny and the rest dim with details obscure. She walked into the sun, knelt, took up her abandoned pad and pen and made a note about the hyssop Bella had planted.

'*Better forget about the car,*' she was thinking. '*Listen to Joe's story and then find out whether a publisher would be interested in it. I've never been any good as a researcher, I'm too inclined to believe what people tell me.*'

She concentrated on Bella and the herb garden. Did it evolve or was it planned? What other plants might spring forth as the year progressed? She was glad she had chosen not to root out anything until a full year had spun round and she had seen everything the modest patch had to offer.

She began considering writing a poem to celebrate her discovery of the garden, a poem linking the lives of the two women who had worked in it. But she caught herself up.

'*No, don't meander,*' she chided. '*The boat poem first, if I can finish it. But before that, Joe's book.*'

Her thoughts returned to her disappointment about the car,

yet having failed to learn where it was she was free to continue imagining. Romantic Delma filled her mind, a fugitive woman living out her life under an assumed name. Maybe a real name. Maybe she had remarried and been correctly and conventionally known as Mrs Someone.

A questioned flickered up. Why would Delma conceal her past? Whether she had remarried or not, there was no reason not to acknowledge she was Delma Ablett, she had done nothing illegal. Alice pictured her now, papery thin cheeks and smiling eyes, an 80-year-old face but perceptibly the same one as in the photograph. What might Delma have to say about Bella and the photograph taken outside Bella's house?

'*Why hide? Because she knew George was dead, that's why.*'

Alice's skin tingled as the idea gripped her. Now she had seen it, it was as clear as the rose in full sun. She grew hot with embarrassment, then thankful she was facing the revelation privately instead of in conversation with Rod or either of the Dottrells. She could not bear to think of Mary's miss-nothing eyes, or Iris squinting through cigarette smoke, as the truth struck.

She stood up, pushing a thick fall of hair away from her face, trying to calm herself and to think, *to think*. And then came the sequel to the sickening idea.

'*If she knew George was dead, does that mean she was involved?*'

Iris Dottrell's words about Joe Keenthorne resounded: 'He had something to do with it, Alice, I'm convinced of that. But I'm not saying he's a murderer.'

Alice shuddered. Questions were springing up as freely as mushrooms after rain, unsuspected until suddenly obvious. For instance, were Joe and Delma implicated together in George's death? And did Delma learn that Joe had been accused of murder?

It seemed impossible for Delma not to have found out about Joe's plight or for her to have a sound reason for not coming forward to clear him.

'Joe was charged with the murder of the farmer and not the wife, and perhaps Delma had thought . . .'

Yet there were no excuses for hiding while Joe was on trial *if she knew he didn't do it.* Only one possibility explained her behaviour: Delma was involved in George's death, either wholly culpable or partly.

'Alice?'

Rod was in the doorway again, this time with the telephone directory in his hand. 'There are Clutton-Wrays at Westowe, near Lydeard St Lawrence.'

'Oh.'

She pored over the page. No Alfreds, though, not even an A.

'Rod, I can't ring up and ask whether they had a relation called Alfred who bought a cheap old car in 1945. They'll think I'm a nutter.'

'No,' said Rod patiently. 'They'll think you're a car fanatic.'

'Oh.'

'Yes. You've found an old photograph and you think the car in it belonged to their Alfred.'

Alice groaned.

Defensive, he asked: 'What's wrong with that?'

'Nothing. It's excellent. But *I* should have thought of it.'

'Well, anyway, with one telephone call you *might* find the car. If it was owned by the Clutton-Wrays, it could be in a barn on their land.' He hesitated, delicately. 'If you like, I'll make the call.'

She was torn between gratitude, because he would be more efficient, and indignation because it was none of his business.

He clinched it. 'A man's voice is more convincing as a car fanatic.'

While he rang she went outside. The sun had edged across to the hyssop. The sea was singing on the breeze. A glorious day, and in a minute or two she might hold a key to the mystery.

Waiting, she challenged her assumption that George Ablett was dead. Justification was immediate: he was a farmer and they do not desert their land. Certainly, he had borrowed too much and faced debt but it was not ruin warranting scarpering. No, George Ablett could have paid his way out of trouble by selling off land, perhaps the Little Farm. He would have sacrificed pride and a few acres, but not abandoned his livelihood. Therefore, George was dead.

From the kitchen she heard Rod's voice, ending one conversation and starting another. Oh, how she disliked standing on the sidelines! She stumped around, urging him under her breath to hurry up and yet dreading what he might tell her.

Rod came out, making the thumbs down sign. 'Nope. I spoke to a Clutton-Wray who was absolutely charming but knew nothing about a Talbot. I asked whether he had *any* old vehicles crumbling away in outbuildings or odd corners and he was adamant he hasn't. Sorry, Alice.'

Her mixed emotions included a sneaky satisfaction that Rod had failed. When she spoke, though, she concealed it, saying it was a pity they had added the mystery of the Clutton-Wrays to an already confusing story.

Rod viewed it from a different angle. He argued this ought to be the end of the whole matter.

'If you'd found the car, Pippin, you'd have had something fresh to write about. As you haven't, there's no point in struggling on with Joe Keenthorne.'

But it did not suit her to appear swayed by his opinion. 'There's one other thing I ought to do,' she said, the words out as soon as the notion came to her. 'Talk to a policeman who searched for the Abletts. His name features several times in the newspaper cuttings.'

Rod looked doubtful.

She said: 'Look, I can't simply copy out the newspaper cuttings and tack on Joe's opinions about his life since. I need to do a certain amount of work.'

Reluctantly, he agreed.

Alice had expected him to put up more of a fight, his opposition to her entanglement with Joe Keenthorne being unweakened since they had previously wrangled about it. She planned to be cautious until she had worked out the reason.

'Time I fixed this for you,' he said.

He held up the catch for the garage door. As he had returned late the previous day, they had decided the job was best left until daylight.

Listening to the clatter of the metal plate and fixings, she remembered his story about meeting someone he knew and going for a pub meal, and then the switch to asking what she had been doing, followed by her headlong plunge into talk of Perrotts Farm and Little Farm. She had been pleased with herself for not divulging details, while accepting it was impossible to have him in her house and not say anything of her adventures.

Fruit flies were chewing a shrub. She fetched an insecticide from the shed, questioning whether Bella would not have relied on herbal hocus pocus. Alice sprayed heartily, muttering that it was her decisions that counted now and no one else's.

She broke off, recognising it was not Bella she was resisting but Rod, and that it was wrong to have him at the cottage. Their marriage was in limbo and so were their separate lives. Stark Point, the place where they had met up, was a gap between proper places. They could not go on like this, and it was her responsibility to end it because he showed no sign of doing so.

She made a decision. '*I can't face being struck with him through the weekend.*'

The kindest way of shifting him, she thought, would be to suggest he returned for a weekend before long. They could, if he liked, settle on a date before he left. Really, she did not care how much she conceded as long as he was gone and she could reclaim her life.

When he had finished with the gate he asked whether she fancied walking out to the headland. She did but said not, preferring to distance herself and, after the slightest persuasion, he set off on his own.

Alice continued to garden but soon realised she was unable to keep her mind on it. So, following Rod's example, she looked up a name in the telephone directory. Then she hesitated before ringing. There were no subterfuges open to her, her request must be stated honestly and if she were refused that would be an end of it.

She took up the photograph of the Abletts, peered at those expressions, static for decades, and wondered what course they might have chosen for her. Different ones, perhaps. George would want her to go ahead, if Joe had killed him. Delma would prefer her not to, if Delma had done the deed herself or covered up for Joe.

'One day I'll ask Joe how he felt when he realised Delma wasn't going to speak up for him. If he's innocent, it was a terrible betrayal.'

Alice made up her mind about the telephone call. There were three people in the story and she might soon be in a position to save the reputation of at least one, although she could not guess which.

She hoped at least to lighten the stain on Delma's character. Depending which story people believed, the woman was an adulterer who left her husband to die, either in the bay or at the hands of his penurious cousin. Alice scowled, fearing she was so beguiled by her fantasies that it was hard to separate reality from conjecture.

Before making the call, she firmly reminded herself that the police, throughout, had believed in two deaths.

The retired police officer did not sound startled to hear from her. They picked a time to talk.

Happy that it was arranged, she resumed gardening but within minutes Rod was beside her, his walk curtailed.

'Cows?' Alice guessed.

'Aren't they?'

'I've only seen heifers in that field.'

'Oh. Well, they were some way off. And frisky.'

They burst out laughing, recalling a picnic with friends ending in panic when a dozen bullocks materialised in an ostensibly vacant meadow.

Alice, recovering, said: 'And you've got the photographs to prove it.'

Taken from the safe side of a five-barred gate, they showed the animals enjoying the picnic: on the rug, snuffling sandwiches and lapping up plastic cups of wine.

'No,' Rod corrected her, 'you've got them.'

'I haven't.'

'I'm sure you have.'

'No, really. *You* have.'

'I wouldn't have taken them, would I? I mean, what for?'

He had a point. Leaving home to live with Ruth had involved numerous complications without seizing snaps of the bullocks' picnic.

'I wonder where they are, then?'

Alice was mulling this over when Rod said, as though it followed on: 'By the way, I phoned Camilla yesterday.'

'How is she?' She was thinking: '*Five years has made her a stranger.*'

'She's fine. Sends you her love. She'd like to come for the weekend.'

Her heart sank. She thought: '*He means he's invited her.*'

He said: 'It's okay, isn't it? I didn't think you'd mind.'

A little flurry of anger was provoking her to tell him, forcibly, how wrong he was! But Alice took her usual way out, quashing her annoyance. It was hardly Camilla's fault if her father had dangled an invitation, so why disappoint the child?

Relinquishing her plan to reclaim the cottage by the weekend, she asked: 'When will you fetch her?'

'Friday, and I'll take her home on Sunday.'

Alice planned anew. '*He can leave then, too.*' But before she could issue the edict he had gone upstairs to the bathroom.

She went back to taming a clump of thyme that was threatening the life of her chives. Ten minutes later she was seething. Resentment had grown in solitude, as it will. Trapped by Rod and Camilla, by Joe Keenthorne and his book, and by the Dottrells . . . Her precious summer, bought for her to learn her craft as a writer, was being devoured and she was gaining nothing.

She slumped on a bench, the sun hot on her shoulders, bees drowsing among the flowers. She was recalling how she had thought about times to drift and times to resist. Stark Point this summer was meant to be a drifting time but, day by day, it was becoming less possible. And now she was to have a second guest foisted on her, and needed to work out what to feed Camilla and where she could sleep. There were only two bedrooms.

Alice had a whim to creep away and let father and daughter enjoy Spray Cottage together. Yet that seemed extreme, and where might she go? To Charles in Bristol? Bad idea, it would encourage Charles to believe she missed him more than she did. Julie? No, Julie was going away herself. Ah, how about declaring an urge for a weekend in Bath and borrowing Rod's flat? But that, she knew, was the worst idea of all. She went indoors.

'Rod? How tall is Camilla?'

'God, I don't know.'

Of course not. This was the man who had never known the child's age or birthday.

She said: 'Try it this way. Is she short enough to sleep on that sofa?'

He grasped why she was asking and sounded encouraging. 'She might be. Yes, I think she might.'

'Think isn't good enough. She could end up with kinked legs.'

'Doesn't the sofa open up?'

'I don't know. Everything in here was Bella's, you see.'

They explored but no amount of tweaking and tugging would persuade it to flip over into a bed.

'That's a shame,' Alice said, understating.

Rod was irritatingly relaxed about it. After he had made three remarks suggesting she was fussing, Alice's riposte was that it was his daughter and his problem so he could work it out.

'There is no problem,' he repeated. 'Kids don't care where they sleep. The floor, anywhere.'

'No, you can't send her home saying we made her sleep on the floor.'

Alice recalled his first wife as a martyr to tidiness, not a woman to countenance her precious only child snoozing on stained carpets on a cottage floor.

Rod said: 'Well, she can have my bed.'

Too late, Alice saw where they were heading. 'Oh, no. I've said no.'

'You've been saying it ever since I arrived.'

'And I mean it.'

She announced she preferred to sleep on the floor herself rather than let him share her bed, then said she had to dash off and thus ended the discussion.

'*Damn him,*' she was thinking as she drove down the lane. And did not know how far he was a manipulative and conniving man who ran rings around her and how far he was a bungler.

Chapter Fifteen

Reginald Pennymoor, retired police sergeant metamorphosed into champion dahlia grower, regarded Alice steadily across his garden wall. The wall was red sandstone like the house, the entire village and the hills.

Her writer's eye registered the warmth of the stone; the comfortable way the houses cuddled close to each other; the pinkish tan of Pennymoor's face, offset by the white sweep of his hair; the blowsy abundance of bloom and blossom; and the luxury of trees that stood their ground instead of cringing from the wind.

'Ah,' he said, managing to pour the full local burr into what might have been one short syllable. 'Alice, is it? Come on in, my dear.'

She went through the gate, a solid wooden one swinging lightly on well-oiled hinges. The path, red sandstone naturally, snaked up to the house and then over the step and down the hall into shaded obscurity. Reg Pennymoor met her on the path, brushed a hand down his trouser leg, inspected it and then held it out fit to be shaken.

'It's good of you to see me today,' Alice said.

She had liked the sound of him on the telephone and in person he was even more promising. Pleasure danced in his blue eyes.

'*I bet he's a wonderful grandfather,*' she thought.

A painted wooden table and chairs stood beneath a pear tree. Impressively, a barefooted young woman was summoned, apparently by discreet signal, and asked Alice how she liked her tea.

'Pop's gone over to Earl Grey in his old age, don't ask me why.' Her glance flicked from the visitor to tease her grandfather as the sentence ended.

'Earl Grey would be lovely,' Alice said.

'Cassie thinks everybody should settle everything by the age of thirty and not change,' he said, looking at Alice although the remark was equally for Cassie. 'She wants everything organised, nobody allowed to trip her up by changing their minds.'

Cassie flapped a hand as if to slap him down. 'Watch it, you, or you will if you want your tea.'

She trotted off chuckling and murmuring: 'Earl Grey.'

'*The happiness here is almost tangible,*' Alice thought, with regret for Stark Point where it was seldom evident at all.

With reluctance she prepared to break the spell. But he spoke first, in his soothing accent that was, she realised, more pronounced than the intonation she had grown familiar with.

'It's been a while since anyone was interested in my opinion about Mrs and Mrs Ablett and Joe Keenthorne. Of course, it was a great talking point for years and every so often something would call it to mind again and they'd say to me: now, Reg, you were there, what do you think to that? But, as I say, it's been a while.'

His blue eyes rested on her. 'I haven't been asked by a writer, though. Never before.'

She was nervous of making the book sound a distinct probability rather than a vague possibility. It would be unfair to build up his hopes of a kind of fame. And if, on the other hand, he was wary of being quoted, it would also be unhelpful.

A neat phrase sprang to her lips. 'This is just preliminary research.' The hurdle was crossed.

'Do you want to tape record, Alice?'

She wished she had thought of it. 'I've brought a notebook.'

He seemed so much better prepared than she was but words she had spoken to Joe Keenthorne came to her rescue.

'Let's take it from the beginning. I've read newspaper cuttings about the search for the Abletts and it sounded as though you were involved from the start.'

He was emphatic. 'Every step of the way. And afterwards, once the trial was over, I kept an eye open. You never know what might turn up, you see.'

A wasp floated down from the fruit over their heads. He lazily batted it aside. Alice flinched.

'Well,' he said, watching the wasp circle before it rose up to the pears, 'the beginning, as far as I was concerned, was hearing a man in the Falcon saying a farmer and his wife had run off. Naturally, my ears pricked up. But all he could say was he got it from a man who reckoned they owed money all over. Then he let out it was at Stark Point, and that put it on my patch.'

'Where were you based?'

'I had the police house at Lambwood, about five miles from Stark Point.'

He stood up and pointed, forcing Alice to her feet too. 'There. That's Lambwood.'

The red hill fell away. Spread below them was the plain stretching to the sea. Lambwood was clear, with its grey church tower of lacy stonework and a cluster of houses round a country crossroads. There was a wood, too, a dark blob but big enough to be useful to the hunt.

'And there,' he said, swinging a few degrees north, 'is a splendid view of your Stark Point.'

The peninsula pointed at the sea like an accusing finger. Alice did not feel the least proprietorial. They sat down again.

He said: 'You told me on the phone you were new to Stark Point. What took you there?'

She explained the curious inheritance and the opportunity to make changes in her life.

His eyes crinkled. 'Don't let my Cassie hear you say that, she doesn't like to know about changes.'

Cassie appeared beside Alice with a tea tray. Alice was glad of the interruption because it saved her from explaining the nature of her changes. Only another writer, she felt, would be sympathetic and, besides, she did not want to reveal herself as a complete novice.

Earl Grey was poured, adding bergamot to the flower-scented air. Cassie promised them the cake was homemade, although not in her own home, busy as she was what with this surly old fool to look after as well as a husband and kids. Their badinage persisted until she was round the corner of the house.

Alice tweaked the conversation back to the Abletts. 'Did you go straight to Stark Point to ask about them?'

He kept her waiting while he sipped. 'Not what you'd call straight away. But the next time I was heading out in that direction I decided to drive up the causeway and see what I could learn. Nobody knew what I was talking about, so they said.'

She could imagine it all too well. 'They don't like questions.'

He caught her dry tone and laughed. 'Ah, so you've found it too. Yes, Stark Point has always been a world to itself. Close, they are, the folk out there.'

He was using it in the sense of silent instead of friendly and involved with each other.

'We are both,' suggested Alice, 'outsiders.'

'I didn't stay long that day, I admit. What was I supposed to do when the handful I asked looked blank? But they knew, of course they knew. It came out later they knew, although I can't say I'm sure to this day who knew how much and when.'

She murmured interest while he sipped again.

He said: 'Well, to hurry this along a bit, because you don't want to spend the rest of your young life sitting here and listening to me, well, the next thing was on the market day. Tuesday, as you probably know. "Where's George Ablett?" the farmers were saying. They look out for each other on market day.

A lot of business gets done, apart from in the market itself, I mean, and it's social too. So, it was market day and the word was going round that George Ablett wasn't there when he ought to have been. There were a couple of men expected him to settle up money he owed, but where was he?'

'Were you there?'

'No, I had a telephone call from a colleague who heard it. He knew I'd been out to Stark Point asking after a missing farmer and his wife. The difference was I had a name now and an address to go to. Mind you, you wouldn't have thought it made a difference, the way they carried on out at the Point. Exactly the same as before. "Don't know what you mean, Sergeant Pennymoor. No idea what you're talking about." '

'Maddening.' She spoke with feeling.

'Then I saw a paper on the noticeboard. A bit faded, been up there some time, but this piece of paper was what I needed to loosen tongues. It was an announcement of an event in the village hall to be chaired by Mrs Delma Ablett two weeks before. And, do you know what, Alice? Her name had been struck through and somebody else's written in.'

The story rolled on, with Reg Pennymoor describing how he went to every door, chivvying people for answers, and gradually pieced together enough of the tale to be concerned. Since he had first heard the rumour, it was nearly a month. Since Mrs Pawlett had replaced Delma on the noticeboard, three weeks.

Reminiscing, he relived the frustration of balancing suspicion against logic. 'Grown-ups are allowed to go away if they choose, Alice. The police can't go hunting them down to ask why they've made themselves scarce. If George Ablett had borrowed money and run off with it instead of repaying, then as far as we were concerned that was hearsay. No one had come to us and accused him of a crime.'

The moment the matter became a serious one, he said was when Delma Ablett's family reported her missing.

'Naturally, they contacted the police station in Taunton, not me or the town nearest where the Abletts lived. Again, I got a phone call from a colleague. What did I know about it, he asked. Not enough, I said. But at last we were able to start a full enquiry. We turned the Point upside down, we put out calls for information about their old car as well as them, but nothing ever came in. They'd just vanished.'

She thought it time Joe was mentioned. 'Did suspicion fall on Joe Keenthorne straight away?'

He batted a wasp away from the untouched cake. 'Alice, you must eat this up before these creatures do.'

As she helped herself to a slice he said: 'You know, you keep asking me about things happening straight away but I'm not sure any of them did. It was a slow process, picking up bits and pieces, looking them over and trying to make sense. We weren't getting co-operation. Often when the police go into a situation there's at least one person brimming with talk. But Stark Point? Never.'

'I know it's ages ago but can you recall what led you to Joe?'

He licked a finger tip and ate crumbs from his plate. 'Mmm. It isn't the time that's the problem, I remember well enough what went on. But you want me to rattle off a list of details because you're hoping for precision. A nice list, and that I can't do.'

Bewildered Alice waited.

'You see,' he said, 'that first time I went out to Stark Point, Keenthorne was one of the men I spoke to. Brusque, he was. Like it was an imposition me walking into his yard and bothering him. "No," he said when I asked. Just that, Alice. "No." And when the inquiry started properly it was "No" again. Didn't give away he was cousin to George Ablett. Oh no, P.C. Rhode and I had to find that out from a woman in a cottage along by the chapel. So we went back to him and said: "Mr Keenthorne, we understand you're a cousin of Mr Ablett," thinking if there's family trouble a cousin might know. And damn me if he didn't stand looking at us as if we were wrong in the head and when we'd finished all he said was: "Don't know anything." And he turned his back on us and walked away.'

Remembered anger lit his eyes. Then he laughed at himself. 'What was your word, Alice? Maddening? Well, that was about right.'

And she thought she was also right to imagine the pair of police officers taking a dislike to the awkward Joe Keenthorne from the outset.

He said: 'Well, Keenthorne didn't gain by it because there was no chance we were going to go away and forget the Abletts. Either they came home safe and sound or, if they didn't, we needed to know where they were.'

Quietly she interjected. 'Which you don't.'

'Ah, well.' He looked up into the pear tree, at the ripening fruit and the investigative insects.

'You think you do, don't you?'

The blue gaze fixed on her. 'There are very limited possibilities, Alice. Farmers don't run off. There were debts but George Ablett could have sold property to pay them or spread them over time, whatever was necessary.'

She loved hearing her own opinion confirmed. 'Yes, I know.'

'He's dead and so's she. Folk said she ran away . . . You've read it all up, I needn't waste your time on that. The crux was: who killed them and what did he do with the bodies? Well, a farm's a farm. A private place where a man, especially one living alone, can operate his machinery and feed his pigs and tip anything he likes down a drain running straight out to sea, or dig a hole on his land and bury it. Nobody ever wonders what a farmer's doing, do they?'

She shuddered. 'No bodies to be found.'

'And one thing Keenthorne kept saying – once he started saying anything at all, that is – the one thing he kept on about was that we wouldn't find the bodies.'

'Did he?' Her voice gave away her dismay.

'Oh yes, although later on his barrister was claiming he meant they weren't dead. What it boiled down to was we couldn't find the Abletts dead and he couldn't produce them alive.'

She frowned. 'I thought . . .'

'Go on.'

'It's just that I thought Joe Keenthorne had cattle, not pigs. If he'd . . . done what you said . . . he couldn't have fed the remains to his animals.'

With a narrowing of the eyes the old sergeant approved her reasoning. 'You're correct, my dear. Keenthorne was a man who raised heifers. I don't believe he's kept a pig in his life.'

'Well, then . . .'

'But there was a man at Stark Point who kept quite a few pigs. And who do you think he was?'

A revolting thought knotted her stomach. 'Oh, no.'

'I'm afraid so, Alice. George Ablett kept pigs.'

'This is horrible.'

'I agree with you there, but that's how it looked. The Abletts were killed by Keenthorne and eaten by their own pigs.'

She pushed her plate away, sickened. 'It's crazy but it makes it worse that they were their own pigs.'

He agreed. 'It doesn't affect the outcome but it's an unpleasant little embellishment. Sorry, I wish I hadn't told you.'

'No, it's all right. I need to know as much as I can.' She hesitated. 'One thing before we leave this nasty little embellishment behind. Was the theory that it all happened at Perrotts Farm? The killing, the butchering and the feeding to the pigs?'

'What are you getting at, Alice?'

'You were saying farmers who live alone can do what they like.'

'Yes?'

'Joe Keenthorne lived alone but not close to Perrotts Farm. Others were going in and out of Perrotts Farm all day. Farm labourers, for instance. If he'd done those things there he risked being noticed.'

'Oh, I see what's bothering you. Well, first off, it was established that George Ablett was probably killed in the farmhouse at Perrotts Farm. Traces of blood were found near the kitchen sink, you see. But don't forget they couldn't do the fancy tests they have nowadays.'

'Before DNA testing they could only indicate blood types, not individuals' blood?'

'Yes. Second, the pigs weren't at Perrotts Farm. George Ablett had bought another farm. It's got a proper name but everyone calls it the Little Farm. That's where the pigs were. Where Keenthorne was living was very near the Little Farm.'

She steeled herself to ask a disgusting question. 'Was there evidence at the Little Farm to show the bodies had been there?'

'No. Nothing remained of Mr and Mrs Ablett except those streaks of blood of George's type on the wall by the kitchen sink.'

His eyes settled on the overhead wasps again but he was absorbed in memory. Alice listened to the summery drone of insects, flustered leaves, and a motorcycle whining up a hill.

At last he said: 'I was amazed when the jury acquitted him. Everybody was, the only argument had been whether he'd hang for it or go to prison. But he got off. He's not an intelligent man, not on the face of it, but maybe we under-estimated him. I honestly don't know.'

Alice gave her view. 'He isn't inadequate. The estate wouldn't have let him take over the farm on his father's death if he hadn't been capable.'

Pennymoor obviously had not thought of this before. 'That's an interesting point, Alice. There are some folk at the Point a bit touched but I haven't heard it said of him.'

She wanted to know what he meant about under-estimating Joe.

He said: 'Killing a couple without leaving evidence lying around isn't easy, and concealing the bodies is usually the hardest part for any murderer. But he managed it. Then, instead of weaving a mesh of lies that would have trapped him, he stuck to "No" and "Don't know". For a stupid man that was very intelligent.'

'But we know he isn't.'

'He wasn't so cunning during interviews, mind. Kept asking whether he was in George's will and insisting we wouldn't find the bodies. But, as I said, his lawyers twisted things, told the jury the words were ambiguous.'

She missed a chance to challenge him with Joe's argument that it was the police, seeking motive, who repeatedly raised the question of inheritance.

He said: 'Uneducated, not very bright, under pressure . . . We expected him to crack. But Keenthorne, he stuck it out. Then there was the decision not to prosecute him for murdering Delma. Not enough evidence, they said, unless he confesses. So they went ahead with one charge instead of two but our expectation was that, after he was convicted, he'd own up to murdering Delma and then confirm what we more or less knew about timing and method.'

'Isn't there a chance he was innocent?'

He gave a twinkly smile that scolded her for flippancy. 'Not a hope in hell.'

'Yet the jury . . .'

'Let me tell you what happened after, Alice. Soon as the trial was over he had his lawyer chasing up the inheritance. He came back to Stark Point, found he'd been turned off his farm by Sir Arthur Devrell while he was on remand, and he went round to the manor house and made a scene. After that hoopla he headed for Cornwall. He lived in a fishing village, hardly spoke to anybody, tried using a false name, that sort of caper. Kept it up for a few years, and I must say I was glad not to have him on my patch. Think what it would have been, Alice, if they'd opted for natural justice and not what he'd had in a court of law.'

She was shocked. 'Are you saying they'd have killed him?'

'Might well have done. Anyway, Cornwall it was. Oh, and a nervous breakdown, whatever that's supposed to be. I mean I know what it is when other folk have them but with Keenthorne it took a different turn. Didn't stop him being sharp enough to have George and Delma declared dead so he could get his hands on the property. Oh, he kept his lawyers busy while he was having his nervous breakdown, I can tell you.'

'So he came back when he inherited?'

'Yes. First off he lived on the Little Farm but that didn't suit him and I suppose we can guess why. He put it up for sale and moved into Perrotts Farm, letting most of the land and living in the farmhouse happy as a pig in shit, if you'll excuse the expression.'

But Alice was wincing at his indignation, not at a description she knew was apt. She asked how long Pennymoor had watched Keenthorne and waited.

''Til the day I left the force. You might say I haven't stopped because I still wonder about him. Since I came to live with Cassie, after my wife died five years back, I look across from this garden and I see Stark Point and I think: "When are you going to tell us, Joe?" '

'Surely you can't expect a confession after half a century?'

'Why not? Say he has another breakdown. The mind's a funny thing, Alice. It will do your bidding for so long but in the end it likes the truth. I wouldn't be surprised if one of these days he can't stand it any longer and starts chirrupping.'

She looked doubtful.

He said Keenthorne had not always been reclusive. 'He tried to win favour when he returned to the Point. Sold things cheap, doesn't charge much rent and one time he gave a plot of land to the council for a bend to be straightened out. But he's a funny one, Alice. Folk don't know how to take him.'

Alice murmured agreement.

'They say he doesn't look after the farmhouse, which you can see for yourself is true. He wouldn't do the work himself and wouldn't let anyone over the threshold. Most farmers who let land make the tenant keep it in good repair but he's the opposite, telling them they shan't do this or that. Tidy hedges, fix gates, I don't know exactly. It's going downhill, everything George

Ablett achieved is being chucked away. And I wonder why, I mean with Keenthorne being so determined on having that inheritance.'

She suggested Joe no longer had the heart for the work.

He snorted. 'He should have sold up and gone away. Somebody else could have bought it and made a go of it. But no, not Keenthorne. He has to hang around the place like a bad memory.'

Cassie came out and offered more tea. They declined. She said: 'Don't forget your gardening programme, Pop. You'll be cross if you do.'

'I'll be cross if they talk rubbish about dahlias, like they did last week. Once they get on television they forget all they ever knew about gardening.'

He rippled with laughter and Cassie teased him about wishing he was on telly instead of the so-called expert.

'You're jealous, Pop, that's all it is.'

When the jokes petered out, and Cassie had padded away barefoot with the tray, Alice mentioned her own intriguing garden.

'Mrs Ablett used to go to my aunt for herbal cures. I wish I knew what for.'

'If it was to ward off the evil Keenthorne, she wasted her money,' he said, looking at his watch, calculating the minutes before the programme.

Rising, Alice admitted: 'You know, I can't help hoping the rumours about Delma running away with her lover are true.'

He looked beyond her, at the hillside tumbling to green splashed with blue water. Stark Point accused the sea.

'A lot believe that,' he said. 'Maybe they need to. But not the Clutton–Wrays. They had a feeling she was dead from the day they were told she was missing.'

Alice gasped. 'Who were they?'

Merry blue eyes studied her astonishment. 'Her family. Before she married George she was Delma Clutton–Wray.'

Chapter Sixteen

'Her *father* bought her the car. Everybody said it was more hers than George's, and they were right. It was a present from her father.'

'Alice, calm down.'

Rod propelled her gently backwards to a chair. Ever since she had burst into the cottage with the remarkable news he had been trying to damp down her excitement.

'Wait there,' he ordered.

'But I . . .'

'No buts. Don't move.'

She heard the fridge open, white wine poured into glasses, the soft slam of the fridge door.

'Now,' he said, handing her a glass, 'let me tell you what happened here while you were gallivanting around the hills.'

His tone made her tense. 'What happened?'

'I found the catch which had been smashed off your garage door.'

This did not sound serious. Her voice was light. 'Oh?'

'You'll never guess where I found it.'

'Quite right, I won't guess. I expect to be told.'

'In the rubbish bin at Ham Cottage.'

She gaped. 'Well . . .' Too many questions, which one

should she pick? This one: 'What in the world were you doing going through Iris's bin?'

Rod took an exasperatingly long time to drink a mouthful of wine before he went on. 'As I was walking near Ham Cottage I picked up a shattered plastic toy. A hangover from your great storm, I should think. The Dottrells' bin was the obvious place to dump it. I lifted the lid and what should be lying in the plastic bag inside it but . . .'

'Good lord.' Then: 'But Iris and Mary wouldn't . . . It doesn't make sense.'

'Not to me.'

Alice asked: 'Was it lying on the top, the last thing dropped in?'

'Yes. The bag was partly full and folded over. I opened it to toss the toy in and there, on top of the usual household dross, was the catch. Smashed.'

Suspicion coloured her every thought. 'The weekly rubbish collection is early tomorrow. If you hadn't chanced to find it now we'd never have known.'

'Yes, but *what* do we know?'

'Not,' she said firmly, wishing it true, 'that Iris or Mary damaged it and messed up my car. Well, we know Iris doesn't go out so it was hardly her.'

'Mary might have found it in the lane.'

Alice frowned. 'Did you mention it to either of them?'

'No, how could I?'

'I'm wondering whether Iris saw you at the bin. The window she uses as her spy hole has a clear view of their gate and the lane.'

'Sorry, I don't know. I wasn't looking up at the first floor.'

A deceptively casual question. 'Were you just passing?'

'I'd been for a walk and decided to call on Mary before coming back here.'

There was a pause. Alice was contemplative. Rod grew wary.

She roused herself. 'I'll ask,' she said.

'Alice, you can't. You can't expose me as a man who goes through people's dustbins. I'm not a . . . a tabloid journalist.'

'You found something of mine. That gives me the right to ask how it got there.'

'Perhaps someone else . . . No, it would be a ridiculous coincidence if two people came along the lane and interfered with the bin.'

'Quite. I'll ask.'

He groaned.

She said: 'Where is it now?'

'Parked by their gate, ready for the bin men.'

She flashed him a look. Was he doing this deliberately? 'My door catch, not their bin.'

'Oh. Still in the bin.'

'You didn't bring it here?'

'No. Honestly, it's no use to you, it's broken.'

'Rod, I appreciate that. But it's also evidence of a crime.'

He rolled his eyes. 'Oh forgive me, love, I thought you only dealt in double murders.'

Which was how they came to speak about the Abletts again. This time he let her tell the full story of her afternoon with the retired police sergeant.

He was unimpressed, though. 'Nothing truly new, then, except Delma's maiden name.'

She opened her mouth to argue, then chose not to bother. He would not understand. Pennymoor had altered her thinking and he had done it without offering precise details of the case but by painting the colour of the prejudice against Joe Keenthorne. Joe had been his quarry and continued to be. What was true of Pennymoor, lovely grandfather though he patently was, appeared to be generally true. And it confirmed her view that Joe was not paranoid in believing people were ranged against him.

Rod produced a bowl of nibbles which she did not remember bringing into the house. Chicken-flavoured? Definitely his purchase rather than hers. '*Oh well, one of those days – Earl Grey teabags and now chicken-tasty potato snacks.*'

Aloud she said: 'Do you know something? If Joe Keenthorne had been given a prison sentence, he'd have been a free man years ago. As it is, he was acquitted yet he'll never be free.'

Rod shrugged. 'Presumably that always happens when people are convinced of someone's guilt.' He added: 'That's a nice line for your book, by the way.'

'Yes, it is.' She cursed silently, knowing she ought to have been thinking as a writer and noticed this herself. Rod, damn him, seemed better suited to the task than she was. She took up his other point. 'Seems unreasonable, though.'

'You can't force neighbours to be nice to each other, and by the sound of it they hate Joe.'

Alice was thinking this was true and it was horrible but there was not much to be done about human nature.

Rod interrupted. 'By the way, I've invited Mary for a drink later on, about nine. She'll settle her mother in front of the film on Channel Five and come over.'

'I'm surprised she can see the screen through all that smoke.'

He laughed. 'Yes, I must admit I encourage chats in the garden if I go round there.'

Alice set down her empty glass. 'Would you mind getting supper, Rod? There's something I'd like to do this evening and with Mary coming later I'd better do it before we eat.'

'You're not going out, are you?'

'Yes, I need to ask Joe . . .'

'Oh no, not him again.'

'It's important.'

'Can't it wait?'

'Look, if this is a fancy way of refusing to get supper, why don't you say so?'

He was extremely indignant, almost convincing her. 'Rubbish! I don't want you hanging around that awful old man, that's all. You hated being at Perrotts Farm so why go back?'

'I won't. He's at the bay. I noticed as I drove by.'

Rod subsided. 'Well, don't be long.'

'I can't believe this,' she muttered, flouncing out of the cottage. 'My own house, my own work, and he barges in and bosses me around.'

Exasperation speeded her on. Lane, wooden bridge, high grass and saltings rushed by in a blur. In her mind's eye she was arguing with Rod or conferring with Joe. She had no space to notice the shades of the wavering grass or the silvering of the line of surf. The observant, reflective Alice, with the urge to preserve the scenery in her writing, was absent. She stumbled over churned-up sand before she remembered the wrecked boat, let alone her boat poem.

Joe was nowhere to be seen but she thought he might be resting, like a lizard on a stone, the far side of the Cat Rock. The tide had turned, there was a dark fringe of wet sand, but she had to judge it finely to get round the wave-slapped outcrop without being drenched in a shower of sparkling spray.

There was Joe, just as she had pictured him, beyond the reach of the waves and staring out to sea. With a jolt she realised he was not peering at distant land, or studying the wailing birds that quartered the bay or watching the ship navigating deep water on the further side of the channel. He was not even dozily enjoying the rush and suck of the tide. No, he stared blankly, seeing nothing but the past and injustice. It was like the moment she realised he was no beachcomber. Plain truth had been obscured by her own stupidity.

'Joe!' She was smiling and waving.

He jerked round, his eyes glinting like quartz. Immediately, he was struggling to his feet, loose stones slithering under his salt-crusted boots.

'Joe, please don't go.'

But he was up and off, making remarkable progress over terrain she found impossible. Practised, he knew where the safe footing was. A novice, Alice blundered. He got away.

She came to a halt, measuring the distance growing between them. Flurries of screaming birds took to the air at his approach, wheeling around his head, diving at him, attempting to drive him back with their fury. He was undaunted, perhaps oblivious. The arms of his torn jacket were flailing stiffly as he fought to keep his balance.

Alice had never walked in that direction but she understood roughly where it led. In George Ablett's day it had reached a cliff path and a track to the coast road.

Massive erosion had reduced it to friable shale dotted with boulders. It ended in a maze created by great shards of fallen stone. Without a backward glance Joe entered the maze and was lost to her.

Cheated, she began the return journey. A feral cat ran past her legs and scaled the cliff, loosening scree. Green eyes watched her from a ledge. More scree, a fine scattering followed by stones the size of her fist. A perilous place, one where she risked a rock on the head. She moved away but only a yard or two because the sea was challenging her with every hiss.

Remembered warnings frightened her: 'It's dangerous by Cat Rock until the tide's well out'; 'If you fall in near the Cat Rock the undertow will suck you right out into the channel' and 'Go in there and you won't stand a chance.'

She listened to the death rattle of the waves on the rocks, and was afraid.

Carefully she crept on. A few minutes later, relieved and safe, she jumped down onto damp sand. It was then that she heard the noise. Voices and vehicles, reminiscent of the day after the storm when the lake formed over the road. She laughed, thinking the place was so peaceful that two cars and a conversation amounted to a commotion.

She took the route through the saltings, skirting the scene of the activity and wondering whether avoidance signified her transformation into a true villager. She met nobody and heard nothing distinct except the waves tamping the shore.

Charles, who disliked every aspect of Stark Point, had one day asked her: 'How long do you have to live here before you stop noticing the waves? When I lived by a railway line it took six weeks to stop hearing trains.'

And she had been bemused. For her, the sea was a constant, like the beat of blood through her veins, a feature she registered with a part of her mind and listened to intermittently day and night.

'Monotonous,' Charles had called it, although that was the last thing it was.

The state of the tide, the direction of the wind, the volume of shipping in the channel, the type of weather . . . Practically everything altered the song of the sea. It wasn't a sound, it was an infinite variety of sounds, and she was learning and enjoying them.

She reached Spray Cottage and found Rod reading.

'You were quick, Pippin. Did Joe tell you to mind your own business?'

She explained she had been thwarted.

Rod said never mind, another day would do. 'It isn't as if there's any real hurry.'

'No.'

She meant yes but could not justify it. The book was a mere glimmer of an idea, its story an old one with the basic facts long established. If she were lucky she would re-arrange prejudices but that was all. Yet she felt impatient, as if a deadline loomed and she was frittering time.

Mary came nearer ten than nine. Light had virtually gone before Alice heard her running footsteps.

Flushed and excited, Mary blurted: 'You'll never believe what's happened.'

She stood there, passing an agitated hand through her cropped hair and tantalising them.

Alice wanted to wrest the news from her. Rod was asking whether Iris was all right.

Mary dismissed her mother with a gesture. 'A car has been found in a rhine. They've been grappling half the evening to lift it out. I've been watching.'

They froze, tacitly demanding more.

Having unburdened herself, Mary asked: 'Can I have a drink?'

Alice snatched up a glass. Rod tilted the bottle.

'What sort of car is it?' Alice asked.

Mary flopped onto a kitchen chair and took several gulps. 'Old. And there's a man's body in it.'

Inevitably, Alice's thought was: '*George Ablett.*'

'Christ.' Rod whispered.

Mary added quickly: 'That's what I heard, a man's body. I didn't see for myself.'

They pestered her for the rest.

She said: 'Bill Chilton lost a piece of machinery in the water when he was working in his big field in the spring and he decided to haul it out at last. He and his son Danny went up there with a tractor and a grab. They found it soon after they began poking around, or thought they did. Danny offered to jump in and fix the grab. He lowered himself into the water and discovered he was standing on top of a car.'

'The body . . .' Rod began.

Mary was markedly less shocked than they were. 'I'm afraid it's what you expect when a car goes in. Unless someone sees it happen and sends for help, the driver's had it. The rhines are too narrow for him to open a door.'

'A window?' Rod suggested.

'If he can't open the door wide enough he can't squeeze out of a window, either. No, the only time anybody survives without help is if the windscreen has gone and they can punch their way out.'

Mary held out her glass and Rod emptied the bottle into it. He was looking sceptical, virtually accusing her of exaggerating.

However, Alice supported her. 'Wasn't there an accident a few years ago in which a group of people died?'

'Yes,' Mary said. 'They were driving late one evening down a causeway – not ours, I'm glad to say – and the car ran down the bank and into the water. There were five people in it. And the worst of it was that people in houses nearby had seen the car lights change direction and then vanish, so they wondered if there'd been an accident and the police were called.'

Rod was investigating the fridge in a vague quest for another bottle. 'If the accident was seen, why weren't they saved?'

'Because the water closed over the car. Next day the police found the tracks the car made as it left the road and they brought their divers. The evidence at the inquests was incredibly horrifying because some of the passengers had survived for hours.'

Distracted, Rod returned with a bottle of milk.

Mary said: 'It set everybody round here discussing whether it's best to keep the windows shut and slowly suffocate or wind them down and drown quickly. Either way, you've had it.'

Alice was frowning. 'I don't understand. You said the car Bill Chilton found was in a drain in his field, not at the roadside.'

She nodded. 'It does sound strange but when I tell you the road used to run alongside that stretch of water, it becomes logical.'

A sickening anticipation gripped Alice. Mary did not elaborate and she was forced to ask.

'Doesn't Bill Chilton rent fields at Perrotts Farm?'

'That's right.'

Rod glanced from one to the other, aware he was missing something.

Alice thought she might as well get it out in the open. 'When Joe Keenthorne inherited the farm he gave a plot of land to the council to allow a bad bend to be straightened. Until he did so the drain was beside the road and ever since it's been on private land. His land.'

In her head Alice heard Reg Pennymoor's voice: 'Always telling them they shouldn't do this and that. Tidy hedges, fix gates, I don't know exactly.'

'I know exactly what,' Alice thought. *'He wouldn't have the drain cleaned out, that's what.'*

Mary was saying, 'Everybody's guessing what you're guessing, Alice, that it's George Ablett's body and Joe's known all along he was there. Oh, it explains a lot of things.'

'Including,' Alice said with resignation, 'why he hangs around here like a bad memory.'

She did not enlighten them that it was a phrase stolen from a police sergeant whose retirement was haunted by Joe Keenthorne's guilt.

Chapter Seventeen

Alice and Rod walked Mary home to Ham Cottage. She had not stayed long with them because her mother was alone and might have heard the news.

'She'll be fretting,' Mary said, and repeated it as she turned in at her gate.

There was no evidence of this, Alice noted. Iris Dottrell's television was sending its blue glow out into the night, as it usually did. Recorded voices were arguing in the sitting room, blasts of music interrupting.

Her eye fell on the dark shape of the dustbin but it was too late to quiz Mary about the broken catch from the garage. There had been no right time, the news from Perrotts Farm having squeezed out the rest.

Once Mary had waved goodnight Alice said to Rod: 'Let's walk down there.'

He gave her an affectionate pat. 'I never imagined we'd do anything else.'

'Am I being disgustingly ghoulish?'

'You have to be, if you're to write the book.'

Voices and bright lights drew them on, as if a subdued funfair had camped in a field.

Alice said: 'I don't suppose there'll be much to see.'

She was praying the body had been removed.

'Perhaps it's possible to recognise the type of car,' he suggested.

'Maybe.' And she thought: *'I don't know how I'll feel if it's obviously Delma's Talbot.'*

A dozen figures were milling just inside the gateway to the field, their voices low and intense. Alice recognised faces from the group who had gathered around the wrecked boat. Her general hello was answered with grunts. Undeterred, she approached the stubble-chinned man who owned the brown and white collie. He did not have it with him now, which she thought wise given the dog's frisky nature.

'I'm told a car's been found,' she said, prompting conversation. This was the man who had one day named Joe Keenthorne for her, although not without a tussle.

'There it is, if you want to take a photograph.'

'Photograph?' An astonishing idea.

'For your book.'

'Oh.'

She felt his disdain and feigned a need to speak to Rod.

'What's up?' Rod was reading her expression.

'I may not be the most popular girl in town.'

'Well, you are with me.' He meant to be reassuring.

Around them conversations faltered. The group shuffled until no one was looking at Rod and Alice.

She touched his arm. 'Come on.'

Striding past the men she went to one of the young policemen whose current duty appeared to be to stand idly in a field. Luckily, her smiling charm worked on him. What had happened? What was going on now? Was it possible for her to see the car?

'You can't get near,' he said. 'Well, you wouldn't want to, not until they remove what they've got to.'

Her mouth twisted in distaste. 'Oh, the body.'

'Yes and no. Not what you'd call a body after it's been in the water for years.'

'How close may I go?'

He offered to take her. Rod tagged on, popping in the occasional question. They moved only a few paces but it did make a difference to how much was visible. Under a harsh lamp lay a hulk that was definably an old-fashioned saloon with a long bonnet and a roof that swooped down at the back. On the far side a door was open and men bobbed in and out of view as they examined the interior.

Rod said to the constable: 'This is probably a daft thing to ask but is there a number plate?'

The three of them craned forward but at a hopeless angle to detect anything attached to the front of the car. The rear was completely obscured.

They agreed they did not believe there was a plate.

Alice said: 'Perhaps they'll dredge for it.'

The constable had a better idea. 'They'll go by the engine number.'

A lorry arrived then and onlookers were cleared away from the entrance to allow it to judder over the grass. Tarpaulins were tied round the car and the operation of lifting it onto the low loader began. The constable became busy and sent Alice and Rod back to the others.

They were ignored, and amused by their implied non-existence. For a while they spoke naturally together, remarking on the progress of the loading and reminding each other of the identities of people who were leaving.

'That's the police surgeon.'

'And that's Sergeant Connolly who was called out here when the car was found.'

They were quoting their expert witness, the young constable. They were also putting on a display of insouciance.

Soon they went away too, breaking into muffled laughter once through the gate.

'Ridiculous!' Rod cried.

'Childish!'

But it was not long before they saw the black side. Rod mentioned it first.

'Now I know what your Pointers have been doing to Joe Keenthorne.'

After a few unspoken thoughts she replied: 'If it's the Talbot presumably it proves their suspicions correct, and they'll carry on believing they were justified in shunning him.'

'Well, it'll be impossible to argue against them now.'

'*Argue*? Who does any arguing around here? If you don't share their view, you can't get them to speak.'

Rod laughed at her rush of indignation. Then: 'How tough will it be for you to accept his guilt?'

'Obviously, I'm sad the accusations are turning out to be true, because it means George Ablett was killed instead of running off.'

'But you believed he drowned.'

'He probably did,' she said.

'Er . . . yes. I can't help thinking of a car smash as being a different sort of death.'

'This evening changes everything. Ask me tomorrow how I feel about Joe, I might possibly have worked it out by then.'

'I'm fetching Camilla tomorrow,' he said.

He drove away from Stark Point very early next morning. Alice heard him tiptoeing about the house, heard footsteps on the path and the hesitant firing of his old runabout. She felt a tweak of sympathy for him and countered it with icy reflection.

'God knows he's brought it on himself. He could have been a real father to Camilla if he hadn't broken up his first marriage. She could have had an adoring stepmother if he hadn't spoiled his second one. And as for picking Ruth . . . Yes, it's all his own fault. And I feel so sorry for him.'

Alice stood at the window, watching the scenery come to life. Birds, a fox, someone's dog out for a stroll, a swinging sea but no beachcomber.

'Never was a beachcomber. Nothing's been what I thought it was. Those who were in the wrong are proving to be right and the man proved innocent now looks guilty as hell.'

Downstairs she dithered, then pulled her jacket on and went out. The lane was deserted but the Stark Point vigilante had been busy. A fresh notice grumbled about householders putting their rubbish bins out overnight, encouraging marauding cats and foxes. In a field, rooks pecked at the ground where the salvaged car had lain. Without a break in her step, Alice hurried by.

She walked down to meet the surf, disturbing waders and involuntarily chasing tiny crabs, and thinking: '*All this will go on regardless of what befalls Joe Keenthorne today, and surely something catastrophic will.*'

She scanned the bay but there was no brown hat ducking out of sight in the scrub or slipping behind the Cat Rock.

'*He's gone,*' she thought, abruptly piecing it together. '*I may be the last person who saw him.*'

She remembered the way he recoiled from her when she sought him out in one of his private spaces. Considered now, it was not the response of a difficult man in a bad mood, it was flight from a tormentor. He must have known about Bill Chilton's discovery and that it was a matter of hours before the police arrested him.

'And this time they've got the body, Joe, and there's no escape for you.'

She spoke the words, telling her story to the surf that never ceased speaking to her. Alice threw a pebble into the water and turned for home.

Jacko, the fisherman, came out of his house as she drew near. Two squat men, compact bundles of muscle, had stopped to speak to him. Alice waved but did not veer towards them.

'Hey.' Jacko was calling her, gesturing.

Alice changed direction. 'Chilly morning.' She followed the convention. Weather first, always.

'Oh, it'll settle,' said Jacko with an eye to the sky. His face was set in a frown. 'Sunny before noon, you'll see.'

'Good.' Alice felt herself beaming, from habit, not because she had anything to smile about.

The weather out of the way Jacko demanded: 'Where's he to?'

'Who?' There was a slim chance he meant Rod and if he did there was no sense in being entangled in darker matters.

One of the men gave an impatient cluck. Jacko said: 'Joe Keenthorne, that's who.'

'I haven't seen him.'

The impatient man said: 'Not this morning, you haven't. We've been watching for him and he hasn't been down to the bay.'

She made a helpless gesture. 'I've no idea where he is.'

Jacko talked over the other man's sarcastic reply, saying: 'You've been meeting him, regular. Seems to us you would know.'

'No, really, I don't.' She moved away a step.

Jacko blocked her. His face was contorted, making him a malign monkey. 'Keenthorne's wanted, Alice. He's been hiding a body on his land and now he's got questions to answer. He's wanted, you mind that.'

She tried to say she entirely agreed but it came out wrong and she sounded dismissive. She dodged around him and got away.

The ill-tempered man yelled after her. 'When you see your friend Joe, you tell him we want a word.'

More circumspectly Jacko shouted: 'And the police, too.'

Her knees felt weak. She stumbled. There was menace in the air. They had not exactly threatened her but they would have no scruples about how they treated Joe. She prayed the police would discover him before they did.

'*I ought to warn him,*' she realised. '*Perhaps I could trace him, persuade him to go to the police for his own safety.*'

But how? And was it possible she could convince him that Stark Point was on the verge of forming a lynch mob?

'Reg Pennymoor thought they might kill him. They've made him an animal at bay and now they want blood.'

Police cars arrived at the field. A delivery van was obstructed so the police pulled their cars inside the gateway. A mixed crowd gathered to watch.

A photographer and a reporter from the local press sifted the crowd for witnesses to the discovery and the loading of the trailer. Bill Chilton posed glumly by the rhine but otherwise co-operation was limited.

Several people, who had not been infected by the idea she deserved to be cold-shouldered, spoke spontaneously to Alice. When they speculated on the identity of the car's occupant and the cause of his death, she brushed the subject aside.

'Sorry, I'm new here.'

A young woman, with a weak chin and hair of an improbable red, looked askance. 'But you're the one who's writing the book.'

Alice demurred. 'It was only an idea. I don't know enough, I'm new.'

She was twisting reality into something they might find palatable but it was a waste of time because the subtlety escaped them. There was a worrying clamour for details of what Keen-thorne had said to her.

'We know you've been talking to him.' The red head wagged, challenging her to deny this.

'Better,' she thought, *'play them at their own game.'*

So she avoided eye contact and brushed their questions aside with an incoherent remark, regretting they were not on the other side of the causeway because she could have included sea-gazing as well.

As they were gearing up for renewed assault a flurry of excitement from the journalists alerted them to police officers going purposefully towards Perrotts Farm. People peeled away from the crowd and followed. Police ordered them back. When the school bus arrived, the lane was blocked by disgruntled pedestrians. Instead of teasing a way through, the driver jumped out to join in.

Mary appeared on the far side of the throng, saw Alice and wriggled her way through, saying: 'What a mêlée! I've never seen anything like it. Not at Stark Point, I mean.'

'Most of them,' said Alice drily, 'have waited half a lifetime for this.'

'I said to Mum last night: "Now they've got the body, they've got the proof." But do you know what she said?'

Alice queried with a look.

'She said: "Mary, it's only proof George Ablett's dead and Joe knew where he was. Where's the proof he killed him?" '

Alice recalled Iris saying she had always believed Joe was involved in the man's death but was not a murderer. 'Your mother's right, but I wouldn't bother pointing it out to anybody here.'

They broke off and listened to the theories being touted. It was common consent the body was George's and Joe Keenthorne had killed him and dumped it there. Where they disagreed was method.

A farm labourer said: 'Hard work pushing a car on your own, steering it off the road and all.'

'Especially with a dead body in the driver's seat,' suggested a chicken farmer distinguished by warts on his nose.

'Ah, but we don't know as he was in the seat. Who heard he was in the seat?' The labourer glanced round.

No hands shot up.

The bus driver voiced his opinion. 'Not easy to do it without being seen either. Anybody could have come along. It's not like it's right out in the country, is it?'

'Why was that?' asked Sam, the young man who had been boringly repetitious about the wrecked boat.

'What's that, Sam?' Mrs Aley's voice rose from the crowd although she was too short to be visible.

Sam clarified. 'Why was it dumped in a rhine in the village? You'd think he'd have driven it over to Lambwood or somewhere else with these big drains and only empty roads beside them.'

Buzzing like furious insects, the crowd fussed with Sam's idea. They divided into those who said it was a good question and those who said questions were of no importance, it was what had happened that counted.

Mrs Aley, invisibly, said: 'We can't say we'll have to see what comes out in court, can we? He won't say anything, will he? Didn't last time and won't now.'

Everyone who heard snickered.

Once he could make himself heard, Sam told them: 'He won't be in court again. That's double jeopardy, that is. You can't be done twice for the same thing.'

Reminded, the crowd grew belligerent.

'Then if the law won't give us justice, we'll see to it ourselves.' Alice recognised the voice of the ill-tempered man who was one of Jacko's cohorts. His words were greeted with cheers.

She shivered. 'I hate this, Mary, I'm going home.'

Mary stayed.

As Alice emerged from the other side of the crowd, the policemen who had gone to Perrotts Farm reappeared and anger erupted.

Cries of 'They haven't got him', 'Why aren't they taking him in?' and 'We don't want him, why don't you take him away?'

A constable was telling them to leave, his pleas drowned by their shouting.

Alice, making her escape, felt queasy. Desperate to put the scene behind her, she ran as soon as she was out of sight around a bend. By the time she was indoors she was shaking.

Unfortunately, her home was an inadequate sanctuary, tainted by her association with Joe Keenthorne. Whatever happened to him, her chance of leading a decent life at Stark Point seemed ruined.

Throwing a camomile teabag into a mug and uttering incantations about calming down, Alice struggled to keep the problem in proportion.

'They're unkind and uneducated but they aren't witch hunters. The worst they can do is make me hate it here so badly I sell the house.'

Sadly, she remembered her pleasure the first time she had driven into the village and seen her cottage. Peaceful, lapped about by water, it had promised tranquillity and she had seized on the opportunity it offered. Poems were to be created here. A writer was to be born.

And look what had happened. No use dismissing it as a patch of bad luck, the Joe Keenthorne affair had wrecked her life. The Pointers would never let her live it down. If they spoke to her at all they would blame her; but they would almost certainly not speak.

Over the weeks she had put out tentative feelers in search of acquaintance, if not truly friendship, and they had been crushed. By excluding her, the Pointers had driven her to seek out Joe's company. Long before she had met him or there was talk of a book, they had slammed the door in her face.

She fetched the photograph from the sitting room and relived the evening she discovered the original in the Falcon. Odd how things had worked out. If Charles had ordered the wood, she need not have gone to the pub. If the woodman had been prompt she would have been in and out without studying the pictures. Oh yes, a series of commonplace details had led inexorably to disaster.

Alice's jaw tightened. *'So it's Fate, is it? Nothing to be done? Well, there's one thing I can do before they drive me out of their village, and I might as well get on and do it. I've nothing more to lose.'*

She went to find Joe Keenthorne. First she tried Perrotts Farm, thumped on the door and pressed her face to the kitchen window, then shouted into the buildings in the yard.

There were no police there, only Bill Chilton's son, the gangling Danny who had blithely jumped into the water and found himself on the roof of a car. Attracted by the noise, he stood in the yard and watched her. They did not speak. His eyes dogged her as she went down the lane.

Police officers were working in the field. The school bus had gone and everyone else had faded back into the landscape. Alice reached the bay. Nobody was there. She upset the birds with her calling but no woolly hat popped into view. She checked the scrubby land and she clambered around the Cat Rock. Again, she shouted. Only the cliff replied.

Next she walked through the scrub, eventually coming, as she had long suspected she must, to a rudimentary path. This straggled inland, near the sheet of water where the swans floated, and ran behind the village. Alice reached the back of Perrotts Farm without a glimpse of its owner.

'*When I find him,*' she was thinking, '*I'll ask who his solicitor was and I'll fetch him. Or I'll bundle Joe into my car and smuggle him out of the village. Whichever way it has to be done, I'll protect him.*'

But for the present, she had to decide whether to continue along the old track or take one of the paths from it to the centre of the village. She went on towards the tip of the peninsula.

The track dwindled to a narrow path and swung round to meet the lane, shortly before the tarmac ended at the gate. Alice realised it was where Mrs Aley and her lurchers had sprung from one day, putting an end to Mary's stories.

She walked out to the headland. He was not there either. So Alice marched back down the lane and turned off through the Little Farm to check that stretch of coast. She averted her eyes from the sties in the farmyard, Reg Pennymoor's hideous theory still troubling her in spite of new evidence that George Ablett had lain in a watery grave instead of being fed to his pigs. True or not, ideas cling.

Home once again, she was exhausted and not simply because of the distance covered. Nervous tension was causing a headache and she wished she had company, even Rod's.

He was fetching his daughter for the weekend but, as usual with Rod, life was complicated. First he was checking mail at his Bath flat and keeping an appointment with a man who might find him work. In the evening he was going to his ex-wife's house to meet old friends. After staying there overnight, he would drive Camilla to Stark Point but had promised to stop in Bristol for her to see an exhibition. Alice expected them late Saturday afternoon.

She occupied herself by working at her computer, transforming her notes on the interview with Pennymoor into a written account that recorded the finding of the car and her last encounter with Joe Keenthorne. The work swallowed what remained of Friday.

When she finished, her confidence was restored because, however Joe's personal story was resolved, she believed she had the makings of a book.

She sketched out a scheme for it, planning to state the current position at the outset: Joe exonerated again or proved guilty, or perhaps a continuing mystery. Although the book needed the excitement of suspense, there was no sense in withholding what most readers who picked it up would already know. Better, she thought, to tease them with the puzzle of the years and its gradual unravelling. Most importantly, the true focus of the story would not be Joe and the Abletts but Stark Point.

After supper she made preparations for Camilla's stay. It had not been decided where the girl would sleep, should she be too tall for the sofa. Alice sniffed a pair of single sheets from the lower shelf of the airing cupboard and detected mustiness. They had come with the house and she had no idea when they had last been used. She pushed them into the washing machine.

Desultorily doing household chores, in between reading a book, she passed a quiet domestic evening. Rod had brought the book, a modern literary novel about colleagues with implausibly complex lives and superficial quandaries. It was hard to take them seriously but she persevered and, page by page, found herself hooked. Alice read in bed for an hour before falling asleep with the light on.

An unidentified sound forced her back to consciousness. Memories rushed in to frighten her. She was alone and she was hated because she talked to the man believed to have killed the Abletts.

A whimper betrayed her fear.

Alert for further sounds, she crept across the room. After a minute, she heard scraping. Footsteps on stone? A door grating? Half a dozen ideas were on offer.

Alice opened the bedroom door. The landing was dark, the spare bedroom and bathroom doors closed. In her head was a picture of a man climbing through the bathroom window. She often left it open. Steadying herself she twisted the handle and looked into an empty room. Then the other room. Empty.

The sound was repeated and now she could tell it was from below. She stared down the stairs into blackness. In the kitchen, her fridge began to hum.

There were two bolts on the back door and she felt a growing certainty they were undone. Worse, she could not remember turning the key. Holding her breath, she listened for her intruder's breathing.

But she heard only the fridge and cursed the worn-out contraption for being the noisiest in the county. How was she supposed to hear anything else with that racket going on?

Soon she was brave enough to venture downstairs, step by cautious step until she was in the kitchen. As she thought, the bolts were undone. The key, though, was turned in the lock. There was one more room to check, the sitting room. Nobody was in there.

Anxiety dissipated and she felt silly for being twitchy. Country nights were full of peculiar sounds. An animal might break free from a farm, a fox wander through her garden, and who knows what cats get up to? Wind whipped branches against windows and sent rubbish on a tour of the village. A sound outside could be anything.

Even so, Alice was convinced she had a prowler.

She turned off downstairs lights and waited in the sitting room checking for a figure at the front of the house. But the sky was overcast and when the moon slipped from behind cloud it lit up her front path and garden. Whoever had been there had gone.

Back in bed, she could not relax. She lay wakeful until, shortly before her usual time for rising, she fell into an untroubled sleep. It was mid morning before she woke. This time she knew what had roused her. The doorbell.

Two policemen were on her doorstep. They looked embarrassed at being greeted so late in the day by a tousled mess in a dressing gown.

'Oh, er, sorry . . .'

'Come in.' She did not haver, it was obvious who they were. Also she wanted the door closed on a brisk breeze.

They went directly to the nub of it. Did she know where Joe Keenthorne was?

'No, although I looked for him myself yesterday.'

Their expressions told her they had heard as much.

Prompted by their questions, she explained where she had looked. 'Then I came home. I couldn't think of anywhere else he might be.'

The one with nice teeth said with care: 'Look, Mrs. Wintle, I don't want you to take this the wrong way but it isn't sensible for you to go chasing after him. He's suspected of killing two people. By anybody's reckoning, he's a dangerous man.'

The other one added: 'You're new around here so maybe you don't know too much about the case.'

She said: 'I've heard about it.'

'Keep out of his path,' suggested the first one.

'Better safe than sorry,' said the other one.

Alice gave an understanding nod. 'I expect you're right. But if he's run off, the risk has gone with him.'

'He might contact you.'

A raised eyebrow.

He explained. 'Because you were befriending him.'

She demurred. 'It wasn't exactly that.'

Their telephone rang, saving her and summoning them away.

Afterwards she marshalled the questions she had lacked the wit to ask. Was the car a Talbot? How long had it been underwater? And was the dead body definitely George Ablett?

Iris was desperate to see for herself but she could not because everyone knew she did not leave the house. If she were spotted she would forfeit sympathy, and worse.

Last evening, when the car was raised from the ditch, she had worked herself into a frenzy of frustration, knowing drama was being enacted close by and she was the only person at the Point who was not free to go and watch. Secondhand news was not good enough and she had voiced wild complaints that Mary was not telling her everything. They had had another harsh exchange this morning and Mary had stormed out.

Fortunately, the vigil at the window soon rewarded Iris with two policemen approaching Spray Cottage, and gave her a fresh topic to think about. She wondered whether Alice would voluntarily tell her about the visit or whether a hint would be needed.

She waited a while after the men left but hope of further activity dwindled and she turned away. In her bedroom were piles of books, pictures stacked against a wall and a heap of bric-à-brac. The doctor, on one of her visits, had joked about it being an Aladdin's cave.

Iris picked up one of the books, sat on her bed and went through the motions of reading. Her mind, though, was fluttering. Soon it settled on one thought.

'If Bella were here she'd understand.'

Her face puckered. Tears brimmed over. Bella was gone, there were only her things to remember her by.

Iris clutched the book to her breast, a poor substitute for Bella.

Everything seemed to be pressing in on her. Secret compartments in her mind, where she hid her old anxieties, were being forced open. She was frightened. Bella would have known what to do but Bella was lost to her. Instead there was Alice. Nosy, interfering Alice who should not be in Bella's cottage anyway.

Iris dried her tears and sat there glowering, the book dropped on the quilt beside her and forgotten while she concentrated on how to get rid of Alice.

Chapter Eighteen

Rod brought his daughter to Spray Cottage late on Saturday afternoon. Camilla wore a grumpy expression as she followed him up the path, and she continued to wear it.

Alice realised she had been expecting a larger version of the ten-year-old with whom she had been on such splendid terms. Instead, Rod had fetched a teenager who had no wish to come.

She measured the girl with her eye. The sofa? Hard to say.

'Come and lie down,' Alice said while they were drinking tea in the kitchen. Luckily, Camilla was keen on herbal teas, if nothing else.

'Huh?'

'Come along.'

Alice drew her into the sitting room and asked her to lie on the sofa. Camilla resisted briefly, then capitulated with sulky resignation.

'Good,' Alice said, much relieved.

The girl wriggled down until her legs were kinked. 'Huh.'

'You've got three inches to spare.' Brooking no argument, Alice turned away.

Camilla sprang up. 'Are you really asking me to sleep on that thing?'

'Yes. It's only for one night.'

A wordless growl pursued Alice as she went back to her tea.

Interestingly, Rod declined to meet her eye. '*He knew, damn him,*' Alice thought. '*He knew she'd behave like this.*'

She mentally repeated what she'd said to Camilla: '*It's only for one night.*' The trouble was, it was untrue. The visit was one evening, one night and a hefty chunk of Sunday. War could break out in that time.

'Tell me about the exhibition,' she said, to kick off a conversation in which the others would do the talking. They had been relying too much on her.

Rod said: 'We thought it was worth the detour, didn't we, Millie?'

Camilla flinched as though he had slapped her. 'Don't call me that, you know I don't like it.'

Alice remembered how she had positively urged it, convinced Camilla was too staid and Millie more fun. But that was five years ago.

Rod, stupidly in Alice's opinion, apologised to her. 'Sorry, I'll try to get out of the habit. Okay?'

'Huh!'

'The exhibition,' insisted Alice, fearing she was to spend the weekend as referee.

'It was all right,' said Camilla, meaning it wasn't.

'*Praise indeed,*' thought Alice sarcastically. 'What did you like best, Camilla?'

'Dunno.'

Rod dived in with a description of a fantastical exhibit, all colour and cutting edge technology and heaps of laughs.

When he came to an end, Camilla said: 'Yeah, it was all right.'

She got up from the table and went out of the back door without saying anything further.

Rod shot Alice an urgent look. Before he could speak Alice leaped in, saying anything just to shut him up. She refused to have muttered adult plotting behind the girl's back, especially as she could see that was precisely what Camilla was aiming for.

'Guess what, Rod? I had the police round here this morning'.

She brought him up to date on the car-in-ditch and Joe-on-the-run tales. Camilla, slumped on a bench outside the open door, was within earshot but affecting not to be interested.

Rod asked: 'What's the next development then?'

'Presumably they identify the body and catch Joe. Any order will do.' Her flippancy startled her and made her wonder whether she wasn't slightly hysterical.

Oblivious, he said: 'Make sure you keep informed.' He was thinking of the book again.

Soon he and Camilla went to saunter through the village. Alice was invited by Rod to join them, but declined, using the washing up as an excuse.

Camilla set out in a T-shirt with nothing to cover her arms although the warmth of the day was fading and Alice had warned there was invariably a cool breeze of the sea. Not long after the crockery was dried they reappeared because Camilla felt cold.

Occasionally, the girl's pose slipped and she behaved like a normal person. This happened when she noticed the old photograph of Spray Cottage on the mantelpiece.

'Were these your family, Alice?'

'No, they were Mr and Mrs Ablett who used to live in the village.'

Alice warned Rod with a look. She had vowed not to disturb Camilla with stories of a murder trial and a body lurking in a ditch.

Rod, failing to catch her eye, said: 'They've just found him in a ditch, right here in the village.'

Camilla gulped. 'Really?' She looked to Alice for confirmation and was rewarded with a reluctant nod.

Rod added: 'And his car. They've been there fifty years.'

Having lit on a subject in which Camilla showed interest, it was impossible not to let the details come tumbling out. Between them they told her the old story and the new one. She greeted each detail with further gasps or squirms of horror.

When the tale was told, Rod introduced a fresh angle. 'Alice is writing a book about it.'

The claim was stated before she could cut him off. She quickly tried to undo it. 'Oh, it isn't definite . . .'

'A book? Cool.' Camilla did not allow backtracking.

Alice, though, regaining control, told her very little. '*Odd,*' she was thinking, '*that Camilla deems writing a book to be cool. From her, it's the highest accolade.*' Alice's work in radio had always, even by the younger and sweeter Camilla, been regarded as second rate, not being television. But now here was hypercritical Camilla giving proper respect to a potential writer. She glowed.

Then Camilla said: 'If it's a very good book, they might put it on television.'

Rod was also in favour of that. 'Yes, that would be great. Pays well too.'

'Who do you think should play Joe Keenthorne?' Camilla demanded.

Fighting down her disappointment, Alice joined in the game of choosing actors for the principal roles. At least, she was *willing* to join in but her contribution was meagre and she was rumbled.

'Alice, what do you mean, you don't know what Peter Sandry looks like? Everyone knows him.'

When Alice said she did not have a television set, Camilla was slack-jawed in amazement. This was followed by suspicion that it was a joke, then by incredulity and, ultimately, pity.

Alice laughed. 'It gives me more time to write my book.'

But the book had stopped being cool. Camilla's emotions had lodged on pity.

Bedtime came and Alice produced blankets, sheets and pillows for the sofa. But Camilla swept into the room with a padded sleeping bag, saying, 'I take this whenever I do a sleep-over.'

'Oh. Fine.'

Alice put her stuff back in the airing cupboard on the landing. Rod was hovering there, conspiratorial. She hushed him with a shake of the head, mouthing, 'Later.'

He seemed glad to be excused from excusing his awful daughter. Alice was wry, thinking it was hardly Camilla's fault she had been encouraged in bad behaviour. No, if anyone was to blame for this rotten weekend it was Rod who had forced an invitation.

In bed, glad to have company in the house and not to be nervous of prowlers, exhausted physically and mentally, Alice drifted towards sleep. All at once, a tiresome thought intruded. She had forgotten to tell Rod not to come back after delivering Camilla to her mother. Worse, it was too late to do anything about it. She did not have the heart to evict him with a few hours' notice, and especially not with Camilla present.

Sunday was a repetition of Saturday, dominated by the girl's general reluctance. Alice ignored it and ignored Rod tacitly apologising for it. They walked round the bay, which Camilla did not enjoy because eleven other people were there and she preferred large sandy bays to be deserted.

'It's only popular at weekends in summer,' said Alice. 'I have it to myself the rest of the time.'

'You and that beachcombing murderer,' said Camilla, and Alice could not tell whether this was intended to be witty or what.

After the walk there were Sunday papers to read, or not if you were too sulky, while lunch was prepared. Camilla said her mother usually took her to a country hotel for Sunday lunch.

'But we're *in* the country now,' said Alice, as if that proved there was no fun in eating out once you left the city limits.

She had abandoned hope of making contact with the previous, friendly Camilla. The detail about Sunday lunch was the only personal information divulged by this one, other snippets having come from her father.

By evening they were pottering together in the garden,

wreathed by gnats while watering the thirstier plants. Rod was walking to the headland.

There was a happy moment when Camilla asked: 'Alice, what are these huge daisies?'

And Alice delighted in the reply, 'Elizabeth, a variety of *chrysanthemum superbum*. My neighbour thinks they're super bums.'

After the laughter, Camilla thought for a while and then announced: 'I hated going to stay when Dad was with Ruth.'

'Oh?'

'I hate Ruth.'

A more moderate 'Oh?'

'But, of course, then Janetta came along and I had to see her too. It was too much.'

Alice risked a sideways glance. Camilla was tense.

Casually, Alice asked: 'Who was Janetta?'

'We have to say is not was. Mum says he doesn't want to marry her.'

'And you?'

'I say I don't care.'

'*Like hell you don't,*' thought Alice.

She hardened her heart against Rod and any nonsense about being sympathetic to him. Unfortunately, she had no means of judging why Camilla had told her. The old Camilla would have said it to be helpful. God knows why the new one had.

Alice caught her eye. 'Thank you,' she said softly.

Camilla blushed.

Rod returned, packed the car and said they ought to be on their way. He and Alice exchanged friendly pecks and Alice squeezed Camilla's hand. It pleased her greatly that the pressure was returned. Rod said he would phone if he was likely to be very late back, and he drove off.

Locking up, Alice realised she had not mentioned the prowler of two nights ago and was nervous of spending a night alone. Her worries were cut short by the telephone.

'Is that you, Alice?'

She recognised Reg Pennymoor's rich accent. 'Yes, how are you?'

'I've been hearing about the body in the car at Stark Point.'

'I was going to ring you tomorrow. I've had weekend visitors until a few minutes ago.'

He said: 'One of the men I worked with has a son in the force and he called me. I thought about going over there but Cassie said: "No, Pop, it's dark and you'll only be in the way".'

She was about to tell him what she had seen by lamplight and what had happened since but he rushed on.

'I had another call from my friend this evening. It's the Abletts' car all right but it's not a man in it, he says. They've decided it's a woman.'

Her head was swimming. His words were going on, adding detail and gossip and conjecture, but all she heard was muddled sound.

'Alice? You there?'

'Yes. Sorry. I'm . . . well, I'm rather taken aback, to tell the truth.'

'You're not the only one. Folk were settled in their minds it was George Ablett. And now we've got to change ourselves around and believe it's Delma.'

Alice failed. For hours after she came off the line she resisted the idea. Delma Ablett dead in the drain meant no race to freedom in her lover's arms, no secret life under an assumed name, nothing, and Alice was not ready to believe that.

She sat, the photograph in her hand, unwilling to give up her wild hopes for Delma. The imagined scenes were vivid as memory, relinquishing them was as hard as denying real events. The little face smiled out at her and the bracelet winked in recorded sunlight. Yet if what Reg Pennymoor said was true, the woman and her wonderful car had lain half a century in a few feet of water in the heart of the village.

The phrase jarred, then the absurdity made her laugh. '*The heart of the village? This village has no heart, not geographically and not figuratively. If ever there was a heartless village, it's this one.'*

A faint sound interrupted her. She cocked her head. Again a slight sound, like a muffled step. Alice cast around for a weapon. The poker. She lifted it from the hearth and moved catlike to the kitchen. The bolts on the back door were undone and they ought not to be. She raised a hand to push one home.

And that was when she knew someone was standing on the other side of the door. A gasping breath broke the silence. She listened to it, uncertain what to do. Her hand was poised by the bolt but a question grew into a certainty and she pressed her face close to the door and whispered his name.

'Joe? Is that you?'

'Yes.'

She flung open the door and pulled him inside.

He was in an appalling state: filthy, bedraggled, his clothes more tattered than ever. And the *smell*.

'Oh, Joe, whatever's happened to you? Where have you been?'

She pulled out a wooden chair and gestured to him to sit.

'No,' he said, indicating his messy clothes.

'It's all right. Sit down.'

He sat, heavily.

'You haven't eaten, have you?'

She did not like the way she was reacting, not the goggling or the pathetic questioning or the mothering. But he was plainly worn out and it was a fair guess he was famished.

There was a pizza in the fridge, bought because she and Rod had assumed all teenagers loved pizza. Camilla had turned it down, so Joe Keenthorne got it instead. Rod had brought beer and Joe got one of those too.

While the pizza was heating up Alice asked had the police seen him or had anyone else? He said not.

She wondered what would happen to her if the police arrived now and caught her giving supper to a wanted man. But they had not exactly warned her against showing kindness. No, they had been stressing the physical danger she would risk in meeting Joe.

Alice looked at him. Broken down. Drained. But not defeated, not that. If he were defeated he would not have come to her, she felt sure.

Then a doubt arose. How much did he know? He had been in hiding and might not be aware what had been happening in the village. How would he respond if she told him what she knew?

She remembered Rod arguing that Joe was an oddball and unpredictable. A tingle of apprehension ran through her as she realised that if she told him things he did not wish to hear, he might lash out. The poker was to hand, a ready weapon. She could be badly injured. Killed.

And she remembered the policeman saying: 'He's suspected of killing two people. By anybody's reckoning, he's a dangerous man.'

Alice sat opposite Joe. 'You realise the police are looking for you?'

'Not now, they've gone away for the night.'

'They went to your house and they're telling people they want to talk to you.'

'They told you?'

'Yes. And . . .' How to tell him this without risking a flare-up? But it had to be said. 'I should warn you there are people in the village who . . . well, they'll harm you if they find you before the police do.'

He shrugged. 'Jacko. Fat friends of his.'

'They spoke to me, Joe. They were really threatening.'

He grunted dismissively.

Alice blurted out what she needed to say. 'Joe, I think you should go to the police. Don't wait for them to track you down, it'll be better if you go to them. You'll be safe then, otherwise you risk God knows what if Jacko catches you.'

He shook his head. 'I can't go to the police, Alice. Not after what happened last time. They picked on me and they'll do it again.'

Exasperated, she argued: 'But, Joe, don't you see it's hopeless for you to stay at Stark Point? Your only chance is to go voluntarily to the police.'

He jerked away from her, but the kitchen was small and there was nowhere to go unless he ran out into the night. Afraid of that, she offered another idea.

'I'll drive you into town or anywhere you want to go.'

'No, Alice, this is my home. I don't want to go anywhere. They want to get the house off me, that's what it is. Blame Joe and get his house. It's worth a lot of money, that house, or will be once a few repairs are done. Bill Chilton wants it. He farms the land now, gets it cheap, but that's not enough for the Chiltons. Oh no, they want me out so they can get the house too.'

'Look, Joe, now the police have found the body in the car they're going to search for you until they find you. Today it was just a few enquiries but once they decide on a thorough search they'll come in with dogs and lots of men and you won't have a chance.'

He stared at her as though what she said was incomprehensible. Alice sighed.

'Oh, Joe, what can I say to persuade you?'

'I shan't tell them anything.'

'*Which is how you handled trouble last time,*' she thought.

Aloud she said: 'Who's your solicitor? At least let me telephone him.'

'He died backalong.'

'Oh.'

Before she could summon another idea, he said: 'I'm not telling the police anything, Alice, but I'm going to tell you. For the book.'

She nodded automatically, although the book was her last concern. 'Yes, we have a lot more work to do on that.'

'Alice, I've come now because I want to tell you the story.' He looked around. 'Where's that notebook of yours?'

'Oh, er, I'll fetch it.'

She ran upstairs, rummaged, returned. He was as she had left him, although mad ideas had chased through her mind: Joe prowling the house, running off or stealing.

Across the table from him she uncapped the pen. 'Off you go, then.' Her voice was inappropriately bright but he did not notice.

'This is the story of how George killed Delma,' he said.

Alice frowned. '*George* killed Delma?'

'Who else would have done it? Of course he killed her.'

'But . . .'

A sneer crept over his face. 'You think I did it, don't you?'

'I . . . I don't know. I don't know what to think.'

He became agitated, alarming her. 'You think I did it. That's what they all think and now they've got you thinking it too.'

He struggled to his feet.

Alice pleaded. 'No, don't go. Please, Joe. Tell me about George and Delma. For the book.'

As usual, mention of the book changed him. Alice felt cheap. She was no writer and a book was unlikely. Even if there were to be one, the chance of it proving his innocence was negligible. But she knew too that dangling the prospect of a book was the only hope of anyone ever hearing what befell the Abletts. She made up her mind to squeeze the story out of him, as much of it as she could before he was arrested or dragged away by the local lynch mob, and to settle up with her conscience later.

Chapter Nineteen

Joe's Story

'See, Alice, they weren't the perfect couple. Some folk like to claim it but they aren't family. I reckon I saw more of what went on at Perrotts Farm than anyone.

Twice when I went over there they were having a big row. Delma crying, George stamping up and down. She wanted summat and he couldn't pay for it, that's what caused the trouble.

The car? Yes, her father owned that car and handed it over to her to drive around in. Delma let folk think George had paid out for it.

"What do I want with a car?" he used to say. I can hear him now. "What do I want with a car when I've got the van?"

But Delma pushed for a car, saying folk would look up to him if he had a nice car, and then one day she drove up in that great big Talbot and said her father had bought it for her to use. George was fuming. Nobody got a fair word out of him for days. Delma was happy enough, though. Got what she wanted, that girl, and if her husband wouldn't give it then her daddy did.

So in a way the trouble between them was money and in another way it wasn't. I think it was more that George was trying to make Delma see sense. She was only a farmer's wife but in her own mind she was summat special.

No, I don't understand why she married George either. But you saw what it said in that newspaper, about how she'd made herself a leading figure – those were the words, weren't they? If she'd married into a bigger place she'd have been nobody. There'd have been up-class families and folk already doing all the things she did here. No nonsense about putting on her hat and driving up to Chapel Field to open the fête, like she was the lady of the manor come from the big house three miles away.

Well, the rows. Like I said, Alice, I heard two bad ones. I reckon the car arrived shortly after the first but, anyway, the second one was definitely after he bought the Little Farm. The council wouldn't let him build her a big new house out there and Delma wouldn't accept it. Got it into her head it was George's fault, either summat he should have done to make sure of it or else he'd done summat to upset a councillor. Screaming, carrying on. I walked out of the yard and up the lane, came back and they were still going at it. But you know how the farmhouse is placed, you have to be close to realise what's going on. From the lane there was only the sea.

Now then, we get to the trouble that put an end to it. This time it looked like she'd been thinking the way I had and asking herself why she was married to George. His money had been spent and since she couldn't get her way over the Little Farm she lost interest. We didn't see so much of her at the Point.

One day I met George on the way to market. Saw his van outside a pub and stopped to have a word. We'd sorted out our differences about grazing the Little Farm and I had an idea I wanted to put to him. He wasn't in the bar so out I went into the garden and there was George, face like thunder, standing under a tree.

Seeing that, I thought I'd better forget asking him and be on my way. But that wasn't easy, with only the two of us there.

"Hello, George," I said. And because of the way he looked at me I said: "Don't look so happy, George."

Then it came out. Delma's having an affair with a man from

over Taunton Deane, she's denying it but George has been told by someone who's seen her with him. Well, I didn't know what to say to him. I mean, if I were honest I don't know why he picked her in the first place, and now she'd made him spend his money perhaps he'd be better off without her. But it didn't matter what I said, he wasn't listening.

What's that? No, Alice, I didn't see her with anybody. George believed the story, though. He certainly did because a few times he mentioned it to me, not coming out with it direct but, because of that day in the pub garden, it was obvious what he meant. Preying on his mind, it was. But they could put on a show, those two. To see George going around, you wouldn't have known anything was wrong. Didn't tell anyone apart from me and I didn't have cause to mention it.

Then one evening, late, there he was at my door. In a terrible state, he was. Panicky, couldn't catch his breath, his clothes soaking wet because it was raining hard. Wouldn't come in, though, and wouldn't say outright what was up.

"Joe, summat dreadful's happened." That's how he put it. Not that he'd done it, just that it had happened, like it was nobody's fault.

"What's happened, George?" But, do you know, he didn't say.

"Listen to me," he said, "you don't know anything."

And I laughed in his face because, of course, I didn't know anything because he wasn't telling me.

Then he got me by the arm, shaking me, pushing his face into mine, very upset.

"For God sake, Joe, you stupid bastard," he said. Yes, that's how he spoke to me then, like we were having a row.

I ripped my sleeve out of his grip. Even in our trouble over the Little Farm he hadn't laid hands on me.

"Listen," he said, "I'm telling you to say you don't know anything. There are going to be questions and you're going to say you don't know anything. Do you understand what I'm saying?"

And he had me up against the door jamb and I was trying to calm him down, saying: "Yes, yes, all right." I could smell the whisky on his breath but I didn't think he was drunk, only very agitated.

"You haven't seen me tonight," he said. "Remember that. I didn't come here. Do you understand?"

And I was saying "Yes, yes, I understand." Only I didn't because he hadn't explained.

Then he said: "I'm going now, Joe. We won't see each other again."

"What do you mean?"

And he said: "Nor Delma, neither. She's gone."

"Gone? Gone to that fellow over Taunton way?" I wouldn't normally have brought that up but this was a peculiar situation, with him hinting and not making himself plain.

"No," he said, the words all coming in a tumble then, "but it's on account of him. She's dead, Joe. And I'm going away now. And you, you don't know anything. Just remember that. Promise now, Joe."

He started to move away. Well, I'd taken my boots off, being indoors, and the yard was wet so I didn't want to go after him. I said: "Wait on, George, you haven't told me what's up."

But he didn't wait. Rushed out into the rain and that's the last I saw of him.

Well, I couldn't believe it, see. I knew he'd said she was dead but I was thinking I'd got him wrong or he was drunk. Because, sure as I was standing there, I couldn't believe it.

You can imagine what I did then.

Oh, no. No, I didn't go over to Perrotts Farm, not right away. I sat there a while thinking what he'd said and how he'd looked and trying to decide what it was all about. George and Delma were going round and round in my head. Same thing when I went to bed. Round and round.

In the morning, though, before dawn I walked the back

way to his place and went up to the house and there were no lights on. And I thought: "*Well, you're a fool, Joe Keenthorne, because if they're all right and in bed they* won't *have any lights on.*" So I went home, walking down the lane but not seeing anybody. And that's how I left it.

A few days later, when I hadn't noticed her driving around or him going about the village, I thought to try again. But I remembered what he said, I wasn't supposed to know anything, so I was ready to say I hadn't seen him since we spoke on market day about the saw. Only nobody saw me and I didn't need to say anything. The doors of the house were closed, there was nothing unusual to be seen through the windows, and the car was gone from the barn.

I had to keep reminding myself: "George said she's dead." And slowly I understood. Because of the state he was in, the business about her being dead and him going away, it seemed he'd killed her, see. If she'd killed herself or had an accident he'd have done things differently.

Ah, yes. I wondered that too, but I can't say why he came to me. He didn't ask me outright to look after the animals or keep an eye on the place. For a while I thought maybe that's what he had in mind to do and then forgot. But he'd been going on about me not having seen him and not knowing anything, so how could I start poking my nose into Perrotts Farm business without showing I knew they weren't there? I let his men carry on with the farm and I kept my head low.

And all the time, Alice, I was expecting a toot on the horn of that car of hers and Delma waving at me and George sitting beside her like a fat rich king. Day by day, though, it was becoming more obvious that what George had spoken was truth. Dead or alive, they'd gone.

Why had he told me? That question burned in my brain and still does. The nearest I came to understanding it was remembering what my mother used to say about him. "Don't you tell George any of your secrets, Joe, because there's a man who can't hold onto his own." I reckon it was simple as that, Alice. He had to tell somebody.

See, there was no call for him to tell me about Delma and her fellow over to Taunton Deane. Yet, George being George, he let it out.

When the police came, and it was official the Abletts were missing, I waited to see who'd come forward to say George had told him about Delma's affair or that George had called on them that last night. Nobody said a word.

Gossip and rumours, as you'd expect, but nobody was willing to say they'd had any of it direct from George. The police went to see Iris Dottrell, I do know that. They asked her: "What's this story about seeing Mrs Ablett with a man in town?" They told me later Iris insisted on it. "Oh yes," she said, "they were having a meal in the County Hotel." She's an odd one, always has been. Touched. Makes up big stories and believes them, even if nobody else does.

No, I haven't forgotten the car in the rhine, Alice, but I wanted you to understand how it was at the time. You see, folk are right when they talk about the mystery. Apart from that strange visit I had from George, they're exactly right. The Abletts just vanished.

George hadn't said about the rhine and I didn't know. When they weren't found, and nobody in the whole of the country had seen their car, I set to thinking. What could he have done with her, and done before he came over to my place? He was untidy and soaked, puffed out, but he wasn't soiled as if he'd been digging. When he grabbed me his hands weren't dirty or blistered.

All the farm buildings had been searched but nobody had thought to dredge the rhines. Mind, it's only local folk who know how deep they can be and what care you need not to slip in. I've lost a heifer that way, and Mrs Aley and her husband lost a little lad who fell in and was smothered with the weed and not found for three hours.

I said to myself: "If George killed her and hid the body, then she's in the rhine."

A body that's in for a while will float up to the top, though. Anybody local knows that too. So if a body isn't coming up, it's held down somehow. Tied with stones, maybe. Or trapped inside a car.

Knowing what George had said, I could work it out. Everybody else was looking for the pair of them, not one murdering the other and going off alone.

But to finish with that, Alice, I guessed he'd done it at the bend because, when I asked myself where I'd do it if it were me, that was the obvious place. A dangerous spot where other vehicles had slipped in. They toppled backwards while trying to pass each other or they tipped in head first if they came up too fast. The verge was just mud, no grip, very easy to slide in. And I thought: "*Yes, George, that's where I'd push her in and I reckon you did too.*" Oh, and another thing, only a local man would know which rhines are neglected and which are dredged every few years. They don't keep them all up, see.'

Oh no, I didn't nose around there. But you're right, Alice, about me giving the land for the bend to be straightened. The story isn't quite as they tell it, though, because Delma got George to offer it a couple of years before, after Mrs Aley's boy died.

As for what became of George, I can't say more than when I talked to you the first time. Nobody saw him walking inland but it's possible he went over the bay to the coast road.

All right, I admit I didn't tell you the whole truth before. But ask yourself, Alice, how could I? Until Bill Chilton's lad landed on the roof of Delma's car, I only had a theory and it wouldn't have done me any good having it proved.

No, I mean that, Alice. No good at all. And it's no use you pestering me to go to the police because I won't go.

No. No, Alice. I can't do that.

It's you that's getting it wrong. Think about it, Alice. They've found the body of Delma Ablett. If it were George, maybe I'd talk to them. But they're saying it's a woman and soon they'll be saying it's Delma. I wasn't tried for murdering her, was I? Which means they can charge me with it now.'

Chapter Twenty

Alice blamed herself for what happened next.

She kept urging him to get away from the village. 'If you won't go to the police, then just *go*. It isn't safe for you here. Jacko and those men, they'll kill you, I know they will. Please, Joe, escape while you can.'

He brushed her concerns away, making her increasingly adamant. '*Please,* Joe, while you have the chance.'

'My place is here, Alice.'

'They don't want you here, Joe. You'll either be arrested or killed. Why won't you believe me?'

She was almost weeping with frustration. That scene he had described, of a frantic George Ablett begging him to grasp the importance of saying nothing, was palpably true. Her own experience was proving it.

'I've got a place they won't find. They haven't found me yet and they won't, you'll see.'

'But you can't live like a fugitive, hiding out God knows where, sneaking around at night begging food.'

Immediately the unfortunate word was out he seized on it, shouting he wasn't a beggar and wouldn't have come to her if he'd thought she'd call him that. His vehemence was frightening.

'I own the farmhouse, I've got the Abletts' money, I was in the will.'

She tried to placate him, but he was raging about being accused of begging when everyone at Stark Point knew he was a rich man.

She thought: '*Oh God, that's not what they think. They think you're mad, Joe. They think you killed to get that money. And I've got to get you out of my house before the predictions come true and you kill me too.*'

On the point of opening the back door, he rounded on her again.

'You aren't fit to write that book of mine, Alice, you don't know how to go about it. You ought to believe what I tell you and write it so other folk believe it too. No use you listening to Iris Dottrell, she can't remember anything. What folk don't know they make up. But *you* – you had a chance to write the truth . . .'

Defending herself, she tried to drag him back to reality. 'Joe, I can't write a book that's only your word. I must hear everyone else's stories too.'

'If I could do the words myself I'd write down what I say, not what the rest of Stark Point makes up.'

'Yes, I know, but autobiography is different. My book is supposed to be about . . .'

'*Your* book? What book's that, then? You're meant to be writing my book down for me. Well, not any longer, you're not. I was a fool to trust you with it.'

She snapped. 'You haven't trusted me. Everything you tell me, you change when it suits you. You let me think Delma ran away in the car, but today you say you guessed she was in the rhine. How can I take your word?'

Her outburst had transfixed him. Eyes hard as pebbles locked on hers, as though he had discovered something shocking.

She moved behind the kitchen table, alert for any movement he might make, but it was his petrified calmness that was unnerving.

Eventually he said: 'You think I killed them. You're like all the rest.'

'I . . . I don't know.' Recklessly she added: 'Do you know the truth yourself?'

This stung him. He flung himself out into the darkness. Alice bounded across and bolted the door.

The kitchen stank of his filthy clothes and unwashed body, a peculiarly rank smell of the sea. She dumped his pizza dish in the sink and ran water on it, tossed the beer cans into the waste bin, and wiped over the kitchen table and his chair. Afraid to open a window, in case he was loitering, she ferreted out an air freshener inherited with the cottage, sprayed, and retreated to the sitting room.

Her mind was in turmoil. She had said things she ought not to have done, knowing his vulnerability. He was under attack, hunted and probably not in his right mind, yet she had thrown those accusations at him because he had made a fool of her. Alice was bitterly disappointed in herself.

The telephone rang. She remembered Rod and his trip with Camilla, and her spirits rose at the prospect of company, to protect her from her folly and Joe's retribution.

'Hello?'

Unbroken silence.

Fear stroked her spine. She left the receiver on the table and walked away. There were tricks you could play on silent callers but the simplest was the most effective: leave them listening to your silence.

Inevitably, she compiled a list of potential telephone nuisances. Joe was not on it because sneaky telephone calls were not made within minutes of heated argument. She entered Jacko and his cohorts and added Iris Dottrell.

'*People make silent calls for two reasons,*' she thought, '*to annoy you or to check you're home before they carry out another act. Time will tell which this is.*'

She made camomile tea, took it to the spare bedroom and switched on her computer. While it was opening the Keenthorne file, she peered out of a window. Visibility was poor, the sky overcast. Beyond the pool of light from the kitchen anything might lurk. She slid up the sash and listened to the comforting rhythm of the sea. Low tide but it sounded close this evening, the other side of her garden wall and encroaching fast.

Back at her desk, she was disturbed by a blank page. Her title, *Joe's Story,* was at the top but nothing followed. The file was available, the text missing. Alice scolded herself, unable to see how she could have been so incompetent. The longer she worried at it the clearer it became she could not. To wipe an entire file was one thing, human error or computer error could account for that. But to retain a file and only two words required intervention.

She asked the machine when the file had previously been opened. It flashed up a date and a time.

Alice groaned. She had been at home and so had Rod and Camilla. Well, she could discount Rod. He could be fairly blamed for many bad deeds but not this one. Camilla it was, then.

Fearful, she systematically checked her other files. Intact. The girl had sabotaged only the book. They had talked about it early on Saturday evening, the one subject in which Camilla showed interest. Later she had deleted the text.

Alice's response was confused, partly because the incident demonstrated how easy it would be for her to abandon the book. The text was safe, anyway, because it was copied onto a floppy disk kept in her bedroom. Camilla had made a gesture but she had not caused damage. Alice fetched the floppy disk to confirm this, then hid it again.

'Tell Rod when he comes or shut up about it? Say nothing unless prodded,' she decided.

Thinking of Rod made her wonder whether he was trying to telephone, as promised, to say what time he would return. She tapped 1471 on the telephone, in the faint hope that whoever had called her had forgotten to withhold their number. An electronic voice chanted that her it had not been recorded, which might mean it was from a mobile. Jacko owned a mobile while Iris, who did not leave the house, had no need of one.

Again the telephone rang and nobody spoke. When it rang for the third time she ignored it, letting it purr twenty times before the caller gave up.

Alice kept busy, making notes on Joe Keenthorne's visit and the bitter words they had exchanged. The prospect of a book seemed dim, although his consent would not be required if she chose to proceed alone. She deferred decisions. It was late, the sabotaged file and the nonsense with the telephone had set her nerves on edge, and she was not in the frame of mind to weigh options. Her plans stretched no further ahead than finishing her notes and having a good night's sleep.

Rod had talked of hiding her key outside rather than wake her if he was extremely late, but she had resisted.

'Pippin, you can put it on the ledge in the woodshed, where you did the other time.'

'Oh no, that was before my car was attacked. I'd be much too worried to do that again.'

So he was to telephone and she was to wait up for him. She looked accusingly at the telephone. *'Suppose it was Rod, failing to get through?'*

But she could not dismiss the silent calls. It might have been Rod the last time but not the others. As if in answer, the telephone chirrupped again.

'Hello?'

'Alice? Hi, Rod here. I tried you just now but there was no answer.'

He sounded peeved that she had not been sitting beside the telephone like a teenager awaiting his call.

She lied that she had not got there in time.

He switched to brisk. 'Look, something's come up and it'll be more convenient if I stay here overnight.'

'Fine.'

'You're sure you don't mind?' Now he was doing apologetic.

'Not in the least.'

'But I'll be down tomorrow.' Soothing, this time.

'Honestly . . .' She avoided saying that honestly she did not care.

He leaped in, misconstruing, thinking he had heard a sarcastic 'Oh, *honestly!*' kind of honestly.

'Yes, I know, love, I promised I'd be there. But I'll get away as early as I can tomorrow. I should be with you by late morning. I'm afraid that's the best I can do.'

Who, she wondered, was listening? Camilla's mother? Or Janetta, the girlfriend Camilla had warned her about? Or yet another? One thing was certain. Rod was speaking to impress someone other than Alice.

She wished she could think of a barbed remark, the sort one only conjures up when the moment has passed. It would have been nice to leave him worrying how much she knew.

As usual, she left it too late. She came off the line dissatisfied. Unprepared, she had let him present someone or other with the impression she was a clinging female fretting at his absence.

Well, she had never been that.

Spurred by her annoyance, she whisked through the wardrobe, intending to squash everything of his into his bag, and hand it over on his arrival, along with instructions to take himself home to Bath without pause.

No bag, though. In fact, there was curiously little of Rod. Paperback novels on the bedside table, a pair of trousers and a few shirts hanging up, plus a muddle of socks and underwear on a shelf. Not even a spare jacket or shoes.

He was travelling light for a man who used to be dominated by possessions: hellbent on earning them, buying them and flaunting them. In a flight of fancy she saw him building a hedge of belongings around himself. Higher and higher it rose, a barricade protecting him from the more sensitive aspects of life.

Then the downfall. A television set buckled under pressure of the pile above it; a camera was squeezed out and toppled down; a car was skewed and teetered, and the CD player balanced on its bonnet slipped sideways. The edifice was collapsing to the accompaniment of a plasticky, crunchy chorus. Rod, encircled but increasingly exposed, was dodging flying debris.

She burst out laughing at her own wicked humour, but did not feel unkind because there had been plenty of occasions when she had been too sore to laugh at his frantic accumulation. When Ruth had swept him away, all his things had gone too, and it was Alice who had suffered from having her surroundings stripped.

'Not suffered equally,' she thought, *'because they were less important to me in the first place.'*

At the time, she had comforted herself that she and Rod might have split up without Ruth's interference because they had already been spinning apart. He had become more absorbed in his work than she had ever dreamed possible, and sacrificed his spare time to tracking down the latest and most expensive baubles. When she had teased, he had declared them the rewards of his industry.

With hindsight she thought it likelier they were his way of affirming his talent and effort. After all, it was not much of a reward to be the owner of a cruiser you were too busy to cruise or a fast car that could never, legally, be driven to the hilt. Pathetically, he was satisfied by being able to glance over his extravagances and tell himself: 'I made so much money I could afford to buy that.'

And now, thought Alice, they were once more travelling in a similar direction, like planets who meet and part and meet again. She lived on little and did not deeply care, as long as there was enough to meet her modest bills. He, if every word he told her was true, currently had even less. They both found qualities they enjoyed in Stark Point, a scene outside the material world. It provided the balm he needed after the most bruising period of his life.

But enough. She hardened her heart and plotted anew to remove him from her cottage the very next day.

Meanwhile, she turned off the room light, which reflected

badly on her screen, opened a file and added a paragraph to an ongoing letter to her mother. Selective in what she reported, she had made up her mind to mention Camilla's visit as well as Rod's, but to skip Camilla's poor behaviour and to say only that Rod's affair with Ruth had broken up and he had taken a liking to Stark Point. Her mother had already heard that Charles detested it.

A sound from outside caught her ear. In the dullness of the cloudy evening she saw movement at the side of the house. Her fists clenched.

'Oh God, don't let it be Joe. I can't cope with another visit.'

Joe, though, had come to the back door and waited to be admitted. Whoever was outside this time was near the woodshed and not approaching the house itself.

Alice debated whether to go downstairs, which meant putting on lights. They would probably scare off her prowler although she would not know because the room she was in was the only one looking down the side of the house. Confident the doors were secure, she decided to stay as she was and have a chance of identifying the figure.

Viewed from this awkward angle, it appeared short and fat, its outfit topped with a brimmed hat. It went out of sight in the shadow of a tree.

She let out her breath in a sigh of sheer exasperation. To have seen the figure so well but not to have identified him!

Straight away, she understood why. *'He's deliberately disguised himself.'*

Realisation confirmed her suspicion this was a person bent on causing trouble, almost certainly the wretch who had messed up her car.

She slipped into her bedroom and checked the garden from one window, then felt her way to the small one overlooking the front. A tree, the one Charles warned was too close to the house to do it any good, obstructed her view of the garage.

Returning to the spare room, she heard a sound she

recognised very well: the creak of hinges in need of oiling. Her front door.

Alice was rigid, even her whirling apprehension was at a standstill. After a moment, during which her ears convinced her someone was below her in the sitting room, she reached out a hand and switched off the screen. She did not want him attracted, mothlike, to where she waited.

The temerity of burglars was mystifying to her. How could a man have the gall to enter a home and help himself to its contents? Well, this burglar was due for disappointment. No television and, consequently, no video. No fancy radio or trendy kitchen equipment. No furnishings or pictures worth carting away. Apart from her computer, there was nothing worth stealing.

Obsolete, it had been bought from a colleague at the radio station when he moved up to classier things. How much of a fight should she put up for it?

'None, better let the insurance company replace it.'

Backing off, she pressed into the gap between the wardrobe and the end wall. Footsteps were crossing the kitchen tiles. Unless he continued out of the back door, he was virtually certain to climb the stairs.

Alice was steady, having taken the decision to relinquish her one valuable possession for the sake of identifying the thief. She felt a spurious power, knowing what was about to happen whereas the intruder would be taken by surprise.

She rehearsed him unplugging the equipment and carrying it away, perhaps in a bag to prevent anyone he met knowing what he was holding. But before he left the cottage, she was going to accost him, switching on lights and terrifying him. Naturally, he would escape because she dared not reveal her presence until he was downstairs. Tackling him any earlier would be foolhardy, especially as she was already trapped in a corner of the room.

Until events began to play themselves out, it did not occur to her that the scenario might be totally different.

A stair creaked. Soon after, a loose board on the landing.

Alice was holding her breath, failing to obey her commands to breathe lightly and quietly. Her pulse was thudding in her ears.

No one approached. From her bedroom came the sound of the top drawer in her chest, the one that stuck and had to be jiggled.

An inventory of its contents passed through her mind: a hairdryer with nowhere else to go, packets of pills ditto, ribbons for her hair, and the one item that mattered – a plastic box of floppy disks. The Joe Keenthorne story was in it but so were personal and, ultimately, more important things.

No other drawers were being opened, the search seemed to have stopped. She was relieved, at any rate, that her burglar wasn't searching for women's underwear. But he couldn't possibly be interested in her hairdryer and so forth, therefore he had come for the disks.

Alice wavered. It was one thing to be a silent witness, ready to spring out and alarm him, but quite another to challenge him as he rummaged in her bedroom. Yet she was beginning to realise she had no choice. Perhaps, even as she dithered, he was damaging the disks, scoring them or forcing them out of shape, rendering them useless.

Logic cut through her fantasy. '*If he's a burglar, why doesn't he put them in his pocket and go?*'

She stifled a moan. Oh, it was impossible to know what to do.

Inaction was out of the question, she must do something. Standing around like a fool while her property was damaged was ridiculous, and calling for help was impossible because the telephone was on the ground floor.

She was poised to charge into the bedroom and take the consequences, when a figure passed between her and the window at the other end of the room. He was here, at last.

Reverting to her first plan, she shrank into the gap beside the wardrobe. She could make out a short bulky shape close to her desk. A second later a button clicked and the screen glowed greenish. By this weird light Alice watched the fat burglar sit down at the computer. All she saw of him was a chunky shape and the outline of a concealing hat. Her horrified thoughts flew to the squat muscular friends of Jacko, and it took a few seconds for her to register the whirring and whizzing of electronic servants following instructions.

A disk was being entered. Realisation galvanised her because she was sure it was one from her bedroom and the intruder was about to wipe it.

She leaped out of her hiding place, catching her elbow on the edge of the wardrobe so that her whoop of triumph blended with a howl of pain.

'Stop that!'

The intruder jerked off the chair in fright and tumbled to the floor. Alice slammed one hand down on the desk lamp, her other plucking the hat and hurling it up the room. Careless of her safety, she charged round the chair and cut off his retreat.

Then she stood and stared, not believing what she saw.

'Iris?'

Iris Dottrell lay crumpled on the carpet. She looked old and defeated, and swathed around her was a leather coat several sizes too large. Now the hat had been wrenched off, her hair sprang out from her head in a raggy perm. She made no effort to rise and when she spoke she was practically whining.

'You've been here all the time!' Absurdly, she was accusing Alice of cheating.

Alice was icy. 'I live here. What's your excuse?'

A toss of the head. Iris proposed to ignore the subject. Infuriated, Alice produced a torrent of lies.

'I've already spoken to the police about my computer being interfered with, my garage door damaged . . .'

'You can't blame me.'

'Oh, yes I can, the broken door catch was found in your bin.'

The dustbin evidence proved conclusive, as far as Iris was concerned. Instead of denying, she justified.

'You were warned, Alice, to keep away from Joe Keenthorne and that Ablett business. But you wouldn't leave it, would you? Now see where you've got us. Delma dead in the rhine and Joe chased away like an animal. If you'd only listened, if you'd left well alone . . .'

'Rubbish.' She held out her hand and spoke bossily. 'Give me my disks, and anything else you've gathered up since you broke into my house.'

Iris bridled. 'I didn't break in here. I come and go with the key Bella gave me.'

'*What?*'

'I've had it years. She didn't leave it to anyone else in her will, did she? So it's mine.'

Gulping down protest, Alice again asked her to hand over what she had stolen. When that failed, she tried to elicit what Iris had been planning to do with the computer.

Iris sniffed. She started to get up but the voluminous coat impeded her and she flumped back on the floor, looking like a hideous doll, a creature with a massive body on spindly legs.

Wearily, Alice said, 'All right, Iris. I can guess what you were up to. You were going to wipe a floppy disk as you previously wiped the Joe Keenthorne file on the hard disk. Every venal act you've done has been to dissuade me from helping Joe write about his life.'

Iris shrugged. She struggled to her knees and stayed there, coughing.

Alice felt no sympathy for this false friend who had deceived her and committed criminal acts against her. Then she softened. The woman was unstable and if Alice had mishandled the situation, it was not entirely Iris's fault. On the other hand, Alice recognised this as her best chance to wring information out of her.

Over the next fifteen minutes she extracted answers, or at least confessions that confirmed answers she suggested. Early on, she was glad to discover she was mistaken about the timing on Sunday, when someone interfered with the Keenthorne file, and Camilla was exonerated. Also, Iris owned up to the silent telephone calls.

'I only come here while you're out. That's how I check.'

'But my car's in the garage. How could I be out at this time of day without it?'

'There's a stronger lock now, isn't there? I couldn't see inside the garage.'

When details had been tidied away, Alice bounced off at a tangent, asking about the impetus for Iris's extraordinary activities. The key to it appeared to be the Ablett business, but how was she to unlock Iris's secrets?

Inspired, she said: 'Sergeant Pennymoor has been telling me all about the Abletts and the failure to convict Joe Keenthorne of murder.'

By using Pennymoor's name she was borrowing the authority of the police. Iris's attention sharpened.

'I remember him.'

Alice said sternly: 'You were too young, Iris.'

'Fourteen.'

'Oh?' Previously Iris had said she was 'only a young girl'.

Being fourteen changed the case. Look how five years had altered Camilla from a sweetly compliant soul to a fractious teenager wielding power over adults.

Alice folded her arms in an apparently casual gesture. 'Tell me what you told Reg Pennymoor, Iris.'

'Why do you want to hear it from me if he's been telling you everything?'

'Because I want to see whether you both have the same story.'

Iris scrabbled but failed to stand up and settled back on the floor, her twiggy legs poking out from the mound of leather. She was wearing the muddy brown shoes Alice had repeatedly noticed in the entrance hall at Ham Cottage, but without spotting the anomaly of a housebound woman getting her footware dirty.

With the half-shrug the Dottrells used when they were ready to deal with a problem, Iris began. 'I told Sergeant Pennymoor I'd seen Delma and that man she was going with. I was a waitress in the Country Hotel, part-time it was, and one lunchtime she was sitting at my table four with a man.'

'Who was he?'

'How do I know? She didn't introduce me. Didn't even say "Hello, Iris", which you'd think she ought to have done, knowing we both lived at Stark Point.'

'Weren't there any clues who he was?'

'He wasn't George Ablett, so what did it matter who he was?'

'I see. And . . . er . . . did you tell people what you'd seen?' Silly question because the rumour had run in every direction and after Delma disappeared it was granted the status of fact.

'Yes, and I told Sergeant Pennymoor too. She must have gone off with him, I said.' A pause, before she added: 'Which he believed, I may say.'

'*Yes,*' thought Alice, '*you're efficient at persuading people to believe what you make up.*'

Iris said: 'I didn't work at the County for long. There was a fight in the dining room one lunchtime and I told them I wasn't willing to put up with that. Folk throwing pepper pots around and all because there wasn't enough salt in their potatoes . . . I said "I won't put up with this", and I walked out. My mother said I was to stay in and look after her. She was poorly, you see, for years and years.'

Alice also saw that it was risky to rely on any of this. The story was a twist on the one Mary had told her, about a fight in a pub where Iris worked. The sickly mother urging the daughter to become nursemaid was an echo of Iris's own pull on Mary. Patterns do evolve in people's lives but, in the Dottrells' case, it was wise to treat all information with scepticism.

Oblivious to Alice's doubts, Iris elaborated on the fight. The more she said, the more closely it resembled the pub story. Alice wondered whether Mary, who had passed on the pub story, realised this. Apart from that, which story had Iris begun to tell first? Perhaps the pub incident was genuine and had gained her attention, encouraging her to invent the other one.

Iris added an episode to the crazy tale of diners lobbing cruets. 'Do you know, Alice, one of the men who was there lives at Stark Point and he didn't lift a finger to help me? I was like a target, with them chucking things and me pinned against the door to the kitchen, but he didn't care.'

Alice's only doubt now was whether both incidents were inventions or only one, but she looked as startled as Iris hoped. 'Who was he?'

A sly look crept over her face. 'You know him, Alice.'

'I do?'

'Oh yes, there's not many you're friendly with around here but you know this one.'

'You don't mean . . .'

Iris pounced. 'Yes! Joe Keenthorne. He was there and he didn't lift a finger.'

'But . . .' The preposterous lie was obvious. Joe had never been a man to eat in the best hotel in town. It was unlikely he had ever set foot over the threshold.

Iris had convinced herself, though, and of worse besides. 'And a man who wouldn't help a woman being attacked, well, you can see how he'd do away with Delma, can't you?'

But Alice was thinking: *'Not easily, I can't. But I can see what a meddlesome nuisance you've been to him. Oh, and to me too and a good few others.'*

She lured Iris into admission. 'You hate him, don't you? Is that why you pestered him by putting newspaper cuttings about the case through his door?'

'He shouldn't be living there. He should have been hanged.'

'By why, Iris? You know he didn't kill anybody.'

The woman blinked at her, then lowered her eyes. More softly she said: 'He could have stopped it and he didn't. He heard her screaming and he went away, up the lane and home. Didn't lift a finger.'

Alice's pulse quickened, because Joe thought he was the only person who had overheard the Abletts' fierce rows.

'Did you tell Sergeant Pennymoor that, Iris?'

'Not him, one of the others. A fat man with a moustache. They went round the houses asking who'd seen anything, and I told him I'd seen Joe running away from the farm in the rain, hiding himself under a sack. I told them everything I knew. And then that Ralphie Aley said it too, how that was the day he'd chased his bullock around George Ablett's farmyard.'

Aghast, Alice was speechless.

Iris decided she had endured enough and made a huge effort to stand, levering herself up by clinging to the desk which rocked and juddered but, fortunately, supported her. Alice saw the unflattering garment properly for the first time. It was a man's leather jacket, a normal size but huge on weedy Iris. There were pockets inside and out, and things jutted out of them. Alice demanded everything was handed over.

Straightfaced, she took possession of her computer disks plus a jumble of envelopes, papers, keys, pens and paper tissues. She made a mound on the desk, everything smelling of nicotine from Iris's fingers. Then she ushered her out of the room and down the stairs. She planned to escort her as far as the lane but a slight drizzle had set in so she locked the front door behind her, bolted it, and hoped for the best.

Chapter Twenty-One

Joe Keenthorne's lair was a fetid cave masked by bushes sprouting from a cliff beyond the Cat Rock.

She found him there, stretched on a ledge four feet above the floor.

'Joe?'

He was instantly awake and squirming away from her.

'Joe, it's all right, it's only me – Alice. Nobody saw me come here, I made sure I wasn't followed.'

'What do you want?'

'To see you're all right. And to bring you this.'

She held a package aloft. Bread, cheese, tins and an opener – it was the best she could do without shopping.

He made no attempt to take it. She put it on the ledge, where his feet had been until he shrank into a defensive ball at the far end.

There was a pause during which she almost decided to leave, driven out by the disgusting smell. But she wanted to warn him about Iris and, possibly, he would want to hear.

He said: 'How did you know where to come?'

'You disappeared from the beach here one day, and I remembered those stories about a cliff path so I came to see if I could find it.'

'It's nearly gone. Used to be cut into proper steps, the path did. But then a storm took the kilns . . .'

'Kilns?'

'They made lime here. That's what this place was for, lime-kiln workers. I reckon you thought it was natural but this type of rock doesn't run to caves. This was cut, like the steps were cut. It's half fallen away now and the rest won't be long.'

As her eyes adjusted to the dimness she saw the rough shaping of the roof and walls, proving it was a relic of industry.

He thought she was noticing something else. 'The tides have changed. That's what brought the cliff down in the big storm of fifty-three, and took the buildings and some of the path. Since then it floods more often but when I was a lad it flooded at spring tide, mind.'

'You came here as a boy?'

'I used to walk up this way. That's how I know all the places round here, walking.'

'*And walking alone,*' she thought. '*All his life a loner. Closer to nature than to people.*'

Quickly, before his mood soured and she was sent away, she told him about Iris, the spying and the newspaper cuttings. But he had known for years the identity of his tormentor.

'I don't know *why* she took against me, mind.'

She suspected he had worked that out too but she let it pass. Joe had turned peculiar because of traumas but Iris Dottrell had always been what they locally called touched. Even Mary, loyal and protective, had said she was obsessional.

Alice described Iris's attempts to prevent his story being published. Again he was sanguine.

'You can't curb folk like that, Alice. Everyone knows she runs around at night doing mischief. Those notices on the board by the chapel, those are hers. Always telling folk what they can't do but nobody's to tell her.'

He gestured at the package. 'What's in there, then?'

Alice opened it. He asked for bread and cheese. While he ate she sat on a stone near the entrance, the swish of the sea in one ear and Joe's burr in the other.

He was talking about the book, insisting that whatever befell him she was to write it. Yesterday he had declared her unfit for the task, so either he was tacitly retracting or had forgotten.

'*He's changed,*' she was thinking. '*Yesterday evening he was full of fire and fury. He's too tired or the fight's gone out of him.*'

Then he changed tack. 'I told you I didn't see George after he left my house in the rain.'

Alice braced herself for more backtracking. 'Was it untrue?'

'Not exactly. I didn't see him alive but, as matters are now, I may as well say I found him dead.'

She felt horribly sick as he peeled away another layer of the innocence he wanted her to prove. Her voice was a whisper. 'What happened to him?'

'I reckon he fell off the cliff. Tried climbing up in the dark and slipped. I found him a few days after, smashed on the rocks.'

Alice's imagination went haywire. She saw Joe explaining to George about the path, and pictured his complicity as vividly as she had once pictured Delma's flight. She saw a panicking George hurrying away into the night only to skid on the muddy steps and crash to his death. Maybe not instant death, either. Perhaps he lay injured as the tide came and went, came and went.

First she wanted to know about culpability. 'Did you send him this way?'

'No, it was like I said, Alice, he told me I wasn't to know anything and away he went. He'd played here as a lad, same as me, knew the cliff path and where to cross the bay ahead of the tide.'

Then she asked the dreadful question. 'What did you do with the body, Joe?'

He swallowed the last mouthful of bread before answering. 'Pulled him in here. Didn't know how to go on from there. He'd been outside for days and he was a mess. Foxes, you know. Rats and eels. Oh, it's no use you making faces, Alice, it's what animals do, how they live.'

She heard an echo of Mrs Aley deriding her for faintheartedness about the eels chewing the face of an angler swept to his death.

Her hand was clamped over her mouth. The very idea of manhandling the corpse into the cave made her retch.

'Oh, Joe, surely you could have reported it?'

'To the police? No. I could see right off it was looking bad for me. You don't need an education to understand those things, Alice. And you can't tell me I was wrong, now can you?'

There were other pertinent questions and she put them too.

He explained. 'For a while, I left it to the animals and the birds. Gulls and crows take carrion, you know. You see, Alice, I couldn't come round here for fear of folk wondering why. Not that they'd missed George or Delma by then, but I didn't know how long that would last. What I did, though, was go looking on the cliff and the beach for anything of George's. When I found him there wasn't anything with him. No money, nothing to say who he was. I thought his belongings had been scattered, by the weather and the animals, and might wash up one day.'

Alice had a vivid impression of Joe as she had first seen him, as a beachcomber.

'You didn't find anything?'

'No. Except the boat.'

'What boat?'

'George got a wooden dinghy along with the Little Farm. Half the people at the Point had a boat back then, nothing fancy, mind, just to do a spot of fishing and be useful in times of bad flooding. Delma had the idea they were going to visit the islands in theirs. Like most of her fancy plans, it didn't come to anything.'

'But, Joe, you've always told me he walked across the bay.'

'No, Alice, I've only ever said *he knew where to* walk across. But I did realise that a man with a boat will use it rather than risk his life racing an incoming tide. At the time he left me, it was dangerous to cross on foot.'

He described how he had discovered the dinghy beached a

short distance from the cave. 'He might have tucked it in there, hidden by a rock fall, or he might have left it floating, hoping it would seem he'd gone overboard and drowned. I dragged it up here. Late one evening when the tide was high, I put what was left of George into it and covered him with pebbles. Then I put the outboard on my father's old boat and towed George down the coast. I sank him where the deep water begins.'

Alice felt her gorge rising again. '*You've looked for a sign from him every day on the morning tide,*' she thought.

He was unconcerned by her revulsion. 'If they'd found Delma or George they'd have blamed me.'

'Oh, Joe. They *did* blame you. They still do. Don't you see, it's hopeless?'

'Not if you write it the proper way. About them plotting to take the house off me. About that daft Iris Dottrell making up tales. About Jacko and his friends coming after me with dogs.'

'*Dogs?*'

'They tried before and they'll try again.'

She could not bear to hear about the persecutions of Jacko, partly because she could be subjected to them too. 'Listen,' she said urgently, 'I'll get you away from here. Is it possible to follow the path to the top?'

'For me it is.'

'Good. Then I'll do what Delma was supposed to have done. I'll drive round to the coast and meet you. Then I can whisk you away to safety.'

He listened to her fleshing out her idea of salvation. He did not contribute and neither, when she finished, did he thank her.

Alice rose. 'I must go.'

'It'll be all right now,' he said, hunkered on the ledge, regarding her keenly.

'Yes.' She ducked out of his stinking lair and filled her lungs with fresh salty air.

She wound through the maze of tall stone slabs deposited in a cliff fall, and then she slithered over the friable shale where Joe had one day outpaced her. The sea was already snagging on the rocks, threatening to cut her off. She was half way to safety before it dawned on her that when he had said it would be all right he was referring to the state of the tide, not her rescue plan. On that he had made no comment.

Alice had learned their secret ways. She could slide through the village on back lanes and coastal paths, and never see a soul. She could melt into the landscape and pretend she did not exist. By example and rejection, they had taught her these skills.

Yet, afraid of revealing Joe's hideaway, she decided not to return to it for a couple of days.

When she came home from delivering the victuals, Rod had arrived and within the hour agreed it was time for him to say farewell to Stark Point. They spent most of the time discussing Iris Dottrell's cheek in stealing his leather jacket from the wardrobe and wearing it on further housebreaking expeditions.

Pedantically he pointed out: 'Not strictly housebreaking or burglary if she had a key.'

Alice replied that it was too good a story to spoil with pettiness. She threw a fistful of papers on to the kitchen table. 'Until I went through these, which came from the pockets, I didn't know it was your jacket.'

Rod pushed the papers around with a fingertip as though they were red hot which, in one sense, they were.

Alice said: 'Don't bother telling me I shouldn't have read them. No one could have resisted it and by the time I discovered they were yours I was hooked.'

There were credit card accounts that ran to several pages and included hefty restaurant bills. The expensive evening at the Foresters had assumed a fresh significance. No wonder he had resisted cheerful pubs which required cash, of which he had been noticeably short.

'*Who,*' Alice was wondering, '*will be unlucky enough to meet these debts?'* And she added a heartfelt: '*Thank heavens I resisted his every entreaty.*'

Rod had abandoned hope of inveigling himself into her life, on other than a once-in-a-while weekend basis, and was nonchalant. Having suffered the great betrayal at the hands of Ruth, he was unwilling to take responsibility for any problems that ensued.

He was far more interested in hearing about Joe, Iris and the increasingly sinister Jacko, than in explaining how he planned to avoid penury. To be fair, he did describe his meeting in Bath, with the man who was a possible source of work, as 'positive'. Alice hoped he meant it.

After he drove away to Bath, she let herself feel melancholy for ten minutes. That allowed her time to reflect on her incompetence at seeking out and holding onto men who were worth seeking out and holding onto in the first place. Provided she kept the thoughts flowing, she could also fit in a swift bout of regret that she wasn't prettier, richer, more popular and, in effect, someone else.

The ten minutes up, she telephoned Julie with a hilarious account of life at Stark Point. Julie, who was low because of a tiff with a client, shared the tonic of laughter and then, astonishingly, announced: 'Stuff it, Alice. I'm going to cancel the rest of the week and come and see you.'

'After all I've said about it being a den of murderers and nutcases?'

'Where else can I get that much entertainment?'

Long after the call ended Alice kept chuckling at the silly things they had said and would, before the week was out, do. She had not said: 'Yes, come before it's too late,' but the thought was not buried very deep. Julie was a permanent feature of her life but Stark Point, which she had embraced with alacrity a few months ago, was eluding her. Once or twice she caught herself weighing up Bella's shabbiness and wondering how much it would command in an estate agent's window.

'I have the luxury of escaping whenever I choose,' she told herself in the bedroom mirror, as she tied up her hair in the way Rod liked but she had avoided in his presence. *'I can take the money and run. It isn't as though I haven't tried, but being here is becoming more of a trial as each day goes by.'*

She had invited Mary for a drink. When Mary arrived it quickly became apparent she was looking forward to seeing Rod. Alice said he had gone home. Mary looked put out.

'Did you send him away?'

'You could say that. He didn't raise the subject and I don't think he was going to.'

'Was it because of me?'

Alice lifted an eyebrow.

A skittish little smirk from Mary who said: 'So he didn't say he took me out one day? We went to a film and then for a meal in town. The day he bought the thingy for your garage door. I wondered whether he'd tell you.'

This was unexpected although Alice immediately saw it should not be.

Mary misread her expression. 'You're not cross, are you? Well, you did tell me you weren't going to get back with him, and he also said it so I assumed it was all right.'

Alice laughed. 'I needn't have been hanging around so much if either of you had dropped a clue.'

She was thinking that duplicity was part of Rod's make-up and the only time he disliked it was when he was the victim. Otherwise he found it exciting, perhaps necessary.

'Will you see him again?' she asked.

But Mary said she doubted it.

Alice moved on to what she considered the point of this get-together: Iris and the nocturnal nuisances. She adopted her most sympathetic tone, saying she appreciated Iris had a problem but it really would not do to have her wandering in and out of Spray Cottage at will.

Mary blustered. 'You've made a mistake. People here will say anything about each other, but you make a mistake if you believe it.'

Alice said there was no mistake and described meeting Iris in the spare bedroom. She edited out the comic details that had reduced Julie to tearful laughter.

Banging down her glass, Mary rose. 'I'm not listening to this.'

'Fine,' said Alice unruffled. 'But I'm offering you a chance to take the situation in hand. If you don't, you leave it to me to handle it whichever way suits me.'

Mary clutched at a tuft of her cropped hair. 'Oh, God. Alice, you don't know what you're saying.'

'If not, it's because you haven't told me the truth about your mother. Until the evening I encountered her upstairs, that wasn't important, but now it's the only thing that matters. Either you face up to it and take action, or I must.'

'What is it you want?'

'First I want to be certain she hasn't any other keys to this house or its sheds. Then I want her to return everything she's helped herself to since Bella died.'

'It's trash.' She was shouting.

'I dare say, but it's *my* trash.'

Mary made the familiar shift with her shoulders, then said in a more measured way: 'Oh, Alice, you didn't know Bella. From what you've said you knew less about her than you do about next door's cat and yet she left you her house. Bella and my mother, well, they . . . I don't know how to tell you this but they were . . . close friends. More than friends.'

A wild laughter bubbled up in Alice. 'Lovers? Is that what you're asking me to believe?'

Mary's colour heightened. 'People noticed how close they were and they were talked about. Well, you know how spiteful people here are about each other.'

'Oh, come on. Was it true or what?' And where, she wondered, did Mary come into the story? She had assumed a dead or deserting Mr Dottrell but perhaps it was more complex.

'It might have been true, I don't know. People always said Bella was gay but that could have been because she lived on her own instead of having a man around.'

'But your mother . . .'

'She says my father had a wife and kids on Exmoor and wouldn't leave them. Bella treated Mum for depression and Mum became dependent on her. She wasn't the only one to react that way, quite a few adored Bella. Her herbs helped them and they became entranced by her. I told you people called her a witch. They saw the hold she had over people. You'll scoff, Alice, but there are women in this village who went to Bella to beg love potions, to make the men they fancied fall for them.'

Alice gave a weak smile, thinking what an unwelcome burden her clients' infatuation must have been for Bella. Teasing, she said: 'I wonder whether the ingredients for the love potion are still growing in the garden. Not that I'd recognise them.'

'Her books said . . .' Mary grew flustered but it was too late, the words had escaped.

'Go on, tell me what's become of Bella's books. Or shall I guess Iris spirited them away too?'

Mary threw an agitated glance at the ceiling. 'Oh, if you knew how I've argued with her about it! But she's convinced Bella meant her to have all those things . . .'

'Pictures off the walls and books off the shelves and half the contents of her desk?' Alice's sarcasm was scathing.

'Please, don't get mad at me. If it was up to me I'd say come and collect them, but you know how vulnerable Mum is.'

'Mary, this can't go on. I want Bella's stuff back. I mean it.'

'But she's got it into her head they're rightfully hers. It would kill her to part with them.'

Alice remembered when Mary's loyalty to Iris had seemed touching. Having been deceived by the pair of them, she viewed it differently now. '*But if they've hurt me it's largely my fault. I was too eager for friendship.*'

Mary's mention of the books had made her implacable. The

pictures and knick-knacks were unlikely to be interesting but the books probably included the manuals of Bella's art, and those she could not bear to surrender.

Abashed, Mary offered to go straight home and tell Iris she was to return everything taken from Spray Cottage.

'Bring the books and any papers first,' Alice insisted.

Once Mary had gone she had qualms about her clumsiness. Too tough, she had offended and now Mary was relaying her demands to Iris who would also be upset. However, the soft approach had failed and the tough stance had been the only one available.

The following day a tight-lipped Mary appeared with two supermarket carrier bags bulging with papers and books. She said flatly: 'I'm not going to describe the ructions before I could leave the house with these.'

Alice, determined not to apologise, brightly thanked her. Tipping books onto the table, she frisked through them. There were indeed annotated herbals, two of them Victorian volumes and one possibly far older. She quelled her excitement but it was difficult because personal items were what she had craved when she arrived at Spray Cottage. Here at last was evidence of the kind of woman Bella had been, her passions and her expertise.

Alice continued to ignore Mary's discomfort. 'I'll be here all morning so you can bring the next batch as soon as you like.'

With a scalding look, Mary went. Unusually, Alice heard the gate shut.

She thought, '*She's letting me see a different aspect of her personality, now there's no longer the possibility of friendship between us.*'

She sifted the books, making a pile of the promising ones and another of old novels and biographies lacking instant appeal. Then the papers. Hope fluttered but a clutch of exercise books proved not to be a journal, only notes on clients. These, however, were treasure. Here Alice could read, for instance, that Iris Dottrell had swallowed valerian when she sought treatment for insomnia.

'*A pity it didn't work!*' She laughed out loud. An Iris abed would be a far less troublesome neighbour.

And then, in one of the earlier books, a faded name dazzled Alice. *Mrs Ablett.*

On her first visit, a leg wound was treated with marigolds. She had consulted Bella several times one year and more often the next, her visits ceasing two months before she disappeared.

The later notebooks grew duller, although the halt and the lame continued to traipse to Bella's door to complain, in the main, of indigestion, depression and coughs, for which they were treated with artichoke, borage and common mullein. Alice forced herself to put the notebooks aside and save up the pleasure of browsing for another time. Besides, she preferred to have them out of sight before Mary delivered the next load.

But where could she put them? Uncertain whether Iris had another copy of the key, she hesitated to put them back on the shelves or in the desk. There was one alternative that was, relatively, safe: her car. Knowing she might be spied on, she disguised the bundles in dustbin liners to carry them out of the house, then locked them in the boot and secured the garage door.

During the afternoon Mary drove up to the gate and unloaded what looked like the residue of an unsuccessful jumble sale. Fuming, she left Alice to ferry it indoors. Before she shunted the car around she snarled: 'I hope you enjoy it.'

Alice, with a chipped pottery jug in one hand and a badly framed print of a ballet dancer in the other, thought it improbable. She began trundling the junk indoors but was soon working out which village was holding the next boot sale, and so she gave up, reopened the garage and shoved the bulk of Mary's cargo just inside.

In the end, she cared to keep a mere handful of the books and a stack of papers. Bella had not had a keen eye for a painting or a pot but, to Alice's amusement, she displayed a great flair for pregnancy: how to achieve it and how to avoid it. Flipping between the herbals and the clients' notes in the exercise books,

Alice learned that Delma Ablett had been trying for a baby eighteen months before she died.

Alice stretched that to 'at least eighteen months' because, presumably, Delma had tried without Bella's wizardry before she resorted to it. During that period two of Bella's other clients swallowed the same concoction and produced babies, while one client with a different problem knocked back a potion that put an end to hers.

Her humour faded as she studied Delma's timing. A two-month gap might mean Delma believed she was pregnant, with a baby who would deprive Joe of his inheritance and provide him with a motive for murder.

'No way of finding out whether that was true, Bella doesn't mention her again. Joe was lucky a pregnancy wasn't mooted at the trial. It could have tipped the scales against him. A matter of life or death.'

An anguished scream shocked her rigid. In the next second she was flying out of the house, dreading what she might find.

Chapter Twenty-Two

She discovered Iris Dottrell, rending her clothes in biblical fashion and hurling stones at Spray Cottage.

Alice yelled back, telling her to shut up. A missile shot past her head. She retreated and heard her sitting-room window shatter. Shaking, she lifted the telephone receiver, then dropped it because Iris was at the broken window, shrieking abuse and taking aim with another pebble.

Alice ran through to the kitchen, guessing she would be safer outside the house than in it, although she was tempted to scamper upstairs and slam her bedroom door. But no, she must get out because Iris had opened the window and was hoisting herself up onto the sill.

'No key, after all.'

Alice braced herself for a dash down the side of the house. She did not have the keys to garage or car so a thorough escape was impossible. Iris caught her, anyway, screeching, her few plain words illogical.

Alice pushed by and reached the lane.

'Where is everybody?' she was thinking, forgetting there had hardly ever been anybody around and, since her championing of Joe Keenthorne, there was definitely nobody who would help. She echoed Iris's earlier lament: 'They won't lift a finger.'

She hit on the strategy of drawing Iris away and ran towards

Ham Cottage. Iris, intent on berating her, was led. Once or twice they grappled in the middle of the lane.

Alice's brain was pounding. '*Where's the school bus? Delivery vans? The man with the tractor who helped Charles escape? Oh God, why doesn't somebody come?*'

Fending Iris off, she was wary of flooring the waif-like woman and causing injury because she was so much the taller and heartier. Her imagined scene of George losing his temper and hitting Delma, with fatal consequences, ran through her mind. She was amazed how many bizarre and unrelated ideas ran through.

And all the while she was saying: 'Calm down, Iris. Please, be sensible, Iris. Listen to me, it's all right, Iris, everything will be all right.'

Iris was abruptly cogent. 'Joe Keenthorne told you I had Bella's books, I know he did, it's all his doing. You wouldn't have known otherwise and I'd have kept them. Bella wanted me to have her books, her herbals and all that, she said I was to be the witch of Stark Point after she died. And then she died and I went and got them. She didn't say it to you – you didn't know her, so how could she? She was my friend and you've stolen them from me and she won't rest easy in her grave until I've got them back.'

She thrust a hand into a pocket and out came a kitchen knife. Alice's eyes followed the golden arc of the blade cutting the sunlit air. Mesmerised with fear, she was idiotically waiting to be slashed.

But Iris took a step away. She taunted. 'That Joe Keenthorne, I know where he is. And I'm going to kill him for what he's done, you'll see. He told you and you took the books, how can I study to be like Bella if you've got the books?'

She spun away, staggered a few yards before she recovered her balance and then ran, light as a feather blown through the air. Once she turned to scream: 'I'm going to get Joe, for what he's done.'

Winded, Alice sagged against a wall and fought to regain her breath. '*She has the energy of the mad. Anyone in their normal mind who can summon such a sustained burst of energy could be an Olympic champion.*'

She gasped, straightened, thrust her hair back from her face. During the scuffles it had come down and the clasp was lost.

Now that Iris was quiet and out of sight her thoughts switched to Mary, about to be subjected to her mother in all her unreasonable fury. Alice hurried to Ham Cottage. The front door stood wide and Mary's car was missing. She remembered then what Mary had said the previous evening before they discussed the difficult topic. Mary had gone shopping.

Alice turned back. '*Well, at least Iris is safe in her own home.*'

When she had taken a few paces she heard a distant cry. The hair on her scalp rose. The noise came from the direction Iris would be taking if she were carrying out her threat and hunting down Joe Keenthorne.

Alice was torn, unsure whether to run after her and try to catch her before she reached the bay or whether to drive down the causeway to the car park and head her off on the sand. '*The car, that'll be quickest.*'

But after pelting a short way up the lane she realised she needed to fetch her keys from the house and, anyway, the car was barricaded behind Bella's junk. She slewed round.

Winding through a bend, she had her first sight of Iris bobbing down the path through the high grass. Alice crossed the wooden bridge in a stride and sped after her.

Unaware she was pursued, Iris was voluble, cackling and cursing as she went but not running out of steam. Alice went pell-mell after her; yet by the time she emerged onto the tufty green saltings, she was lagging by hundreds of yards.

She paused ready to hail her but the wind was whipping up and she saved her breath for the chase. And that was the moment she realised exactly what Iris was doing. Instead of skirting the bay, she was making a beeline for the Cat Rock. Lingering doubts vanished. Iris did know where Joe Keenthorne had his lair.

'Iris!' Alice used the full power of her lungs.

Iris Dottrell's head swivelled. Her steps faltered. The wind snatched away her reply. She ran on, faster, straight towards the Cat Rock.

A shocking reality hit Alice. '*She can't do it. The tide . . .*'

Wildly, she scanned the bay. Nobody. Sun winked on a windscreen as a car climbed the hills. In the deep water channel a tanker was sliding west. But there was nobody to help.

'*Except me,*' thought Alice, desperate, knowing she was all that stood between crazy Iris and disaster.

The white line dividing land and sea was already breaking at the foot of the Cat Rock. The tide came in along this coast at tremendous speed.

Iris, she presumed, did not realise her predicament. It was worse for Alice that she did and knew too that if she failed they both would die. Drowning, the death she most feared. A terrifying panic-stricken death, fighting to the last ounce of energy and willpower, yet doomed because human beings are frail and the sea is the most powerful thing in all creation. And after the dreadful death is accomplished, the revolting corruption of the body, its exposed parts a meal for sea creatures, so that fingers and faces are no use for identification should any remains come ashore.

Alice steeled herself not to dwell on that. '*I mustn't fail. I just need to go faster and wrench her out of harm's way.*'

Even so, the distance between them was growing. Once clear of the saltings she ran full tilt over the sand, compelled by Iris's footprints to cross the bay at an angle to meet the sea.

'*This is madness,*' she thought, and it could have been a comment on Iris or the route or the dismally inefficient rescue operation.

The wind blindfolded Alice with her hair. She twisted this way and that to free herself, running on, not daring lose a step, and she clutched her hair away from her face and stuffed it down inside her collar. She skidded. Mud. Grey streaks protruded from a film of yellow sand, evidence of the peril beneath the surface.

Iris's scream tore at her. Alice swung up her head, forgetting her own risk when she saw Iris reduced to blundering instead of running, her skinny legs lifting heavily and awkwardly, all her lightness gone.

'I'm coming,' Alice bellowed although the onshore breeze rendered her mute.

She glanced nervously at the rushing surf. The wind sent the hissing threat ahead of it but she did not need that warning. Unless she and Iris changed course, they were running to meet their deaths.

What she had to do was obvious. Run on. Pluck Iris out of the mud. Haul her inland away from the Cat Rock. Never mind if she fought and scratched. Knock her out, if need be. But get her, that's all. Just get her.

Alice was moving ahead, steady and circumspect for fear of copying Iris's folly. Luckily, the footprints offered her a guide and it was going to be easy to spot where Iris ran foul of the mud. But when she raised her eyes she saw her moving freely once more and going like a dart for the Cat Rock.

'Damn!'

Shoving her hair down inside her collar again, although it was escaping before she had finished, Alice charged on. Sand became soft and damp, with silvery runnels that never dried from tide to tide. Straggles of sodden weed littered it, along with the crinkled carapaces of tiny dead sea creatures. Most people would have sidestepped these awkward areas but Iris had barged through them because, undeniably, she had not veered a single degree from her target.

Alice's shoes sank into sand that had crumbled at Iris's passing. She splashed through the rivulets of a seeping spring. She plunged into sticky brown oil, evidence of shipping. And she jumped over the decomposing body of a small creature. But she could not gain on Iris.

And then Iris skidded, her feet shooting out from under her so that she landed flat on her back. She moaned cursing the sky and making no attempt to rise. Alice approached with increasing care. She called but Iris ignored her or perhaps did not hear.

Beyond Iris, a great wave smashed against the Cat Rock. Flecked water rushed inshore, swirling close to her body. Horrified, Alice saw how the wind was thrashing the waters of the channel into whitecaps, and how few big waves it would take for the bay to flood. The advance of the incoming tide was awesome.

Urgency speeded her on. She panted up to Iris. But Alice's sudden appearance shocked the woman into convulsions of rage.

Shouting her down, Alice tussled for a hold on an arm and tugged. Iris, wriggling to free herself, nestled into the grey mess. It oozed into her hair and smeared her skin, painted her clothes and richly plastered her shoes and legs. It was eating her alive.

Alice had to fight down an impulse to flee. She would have been justified in abandoning Iris and saving herself because Iris was resisting rescue, but Alice would never have forgiven herself if she had done that. She even felt guilty to have allowed the thought.

'Come on, Iris. It'll be all right. Just let me help you up . . .'

The boom of a wave battering the rock killed the rest of her plea.

She latched onto Iris's left arm and leaned away, to force her to sit up. From sitting she hoped to coerce her into standing. Cold silt made the arm slippery and Alice lost her grip. Another minute was wasted while she struggled to grasp it again. Another minute and another wave.

'Leave me alone.' Iris hit her in the face.

Alice implored. '*Please,* Iris, give me your arm. Let me help you away from the water.'

'Go away.'

Iris flopped her head aside. There was a declivity where it had lain. Water began to fill it.

Alice felt sick. The mud was sticky and unpleasant but it was not a sucking mud, able to swallow them like quicksand. Their only danger was the incoming water and, if either of them drowned, it would be an avoidable tragedy. They had time to get up the beach to safety, but not *much* time and it was running out as fast as the sea was coming in.

The responsibility appalled her. '*It's up to me. Iris isn't rational. Whatever happens is going to be my fault.*'

For a couple of seconds she took stock. The Cat Rock was virtually cut off. The direct route to safety was inland and up the beach ahead of the tide, but between the safe yellow sand and where they had come to rest was a vast area that was suspiciously dingy. Mud. It might slow them sufficiently for the tide to overtake them. She cast around, checking for fingers of yellow poking into the grey. There were some but they were narrow and spread out, and not near enough to where she stood to be useful. The other possible escape route was back the way they had come.

Alice pounced, heaved on Iris's arm, yanked her up, manhandled her until she was sitting. Iris was bawling, flailing about, forcing tears down her cheeks.

'I don't care,' Alice growled. 'I really don't care. You just do as you're told or you'll kill the pair of us.'

But Iris threw herself sideways. She ended up kneeling. Alice seized a handful of hair, pulling and urging her up. Iris seemed impervious to pain and ignorant of the meaning of the water that edged up to them.

A few more waves, a few more minutes of badgering and levering, and Alice began calculating how soon she must leave Iris to her chosen fate.

'*Not chosen, not really. This isn't suicide, it's madness.*'

Foam encircled Iris. Alice stood ankle deep while it receded. She made another tremendous effort to shift her but could see she was embedded. One of Iris's hands was in above the wrist.

Tentatively, Alice changed the position of her own feet. The mud clung but by stepping high she was able to lift them. Like that, slowly and with luck, she ought to get ashore. *If* her stumbling steps could outpace the rushing tide.

She renewed her efforts with Iris. No use. Beyond endurance, she struck a stinging blow on the clownishly plastered face.

This shocked them both. The light in Iris's eyes brightened, like someone waking from reverie.

Iris howled but at last it was the desperation of a human being confronting danger. She tried to stand up and discovered her hand was trapped. Attempting to free it, she slumped face down. Water flowed in, lapped her head and deposited foam in her hair.

'Christ! She'll drown in this.'

Alice crouched down and scrabbled around the trapped hand. Using her hands as a scoop, she dug around it, then seized the wrist and worked her free. During this Iris was docile and compliant.

'Iris, you're free. You can get up now.'

No movement.

'Iris?'

Alice lifted her shoulders. The head swung down, like a woman asleep. Or unconscious. Or dead.

Alice screwed up her eyes and prayed to be helped out of this mess. She was not competent to say whether Iris was dead or alive but if she were dead – of a heart attack, say – there was no point in loitering and losing her own life.

She stood there, the water over her ankles, and held Iris up so her head was clear of the water. After that she did not know what to do.

In normal circumstances she would have recognised the colourful signs of a heart attack but with Iris smothered in mud her skin was invisible. Alice investigated her nose and mouth but they were not blocked.

She pushed back an eyelid. Iris flinched. Alive, then.

'In that case,' thought Alice, very matter of fact, *'we press on.'*

She clutched her beneath the armpits and dragged. This was back-breaking, especially as she had to do the high-stepping motion if she were to move her feet at all. The water kept up with them.

After a while, she let Iris fall back, then raised her ankles and lugged her along that way. She was past caring whether it was less comfortable for Iris because it was certainly easier for the rescuer.

Progress was wretchedly slow. Encouraging moments, when they seemed to be outstripping the tide, were wasted each time Alice needed to pause to alter her grip, or tripped, or blundered into a particularly sticky spot and began to believe it was the sucking kind of mud after all.

The surf raced past them with a triumphant roar, swilling over Iris and making it senseless to drag her by her legs. Alice heaved her upright. Iris blinked and appeared conscious so Alice ordered her to lean against her and attempted to walk on. They collapsed. Rising, Iris wailed, a hideous incantation that Alice was unable to stifle. Above the goading of the wind and the boisterous challenge of the sea, there was the wretched descant of Iris Dottrell's misery.

One of the bigger waves galloped ashore, buffetting Alice and sending Iris sprawling. Iris flapped about, rose up spitting defiance at Alice and suddenly she was flourishing the knife. Alice backed off. Iris lunged at her, twice, and then another wave bowled her over. Alice saw the knife, flung like a spear as Iris fell. It went wide, no real threat, and immediately Alice was moving forward to retrieve Iris, but she was losing her own footing and could not be quick.

The squally breeze used her hair as a blindfold and she had to spin around to unbind it and make her hair stream away from her. When she opened her eyes, Iris was gone.

A wave slapped hard at Alice, buckling her knees, and she slapped down into water slightly too deep for her arms to save her. Her head went under. Cold water was a shock to her skin and every inch of her was soaked. For the first time, she forgot about Iris.

Having lost a shoe, she kicked off the other one. Running and walking were ruled out, there was only swimming.

She was an average swimmer and that was in pools, not

British coastal waters, but she did not waste time considering whether her ordinary skills were enough save her. There was no choice but to try.

The crucial decision was whether to toil towards the beach. She did not think long about that either. If she made an effort to go straight to the beach she would be fighting the current, but if she swam towards the saltings she would travel with it. She started moving that way, being raised off her feet now and then and bounced along. The water was taking her weight, she realised, and she was unlikely to become bogged down. The waves were waist high with a tidal drift which remorselessly pushed her across the bay.

For a while she felt in danger of being rolled in the surf. Waves flattened her and the suck of the receding water made her scared of being dragged out into the channel by the notorious undertow. But soon she was in water too deep for her to stand and was swimming properly at last.

She dared to drift, testing the direction of the flow. From the water Stark Point and its causeway looked extraordinary, just a dark line barely above sea level. It was incredible that those few feet of earth made the difference between habitation and water, between life and death.

'If I miss the saltings, I'll be carried past the Little Farm. I might get onto one of the outcrops there.'

The darker thought was that if she could not keep close to the shore she would be swept alongside the tongue of land, beyond the lonely headland and out into the expanse of water between it and the seaside town. She knew this because she had heard where dead animals fetched up after storms and where the crews of capsized boats were found: either in the bay or in a cove by the seaside town. They were invariably dead.

The sea was pitiless. It tossed her about, tempted her to believe she was going to be lucky and then cheated her. She saw the green of the saltings grow near and then fade away, ending her hope of a simple crossing of the bay.

She went under, choked, grew panicky and squandered her strength. The bay was a memory and the rocky outcrops were feeble possibilities viewed from her new angle. But the tide, it was the tide that changed it. Water was rising and the rocks were partly submerged, so if she could strive to keep close in she might touch land quite soon.

Then she recognised the white surge from a big drain, and knew she could not withstand a rush of water pushing her out to sea. With a massive effort, she battled to get ashore before she reached it.

Her lungs were burning. Pressure on her body was intolerable. Her limbs were numb but, like automatons, they slaved for her and she concentrated on how well they were doing instead of giving in to despair because the rest of her was cracking up. And so her initial reaction when her leg was grazed was indignation.

She thumped the obstacle a second time but gladly, proving it was not an illusion. Alice bumped along beside it, not caring that it gouged her. And when the hunk of sandstone broke the water and she could crawl up it, she hung there instead, tears scorching her face, their heat shocking as the coldness of the sea had earlier shocked.

The wind lobbed spray in her face. A wave teased, tweaking so hard at her clothes that she clung limpet-like, in dread of being reclaimed by the sea.

Alice raised her upper body onto the rock and summoned her strength. She went slowly but eventually she was upright and swaying uncertainly ashore. Water chased around three sides of the rock. She bullied herself to get away from there, not trusting the sea to leave her in safety. A scraggy field ran down to the rock. Alice wrung water out of her hair and stretched out on the grass.

She had no idea how long she lay there. Behind closed eyelids, she saw the restless water and marvelled at its complicity with the wind. One alone was powerful enough, together there was nothing of which they were incapable. It was a miracle they let her survive.

A blast of wind, making her pungent clothes freezing, reminded her it would be stupid to die of pneumonia after everything she had endured. Head whirling, she sat up. She felt too weak to walk and started inland on hands and knees. After two or three minutes she flopped down and this was when she noticed blood trickling from gashes on her battered feet and legs.

She had nothing to bind them. Everything was drenched with dirty water. Worry about the bleeding galvanised her and she managed to walk, almost to hurry. Along the paths and the back ways she made her way home. The light was dying and the frisky wind made it an evening when people preferred to sit around their television sets rather than stroll in their gardens. She did not see anybody.

Alice joined the lane close to Spray Cottage. As she drew closer she saw an unfamiliar vehicle there, a chunky lorry she supposed belonged to a visitor at one of the other houses. But as she turned in through her gate a man gave an exclamation. He was on the path at the side of the house, a brawny man squeezed into a T-shirt. She did not know who he was or why he was there, only that whatever he wanted she was too exhausted and ill to resist.

'Is it you, Alice?'

'Yes.' The voice was thick and slurred, unlike her own.

Her legs gave and she flapped a hand in the general direction of the wall. She missed and was sinking down when he sprang forward and caught her.

'My God, you're in a mess.'

'Mm.' She was letting him take her weight.

He lowered her carefully onto a large log. She did not remember a log being in her garden but lots of things were escaping her mind, including who on earth he was.

'They said you were drowned,' he said, his voice shaky.

'Who said?'

'Folk who saw your trouble in the bay. Two women drowned, they said. And I said what am I to do . . .'

Pain was drumming her skull. She clapped hands to her head. 'Sorry, I don't understand.'

'Where are your keys? Let's get you indoors.'

'Keys?'

He risked leaving her side for as long as it took to turn the handle on the back door and discover the house was unlocked.

The next thing Alice knew she was plonked on one of her kitchen chairs and this stranger, who was not quite a stranger, was boiling a kettle and rummaging through her cupboard for tea bags.

'Camomile,' she said, pointing.

'Oh?' Very doubtful, he did not know what to do with those.

She fumbled instructions. Then: 'What are you doing here?'

He gave her a studied look. 'Ah, you don't remember me. Well, I did say it would be a week or two and I've been that busy, what with one thing and another.'

Bewildered she shook her head. A mistake. It hurt.

He said: 'Fred Partridge. You came up the Falcon one evening and ordered logs.'

With distaste he watched her sip the camomile. 'Smells funny, if you ask me.'

For the first time in hours, she smiled.

He wanted to telephone a doctor and when she said she was not registered locally he said she needed the once-over in hospital anyway and it was hardly out of his way to drive her there.

They bobbed along in the cab of the lorry while he told her how he had arrived to find a handful of people on the beach looking intense. He had pulled up pretending to need directions but actually to satisfy his curiosity. The fisherman told him a couple of women were drowned.

'He said the state of the tide meant you hadn't a chance, and it was a mad thing to do but Iris Dottrell had always been touched and Alice Wintle was an incomer who didn't know any better.'

Changing gear at the foot of the hill, Fred Partridge laughed richly. 'I reckon you know more about the tides at Stark Point than that Jacko does. All mouth, I'd say.'

She was warmed by this curious compliment, especially as there was a shade of truth in it. Jacko had once boasted he had never swum or walked there so, really, what did he know? Yet he ruled the roost. Except that . . .

Alice shut her eyes. She was thinking that her special knowledge of Stark Point affairs was equal to anybody's. She knew most about Joe Keenthorne, the Ablett business, Iris Dottrell, Bella and, as she owned Bella's books, about the mysteries of herbalism and who had been treated for what.

She murmured. He did not catch her words but she said it did not matter. To a stranger it would make no sense, only to someone who intended to go on living at Stark Point.

The words repeated silently in her head. '*Knowledge is power.*'

So it was and in future they could not touch her.

'What's amusing you?' he asked, grinning at her but slightly alarmed.

But she could not say, she was laughing too much.

Chapter Twenty-Three

'Three days, Julie!'

Julie's plump little fingers ran along Alice's instep. 'I wouldn't have been surprised if they'd kept you in longer.'

'But there was nothing wrong with me.'

'They said you were half-conscious and rambling about a wrecked boat.'

'That was my poem!' She was shaking with laughter.

'How were they to know? It sounded like an accident.'

'Ouch!'

Alice tugged her foot away. Julie collected it and stroked more lightly.

'That's your kidneys, Alice. No wonder it's tender. Just relax.'

'I might if you didn't keep hurting me.'

'You'll feel wonderful afterwards. I'm channelling your energy so you'll be stress-free and rested.'

'Ow!'

'Sorry, that's your lungs.'

'Can't you find any bits of me that aren't suffering?'

'You *look* good, though. Three days on hospital food and you're positively gaunt.'

'Since you mention food . . . Have we got anything for supper?'

'Plenty, I went shopping while you were away. Relax, Alice. Stop fussing, everything's all right.'

Alice made gestures of surrender and tried to relax.

The telephone rang. Julie, whose life was incomplete without telephone calls, sprang up. A chocolate wrapper popped out of her pocket as she dashed from the room telling Alice: 'Stay there.'

Alice lay on her bed languidly watching the shadows of leaves dancing on the ceiling to the erratic rhythm of the breeze. Through the open window she heard the beat of the waves. Chaffinches were gossiping in her garden. She felt content.

During the compulsory idleness of a hospital bed she had come to decisions. Specifically, she was going to divorce Rod and leave Charles. Broadly, she was going to bring this period of drifting to an end and pay more attention to her future than to the past. She had recognised strengths she did not previously know she possessed but weaknesses too. And she had learned the difference between enjoying life-threatening drama from the safe side of a window pane and being the principal actor. Oh, and the boat poem was a hopeless intellectual game: head rather than heart, ideas instead of passion. She knew better now.

Before she had left the hospital Rod and Charles, who had both heard about her on the news, had telephoned, greatly concerned. Rod had invited himself to return to look after her, an offer she was able to decline gratefully because Julie had already been appointed to that role. Charles, by contrast, had been glad to learn Julie was healing Alice because he was too busy to.

Julie was running upstairs. 'That was the evening paper wanting to interview you about your brush with death.'

'I trust you said no.'

'They're coming at six.'

'Oh, Julie!'

'Listen to me, Alice. You need to speak to them. What's that awful expression about putting the record straight?'

Suspicion clouded Alice's eyes. 'What are you keeping from me?'

'The story that's going round is that you and Iris Dottrell had a fight and she was tearing across the bay to get away from you.'

'But I was trying to save her life!' Alice was bolt upright.

'So put the record straight. Okay?'

Alice swung her legs off the bed and went to the window. The sky was cloudless, the surf glittering. A man and his dog ran along the curve of sand.

She said: 'It was Mary Dottrell, wasn't it?'

'Yes. I heard that from the policemen who came to see if you were fit to talk about the inquest on Iris.'

'Mary wasn't even here, she knows less about it than anybody.'

There was a thoughtful moment before Alice added: 'I do wish it hadn't been Joe Keenthorne who found Iris's body.'

'She wasn't in the water long enough for it to be really hideous. They found her as the tide went out.'

Julie cancelled the rest of the reflexology session and offered to make a tisane to speed healing.

'With Bella's herbs,' she emphasised. 'I don't know why you bother buying sachets when you've a splendid crop of the real thing.'

'Laziness,' said Alice. 'Plus ignorance.'

They went into the garden together. Julie, delighted with the collection of useful plants, had been titivating them ever since her arrival.

She asked, a little nervously: 'Are you planning to sell up? I wouldn't blame you, after everything that's happened.'

'Oh, no.' Alice had settled the question in her own mind days ago. 'My radio work will keep me away a lot but I'll manage to spend plenty of time here.'

'Good, because I'm scheming to cadge herbs from you. Clients like to hear you have your own special supply.'

Alice beamed, inordinately pleased that Bella's work was appreciated and about to be useful again.

She sat on one of Fred Partridge's bigger logs and watched Julie busily selecting leaves. For two days Julie had been protecting her from inquiring policemen and insensitive Pointers, and it felt good to have a champion. Now, though, Julie had thrown her to the press. Putting the record straight sounded easy but *which* record and what was straight?

She said: 'I suppose the paper's aware Joe was released after being questioned by the police about Delma?'

'Sure to be, it was on the television news.'

'But do they realise Iris was instrumental in having him charged with murder? She claimed to have seen him at the Abletts' farm on the supposed date of their disappearance, you know.'

Julie straightened, holding the leaves delicately to prevent bruising them. 'Yes, and she was on her way to kill him when she was drowned. If they don't already know that, are you going to tell them?'

'I can't decide. Of course, I told the police everything when they interviewed me in hospital.'

But that was untrue. In an attempt to help Joe, she had kept to herself his revelation about the death and disposal of George Ablett.

Julie peered at her solemn face. 'You're not cross I said yes to the paper, are you?'

'No, I can't let Mary's crazy accusations go unanswered.' She gave a self-mocking laugh. 'I remember an innocent time when I used to think it was admirable how she protected Iris. Now I believe she's as inventive and obsessive as her mother was.'

She was thinking especially of the stream of disparaging stories about the Pointers. They had been tiresome when she was subjected to them but, in the light of Mary's other deceptions, they looked questionable too.

Julie said, 'You can't have her traducing you because of an unfounded grudge, as Iris did Joe. Kill her story before people get used to believing it.'

Cupping the leaves in her hands, Julie inhaled their mild scents and then asked: 'What's your feeling about Joe now? Guilty or innocent?'

'I'm convinced he's an innocent man destroyed by circumstances, one of which was Iris's finger-pointing. I wish I could tell you I had a dollop of conclusive evidence but I don't. Anyway, it's meant to be the other way round, isn't it? Innocent until proven guilty.'

'Nothing's really changed, then, since the trial?'

But Alice was quick to say: 'Oh, the body in the rhine makes a huge difference. If Joe killed the Abletts, both bodies would have been in the car. It was an excellent method of disposing of a body, so he'd hardly bother to think up a second one.'

Julie elaborated. 'Even if he'd killed them at different times, he'd have dumped them together.'

She went indoors to make the tisane. Alice stayed there, letting the comforting warmth of the sun ease her aches. She fancied walking out to the headland but her energy was depleted and, besides, she would not want to rush back for her six o'clock appointment.

'*Tomorrow*,' she thought, '*I'll tell Joe I'm ready to start on the book. Now it's my story, as well as his.*'

Deciphering the past had been like reading a book under water, confusing and surprisingly hard to do. Imaginative leaps had led her astray. Prejudice had been presented to her as unadorned fact. Now, though, she had her own legitimate perspective and that would give her writing authority. Nobody else could tell this part of the story, it was hers.

She closed her eyes and tilted her face to the sun. As darkness replaced the bright flowers of her garden and the brilliance of a summer sky, her only sense was sound. Bees murmured about her lavender. A lark rose singing from the field beside the cottage.

Papery stirrings were fronds gesturing in the breeze. And she heard the sea, a lazy tide on a hot afternoon as the surf hushed the shore, and hushed, and hushed, like history wearing away at the truth.